THE SMUGGLERS AT SEA

Book 2 of The Company Series

HARRY FINKELSTEIN

March 28, 2021
To Millicent McKinley
Thanks for encouragement

Hary Finkll

1

DEDICATION

To my wife Sandy
who has kept peace around me
so I could finish
SMUGGLERS AT SEA
Book 2
Of
The Company Series

Acknowledgements
My thanks to the following for their help and expertise

Christine Giblin, RN.,   Cranston Rhode Island
Jon Forcht,   Plano Texas
Cheri Hodson,   Montgomery, Alabama
Norma Pitman,   Bath England

<u>And especially to my wife for her patience.</u>

This is a work of fiction. Names, characters, places,
and events are the product of the author's
imagination or are used fictitiously and
resemblance to actual persons, living or
dead is entirely coincidental.
All the errors are mine.

Chapter 1

At 0700 hours Thursday morning, the phone rang. Ron Sullivan leaned over, picked it up and said, "Ron Sullivan."

"Ron, this is Harry Blank."

Ron sat up straight. Harry Blank was the Chairman of the National Intelligence Advisory Board and one of his main clients. "Good to hear from you, Harry. What's up?"

"We have a problem in Florida," said Harry. "We need you there in less than forty-eight hours. You and your people are going to be taking a cruise to the Caribbean."

"That sounds good. What exactly is the problem so I will know who to send, how many to send, and what equipment to send with them?"

"That is going to be the problem. I was only able to get four cabins. That means room for eight people or four couples. The ship is fully booked. I have two people already on board as part of the crew. One is an officer, and one is a cabin attendant. You won't need any special communications equipment," Harry said, "since you designed that miniaturized equipment that is installed under the skin. I'm scheduled to get my unit inserted under the skin tomorrow. How is it working out for you?"

"It is performing better than we thought it would," said Ron. "It's a two-way communications system and a tracking device as well. With the new communications satellite, all of our people are in contact with each other, and New York is able to monitor everything. Now that the Cray computer is almost online, we are in great shape. Every Center will be connected to each other and routing will we three times faster than the old system. You still haven't told me why you are being so generous to give four couples a prepaid cruise to the Caribbean."

"When your teams raided that New York operation last year, you took away a tremendous amount of material. We have spent many hundreds of man hours going over it. We uncovered part of a smuggling operation that they had set up and sold to a Mexican cartel. They are moving material from the United States to the Caribbean. All we know right now is that they are using a number of cruise ships. We're not sure which cruise ships are being used at this time. We suspect the Valley Forge might be one of the ships. What we do know is that they are smuggling the goods onboard cruise ships. We don't know how they are doing it. We don't even know how they are getting the goods off the ships. We know it isn't weapons that are being smuggled. We suspect gold, money or drugs. What we need you and your group to do is find out how they are bringing the material on board, what the material is and where it goes. We'll take it from there. We do have observers on the other ships of this line, but they have found nothing so far. We put you on the Valley Forge for two reasons; first, the observer team got sick, not on the ship, but ashore. Second, we had no one else to send. It doesn't sound good, but it is the best I could do on such short notice. You don't mind the 'vacation' do you?

"No. I'm sure no one I pick to go, will mind. I'll get back to you in a couple of hours with the names." He disconnected and sat there thinking. *'Who should he take with him?'*

He said "Computer, get me Lucinda."

"Lucinda is online," said the Computer.

"What's up Ron?" she asked.

"Can you come up to the office, please?" he asked.

"On my way," Lucinda answered. "I'll be there in five minutes."

Five minutes later Lucinda walked into the office. Ron got up and met her halfway. He held is arms out and Lucinda walked into them and he hugged her. Then he loosened his grip, leaned down and kissed her.

"What brought that on?" she asked, smiling.

"How would you like to go on a Caribbean cruise, all expenses paid, for three weeks?" asked Ron.

"Did you win the lottery?" she asked.

"No," he said. "We have a job. I just got a call from Harry Blank." He went on to explain what Harry wanted them to do. He continued, "Who else should we take with us? We need three more couples. Who would you recommend?"

They both walked into the conference room. Ron filled two cups with coffee and brought one to Lucinda, who sat at the table. Lucinda thought about it for a few minutes. *'This is the first time since Melinda Dash*

6

left her in joint command with Ron that they needed a team put together. It seems so strange to give orders.' She mentally went through the list of names and their qualifications. With the cross training they all had, she could put together four couples to form a good team.'

"I would recommend Jose Martinez, John Mason, Benjamin Britain, and for their partners, without playing matchmaker, Susan Bart, Marsha Abrams, and Sheena." Ron smiled at the 'matchmaking' remark. Melinda Dash played matchmaker ten months ago ending with Jason Fink and Lucy getting married. Melinda and Martin ended up getting married at the same time.

"Sounds like a solid team. I will call Harry Blank and let him know the names we chose. He can fill in the names for the cruise ship and get the paperwork to us. You contact the crews and tell them to pack for twenty-four days. Tell them no weapons, not even a knife. Harry told me that we would find our weapons delivered to us on board the cruise ship. It will be the new dart guns that Dr. Wellfleet developed last year which we used on the raid in New York."

Lucinda nodded and went to her desk. "Computer online," she said.

"Computer online, Lucinda," the Computer said.

"Connect Jose Martinez, John Mason, Benjamin Britain, Marsha Abrams, Susan Bart and Sheena on a conference call."

"Jose Martinez online, John Mason online, Benjamin Britain online, Marsha Abrams online, Susan Bart online, Sheena online."

"Okay everyone; I have a big surprise for you," said Lucinda. "We are all going on a Caribbean cruise for twenty-four days. It is leaving this Saturday." She waited for all the questions to subside and continued. "I want you to pack for three weeks plus three days. You have to be ready to leave at 1000 hours tomorrow. We will fly down on the Gulfstream and stay at a local hotel. The following morning we will leave the hotel in pairs by cab to the cruise ship. Do you have any questions?" A flurry of questions followed.

"Do we need fancy clothes?"

"How many outfits do I need to pack?"

"What ports are we visiting?"

7

"Are we going to be able to go on any tours?"

"Do we need our weapons?

Lucinda waited for the questions to run out and then said, I will answer all your questions over lunch. Meet me in the conference room at 1300 hours today. I will explain everything to you. Computer off." The computer disconnected the conference call.

Lucinda walked over to Ron. "I have a small problem."

"What is it?" Ron asked, looking up from reading a report on his tablet.

"I am being asked questions about the cruise," Lucinda said. "Like what they should wear, how fancy, and how much to bring."

"So what's the problem?"

"I've never been on a cruise," Lucinda replied," so how can I tell the crew what to take?"

"I don't know the answer," Ron said. "I'll call Dr. Wellfleet. He will know or will know someone to ask."

"Computer," said Ron.

"Computer online," said the Computer.

"Dr. Wellfleet, please."

"Dr. Wellfleet is online."

Ron explained Lucinda's small problem to Dr. Wellfleet and told him that she is meeting with the crew at 1300 hours in the conference room to answer their questions. "Could you join them and help out?" Ron asked.

"Sure. I'll meet them in the conference room at 1300 hours."

"Computer off," Ron said.

Lucinda leaned over and gave Ron a peck on the lips. "Thanks," she said. "Are you going to join us?"

"You bet." He said. "I've never been on a cruise before, either."

At 1300, everyone was in the conference room just as Beth, Ron's secretary, wheeled in the food cart. Everyone thanked her and started filling their plates. As they were eating, Dr. Wellfleet walked in with Melinda Dash on his arm.

Everyone stopped eating and stood up. They all went over to welcome Melinda. They had not seen her for ten months, ever since she

8

took leave after marrying Martin. After all the greetings and all the hugs, everyone sat down. Melinda sat at the head of the table. Ron brought her a plate of food, while Dr. Wellfleet filled his own plate.

When lunch was finished and the dishes cleared, Dr. Wellfleet stood. "Okay," he said. "You wanted information about what to bring for a twenty-four day cruise. Just to clarify the length of the cruise. It is really two seven and one fourteen day cruise. I don't know all the answers so I called someone who did." He pointed to Melinda.

"I can speak for the men," Dr. Wellfleet said. "They need basic daytime clothing such as shorts, bathing suits, T-shits, and slacks. Evening clothes are different. No shorts, T-shirts or bathing suits inside the ship in the evening are permitted. For formal nights, you need a suit or a tuxedo. If for some reason you do not want to wear either, you can eat dinner at the buffet. If it is like other cruises I have been on, you will receive a daily schedule the night before with all the information you will need for the following day. It will tell you what events are planned and what entertainment is available. It is my understanding is that if you are not on duty, you may avail yourself of all that the ship has to offer. That is all I have to say to the men. For the women, I have brought you Melinda." Turning to Melinda he said, "It's all yours!" and sat down.

Melinda got up slowly. "I thank you all for that marvelous welcome. I won't be standing up for very long for as you can see I am pregnant. Eight months plus. I will be having twins, a boy and a girl. We have not picked out names yet. Martin is thrilled to death, and he treats me like the Queen Mother."

Marsha asked, "Do you like being pregnant?"

"Yes, I am enjoying being pregnant. It has done wonders for my skin, and I've had no morning sickness. I don't expect to be coming back to work anytime soon. And although Martin and I would love to go with you, we were not chosen to be part of this team."

"That's enough about me. Let us get back to the subject of what to pack for your twenty-four day 'vacation'. She paused hearing the Computer say, "Harry Blank online."

"Hi, Harry," said Melinda. "I thought you weren't going to be connected until tomorrow."

"I figured you might need me in a hurry, so I had the clinic advance my appointment to install the communications equipment under my skin. Melinda, how would you and Martin like to join the team?"

"That's a silly question," said Melinda. "We would love to join the team. We both love to cruise. Of course, I would love to know what ports we will be going, not that it would matter."

"The ports are St. Maarten, St. Kitts, San Juan, Labadee, Grand Cayman, Jamaica, St. Lucia and Curacao, a total of twenty-four days," replied Harry.

"All right, I'll inform the crew. I assume Martin and I will be traveling under our own names. That means I will be playing Den Mother, and in my condition it shouldn't be too hard."

"You got that right," replied Harry. "Of course, you will have to disguise your condition. Talk to you later about that. Computer off."

Melinda continued, "OK, clothing for the females. Casual clothing like shorts or bathing suits is fine for day wear. If you plan to walk around the ship in your bathing suit, you must wear a coverall. There will be two formal nights each week. In the daily planner, that you will receive the night before, you will be informed what the dress code is for the next evening. For those who want to participate, that will mean six dress-up outfits. It can be pantsuits or dresses. Since this is a back-to-back-to-back cruise, you can wear the same outfits three times. Heels or flats are okay. Make sure you can move in the clothing you take. Remember, you are always on duty and might be called at any time to participate in a particular operation. You will be armed with the new dart guns after you board the ship. The dart gun is the same model that we used in the New York raid. Some of you were in on that raid. You know how effective those dart guns are. They are small enough to hide on your person. Do not leave your cabin without it. You will have laundry service. You can send it out as often as you want. That means you only have to pack for five days. You can have two suitcases. Maximum weight is fifty pounds for each bag. Are there any other questions?"

"Are we going to have a contact on the ship?" John Mason asked.

"The Head of Housekeeping is one of your contacts. I'll explain about that later," replied Melinda.

"Why is there a fifty pound maximum on suitcases?" Jose asked.

"The cruise line doesn't want its employees getting hurt lifting heavy suitcases," answered Melinda.

"Do we take our own weapons?" Susan asked.

"No. Absolutely not," Melinda said. When you go onboard the cruise ship weapons will be brought to you. Dr. Wellfleet is going to be one of the ships doctors. Suzy Quentin will be the officer in charge of Housekeeping. She will be wearing three gold stripes separated by two white stripes. She will be walking around the ship, and you can approach her with questions like any other passenger. The Captain will introduce her when he introduces his officers the first night. The Captain has no knowledge of this operation." Melinda paused as the Computer asked for her attention.

"Melinda, Harry Blank online," interrupted the Computer

Melinda stopped talking, held up her hand and said, "Yes Harry. Were you able to get us a cabin?"

"I'm sorry, Melinda. I couldn't get you and Martin a cabin."

"I'm kind of disappointed," she said.

"I got you the Owner's Suite instead," he said laughing. "It is room number 1640. I hope you don't mind."

"You had me, Harry," Melinda said with laughter in her voice. "Thanks. I'll call Martin and tell him to start packing."

"Don't bother," Harry said. "I already spoke to him. I love this subcutaneous communication equipment. They should give Ron a medal for all the work he did. The design and implementation of this equipment is unbelievable. I'm able to contact anyone that is 'connected' and still have privacy."

"Be careful," warned Melinda. "He might come up with something that gets connected to other parts of the body."

"Never you mind. Have you figured how you are going to disguise yourself? I spoke to Dr. Wellfleet. He's going to certify that you are only six months pregnant and that you are just obese," he said, laughing, as he disconnected.

Melinda hesitated a moment and then continued, "It looks like Martin and I are going to be on this cruise after all. We will be in the Owner's Suite, cabin number 1640. Are there any more questions?"

What about our cabins?"

"I was told that when you get on the ship you will be assigned your cabin. The numbers are 2309, 3336, 6326 and 7331. That is all I know. Are there any further questions? No. Good. Then I had better get home and help pack. We will see you on the ship or at the hotel." She got up, turned and left the conference room with Dr. Wellfleet.

Outside the conference room, Doctor Wellfleet pulled Melinda aside. "I had to fix the papers," he said. "There is a rule that no one in their third trimester can travel on a cruise ship. I wrote that you are just six months pregnant. It made it easy since you are not showing that big. How many months pregnant are you, really?"

"We were told eight months," Melinda replied. "Don't forget that it is really an estimate. I could be almost nine months. I guess I am lucky. I feel no distress and have plenty of energy. Besides, I will not be running around the ship. I am going on the cruise ship as an obese, pregnant woman."

The doctor looked at her, smiled and gave her a peck on the cheek. "You will let me know if anything changes, won't you?"

Melinda told him she would. She took the elevator down to the garage level and walked to her car. The driver got out and opened the passenger door for her. She slid across the seat and put on her seat belt. The driver closed the door and got into the driver's seat. He closed his door and put on his seat belt.

"Where do you want to go, Melinda?" He asked.

"I'm getting very tired," she replied. "I think home would be the place to go."

The driver nodded his head, started the engine and drove out of the garage.

12

Ron looked at the remaining team. "Were all your questions answered?" he asked. Seeing the heads nod, he closed the meeting. Everyone got up and left the room. Ron went to the conference room, fixed a cup of coffee and returned to his desk. He turned on his tablet and wrote a summary of what just took place. He sat back, turning his chair to face the window. He looked out at the broad expanse of the Hudson River. He watched a ferry go up the river. He followed a cruise ship pulling into the dock on fifty-fourth Street. The weatherman had said 'chance of rain'. It was raining, and raining hard. The buildings glistened. It was a perfect time for a cruise.

Ron thought about the group they had put together for this operation. *He had never worked with most of these team members before. According to their files, they were on Melinda's team for five years, so they must be good.* An hour later, on his way to his room, he contacted Martin to get his opinion of this operation.

"Computer, Martin online," said Ron.

"I'm online, Ron," what do you need?"

"I see that Harry Blank found room on this trip for you and Melinda. What do you think of this trip?"

"Hey guy," he said, "I'm only an escort on this trip. I am not even the pilot since Dennis got his fourth stripe. The only thing I was great at was being a pilot. I feel like I've been put out to pasture. They might let me be the co-pilot if I promise to make coffee."

"Enough. You are going to make me cry and rust my pens." They both laughed and said, "Computer off" at the same time.

At 0800 hours Friday morning, everyone met in the conference room next to Ron's office.

Ron stood up and the room got quiet. "As of 1800 hours last night the information is as follows: We will be traveling together to Ft. Lauderdale on the G650 which is parked at General Aviation at Newark International Airport. We will leave here by helicopter at 1100 hours. That will give you a little more time to finish any work you started. We will be staying overnight at the Hilton Hotel next to the airport in Ft. Lauderdale. The following morning each couple will leave for the cruise pier at twenty-minute intervals. You will be strangers to each other. Once on the ship, you can become friends. Just be aware of your surroundings. Are there any more questions?" There weren't any. "I will meet you in the underground garage at 1000 hours."

At 0930, everyone was already in the conference room. Ron walked into the room and motioned to everyone to proceed to the elevator. The elevator doors opened when they got there. They rode to the basement where the electric carts waited. The drivers transported them through the underground passage to the basement of another building. They rode the elevator up to the roof to their private heliport. They loaded their luggage as the engines roared to life. A few minutes later, the helicopter lifted off, heading west to the Old North Terminal at Newark International Airport. The rain was still heavy and visibility was limited. They landed at General Aviation next to their Gulfstream 650. It took fifteen minutes to transfer the luggage to the airplane. While they were loading the plane, Dennis, the pilot, did a walk around. He entered the plane, took off his raincoat and took the left seat in the cockpit. He looked back and saw Martin watching him. "Do you want to take the co-pilot's seat?" asked Dennis.

Martin smiled. "Do you really need an answer?"

"Okay. Close the door, come on up, and take your seat."

Martin closed the door, secured it and went into the cockpit. He sat in the co-pilot's seat, leaned back and buckled up. He had a broad smile on his face.

As Dennis started to call ground control for permission to taxi, he turned to Martin and reminded him to tell the passengers about the safety features of the G650. Martin unbuckled his seat belt, got out of his chair, went back into the main cabin and just stood there. It was nice to be home for ten months, having recuperated from the wounds he had received in the New York raid. Melinda was wounded in the same raid, but had recovered more quickly than he had. It was nice to be in action again, even though it was as the Den Mother's assistant.

"May I have everyone's attention, please?" It got very quiet. All you could hear was the purr of the engines. "Most of you have never flown

14

with us before in this aircraft. So let me tell you about the safety features of the G650."

Three minutes later Martin entered the cockpit. He heard Ground Control say, "Delta 267, you are number seven."

Dennis picked up the microphone and said, "Ground Control, this is Gulfstream 202Tango, ready to start engines and taxi."

"Roger 202Tango. Request permission to start engines and take taxiway Mike 2 to Echo 3 and hold."

"202Tango Mike 2 to Echo 3 and hold," Dennis repeated.

Turning to Martin, he said, "Just in the last ten minutes the runway got busy. We will have at least a fifteen to twenty minute wait."

A message then came from Ground Control. "202Tango, follow Delta 267. You are now number seven."

Twenty minutes later, they found themselves holding at the end of the runway waiting for Ground Control. "This is 202T, ready for departure," Dennis said into the microphone.

"202Tango, you are clear to flight level 30 (3,000 feet). Contact Departure Control 119.1 for final vector and level. Have a good day."

Dennis brought the engines to full power and released the brakes. Thirty seconds later, they were airborne, climbing to 3,000 feet. Dennis told Martin to switch the channels and call Departure Control.

Martin switched the channels and picked up the microphone. "Departure Control, this is 202Tango. Request a final vector and level to Ft. Lauderdale."

"Roger 202Tango. Set course to 090 cleared to flight level 230 (23,000 feet)." Dennis put the information into the autopilot, and the aircraft climbed. Moments later Dennis heard from Departure Control, "202Tango cleared to flight level 280 (28,000 feet)." Dennis put this information into the autopilot, and the aircraft continued to climb. Just as the aircraft reached 28,000 feet, they heard from Departure Control. "202Tango, you are cleared to flight level 330 (33,000 feet), final vector 180, have a good day."

Martin acknowledged the receipt of the information and hung up the microphone. He was still smiling, even though he was not flying the plane.

Just sitting in the cockpit was enough. Just then, Dennis reached over and poked him.

"You want to fly it?" Dennis asked.

Martin's smile would light up Grand Central Station as he nodded his head. Dennis lifted his hands off the yoke, reached over and turned the autopilot off. "The ship is yours," he said.

Martin put his hands on the yoke and just sat there. He started looking at all the dials and noted the position of the switches. He had not flown in more than ten months, and it seemed so strange to be sitting in the right hand seat. He had been flying in the left seat for over 10 years. He slowly became comfortable and started enjoying himself. Dennis did not say anything. "Now you can fly the plane yourself. It is less than three hours to Ft. Lauderdale. Can I buy you a cup of coffee?"

Martin laughed. "Sure, why not."

As Dennis unbuckled his safety harness, Martin said, "I almost forgot. Congratulations on getting that fourth stripe."

"I got that stripe almost a year before I would have gotten it on my own," said Dennis. "You even made sure I would have this job."

"You did the work, so enjoy the results. Do the same for your next co-pilot. Speaking of which, have your found one yet?"

"I interviewed a number of great candidates. One really stood out. He just retired from the Air Force as a Major. He flew F15's. As soon as his security clearance is renewed he will fill that chair," pointing to the chair Martin was sitting in.

"I hope he works as well with you, as you did with me."

Dennis smiled. "I'm pretty sure he will. I spoke to some of the pilots with whom he worked. He has a great reputation for keeping his cool and for being fair to those he commanded."

They were suddenly interrupted. "202Tango, this is Atlanta Center. Change course to 183, confirm flight level 330 (33,000 feet)."

Martin went on the radio and confirmed the information. He made the adjustments and continued flying the plane.

16

An hour later, Dennis picked up the microphone and said, "Ft. Lauderdale Center, November 202Tango with you at flight level 330 (33,000 feet). We are requesting landing instructions."

"202Tango, you are fifth to land. Use racetrack pattern 090 at flight level 200 (20,000 feet). You have four aircraft in your airspace." Martin confirmed receipt of the information.

Twenty minutes later, when they were at 3,000 feet, they received a final call from Arrival Control giving them permission to land. Martin took his hands off the yoke and said, "I give you back your airplane in one piece."

Dennis smiled, made minor adjustments and took over control of the Gulfstream. He reduced his speed as he came in over the outer marker. As soon as the wheels kissed the ground, Dennis applied the reverse thrusters and slowed the plane. Ground Control gave him instructions to taxi to General Aviation. It was necessary to taxi the length of the airport to get to General Aviation. He parked the plane next to another G650 and shut the engines down. Martin went into the main cabin, unsecured the door, opened it and pressed the button that let the steps descend.

As soon as the stairs were fully descended, a messenger ran up and handed Martin an envelope. Martin nodded and tore it open. It was from Harry's assistant.

> *'Harry wanted all of you on the ship as soon*
> *as possible tomorrow. A van will be available*
> *to take all of you to the hotel today and to the ship*
> *tomorrow. Since there will be many vans there,*
> *Harry did not think you would be noticed.'*

Martin turned to the passengers and said, "Change of plans. We are traveling to the hotel together, and tomorrow we will be taken to the ship." As he said this, a large green van towing a trailer pulled up to the plane. "Okay, this looks like our transportation."

Everyone stood and went down the stairs. They retrieved their luggage from the cargo hold, put it in the trailer and took a seat in the van.

17

Martin shook Dennis's hand and thanked him for allowing him to fly the airplane. Martin helped Melinda down the steps and into the passenger seat of the van next to the driver. He got in the seat behind her. Melinda took out her makeup kit and started applying the disguise that would make her face and arms look obese. The ride to the Hilton hotel lasted only fifteen minutes. Each couple checked in and went to their rooms to drop off their luggage. They met back in the lobby and went for lunch. When lunch was completed, the couples separated and toured the area. There wasn't much to see but they wanted to stay out of their rooms as much as possible.

Day 1   At 1100 hours on Saturday, as the van approached the cruise ship Valley Forge, a police officer from the Sheriff's Department directed them to the V.I.P. parking. The van pulled up and two porters came over to unload the van. Martin tipped the porters, and everyone got out of the van and headed to the terminal. Martin retrieved a wheelchair for Melinda, which was sitting by the door.

Since they were in the V.I.P. parking lot, they were directed to the V.I.P. check-in. They had to walk the entire length of the terminal to find the correct check-in line. There were twenty-five people on the line ahead of them. Twenty minutes later, with all the paperwork finished, the cabins assigned, their key cards received, they headed towards the gangway. They finally made it to the top of the steep gangway where Security scanned their key card. Martin struggled with the wheelchair until an attendant came from the ship and assisted him. Everyone was escorted to the elevator and they went to find their cabins. Ron and Lucinda had cabin 7331 that overlooked the Promenade. Jose and Susan had 6331 which also overlooked the Promenade. John and Marsha received cabin 3336 and Sheena and Benjamin received cabin 2309. Martin and Melinda went to deck 10, the Concierge level. There they were welcomed by their cabin attendant and escorted to their suite. Martin put his key card in the slot and heard a click as the green light came on. The cabin attendant held the door open as Martin pushed the wheelchair into the cabin, and stopped short.

Melinda was transfixed. Martin stood next to her. "Harry Blank really knows how to spoil us," said Melinda.

"As soon as the luggage comes up," said the cabin attendant, "I'll bring it in." He turned and walked out of the cabin letting the door close.

Straight ahead of them was a baby grand piano. On the room to the right was a large mahogany dining room table on which you could land a small airplane. Twelve matching upholstered high back chairs surrounded the table. Melinda got out of the wheelchair, and they both walked further into the cabin. Melinda saw two doors on the left. Martin opened the first door, and they entered a large bedroom with a round king sized bed. To the right of the bed was a large bathroom in which there was a whirlpool bath, a large glassed in shower, a toilet, a bidet, and double sinks. From the bedroom, a door led onto a large private balcony on which there was a hot tub and four lounge chairs.

"Can we move in permanently?" Melinda asked.

"Wait," Martin said. "Before you make any decisions we should look at the rest of the suite."

They walked back into the living room, through the sitting room and into the second bedroom. This was not as grand as the first bedroom. It had a small sitting room with a glass table and two small upholstered chairs. Through the door were a standard bed, a small dresser and one chair. The bathroom was quite small compared to the master bathroom. It didn't even have a whirlpool bath. "I guess this is a guest bedroom," Martin said as he put his arm on Melinda's shoulder. "Let's see what behind door number three." The third bedroom was larger than the second bedroom. What made it seem even larger was that it did not have any windows. It contained two double beds, a wide walk in closet with sliding doors that were covered with a large mirror on each door. The bathroom was smaller than the other rooms. It had a toilet, a shower, and a single sink mounted in a black marble counter. They walked back to the main sitting room. In an alcove there was a small kitchen. It had a miniature refrigerator, a small two burner electric stove, a sink and a microwave that was mounted under the cabinet. Sitting on the black marble counter were a tray of snacks, a bottle of champagne in an ice bucket and two flutes.

"I think you're right," Martin said as he held Melinda in his arms. "We should move in permanently. Since we can't, I guess we should enjoy it now, unless we win the lottery."

There was a knock on the door. Martin let Melinda go and went to open the door. Melinda went into the bedroom to start unpacking her carry-on bag. Martin looked through the peephole and saw a petit woman in a white uniform with three gold stripes on her sleeve. He opened the door, and the officer walked in wheeling a large suitcase. She was about five foot four, with short black hair surrounding an oval face. She had dark eyes that sparkled when the light hit them.

"My name is Quentin," she said. "Susan Quentin. My friends call me Suzy Q." She put her hand out to shake Martin's hand. "I have some information from Harry Blank."

Before she could say another word, Melinda walked into the living room and stopped. She looked at the woman in uniform and said, "Suzy? Is that you?" She rushed over and pulled her into an awkward hug. "What are you doing here? Why are you in that uniform? Where are you living? Are you married? Do you have any kids? What have you been doing and with whom? Talk to me."

"I would, if you would just give me a chance to get a word in."

Melinda let her go and stepped back.

Suzy laughed. "You haven't changed and neither has your corny greeting."

"I haven't seen you in five or six years. By the way, you look good in that uniform."

"Thanks. I worked really hard for it," she said, looking Melinda at Melina's large stomach. "How far along are you?" she asked.

"For the record, I am six plus months pregnant. Actually, I'm more than eight months pregnant. Dr. Wellfleet is aware of this. We don't expect any problems since I am only going to be the 'Den Mother.'"

"What's a 'Den Mother'?" Quentin asked.

"Like a mother wolf taking care of her cubs," said Melinda.

Suzy looked at her again and smiled. "Yeah, I can see that. If you need me, I'm connected." She reached down and started to lift the suitcase.

Martin reached over and helped her put the suitcase on the dining room table. She opened the suitcase and took out a small portable television set, a batch of wires, a small antenna and a small cardboard box.

She opened the small box and took out four guns. "These are the dart guns that were sent for you," Suzy said. "Each of your teams will get a set when they get to their cabin. I don't know why they sent a portable television since all I have to do is attach the antenna to the converter and plug it into your television in the living room. When I get done, you will be able to use the monitors in all the bedrooms." She took the antenna, took the tape off the back and mounted it to the balcony window behind the curtain. She fastened the wires to the wall and snaked them behind the furniture. She attached the converter and then plugged it in to the television. "Now you have access to all the ship's cameras. You can control them with the joystick or just run your finger across the screen. If you need to add cameras to the system, enter their codes, and that will bring that camera online."

"I don't know why Harry didn't contact you directly since he's now connected," continued Susy Q. "I guess he isn't used to it yet, either. I know I'm not. Harry asked me to tell you that he wants Martin to use a wheelchair. That way his six foot, five inches will not appear to be threatening, and no one pays any attention to someone in a wheelchair. We know that many people saw Martin walking onto the ship, so you are going to have an 'accident' in the hallway. You will lie down and Melinda will dial 911. An emergency team will come get you and take you down to the Medical Center. Dr. Wellfleet will give you the rest of the information. He has a wheelchair especially for you. It has helper motors so that Melinda won't kill herself trying to wheel your 300 pounds around the ship."

"I only weigh 250 pounds," Martin said innocently.

"Yeah, right, sure you do," said Suzy Q. "I guess that's your story and you're going to stick to it." Everyone laughed at that.

"Wait fifteen minutes after I leave so I won't be near the 'accident'. I'll get a chance to talk to you later." She patted Melinda's belly lightly, said her goodbyes and left the room.

Fifteen minutes later, Martin went out into the hall, making sure no one was around. He also made sure he was out of sight of the surveillance camera that was mounted to the overhead twenty feet away from their suite. He lay down on the floor. Melinda picked up the phone and dialed 911. The rest of the charade went as planned. Within minutes, one could hear over the loudspeaker, "Mike, mike, mike, Deck 10 forward." This alarm was repeated twice more. Within minutes four members of the emergency medical team showed up, put a collar on Martin's neck, slid Martin onto backboard, lifted the board, and moved through to the inside passage. They lifted the backboard onto a gurney and strapped it in place. They moved the gurney into the elevator and pressed 1 on the panel. That was the deck for the Medical Center. The elevator descended and the doors opened on Deck 1. They wheeled the gurney out of the elevator and towards the Medical Center. As they approached the Center, the doors opened and they wheeled the gurney into an examination room. They unstrapped the backboard from the gurney and slid it onto an examination table. They split the board and removed it without moving Martin who was laying there moaning. They made sure Martin was safe on the table and left the room. As they left, Melinda and Dr. Wellfleet entered. The doctor locked the door. Martin lay on the table and moaned and groaned some more.

"That is the worst performance I have ever seen, or heard for that matter," said Dr. Wellfleet.

"I agree," Melinda said.

"You're all a bunch of critics!" said Martin. "You didn't see how they struggled to lift me onto the gurney? I think they need to exercise more or you had better get bigger and stronger medics. I am not the largest passenger on this ship. Have you seen some of them?" Both Dr. Wellfleet and Melinda laughed at his description of some of the passengers.

Martin sat up and put his legs over the edge of the table. Doctor Wellfleet walked to the back of the room and wheeled a black wheelchair with balloon tires next to the examination table.

"Melinda," he said, "I want you to try pushing this wheelchair."

Melinda got between the handles and tried to push. She could barely move the chair. "If you think I am going to push my husband in this chair, you're out of your mind."

The doctor laughed, leaned over the chair, and pushed a button that was under the handle. "Now try it," he said.

Melinda got between the handles and again gave it a hard push. The wheelchair flew across the room and banged into the wall.

"What just happened?" she asked, as she walked to retrieve the wheelchair.

"Watch," said the doctor. "Martin, get in the chair,"

Martin got off the table and sat in the chair. The doctor motioned for Melinda to try to push the chair. She couldn't move it. Then the doctor leaned over again, and pushed a button under the handle. Melinda tried moving the chair, and it moved with no effort.

"The chair has helpers that multiply the force used," he said. He turned a couple of knobs, and the back of the wheelchair opened. Clipped to the board were four dart guns and four rows of extra darts. He closed the panel and said. "Try practicing with the chair Martin, while I get the special brace for your leg. If anyone asks what happened to you, you tell them you slipped in the hall and broke your ankle, the doctor set the bones and put on a cast. The doctor said it will take months to heel. Now we all can tell the same story." Wellfleet put the cast on Martin's ankle and snapped it closed. "You can take it off by pressing the top edge in," the doctor told him. He demonstrated the procedure until Martin and Melinda understood. "I made it look very heavy but it only weighs ounces. It is strong enough that you can put your entire weight on it. You can even run with it on your foot."

Martin moved the chair around the room until he was comfortable using it. "Okay. I'm ready to be seen in society." Melinda held the door open and Martin wheeled through it.

"Before I forget," Doctor Wellfleet said. "Don't tell anyone about the helper motors. It is still a work in progress."

Meanwhile, the other four couples were settling into their cabins. Quentin visited them in turn as the luggage was being delivered to their cabins. She let them know what was happening around the ship and what they were allowed to do when they were off duty.

"Martin," said Melinda. "New York just called. They said that the crew of the Valley Forge had only cursory background checks. Maritime Service does not do background checks like the FBI. The New York office is going to do a more thorough background check on the entire crew and will keep us informed."

Ron looked at his watch. "Isn't it time for lunch?"

"Of course it is," said Lucinda laughing. "It is always lunch time with you. Just remember, this is not an eating cruise. We're here to work."

Meanwhile, on another deck, in another part of the ship, Jose Martinez, a five foot eight, wiry built thirty-two year old, with brown eyes, sporting short brown hair was unpacking his carry-on bag. Doing the same was his partner, Susan Bart. She was a thirty year old, five foot seven fine boned well-proportioned woman. She had beautiful brown hair cut just above her shoulders and golden specks in her eyes. "When we're finished here I would like to tour the ship and see what there is to see," she said to Jose.

"I'm almost ready," Jose replied. "Not enough drawer space here to make unpacking easy. I can't imagine the problem we will have when we get the rest of our luggage."

"Computer"

"Computer online Susan," answered the Computer.

"Melinda, please," asked Susan.

"What's up Susan?" asked Melinda.

"I still can't get over this communication system. We have unpacked our carry-ons and are going to tour the ship. Is Quentin connected?"

"Yes she is. Why?"

"When she met with us, she told us she would keep us informed as to what is happening. We get that direct. We didn't know what to say to her."

"She only got connected two days ago. She is not used to using it as often as we do. She told me that she forgets that she has the system under her skin. I'll remind her. Is there anything else?"

"Yeah, this is some monster ship. Five couples are expected to cover it all?"

"I know," said Melinda. "It sounds strange. We only have to try to find out how they are smuggling stuff on and off the ship. We will have teams wandering around at all hours of the day and night, especially when we approach a port. We have twenty-four days to find out how they do it. If we don't solve it on this trip, then Harry will have to figure out another way to do this. Hang in there. We are not at sea yet. Enjoy your tour. Computer off."

Jose and Susan left their cabin, turned left, and walked to the elevator. "Let's start at the top of the ship and work our way down. I've looked at the ship's plans and we'll have a lot of area to cover," Susan remarked.

"You should walk three paces behind me like a perfect 'wife,'" laughed Jose.

Susan smacked him on the shoulder and laughed. "Just remember who has seniority in this 'marriage'."

They took the elevator to Deck 14 and went outside on deck. The sun was shining, reflecting off the water. The air was so clear you could see forever.

"What a view," Susan said, putting her sunglasses on. "It is a shame we have to work."

"It's real hard work," Jose said smiling. He took his sunglasses out of his pocket, put them on and started walking. Susan turned and joined him.

"Team, this is Ron. Check your room cards for your table number and time for dinner. Start touring the ship after you have unpacked your carry-on bags. Keep your eyes open." Each member acknowledged the message.

John Mason was a twenty-eight year-old, five foot nine with blond hair and blue eyes. His shoulders were so wide he had to turn sideways to go into the narrow cabin doors. He was the team's medic. He held the hand of Marsha Abrams, his thirty-year-old, five foot six inch red haired freckled 'wife'.

"Don't get overly friendly, my 'husband'. Just remember I can still take you down, even if we are 'married'.

John laughed, pulled her close and kissed her on the cheek. "Yes dear," was his only reply. They both laughed as she put her arm in his.

They entered the dining room and showed their key card to the waiter who escorted them to their table. The table was in the corner of the lower level dining room. They both looked around as if they were tourists, pointing to different things in the dining room. The dining room was three tiers high. What they were really doing was whispering about the different vantage points that were in the dining room if someone wanted to cause havoc.

"This is a very large dining room," said Marsha. "There is no way we can cover it by ourselves, Even if all of us sat in here each meal we couldn't do it. It's going to be mostly luck."

"Maybe not, but once the security checks are finished, we will have an idea whom to watch."

The other teams were checking in, unpacking their carry-ons and doing a tour of the ship. They took turns breaking for lunch. When lunch was finished, they checked in and continued to tour the ship. They were to walk each deck and comment as to what they saw. New York will act as recorder, and at the end of the day will relay the information to everyone's tablet for review. They will have the watch stander's schedule on their tablets by dinnertime.

At 1700 hours, the Valley Forge got underway, heading out of the harbor. There were four ships ahead of them leaving the harbor. They were all monster-sized ships. They were each more than eleven hundred feet long and as high as seventeen decks. One ship had eighteen decks. The sun was setting and it made for a romantic picture. The Valley Forge passed the Coast Guard Station and turned right, into the channel. Once out of the harbor, the Valley Forge turned south towards its first stop, St. Kitts. Ron notified the teams of the ship's schedule. They would be at sea for the next two days, and allowed to participate in the ship's activities. He advised them to keep their eyes open and remain vigilant.

Chapter 2

Day 2 On Sunday, their first day at sea they all met for breakfast. While eating a leisurely breakfast they discussed which assignments they had for the day. Who was walking the deck and who would be watching the monitor. When they finished breakfast they got up, separated and went to their assignments. Each team took a deck and walked the length of the ship, taking notice of everything that was going on about them. They exchanged decks and did the same thing again, getting very familiar with the Valley Forge. After walking around the ship for a couple of hours it was decided that one pair could take a break for a couple of hours. They met in the lower atrium to choose straws. Jose and Susan won the first round.

"We will meet you people at the lunch buffet," said Susan. "I don't think the world will end if there is no one patrolling the ship for twenty minutes out at sea, do you?"

No one answered. Marsha smiled, gave Susan a hug, and they all separated. Susan and Jose walked to the elevator and took it to their floor. They turned left and entered a long corridor. They walked two hundred feet down the corridor to their cabin. Jose took out his key card and put it in the slot on the door. A red light blinked. He tried the card again. Again, the red light blinked. He pulled the card out of the slot and looked at it to make sure he was putting it in correctly. He tried it one more time and the red light blinked.

"Let me try my key card," said Susan, taking it out of her pocket. She slid her key card into the slot on the door, a green light blinked and a click sounded. She turned the handle on the door and pushed it open. "You are going to have to go to the Customer Service desk and have them issue you another card."

"I wonder what I did to cause it to not work," asked Jose. "Everything I have is in the safe. All I carried was the key card and the dart gun. I'll go to the Guest Relations desk later. Now I have the excuse to stay with you all the time."

Susan looked at him, and smiled. She liked Jose, but he always seemed so shy around her. I wonder, she thought *what I should do to make him feel less shy around me. I'll think of something. We'll be eating all our meals together, relaxing together, and sleeping in the same cabin. We'll see.* They laid out their bathing suits and took turns using the bathroom to change. They both knew what they wanted to do. They wanted to use the pool for a short time and then lay out in the sun.

Susan came out of the bathroom wearing a very small bright orange bikini. Jose stood there and stared at her. He nodded his head in approval, picked up her coverall and handed it to her. Jose ducked into the bathroom and put his bathing suit on. As they left the cabin, Susan reached over, grabbed Jose's hand and held it as they walked towards the elevator. She didn't look at him, just kept walking, holding his hand. She noticed he held her hand as well.

They took the elevator to the pool deck and were lucky enough to find two empty lounge chairs next to each other. They put their things on the chairs and walked to the stairs that went into the shallow end of the pool. Jose went down the steps first and turned around. He reached for Susan's hand to help her down the stairs. She took his hand, walked down the stairs, and pushed against him. He put his arms around her, to hold her steady and she kissed him. They stood there, looking at each other. She smiled up at him, kissed him lightly on the lips, dove into the water and swam away. He stood there for a moment, wondering what had just happened. Shaking his head, he dove in the water swimming after her. After swimming for a while they both got out of the pool and walked over to their lounge chairs. Jose picked up Susan's towel, put it around her and started drying her back and shoulders. He did this very slowly. He was enjoying doing this to Susan. He really liked her but felt so shy around her. *I have to do something about that,* he thought. *After all, she did kiss me, didn't she?* He took the towel and started drying her legs, very, slowly. She didn't stop him, either. When he was finished, he helped her into her lounge chair, then took his towel, and dried himself. He got into his lounge chair and laid back. He reached out for her hand and she placed her hand in his. They lay there quietly and dozed off. An hour later, Susan woke up, and looked around. She saw Jose was still sleeping in the lounge chair next to her. She quietly got up, walked around the lounge chair, bent down and gently kissed Jose on the lips. He smiled, opened his eyes and kissed her back.

Susan placed her hands on his chest and pushed away. "You can't do that in public," she said, out of breath." It is time we went back to the cabin and changed for work. She reached out for his hand and helped him out of the lounge chair. They walked hand in hand back to the cabin.

Susan put her key card in the slot, the green light blinked on, and the door unlocked. She pushed the door open and they both entered the room. As soon as the door closed, Susan turned and fell into his arms. They kissed for what seemed hours but were only minutes.

"What's happening?" asked Susan, startled at her brashness.

"I don't know," answered Jose. "I really don't want to have a debate over it, I just want to enjoy the feeling."

"Who gets to use the shower first?" asked Susan.

"If you don't mind," said Jose. "I would like to use it first. I got chilled walking through the passageway to the cabin."

"You go ahead, then" said Susan. "I'll take out my clothes while I'm waiting."

Jose went into the bathroom and walked to the shower. He turned it on, took off his bathing suit and got under the spray. He started shampooing his hair when he felt a pair of hands wrap themselves around his chest. He let the water rinse the soap off his head and turned around. He leaned down and kissed Susan deeply. She kissed him back. They stood like this for many minutes before breaking apart. He took the soap and started washing her shoulders. He massaged her back and moved his hands down her buttocks and down her legs. While he was on his knees washing her legs, she turned around. He started washing the front to her legs until he got to her upper thighs. She grabbed him by the hair and pulled him up. They stood there kissing for a few moments. Susan turned the water off and took Jose's hand. She pulled him out of the bathroom and walked to the bed. She put her arms around his neck, kissed him and then gave him a push. He fell onto the bed. She fell on top of him and started kissing him.

"I don't think we will make it back on time," said Susan, as she kissed him again.

Jose pulled away from her and sat up. "I don't think this is smart,"

30

he said. "The rules are very strict. If the boss found out we were messing around during an operation, she would fire us. The punishment could be worse. We could be made to sit at a desk. I want you so much, but I don't think this is the time or place. We'll be finished in a week and then we both get at least a week off."

"You're right," said Susan. "I don't know what got into me. As soon as you touched me I felt sparks between us." She leaned over, gave me a light kiss on the lips and got off the bed.

New York notified Melinda that Suzy Q's second in command, Frank Barber, in the housekeeping department did not pass the deep security check. They are also investigating Barber's assistant, Casandra Niki, since they came on the Valley Forge together. Quentin will try to keep them under observation as best she could. She still had own duties to perform. It would look very suspicious if her work was not completed. In addition, it would raise eyebrows if she wandered into areas that she had designated to someone else, and it might raise questions if she made any operational changes. At least New York was able to identify one definite suspect and one possible suspect. New York will try to keep those two under observation. New York is also going to see if anyone else came on the ship at the same time as Frank Barber and Casandra Niki. It made sense that it had to be someone who could move around the ship without anyone paying attention to them. No one pays attention to someone wearing a uniform on the ship, only other uniforms. One question that was asked earlier, however, was, "Who else was working with Frank Barber, the assistant housekeeper? Would it be crew, other people in uniform or some passengers?"

Day 3 On Monday, their second sea day. Martin and Melinda met with three couples for breakfast in the dining room. The placed their orders and started discussing what they wanted to do that day. Cruising was a new experience to all the members except Martin and Melinda. It was a relaxing breakfast. When it was over, Susan stood saying it was her turn on the monitor. She went to Melinda's cabin to relieve Lucinda, who was watching the monitor since midnight. The rest of the teams went to their assigned areas around the ship.

That afternoon the weather changed. The wind picked up to thirty miles an hour and many passengers went indoors. The teams took turns going back to their cabins to get heavier jackets. They had to stay on deck to keep an eye out for any unusual activities. A black cloud moved swiftly past the ship dropping cold rain which caused the rest of the passengers to go inside. By lunchtime, the sun had come out and the wind died down to a mild pleasant breeze.

Everyone took his or her turn watching the monitor. The ship was a little more than two hundred from land and the teams were getting anxious. They didn't have any idea what to expect. They had never operated on a ship this large. It was over a thousand feet long. They took turns going for lunch. Every couple of hours, one pair would take a break and head for the pool. When it got close to dinner, one-half of a pair volunteered to stay on deck and the other half went to watch the monitor.

Those people who were not assigned to walk the deck met in the main dining room for dinner. After a leisurely dinner, Melinda and Ron assisted Martin into his adapted wheelchair. Melinda wheeled Martin on Deck 4. They were walking towards the back of the ship when she noticed two deck hands wheeling a cart past them. The cart was loaded with cardboard boxes and each box had a wide black diagonal stripe on it. The men stacked the boxes by the railing and then covered the boxes with a canvas. They tied the canvas down and walked away. They had ignored Melinda and Martin. Martin thought it strange for them to be working on deck during the passenger's dinnertime and that they left boxes on deck where it would be protruding into the public areas.

Martin and Melinda relayed this information to New York. Melinda pushed the wheelchair back to their suite. She opened one of their carry-on bags and removed a miniature digital camera. They returned to Deck 4 where the boxes were stacked. There was no one else on deck. Martin stood up from his wheelchair, placed the video camera between the overhead beams, pushed a button on the side of the camera and heard a click. He tried to tug the camera and found the magnet did a good job. He aimed the camera at the boxes and quickly sat down. Melinda continued to push the chair slowly along the deck. They looked around to see if there was anyone else on deck. The coast was clear. Back in their cabin, they turned on the monitor, the converter, and entered the camera code. Within moments, they had a clear video picture of the boxes. A few more clicks on the computer keyboard and New York had the video feed.

"With both of us watching," Martin said, "We shouldn't miss much. I have notified everyone about the boxes. I was wondering if we should take one of the boxes to examine."

"I don't think it would be a good idea," Melinda said. "If I was smuggling goods in boxes, I would have dummy boxes with traps."

"I think you're right," said Martin. "We'll let the camera do the work. We are about two hundred miles from St. Kitts. I don't expect anything to happen until we are less than twenty-five or thirty miles from shore, when the pilot boat comes out. Speaking of which, did they clear the pilot and his crew through security?"

"Yes they did," said Melinda. "That was one of the first things Harry said they did. The way I figure, if they are going to do anything, it will be before the pilot boat comes out. I don't think they would want anyone to see them gathering the boxes. That means we need our people up by 0530 for an early breakfast. Sunrise is about 0630. Two couples should be on each side of the ship. You and I will be watching the monitor from our cabin to see what happens to those boxes." Martin thought, *'Here she goes again. If she said we will have action tomorrow morning, then we will have action tomorrow morning.'* Melinda relayed all the information to New York and to the team's tablets. Everyone gathered in the dining room for dinner. They discussed what would happen in the morning, who would get what assignment, in what part of the ship. After a quiet dinner, everyone went to their cabins. They had to be ready for a 0500 wake up call.

After Martin and Melinda returned to their suite, Martin checked with New York to see if there had been any action that he should be aware of. He shut down his monitor and prepared for bed. He got undressed and walked into the bathroom. Melinda was already in the shower, and Martin stood admiring her swollen body. Even though Martin was six feet-five and Melinda was five feet-ten, she folded perfectly into his arms every time he held her. She radiated such loveliness since she became pregnant. Now that she was eight months along, she just glowed. He smiled as he opened the shower door and stepped in. She leaned into his strong body and stood there under the shower. One of Martin's favorite things to do was to massage Melinda's belly now that she was pregnant. When he did that, Melinda moaned in delight.

Day 4   At 0530 hours Tuesday, the four teams were up, dressed and had a light breakfast. After breakfast, they went out on deck to their prearranged positions. They would stop occasionally and do stretching exercises. None of the teams was going near Deck 4, since they knew it was under observation. Melinda and Martin were taking turns watching the video monitor as the sun started to rise over the horizon. "I hope the angle of the sun doesn't reflect into the lens of the camera," said Martin, as he took his turn at watching the boxes on the screen. Just then, he saw two deckhands untie the canvas cover, remove it and start throwing the boxes off the ship. Within minutes, all the boxes were gone. They folded the cover, looked around to see if anyone was watching and walked away. In doing so, they looked directly into the camera. Now Martin had pictures of two of the suspects. New York notified Martin that the facial recognition program was now processing the pictures. Ron had the other three teams continue walking around and taking turns eating a second breakfast. He wanted them prepared to leave the ship as soon as it docked in St. Kitts. He wanted one team at the taxi stand, one team at the dock next door, and one team in a cab on the outside of the terminal. He and Lucinda would be wandering around the pier.

A call suddenly came in.

"Ron, New York is online," said the Computer

"What do you have for me?" asked Ron.

"We have identified one of the two suspects. His name is Rayson Grith. His file shows an arrest eight years ago as part of a group that was smuggling young children into the United States from Haiti for the sex trade. The file also shows he received a sentence of fifteen years. He got out after serving only three years and dropped off the radar. We are checking to see how long he has been attached to the ship."

"We also have a drone from the Air National Guard flying over the Valley Forge. We watched them throw six boxes off Deck 4. With this stiff breeze, the boxes have spread out. They are just below the water level. The drone is being operated from Puerto Rico and is good for three more hours. Its call sign is Special One. Special Two will be on station at 0730. They are not connected. Communication will be through New York. Computer off." "Melinda, did you monitor New York?" asked Ron.

"Yes," replied Melinda. "Both Martin and I did. Since everything is being monitored, why don't we take a turn on deck and get some coffee," Melinda suggested. "If something happens, they will call us. Martin finished dressing, put on a light jacket, and sat in his special wheelchair. Melinda opened the door, and Martin wheeled himself out into the passageway.

"What deck do you want to take a walk on?" inquired Martin.

"Deck 5 would be nice," Melinda replied. They took the elevator to Deck 5 and stopped for a cup of coffee for Martin and a cup of tea for Melinda. They sat and checked in with the teams. They did not see any suspicious activity as they wandered around the ship. Even Frank Barber, the Assistant Housekeeper stayed in his office.

"Melinda, Sheena online," said the Computer.

"What is it Sheena?" asked Melinda.

"I'm on Deck 14, with Benjamin," she said. "We see land on our starboard side, and we see three boats heading in our general direction."

"Okay. I will check with the New York office," said Melinda. "They should have it on their screen."

"Computer, get me the New York office," said Melinda.

The New York office came online and said, "We have Ron on as well. Special Two reported two small boats converging on the boxes. We are relaying the video to your monitor. The two boats are picking the boxes out of the water and placing them in their hold. One boat has finished loading and is heading to shore. It will dock twenty minutes before you do. We do not have anyone in St. Kitts at this time. We notified Charlie Pile. He's still in charge of the Caribbean desk. If anyone can help us at this time, it will be Charlie. He is connected."

"Melinda, Charlie Pile is online," said the Computer.

"Hello Charlie," said Melinda. "Did you get the messages from

New York?"

"Yes. I didn't answer because we were a little busy sorting out our teams. We flew four teams into St. Kitts late last night, in case they are needed. They will be looking for your teams. New York sent a set of pictures of all your teams, and I passed them out to my people. They have their assignments. My people are not connected. You and they will have to relay information through me. Your teams will not have to rush getting off the ship. By the way, I love this new communication system. I wish we could have had it last year. It saves us a lot of time. I wish my people could have been connected."

"Don't tell me, I know it. Tell Ron. He was the one who developed it."

"Melinda, Sheena is online," said the Computer.

"Okay, Sheena, what do you have?"

"After breakfast," Sheena said, "we went back up to Deck 14 and saw one of the small boats New York notified us about this morning. I notified Charlie Pile, and he was able to get a team down to the docks. We can see them still unloading the boat and putting the boxes into a light green van that has some advertisement on its sides. We are too far away to see the license plate."

"All teams from the Valley Forge, Charlie Pile is online."

"We have the light green van in sight," Charlie Pile said. "We don't know if they are going to wait for the second boat, or not. We are prepared to follow the van. One of my men is going to try to get a tracker on the van."

"Valley Forge, this is Special Two. The second suspect boat is slowly pulling into the harbor now. It is heading for the same dock as the first suspect boat."

Five minutes later, Special Two came back on the air. "The second boat has tied up in front of the first boat and is starting to unload their boxes onto the pier. One of those boxes appears to be very heavy. It is taking two men to carry it."

"How much time do you have left on station?" Ron asked Special Two.

"We have sixty minutes," he replied. "Special One is still on the ground."

"Okay," Ron said. "We have everything under control. You have permission to return to base. Thanks for your help, Special Two."

"This is Charlie Pile. The van is leaving the parking lot. There are many vehicles leaving the parking lot that resemble us. I guess the tourists have arrived. There is another ship docked in front of you and passengers are leaving that ship. We have the tracker on the green van and it is working, so we are falling further behind. We should be able to follow them without a problem. The tracker is working well even if we have to stop following the van."

"Attention all teams," Ron said. "Keep a loose patrol on the pier just in case they have people watching their back. Enjoy your break, but keep your eyes open."

"Melinda, Marsha online," said the Computer.

"How are you doing, Marsha? How is your 'husband' John."

"Everyone is good," she replied. "We relieved Sheena and Benjamin on Deck 14. We see the two boats in question. They are loading many small black objects the size of shoeboxes onto the blue boat. We cannot make out anything else. I took a few pictures and sent them to your tablet."

"Melinda. Charlie Pile online," the Computer said.

"What do you have for me, Charlie?" Melinda asked.

"Not a whole lot," he replied. "We were able to follow the green van to the other side of the island where it stopped at a small garage. They transferred the black boxes to a white van. We left a team in the neighborhood to watch the garage. They'll take pictures and make notes of anyone approaching the garage. If they get a chance, they will snoop around. We could not get a tracker on the white van. We followed the white van to a gas station where the driver stopped to get fuel. We then followed it to a small white house that had red shutters and a tan roof. There was a satellite dish mounted on the left side of the house. The driver opened the garage door, pulled in and closed the door. We noted the address, took pictures, and forwarded the coordinates to New York."

"We parked down the block to observe the house when we saw another van pull up to the garage door and four men got out. All four men were holding weapons in their hands. We were too far away to see what kind of weapons that had. They rushed to the front door and broke in. We heard gunfire and decided to get out of there. We started our engine, and slowly drove away. Before we got to the corner, the van passed us. A man leaned out of the passenger window and started shooting at us at it passed. We slowed down and waited for that van to drive away. When the van was out of sight, we came back to the docks where we saw one of the boats being loaded with small boxes. We couldn't get close enough to see what they were loading. When we got to the dock, we examined our van and found a row of bullet holes down the side. I am glad this van had reinforced sides. I'm going to leave two teams here and fly out to St. Maarten with the rest of my people to set up surveillance in case there is another episode of 'boxes in the water'. I notified San Juan to have two drones available, in case there is a problem."

"Okay Charlie," Melinda said. "We'll keep you informed if they drop anything off the back of the ship. We still have the Deck 4 camera online. We tapped into the ship's Security cameras as well. We did not think to do it when we came on board Valley Forge. Now we will be able to follow everyone throughout the ship. New York hasn't identified the second suspect, which bothers me. Neither one got off the ship in this port. We suspect there will be others working with them on the ship. We just haven't spotted them."

All the teams were back on board by 1700 hours. They went to their cabins, showered, dressed and met at the dining room entrance. At dinner, four of the five couples sat at the same table. After they sat down and their food orders taken, Ron told them that they were eating together because it was easier than trying to ignore each other. He said to them, "Just remember not to discuss any part of the operation when there are other people around." Everyone agreed and it relieved the tension. After dinner was finished, they got up from the table and went for a stroll on the promenade. Ron came online and told them to relax for the evening but to resume their duties at 0530 tomorrow. At 1700 hours, the Valley Forge got underway to St. Maarten.

Day 5   On Wednesday at 0530 hours, the Valley Forge was thirty miles off the coast of St. Maarten. Martin got up and made a pot of coffee in the little kitchen. He poured a cup and went out on the balcony, sat and watched the sun start to come up. He could see three large cruise ships following them into port. He finished his coffee and went inside the cabin, turned on the monitor, and noticed that there was something under a canvas on Deck 4. He reviewed the recordings of the night's activities and found that the boxes were placed on deck at 0430. The boxes were covered and secured. Martin notified New York and asked why they had not contacted him when the boxes were brought on deck. New York assumed he had been watching the monitor. Martin called Ron to let him know that it looked like we were going to have some action this morning. He no sooner notified the teams to be on alert when he saw two men approach the boxes. He watched as they took the cover off, threw the boxes over the rail and quickly left the area. Ron called Charlie Pile and notified him about the action that just took place on Deck 4. He also told all the teams to be on the lookout for any small boats heading for the ship. He notified San Juan and requested they launch a drone as soon as possible. Charlie Pile called back and said that all three marinas would be covered. Charlie called Melinda and told her that the team he had left on St. Kitts had not reported in. He is sending another team to try to find out what happened. At 0645 the sun broke free of the horizon. San Juan notified Ron that Special One was in the air and she was watching the boxes floating behind the ship.

"Valley Forge, this is Special One. If you hadn't told me what to watch for, I would have missed the boxes. They were floating just below the water level."   Special One continued commenting on what was happening on the water.

"Valley Forge, Valley Forge, this is Special One. A blue boat is taking boxes out of the water. One of the boxes seems to be extremely heavy as it keeps slipping out of their hands and back into the water. They have taken all the boxes out of the water and are speeding towards shore. They have slowed down. They are pulling into the same dock as your cruise ship."

Charlie Pile cut in and told everyone that he had the boat in sight and had a team on the dock. Thirty minutes later, Charlie came back online and let everyone know that his team was watching the suspects load the boxes into a multicolored van that had just pulled onto the dock and parked next to the fence. Sheena told everyone that they were letting the passengers off the ship and that Suzy Q arranged for Benjamin and herself to be in the first group off the ship. Suzy Q was staying at the gangway to see if any of our suspects sign out and leave the ship. Sheena watched Charlie follow the multicolored van out of the parking lot. She and Benjamin walked around town watching the tourists. Three hours went by when they noticed Charlie Pile driving down the main street towards the parking lot next to the Valley Forge. They turned and headed toward the dock where the Valley Forge was. They met Charlie in the parking lot. He explained what he had done all afternoon. He followed the multicolored van when it left the parking lot. That multicolored van had made several stops. At each stop, the passenger got out of the van, delivered a small package and returned to the van. Two hours later they appeared to be finished and the van drove into a garage and stopped. Two men and a woman got out of the van and walked into the house next door to the garage. One of Charlie's men was able to get pictures of the three people from the van. Charlie forwarded the pictures to New York for identification."

By early afternoon, Sheena and Benjamin came back onboard the Valley Forge and returned to their cabin. By 1800 hours the Valley Forge was underway. Everyone was at the dinner table except Marsha and John. They were in Melinda's suite watching the monitor. After a delicious dinner, Jose and Susan left the dining room to relieve Marsha and John. Marsha and John went to dinner and then wandered around the ship. As they were walking down the hallway on Deck 6, Marsha happened to glance into one of the storerooms and saw a stack of brown boxes. What caught her attention was the black diagonal stripe on each box. She called Ron, told him the location of the storage room and kept walking with John. By the time they reached the end of the passageway and turned back, someone had closed and locked the storage room. They kept walking around Deck 6 and passed the storage room every fifteen minutes. By the third trip around,

Suzy Q and Ron showed up. Suzy took out her ring of keys and unlocked the storage room door. Ron went into the room, reached up and mounted a miniature digital camera on the overhead, in the corner out of sight. They counted the boxes, took a picture, and locked the door. That entire operation took less than three minutes. Ron went to Melinda's room. He knocked and she let him in. He went quickly to the converter and entered the camera's code. Within moments, the video of the inside of the storage room showed up on the screen. With a few clicks of the keyboard, New York now had the camera online.

"Now maybe we will find out who else is smuggling this material," said Ron. "I would like to know how these boxes got on the ship." Ron called New York and told them about the storage room. He called the teams and told them to keep an eye out for those boxes with the black diagonal stripe when we arrive at the next port.

Day 6   On Thursday, the Valley Forge slowly passed El Morro Castle on its left and entered San Juan Harbor. It slowly worked its way to pier one. It looked like it was going to be a hot day. The sky was a clear blue, and the sun was very bright. The ship docked, the lines were tied to the bollards, and the gangways were put in place. The passengers started streaming off the ship. Susan and Jose stood at the railing watching as the passengers left the ship. They received a call from Suzy Q that one of the suspects was leaving the ship and that Sheena and Benjamin were following him. She suggested that it might be a good idea if Jose and Susan follow behind, as backup. Susan and Jose quickly walked to the elevator and rode in to Deck 4. They walked to the Security post, scanned their key cards and left the ship. They could not see Sheena or Benjamin. They walked to the main sidewalk and looked in both directions. Jose nudged Susan, and she looked in the direction he was looking. She nodded her head and called Sheena to let her that she had them in sight. Just past the pier, where two Coast Guard boats were tied, the suspect turned right and walked up the hill. Sheena and Benjamin followed the suspect for six blocks. They had to break off following him since there was no one else around. If the suspect turned around, Benjamin and Sheena felt they would stand out since they were over six feet tall and black as ebony. In all the time in San Juan, they have not seen anyone that was as dark as they were. They turned right, stopped at a jewelry store, admiring what was on display, and then continued walking. Susan and Jose kept walking straight. They were holding a tourist map and were looking around as if lost. Susan started berating Jose in a loud voice as they started to pass the suspect. Susan stopped the suspect and asked if he could show them where they were on the map. The suspect stopped, answered their questions and went on his way. Susan notified Ron that she and John were coming back to the ship. Charlie Pile called and told Ron that he had still not heard from his men that he left on St. Kitts to observe one of the houses, and was concerned.

Day 7 On Friday, the Valley Forge tied up at the pier in Labadee, Haiti. The sun was shining, and by nine in the morning, the temperature had risen to eighty-five degrees. It was going to be a good beach day. The teams got off the ship and spread out along the road that was the length of the 'island'. That piece of land was advertised as an island but in truth in was a spit of land that stuck out into the ocean. Sheena and Benjamin blended right in with the natives, as did Jose. Everyone else played tourist going into all the shops. After a while they spotted two of the suspects carrying boxes with the diagonal black stripe off the ship. They would not have paid attention to the men carrying the boxes if Marsha had not noticed the diagonal black stripe on the side of the boxes that they carried. She notified everyone to watch for those boxes. Twenty minutes later, Suzy Q called saying that two more of the crew had left the ship carrying boxes that had a black diagonal stripe on them. She notified New York and sent the names and pictures of the two crewmembers. Now they had four crewmembers on the ship plus an officer that were part of the smuggling ring. The next question to be answered is *'what are they smuggling' and 'to whom?'* Four boxes were stacked in the shade of a tree and the suspects walked back to the ship. The teams set up surveillance. They mounted a digital camera under the bench near the boxes. They were able to install the camera while they were playing a game of 'catch'. New York now had a visual on the boxes. The camera codes was sent to whomever was watching the monitor on the ship and entered into the computer and now everyone can watch the boxes. Two hours later, as the sun was starting to go down, a sand buggy approached the tree that the boxes were stacked against. It stopped and two men got out and quickly loaded the four boxes on the back of the buggy. They got back in the buggy, did a three point turn and left the way they had come. Sheena notified Charlie Pile about the sand buggy. He told everyone that he had two teams at the entrance and they would try to plant a tracker on the buggy.

There was a pause, and Charlie came back online and informed everyone that one team had stopped the buggy to ask for directions. The second team planted the tracker.

San Juan notified Ron that they had launched a drone thirty minutes ago, and it should be overhead in less than fifteen minutes. Twelve minutes later the drone operator, whose call sign was Special Two, notified New York that they had the buggy on the screen. The tracker was showing up on the screen as well. New York put everyone on the circuit so they would have the information at the same time. They listened intently to the operator as he described the actions of the buggy. It was a good thing no one had tried to follow the buggy. It backtracked the way it had come, then drove through a parking lot and then around the block to see if anyone was following them. The sand buggy finally pulled into a circular driveway in front of a large ranch style house. The house had a light brown roof and dark brown shutters. Special Two told New York that they could only stay over the area for two more hours. Special Three was getting ready to launch in case it was needed. Ron told the teams to return to the ship and meet in Melinda and Martin's suite. When everyone was in the suite, Ron started the meeting. "We now have a slight problem," Ron said. "We should raid the house and find out what they are smuggling. However, the ship leaves in less than an hour. I contacted Charlie Pile and requested he have one of his teams enter the house and find out what was in those boxes. He is working on it as we speak. He mentioned that he still hasn't found out why the team he left on St. Kitts has not checked in."

"I spoke to the New York," Ron continued. "They are still having trouble identifying the second suspect. Suzy Q is trying to get the ship's records, but it is not her department, so she has to be circumspect. It would have been much easier if the Captain was in on this operation." Ron's tablet beeped and he looked down. "They finally identified the second suspect. His name is Stephen Van Deer. The ship's manifest lists him as a deckhand 3rd class, and he is from Holland. His job is below decks, not on decks four through fifteen. According to the ships rules he is not allowed to be in the passenger areas except to handle luggage when the ship is in port. That is everything I have for now. Tomorrow we will keep the same schedule." The meeting broke up and everyone went back to their cabins. At 1730 hours the Valley Forge got underway. All the teams settled into their routines. After dinner, they wandered into the showroom and enjoyed the entertainment. It was a production show with singers and dancers.

Day 8   Saturday at sea. As dawn approached, the weather turned cloudy and some rain clouds appeared. The sky turned black and a rainsquall swept across the deck. The temperature dropped, and the winds picked up to gale force. Very few people were out on deck since the weather had turned so nasty. Each of the teams kept walking around the ship clad in rain slickers and hoods. New York was monitoring all the digital cameras. They would notify Ron if anything happened.

Melinda went to Martin and put her arms around his neck. "I'm going to stay in the suite this morning. I'm very tired." She no sooner got those words out of her mouth than she passed out. Martin caught her before she hit the floor. He lifted her up as if she was a child, walked into the bedroom and placed her on the round bed. He reached for the phone and dialed 911. He explained what happened. A moment later, he heard over the loudspeakers, "Mike, mike, mike and his cabin number." In less than five minutes, there was a knock on the cabin door. Martin opened the door and four people from the Medical Clinic entered, pushing a gurney. Martin directed them to the bedroom and he followed. The medical team lifted Melinda off the bed and put her on the gurney. They strapped her down and started moving quickly towards the door. Martin rushed ahead and held the door open as they wheeled Melinda out of the cabin. They wheeled her quickly through to the inside elevator that was being held open by one of the security people. They told Martin to take the passenger elevator that was opposite his cabin and to meet them in the Medical Clinic on Deck 1. The elevator door closed, and Martin went back into the passenger corridor and to the elevator across from his suite. He pushed the down button. He waited for what seemed like an hour but was only two minutes. He got in the elevator and pushed the button for Deck 1. The elevator descended quickly. When the elevator doors opened, Martin rushed out. Looking in both directions, he saw a sign for the Medical Clinic and rushed in that direction. When he arrived, the door was open, and a nurse was waiting for him. She asked for Melinda's insurance card. The nurse picked up a clipboard and started asking Martin questions about Melinda's health. He answered most of the questioned asked. The nurse asked if Melinda had any allergies and what medicines she was taking. Then the nurse wanted to know how far along her pregnancy was. Was she having any problems with the pregnancy? The questions went on for more than ten minutes.

The nurse left Martin in the waiting room. He paced back and forth. He sat down and then got up and paced some more. He kept looking at the clock, but the hands on the clock were not moving. Finally, the doctor came out and told him that he needn't have worried. Her blood sugar was extremely low, thus causing her to pass out. Since she was so far along in her pregnancy, she should be eating many small meals. The doctor wanted to know if she had breakfast this morning. Martin thought about that and realized that Melinda had not eaten breakfast.

The nurse wheeled Melinda into the waiting room in a wheelchair. Martin kneeled down, took both her hands in his and looked into her eyes. "How are you feeling?" he whispered to her.

"I'm alright," said Melinda. "What's all the fuss about? The doctor said I had low blood sugar. I would like to go back to the suite, Martin. I still feel a little tired." Martin looked at the doctor who nodded his assent. He wheeled Melinda back to their cabin. He lifted her out of the wheelchair and put her on the bed. He pulled the comforter over her and closed the drapes. He leaned over his wife and gave her a kiss on her forehead. He noticed she was already asleep. He went into the living room and closed the door.

"Computer," said Martin.

"Computer online, Martin," replied the Computer.

"Call Ron," said Martin.

"Ron is online," said the Computer.

"What's up Martin?" Ron asked.

"Melinda passed out," Martin said. I called the 911 number and they came and took her to the Medical Clinic. The doctor said it was just low sugar and that she'll be okay. He also said that stress could be one of the factors that caused her to pass out. I didn't agree with his diagnosis. She is only acting as a 'Den Mother'."

"You sound worried," Ron said. "I'm on my way up,"

Five minutes later, Ron knocked on the door, and Martin let him in. Ron said, "I guess after being away from the job for a while, she forgot what stress she was under. Even here, she took over. She just normally takes over."

"You know she didn't do it on purpose," Martin said. "She is happy the way you and Lucinda are running the outfit here on the ship."

"I know," Ron replied, "but once a boss always a boss," he said, with a laugh in his voice. "I have no trouble sleeping when she's around. When she is here, everyone reports to her anyway, out of habit." Martin got up and went to the kitchen. He made a pot coffee, poured two cups and brought them to the sitting room. He handed a cup to Ron and then sat down. Thirty minutes later the bedroom door opened and Melinda walked in. Martin put his cup down, got up quickly and went to her.

"I'm alright," she said, holding Martin's hands. "I heard what the doctor said about the small meals. Speaking of food, will you order a snack for me?"

"What would you like?" asked Ron.

Melinda said she would like tea and toast with marmalade. Ron could have had one of the team members get the food, but he wanted to give Melinda and Martin some privacy.

When they were alone, Melinda told Martin she wanted to take a shower but didn't feel secure enough to do it herself. Martin helped her into the bathroom. He sat her on the stool and turned on the shower. He adjusted the temperature and helped Melinda get undressed. He helped her into the shower. She held onto the safety bars and let Martin bathe her. He soaped her down, washed her hair and rinsed her off. He shut the shower off, reached for the heated towel, and put it around her and held her tight. A minute later, he took a second towel and dried her hair. He helped her get dressed in her maternity slacks and a short sleeve over blouse. He helped her to her dressing table and left her brushing her hair.

Twenty minutes later, Ron returned carrying Melinda's requested snack. "Where's Melinda?" he asked.

"She's in the bedroom doing her hair. I'll go get her." Martin went into the bedroom and found that Melinda was sound asleep stretched across the bed. He pulled the coverlet over her and went back into the living room.

"She was brushing her hair when I left her," he told Ron. "Now she is in bed fast asleep."

"You still look worried," said Ron.

"I am," said Martin. "I have heard so many horrible stories about all the problems pregnant women have. I don't even know how capable this doctor is. Dr. Wellfleet wasn't even down there and I never thought to call him.

Ron raised his hand to stop Martin from talking. "Computer," said Ron.

"Computer online," said the Computer.

"Get me the New York office," said Ron.

"New York office online, Ron," said the Computer.

Ron explained the situation to the New York operator, and New York promised to call back in a few moments. "I'll leave you alone," said Ron. "Let me know what New York has to say. I notified everyone else to contact me directly and not to bother Melinda."

"Martin, New York is online," said the Computer

"What did you find out about the doctor?" asked Martin.

"We checked on the doctor," New York said. "He has an impeccable reputation. He retired last year and according to his file he didn't want to stop working. The hospital wanted him to take over the department he was working in. He did not want the pressure of running an entire department. They didn't give him a choice. It was take charge of the department or leave. So he walked away. He retired and was offered a berth on the Valley Forge. We even spoke to him and he convinced us that all Melinda needs is rest and many small meals. In forty-eight hours she will be as good as new."

After hearing this news, Martin relaxed, sat down and put his head on his folded arms. Within seconds, he was sound asleep with his head on the table. Ron smiled, turned and left the suite. Two hours later, Melinda came into the living room and saw Martin asleep at the table. She smiled as she walked to the table. She was going to wake him then changed her mind. She went back into the bedroom, picked up the phone and ordered lunch for two. She washed up, brushed her hair and walked back in the living room. There was a light knock on the door. Melinda looked through the peephole. She recognized their room steward. She let her in and directed her where to set up the lunch. When she was finished setting up the lunch, she wheeled the cart out of the room and closed the door. Melinda walked over to the sleeping Martin. She kissed him on the neck, and he woke up.

He stretched and moaned. "Oh my aching neck," he said. He massaged his neck for a moment and then looked up. He jumped up and put his arms around Melinda. "You scared me this morning," he said. "I was so worried about you and the babies."

"Yeah, I got that," Melinda said, smiling. "I really didn't eat breakfast this morning or dinner last night. I figured I didn't have an appetite because of the twins. Now I know better."

Martin nodded and said, "Our entire group and the New York office are aware of what happened. I even had New York check on the doctor." They sat and continued the conversation over lunch. They discussed the investigation of the smugglers and what they felt was happening. While they were sitting over their coffee and tea, Charlie Pile called. One of his surveillance teams observed a middle-aged couple leaving the house which they had under observation late last night. They took pictures of the couple and forwarded the pictures to New York for identification. They had two of his people follow the couple, while the rest of the team broke into the house. They found four boxes that had the diagonal black stripe on the side. They boxes were hidden in a closet under a blanket. They checked the boxes for booby traps, found none, and carefully opened the boxes. The boxes were waterproof and had a built in floatation device attached to the inside walls of the box. Inside that box, they found four packages. Each package weighed one kilo each. They tested the contents using a needle extractor and found the contents to be almost 100% pure cocaine. They painted each of the packages with a slightly radioactive powder to make it easier to track and trace. They also hid a tracker in each of the boxes. They could not open the packages safely to put in a tracker. They left the house leaving no trace of anyone being there. Charlie notified New York as to what they found in the house. He gave them the address and requested the owner's name.

Martin told Charlie that his people did a great job. Maybe next time they should try to mark the boxes before they leave the ship. He hesitated and then called Suzy Q. He discussed getting back into the storage room to mark the remaining boxes, then notified Charlie Pile and discussed it with him. Suzy Q cut in and said that it would not be a good idea to do this now. The best time would be when they have the crew emergency abandon ship drill. Those four suspects are on the same emergency team and would be busy for ninety minutes. If they needed more time the drill could be extended by two hours. There was a pause and they finalized the plans and disconnected. While everyone was talking, Melinda sat on the couch. She put her head back and closed her eyes. She was asleep before her head hit the back of the couch. Martin turned to speak to her and saw she was asleep. This concerned him. She was sleeping a lot.

He picked up the phone and called the Medical Clinic. He spoke to the nurse. He explained his concern, and the nurse said she would have the doctor call him back. Thirty minutes later, the doctor called. Martin again explained his concern, especially since she was seven months pregnant. The doctor told him he would be up in ten minutes. Five minutes later the doctor knocked on the door. Martin let him in, and he went to Melinda, who was still asleep on the couch. He checked her pulse and took her blood pressure. Melinda slept through the entire procedure. The doctor picked up the phone and called the bridge to speak to the Captain. He spoke to the officer of the deck and explained the situation. Martin did not hear the conversation, as he was sitting on the couch holding Melinda's hands. The doctor hung up the phone, pulled out a chair and faced Martin. The doctor explained that Melinda's condition had become very serious, and it was advisable to get her to a hospital as soon as possible. Martin had to make a decision. The doctor told Martin that the ship was more than twenty-four hours away from Ft. Lauderdale, and it was not prudent to wait that long. He recommended a helicopter evacuation.

"You said she was okay after you examined her this morning," said Martin.

"At that time, she was," said the doctor. "Now her blood pressure is even lower than before, and I was unable to wake her. I consulted with some of my colleagues by phone before I came in and explained the situation, and they had never heard of this problem. They didn't even have a recommendation for me. I called Jackson Memorial in Miami and had a consult with their head OB/Gyn. The doctor thought, based on the information I gave her, that it sounded very serious. She wanted to know when we could get her there for an MRI. I recommend that we do a medivac to Miami."

Martin didn't even have to think about it. He asked the doctor to set it up. The doctor picked up the phone and spoke to the officer of the deck. He told him what the Miami doctor recommended. The officer of the deck called the Captain and explained the situation. He told the Captain that the Valley Forge is four hundred miles south of Ft. Lauderdale. The Captain instructed the officer of the deck to place a call to the Coast Guard and request a medical evacuation for an unconscious woman who was seven months pregnant. The officer of the deck called the Coast Guard and gave them the pertinent information and he would stand by on 116.32. The Coast Guard informed Valley Forge that they were a hundred miles outside the maximum range of their helicopter, but at the speed the ship was traveling, and time of flight to the ship, they would have thirty minutes on station. Any increased speed of the Valley Forge would increase the safety factor for the helicopter. A C130 has launched from Key West. They would be overhead in less than two hours. The medivac helicopter's call sign was Rescue 7. It was now warming up on the helicopter pad at Key West. The Valley Forge was kept informed of the rescue procedures and they in turn kept the doctor informed. The doctor called for a gurney and extra blankets. They wrapped Melinda up tightly, put her on the gurney, strapped her down and moved her to the helicopter deck. The C130 called and said that the helicopter was less than thirty minutes out.

"Valley Forge, Valley Forge, this is Rescue 7. We have you in sight. Request you change course to 095 and maintain fifteen knots. We are approaching from the northeast at 130 knots. We will be with you in ten minutes."

"Roger, Rescue 7. We are changing course to 095 and maintaining fifteen knots. Helicopter pad clear of all obstructions. Helicopter Fire team standing by. It is clear for you to land."

"Roger, Valley Forge. We are now over the landing pad. Maintain your course and speed."

"Valley Forge, this is Rescue 7. We are on deck. We are keeping the engines running. Send out the patient."

As he said that, one of the crewman motioned Martin, Ron and the doctor to wheel Melinda across the deck to the open door of the helicopter. Two of the helicopter crew jumped out, assisted sliding the gurney into the helicopter and secured it. Martin climbed in and sat in the jump seat. He was not able to hold Melinda's hand, as his jump seat was far away from her. One of the pilots handed Martin earphones with an attached mike. The medic asked if Melinda had any allergies as he hooked her to a saline drip. Melinda had not moved at all, and Martin was extremely worried.

"Jason is online, Martin," The Computer said.

"Yes Jason," said Martin.

"How is Melinda?" asked Jason.

"She is still unconscious," replied Martin. "We are thirty minutes out of Miami. We are heading to Jackson Memorial in Miami for an MRI. I've been in combat, I've flown off the deck of a carrier at night, and I have even jumped out of airplanes. I have never been this scared."

"I guess when you love someone things are different. When Lucinda went on a mission, I worried. We signed on for that job. You did not sign on for what is happening to Melinda. That is part of the package. If you think of anything you need, let me know."

"Thanks, Jason. I'll keep you informed. The pilot just told me that we are going to land at the Jackson Memorial Hospital in northwest Miami.

He said we will land on top of the Ryder Trauma Center and that they are waiting for us." The Coast Guard helicopter landed on the roof, two of the crew jumped out, unhooked the gurney, slid it out onto the roof, being careful not to disconnect the saline drip. Martin followed the medic. The medic informed the doctor of Melinda's condition as they moved her into the elevator. The crewmembers climbed back in the helicopter and closed the door. The helicopter took off and headed east to Miami Airport. It would then be ready for its next call. Because of the time it took to load and unload Melinda, they would not have enough fuel to fly back to Key West, so they continued on to Miami Airport to refuel.

As the elevator was descending, the doctor started examining Melinda. He was concerned because she had been unconscious for so long. He needed to check on the babies. They rolled the gurney into the MRI department and prepared Melinda for the MRI.

The nurse escorted Martin to the waiting room while preparations were being made for Melinda. He poured himself a cup of coffee and just stood there. He was exhausted but was afraid to sit down. When he finally did sit down, he put his head back and fell into a deep sleep.

Thirty minutes later a nurse came into the waiting room and woke him. She escorted him back to the emergency room. "We found the problem," said the doctor. "The MRI showed that the boy has shifted, and his foot is pressing on an artery that is a branch of the aorta. That's what is causing Melinda to remain unconscious. The medical name for it is Inferior Vena Cava Compression. It is not stressing the babies, so far. The boy's foot has to be moved away from the vein, and that would require a very special operation, which we are not equipped to do at this hospital. We had our team of vascular surgeons look at the MRI, and they all admitted that they had never done that type of operation. We are calling all the hospitals on the east coast to find someone who is qualified to do that operation."

"Is the helicopter still on the roof?" Martin asked.

"The doctor reached for the wall phone, picked it up and spoke into the receiver. After a moment, he turned to Martin. "The helicopter left for refueling. It will take them forty five minutes to an hour to get back here."

"Jason, you heard it all. I need a recommendation. They claim that there is no one here that can do the procedure."

"You have to get her here to Ft. Lauderdale airport," said Jason. "It's too far by ambulance. Have them get Melinda ready to transport by helicopter. I will let you know when the helicopter will land. I have a jet available, and it's parked at General Aviation at Ft. Lauderdale Airport. Hang in there, Martin. Have Melinda's medical records and MRI's with her. I will find a medical facility for her."

Martin told the doctor that they would be moving Melinda by helicopter shortly and to have her prepared for transport. The doctor told Martin that it would be very dangerous to move her in her condition. If Martin had to move her, the doctor recommended that he get a qualified nurse to take with him, since he will not be on a rescue helicopter. One of the emergency nurses overheard what the doctor had said. She interrupted the doctor and told him that she is qualified for air rescue, and if he didn't mind her leaving, she would volunteer.

Martin looked at her. She was a tiny thing. Five foot nothing. As she removed her cap he saw that she had bright red curly hair and freckles on her nose. She stood there dressed in blue scrubs. She looked like a doll. The doctor nodded and walked over to the phone. He called the head nurse and explained the situation.

"What's your name?" Martin asked, turning to the red headed nurse.

"Rosemary, Rosemary Klein."

"I want to thank you for volunteering," said Martin. "I don't know when I'll be able to get you back here."

"That's all right," Rosemary said. "I needed a break. The emergency room at this hospital is extremely busy. They have plenty of personnel so I won't be missed. Just so you know, I am also qualified as a jumper."

"That sounds good to me," replied Martin, smiling. "I hope that we won't have to jump. There is a helicopter heading our way, so I need my wife prepared for transport. We are going to fly to Ft. Lauderdale and transfer to a private jet that is standing by. The jet has been reconfigured to transport a gurney. The gurney will fit without any problems. I still don't know where we are going to land, or what hospital will have the facilities to operate on Melinda. This hospital is contacting every hospital on the east coast."

The hospital staff attending to Melinda prepared her for travel. They wrapped her in blankets and strapped her down securely on the gurney. Now they waited. Martin walked back and forth in the lounge waiting to hear from Jason.

Finally, Jason called him. "The helicopter is ten minutes out," he said. Martin thanked him and walked back into the emergency room. He told everyone that the helicopter would be landing by the time the gurney was brought to the roof. That statement activated the staff, and by the time Martin put on his jacket, they had the elevator doors open and had moved Melinda into the elevator. Martin had to run to catch up. Rosemary yelled that she would meet them on the roof and disappeared behind a green door to get her jacket.

As the elevator doors opened on the roof, a black helicopter was landing on the helipad. It was a large twin rotor machine with no lights showing. If it were not for the lights around the helipad, it would be almost invisible. The side door of the helicopter slid open and four very large men in full combat gear jumped out. They each took a corner of the gurney, snapped the legs in the travel position, and lifted the entire unit into the helicopter. They reached down and helped Martin and Rosemary into the strange looking machine. The door was closed as soon as everyone was strapped in. The helicopter lifted off, tilted forward and started flying north. The staff on the roof stood stunned. They had never experienced that type of emergency evacuation before.

Rosemary watched the men in black work on Melinda. She realized that these were qualified military medics and that she was redundant. She unstrapped herself and shifted over to where Martin sat. "I don't think you really need me. These guys are qualified to care for her."

"I didn't know who or what they were sending," Martin said. "I thought the Coast Guard helicopter would be coming back. I would like you to stay with her. When she wakes up, I'm sure she would like a woman to talk to. Besides, I don'tt think these people are going with us after we land."

"I just realized that you didn't get a chance to pack," exclaimed Martin. "If you give me your sizes, I can have some clothes brought to the plane."

"Promise you won't laugh?" Rosemary said.

Not knowing what she was going to say, he said, "Okay, I promise."

"I wear a children's large," she said. "I even have to get special size scrubs and gloves."

"That has to be tough," Martin replied. "How do you solve that problem?"

"I shop mostly in children's stores. I have a friend who goes with me because the stores don't like children wandering around the store alone."

Martin could not help it. He burst out laughing.

"You promised," said Rosemary, with a smile on her face.

"I'm sorry," Martin said, "but you must admit, that to a stranger it does sound funny."

"Yes, I know," Rosemary said. "Sometimes I feel like a butt of a joke. Even in nursing school. I had been stopped many times, going from one class to another, and told *'you have to wait for your mother outside'*. Alternatively, I was told *'visiting hours are over.'* It took a while for the staff to get to know me, and then things went smoothly. When I came to this hospital, it started all over again. It's gotten better. Everyone knows I am a qualified Emergency Trauma Room Nurse. When patient's families have questions about who I am, the head nurse intervenes. This is a good hospital. It's a shame that they can't do the procedure here to help your wife."

Martin explained that his New York office has not found a hospital for this procedure. They are also having a problem finding a qualified doctor.

"I meant to ask you," Rosemary said. "How did you know the helicopter was going to land?"

Martin realized he had gotten careless. He really did not know this nurse. He will have to have her checked out. He thought, *'I will have to downplay it'*. "I spoke to my office," he said. "They told me when the helicopter was scheduled to land."

"Where do these guys come from?" she asked, pointing to the four medics."

"I don't know." Martin replied. "A rescue helicopter was needed. This one was the closest to us." Martin smiled to himself. He turned his head away from Rosemary, contacted New York and asked them do a thorough background check on this Rosemary Klein.

At 0400, the black helicopter touched down next to the G650 at General Aviation at Ft. Lauderdale International Airport. The door slid open and the four large medics jumped down, unhooked the gurney and lifted it out of the machine. They didn't even put the wheels down on the gurney. They carried it to the Gulfstream, trotted up the stairs and carried the gurney into the main cabin. They held the gurney while the wheels were dropped and locked in place. They held onto the gurney until it was secured in the aircraft. The leader of the medical team turned to Rosemary and told her that the patient was all hers. She gave Rosemary a salute and left the aircraft. Rosemary looked out the door and saw the four medics trot to the black helicopter, jump in, watched it take off as its doors were being closed. Rosemary made sure Melinda was comfortable, checked her saline drip and sat down next to her. She put on her seat belt and reached over and took Melinda's hand in hers, put her head back, and closed her eyes. '*Now it was a matter of finding a hospital and a qualified doctor to perform that procedure*', she thought.

At 0500, Martin received a call from Jason. He said, "We found a hospital and a doctor for Melinda. It's North Greenville Hospital in South Carolina. We called them, and they will be waiting. They already have a copy of the MRI's and the radiology report. So get that bird in the air."

Martin walked to the cockpit and told Dennis the destination. Dennis contacted Ground Control and received permission to start his engines. Within twenty minutes, they were rolling down the runway. At maximum thrust, they would be there in less than ninety minutes. As soon as the airplane leveled off, Dennis picked up the microphone. "Spartanburg Control, this is Gulfstream 202tango. We are with you at 18,000 feet. We need a straight in approach, priority one."

"Roger 202 tango. We were expecting you. Please standby for Approach Control." Approach Control came on and gave Dennis his instructions. Dennis landed the plane on the longest runway, slowed with the reverse thrusters and was directed to General Aviation, where the medical helicopter was waiting with their engines running. They carried the gurney down the stairs, and lifted it into the helicopter. The medics secured the gurney. Martin and Rosemary jumped in, the doors were closed and the helicopter took off. It took only fifteen minutes to get to the heliport on the top of Greenville Hospital. As they landed, four people came running towards the helicopter. The helicopter door was opened and the gurney lifted out. They snapped the wheels down, and two orderlies started wheeling the gurney into the elevator. Martin and Rosemary had to run to catch up. Martin turned his head to make sure Rosemary was with him and noticed a beautiful sunrise. Rosemary turned her head and saw the same beautiful sunrise. They looked at each other and smiled. They got on the elevator, and the doors closed.

Chapter 3

Day 9   On Sunday at 0600, the Valley Forge pulled into Ft. Lauderdale as the sun was starting to rise. Two passengers, Melinda and Martin Xavier, were missing. The passengers were eating breakfast and getting ready to go ashore. The teams gathered in Martin and Melinda's suite.

"Okay," said Ron, as everyone sat down. "You all know what's going on. We are going to continue with the mission. Melinda and Martin were only to be our 'Den mother and father,' so the mission is not compromised. I want the patrols on deck continued. We know that drugs are being smuggled. I want everyone to watch all the material coming onto the ship. I want to find out how the drugs are being brought on. We don't know how the brown boxes with the black stripe were smuggled aboard this ship. Suzy Q got us a copy of the ship's material manifest, so we have to make sure that the material coming on is the same as what is on the list. How the drugs get by the dogs is beyond me. Are there any ideas?" No one answered.

They talked among themselves for a few minutes and then Jose said, "It might be a new kind of packaging that the dogs can't smell."

"Maybe they pick up the merchandise while we are out at sea." Marsha added.

"Then why not deliver it direct without all these charades?" John remarked.

"Keep thinking," said Ron. "We will meet at 1000 hours and be escorted off the ship into the lounge. It shouldn't take them too long for debarkation."

By 0630, some of the passengers were leaving the ship. One team was stationed on Deck 1 aft, and one team was stationed on Deck 1 forward, both teams watching everything that was coming onboard the ship. The crew of the Valley Forge thought Melinda's people were 'health inspectors' so they didn't think anything was wrong when a pallet of goods was stopped and checked.

Ron was still in Melinda's cabin watching the video monitor. He had a large pot of coffee sitting on the table, next to him. Lucinda and Ron took turns watching the monitor. They had even brought in another monitor to help break up watching so many videos on one screen. As Lucinda was taking her turn at the monitor, she noticed one of the suspects, the person from Holland, check out a particular pallet and then walks away from it. She told Ron to take over and she left the suite. She boarded the elevator and went down to Deck 1. She motioned to one of the 'health inspectors,' and when he came over, she told him about the pallet. He had the pallet moved to vacant storage room to 'be examined for rodent droppings.'

Ron continued to watch the monitor as Lucinda went into the storage room where they had moved the pallet. The entire pallet was shrink-wrapped. She examined what she could without cutting open the shrink-wrap. She noticed gallon cans of pinto beans from Columbia. She checked the manifest. There were barbecue beans, green beans, but no pinto beans. She took a small knife and slit the shrink-wrap. She took one of the gallon cans and pried it open. Inside were packages of a white powder. She called Ron. "That is how they got it past the dogs. The material was in cans, and the contents have no smell. I am going to leave the storage room locked up until we can coat the cans to make it easier to track when they are taken off the pallet. Just so no one gets suspicious; we're going to have an accident when the pallet is moved. This way, the wrap can be broken and the cans coated. Then we will leave the cans in the storage locker. Have a camera mounted on the overhead so we can see and record who enters the locker. How does that sound?"

"Now I know why I love you," said Ron.

"Why is that?" asked Lucinda. "Is it because I'm beautiful?"

"No, It's because you are so sneaky, that's why." Ron replied, smiling.

"In fact," said Lucinda. "Why don't you give the coating material and the camera to John and Marsha, and they can bring it here to me in the aft storeroom. We'll coat the cans right now."

Ron contacted John and Marsha. They came to the cabin and gathered the material as well as another digital camera. They met with

Lucinda in the storage locker and mounted the camera. Then they cut away the shrink-wrap and started coating all the cans. Instead of restacking them, the cans were laid around the floor. Lucinda had the 'health inspector' lie down, and she piled a few cans around him. She broke open a bag of blood that she had taken from the Medical Clinic. She put some on the blood on the side of his head and on one of his legs. Then she went out and found one of the ship's officers. She told him about the 'accident', and he got on his walkie-talkie and called for help. "Mike, mike, mike, Deck 1 aft," sounded over the ships speaker system. This alarm was repeated twice more.

The medical team appeared, placed him on a gurney and transported the 'injured health inspector' to the Medical Clinic. Lucinda threw some of the cans around so they developed deep dents. She closed the storage room door but neglected to lock it. She looked around the passageway but it was clear. She went back to her cabin. When she entered the cabin, Ron gave her a hug and a kiss. "You are something," he said, swinging her around the room. He went back to watching the monitor. The rest of the loading went without incident. "I hope we got it all." Ron said.

"I don't think we missed anything," Lucinda said, "but time will tell."

"We will be at sea all day tomorrow," Ron remarked. "Why don't I call for a meeting at 1000? This way everyone will have time for a leisurely breakfast. You and I can take turns watching the monitor."

"The meeting at 1000 is okay," answered Lucinda, "but I really don't feel like watching the monitor four hours on and four hours off. Since you don't expect anything to happen, why don't we share the pleasure of watching the monitor with everyone?"

"Okay," Ron replied. "That's a good idea." He called the team and told them the schedule. They acknowledged the assignments and signed off. Lucinda nodded and smiled. She walked to Ron and gave him a big kiss. He held her and returned the kiss and then some.

"Stop," said Lucinda. "At that rate we won't get anything done."

"Sure we will," said Ron. "We just won't get done what we were supposed to get done." They both laughed.

At 1630, the Valley Forge performed the mandated abandon ship lifeboat drill. Ron attended the drill, and Lucinda stayed behind to watch the monitor. She did not expect anything to happen, but you never can tell. Right after the drill started, Lucinda noticed the door to the storage locker on Deck 1 aft, opening. One of the suspects, the man from Holland again, walked into the storage locker. He turned on the light and looked around. He started counting the cans. Lucinda called John and told him rush to the storage locker and secure it.

"Make a lot of noise doing it," said Lucinda. Let's see if Mr. Van Deer can come up with a good excuse for being where he isn't supposed to be. Meanwhile, I'll call Suzy Q and ask her to meet you at the storage locker. I know it's not her department, but let her step over the line a little." Lucinda called Suzy and explained the situation. Suzy laughed and said, "These people aren't very smart! I'll be there in five minutes."

"Make sure you keep him busy until we are underway," said Lucinda. "I don't want him to slip through our hands, and I don't want him to contact anyone." Suzy said she would have a Security team with her.

Suzy Q and the Security team met John at the storage locker and started locking it. Instead of a lock, they used a steel pin. It made a lot of noise, and Van Deer started banging on the door. Everybody stepped back and ignored him. The three of them just stood back and stayed quiet. When the banging finally ceased, Suzy said in a loud voice, "Show me where the accident happened." The door was unlocked and they all went in. Everyone showed surprise at discovering a member of the deck crew in the locker. Security started questioning him. Van Deer became very hostile and took a swing at one of the security guards. They grabbed his arms, forced them behind his back, handcuffed him with a zip tie and took him to the ship's brig.

Lucinda told Ron what she had done, and he laughed. "That's better than you planned, I bet."

"I was trying to figure out a way to keep one of them out of circulation. This worked fine. I am going to ask Dr. Wellfleet to question our Mr. Stephen Van Deer.

The rest of the day was uneventful, and at 1700, the Valley Forge pulled away from the dock, escorted by a Coast Guard vessel. Four other large cruise ships were ahead in the channel. The sun was just setting as they passed the last spit of land.

At 0630, at the North Greenville Hospital in South Carolina, Melinda had been undressed, examined, and dressed in a hospital gown. When everything was completed, they moved her into a private room. Rosemary stayed with her the entire time. They relegated Martin to another waiting room. When the doctor was ready, she had the aide bring Martin into Melinda's room. Rosemary ordered breakfast for Martin and herself. While Martin and Rosemary were eating, the doctor introduced herself, "I'm Nancy Troop. I'm a Pediatric Neurosurgeon." She explained what the problem was and what she planned to do to solve it. "The operation itself is straightforward," she said. "I have to make a small opening in the uterus and insert a camera to find the nerve. Then I have to move the boy's foot away from the nerve. That's all I have to do to solve the problem."

"You make it seem so simple," Rosemary said, "but I've been in the OR for more than five years, so I know it is not that simple.

"Actually it is," the doctor replied, smiling at her. "The surgery is easy. I have studied the radiologist's report of the MRI that we received before you came, and the new report from the MRI that we took after you arrived. I have plotted out each step of the procedure. My team has trained for this type of operation. The worrisome problem is always infection. To reduce that possibility, we are going to use the robot to do the actual work. In this way, there will be only three people in the sterile room, and we reduce the chance of infection by more than seventy percent. I do have to tell you that even with all that we do to keep the patient safe, complications may occur, even with da Vinci surgery. I will be making two incisions. I will be operating through one incision and observing, using a 3D camera, through the second incision. You can watch the entire operation on the monitor. One other thing, you won't be able to touch your wife for at least four hours, unless you want to go through the same process that we do."

Martin looked at Rosemary. "Are you going through that process?"

Rosemary nodded. "That's what I'm trained for. If you want to go through the process, I can help you with it. This hospital has accepted my credentials, so I will be in the actual operating room as a redundant nurse with the robot, the anesthetist and a charge nurse.

Martin thought about it for a very short time and said, "Lead me to it."

With the doctor's permission, Rosemary led Martin to the locker room. She told him to take a shower, scrub his hair thoroughly and come out wrapped in a towel. When he finished showering, he came out and put on the scrubs that Rosemary had ready for him. While he was dressing, Rosemary took her shower and put on her scrubs. She couldn't believe that the hospital had scrubs her size. Then they went to the scrub sink and Rosemary showed Martin how to scrub his hands and arms.

They walked to the operating room together. "This is where I leave you," said Rosemary, pointing to a double green door that had a sign on it, reading '**No Admittance - Authorized Personnel Only – Proper attire is required**'. "You go through that door," she said, pointing to a single door ten feet down the hall. "Someone will come for you." Rosemary turned and backed through the green door. It swung closed behind her.

Martin walked down the hall and through the door into a small waiting room. He sat down and waited. Ten minutes later a nurse called him. She took him into a dimly lit room with a row of chairs facing a large monitor and a number of smaller screens. On one of the smaller screens, he could see his wife, who was in the other room. She had a clear mask over her face. The nurse explained that Melinda was lightly sedated because she was so far along in her pregnancy.

The nurse pushed a number of buttons on the wall, and the large monitor came to life, as well as the blood pressure monitor, the heart monitor, and the activity from the fetal monitor.

Dr. Troop, the surgeon, walked into the operating room. The scrub nurse said to her, "Everyone is ready." She assisted the doctor in putting on an OR gown, mask, and head covering, She looked at the anesthetist, who nodded and said, "The patient is ready."

The doctor nodded, put her head inside the hood of the robot and put her hands on the controls. On the big monitor, the edge of the cautery knife could be seen as it moved towards the operating site. A three quarter-inch incision was made through the skin. The scalpel moved aside, and another tool took its place. Thirty minutes later the doctor told her audience that she was through the wall of the uterus. "Now we look for the vein," she said, as she inserted the camera. She moved the camera around in very small increments and then stopped. "There it is. I am going to try to nudge his foot with the camera." Two very little toes came into view. The doctor pushed the toes with the camera, and the foot moved back and then down. "Okay, that's the way I like it." The doctor waited a few minutes to see if the foot would move back. "I am coming out," she said. "Okay. I'm out. Someone read the numbers. Through the microphone, she told Rosemary to put a small bandage on the incision and told the anesthetist to bring Melinda out of her beauty sleep. "Bring her out very, very slowly. I don't want to disturb the babies. I'll be back in thirty minutes, unless you need me sooner." The doctor turned to Martin and said, "I told you it was a straightforward operation."

Martin got up and hugged the doctor.

"Hey. I'm sterile," she said.

"I'm not," Martin said. Everyone laughed.

Martin asked the doctor if Melinda would be able to fly after twenty-four hours. The doctor told him that there should not be a problem, especially if he is traveling with a nurse. Martin looked at Rosemary, who nodded her head.

"Yes Doctor," said Martin. "Melinda has her own nurse. The nurse will be with her for the next couple of weeks, at least."

Dr. Troop left the operating theatre and left Martin watching his wife on the monitor. He watched as she slowly woke up. "You scared me," he said into the microphone.

"Hey, blame your son." Melinda answered. "He's the troublemaker. Your daughter was very quiet."

"Speaking of our babies, have you thought of names for them yet?" Martin asked.

"I would like the boy's middle name to be Thomas, in honor of Tom Marcus."

"I like that. What about first names?"

"How about naming our daughter Annabelle?" Melinda asked.

"That is a beautiful name," said Martin. "What about our son?"

"I know you wanted Edward for our son name?" Melinda said.

"I can live with that, "said Martin, smiling. "Don't forget a middle name for Annabelle."

"I'll take care of that," Melinda replied. "Computer, get Sheena online."

"Sheena is online," said the Computer.

"How are you Melinda?" Sheena asked. "Everyone has been worried."

"I'm fine," she replied. "The operation was a complete success. Edward came through it like a champion. I called because we need some help with a name. Annabel needs a middle name, and I thought her godmother should do the honors."

Sheena was silent for a moment. "I'll have to get back to you on that. I'm crying too hard to make any sense."

"That was the head of our combat teams? Martin asked. "What a softie."

"Don't let her let you hear say that," Melinda chuckled.

"I won't tell, if you won't tell," Martin answered.

Melinda dozed off and Martin watched her. Twenty minutes later two orderlies came in and wheeled the gurney to the ICU. The report from the new MRI had come back saying that the operation was a complete success. Edward's foot was no longer near the vein. The doctor told Martin that by the end of the day Melinda would be fine. They would advise keeping Melinda in the hospital for twenty-four hours to make sure that Edward's foot does not rotate back and press on the vein. An hour later, Martin, who was now wearing a sterile gown over his scrubs, went in to see her. She was wide-awake and held her hands out to him. He walked over to the bed and sat down. He did not say a word. He just sat holding onto her hand. It did not take long before Martin's eyes closed and his head hit the bed.

Two hours later Melinda pushed at Martin, waking him up. "What's wrong? What's the matter?" he asked her, with concern on his face.

"My water just broke and I have awful stomach cramps. It hurts." Then she screamed, as tears started coming out of her eyes.

Martin pushed the call button for help. Two minutes later, Dr. Troop and another doctor came in. They moved Martin aside and examined Melinda. The other doctor whispered something to Dr. Troop. She in turn asked Martin to go into the waiting room. She would come to him as soon as she was finished with Melinda. He was not to worry. "We expected those cramps," she said, "just not this soon."

Martin went to the waiting room and sat down on the couch. In less than 10 minutes he was sound asleep. He no sooner fell asleep than a nurse came in and woke him up. She took him to the elevator and up one floor to the maternity ward. Martin's head was swiveling back and forth, not seeing what he was looking at.

"Why are we in the maternity ward?" he asked.

"Your wife is in labor," replied the nurse.

"How can that be? That is not why she was brought to this hospital." Martin followed the nurse to the end of the hallway, turned right and entered the second door on the right. Melinda was in the bed with her legs in stirrups and the doctor sitting under the drape between her legs.

He heard the doctor say to the nurse, "She is dilated10cm."

The nurse pulled a chair over to the head of the bed and motioned for Martin to sit down. He reached for Melinda's hand and closed both of his hands around her hand. He leaned over and kissed her on the forehead.

"This is a fine mess you got us into," Melinda said, and then let out a blood-curdling scream.

Martin turned white, and looked at the nurse. "Can't you do something to help her?"

"Your wife did ask for an epidermal, but her contractions were too close together. If we put in a needle at this point she could risk spinal injury."

Melinda squeezed his hand so hard; he thought he would lose a couple of fingers. She let out another blood-curdling scream. Martin did not know what do. The doctor told Melinda to push, then to breathe, then to push again.

"I see the crown," the doctor said. "The head is clear. Here comes the right shoulder, now the left shoulder. Here she is." The doctor clamped the cord and cut it. He handed the baby girl off to the nurse and turned back to Melinda.

"Melinda," he said. "I don't want you to push. Wait until the pressure builds up, then I want you to take a deep breath and push." He looked down and then said, "Forget what I just said. This little one is not going to wait. Here he is now." The doctor cut the second cord and handed off the little boy to the nurse. He then stood up and said to Melinda, "You are the mother of two lively babies, a boy and a girl. Congratulations."

Martin was able to pry Melinda's fingers open. He reached over and wiped her face. He gave her a kiss on the lips and plopped into the chair to catch his breath. Fifteen minutes later, the nurses brought the wrapped babies to Melinda. They placed one on each side of her. Martin stood up and looked at his wife and his two little babies. They were so tiny. There were tears streaming from his eyes. He was so happy.

They told Martin to go into the waiting room, and they would come to get him when Melinda was in her room. Thirty minutes later, Rosemary came in to the waiting room to get Martin and take him to Melinda's room.

"What the heck happened?" Martin asked. "One minute I'm sitting with Melinda as she was recuperating from the operation, I fall asleep and the next minute she is complaining of cramps. They throw me out of the room, and as I'm leaving, they tell me that they expected the cramps."

"I gather even you didn't even know she was that far along," said Rosemary. "Your wife went into what is called 'precipitous labor'. Her water broke six hours after the operation, she had severe labor pains and then she gave birth. The entire procedure took less than two hours."

They walked down the hall and into Melinda's private room. Martin walked to the bed, leaned down, gave his wife a kiss and then kissed the forehead of each of his babies.

"You make some beautiful kids, Melinda," he said, with a smile on his face.

"I had some help," Melinda replied, smiling back at him.

Martin sat next to the bed and held one of Melinda's hands to his cheek. His tears started to flow again. She wiped the tears from his cheeks and started crying herself.

Rosemary walked back into the room, looked at both of them and started to laugh. "You are supposed to be warriors?"

Both Melinda and Martin turned and looked at her and started to laugh.

"Okay, the pity party is over." Rosemary said. "We have a lot of work to do." Turning to Melinda, she said, "I just got a call from Sheena. She said I should tell you that Annabelle's godmother wanted her middle name to be Sandra." Turning to Martin, she continued," Why don't you find a hotel room, get some sleep and don't come back until the bags under your eyes are gone. You are no use to your wife or your babies if you are not clear headed. I've made arrangements for another nurse to spell me for a while, so I can get some well needed sleep and another shower."

Martin walked out into the hall. "Computer, get Ron."

"Ron is online," said the Computer.

"Martin how is Melinda?" Ron asked.

"She's fine. She gave birth to twins, a boy and a girl."

"That is fantastic."

"That's not why I called. You know where I am, right?"

"Yes, the hospital in North Carolina. Why? What do you need?"

"I need a suite of rooms as close to the hospital as possible and transportation from here to the hotel. I will need a change of clothes for myself and for Rosemary, the trauma nurse. By the way, has her security clearance come in yet?"

"Her security clearance came in, and she is clear to top secret. She can be connected at your convenience."

"Okay. Call me when the transportation is outside."

"I'll do that. Give Melinda our love and give the babies a kiss. I'll let everyone know, and I'll tell them not to bother her for a couple of days."

Martin walked into the room, told Rosemary that she has a room at the hotel, will have a change of clothes by the time she wakes up and that transportation will be here soon to take them to the hotel. He told Melinda that Rosemary's clearance is top secret. He turned to Rosemary and then started to explain about being 'connected'. She looked thrilled.

"Martin," Ron said, "Transportation is at the front of the hospital."

Martin kissed his wife and started to leave the room.

"Some husband you are," Melinda remarked. "Knocks his wife up and goes to a hotel with a younger woman."

"He's safe with me," said Rosemary.

"It's not him I was worried about," laughed Melinda.

They left the hospital through the Main entrance and climbed into a black SUV that was idling at the curb. As soon and Martin and Rosemary put on their seatbelts, the SUV left the curb and headed out of the hospital property. Twenty-five minutes later, they pulled into the driveway of the Hyatt Regency. The door attendant rushed to the SUV and opened the rear door. Rosemary and Martin got out, entered the lobby, walked to the desk, identified themselves and were given keys to the suite. They took the elevator to the penthouse floor and found their suite. Martin opened the door, and Rosemary walked in with Martin close behind. Rosemary stopped short, and Martin banged into her. "What's the matter?" he asked her.

"Look," she said, pointing to the sitting room. The room was very large. On one side was a large table surrounded with six upholstered chairs. At the other end was a leather upholstered couch against the wall with a mahogany coffee table sitting directly in front of the couch. Across from the couch were three upholstered chairs. The far wall was covered with silk drapes. They both walked all the way into the suite. Rosemary walked to the far wall, opened the silk drapes and looked out. The wall had a glass door, which went from the floor to ceiling. The view was of downtown Greenville. Rosemary stood there with her mouth open. "I thought we were going to a motel," she said.

"This is what you get when you joined us. We each have our own bedroom and bathroom. I don't see any packages here, so I guess we don't have clean clothes. We will have to make do with the hotel's bathrobes. Hope you don't mind. Are you hungry?" he asked Rosemary.

"Yes, I am," she replied. "I'm so hungry I could eat a horse."

"I'll order us something to eat, and by the time we finish showering the food should be here." Looking at the doors, he asked her which bedroom she wanted. "I didn't even look," she said. "I'll take this one," pointing to her right. "See you in a few minutes." She opened the bedroom door, went in and closed the door. Martin picked up the phone, placed the order for food and went into his room.

Twenty minutes later, both Martin and Rosemary were sitting in the living room when there was a knock on the door. Martin got up, checked the peephole and opened the door. A waiter stood there with the food cart. The waiter was dressed in a tuxedo with shoes so shiny; one could shave using them as a mirror. The waiter pushed the cart to the sitting room area and laid out place mats and silverware. He opened the little door on the side of the hot cart and brought out heated plates. He finished setting the table, went back to the cart and brought out the food. When he was done, he asked Martin if there was anything else. When told there wasn't, he bowed slightly and turned to the cart. He wheeled the cart to the door, opened it and moved out into the hallway. The door closed and locked.

Martin walked over to Rosemary and offered his hand to assist her to the table. He held her chair while she sat down. She was in awe. Martin walked to the other side of the table and sat down.

"Didn't I get anything you like? I can order something different if this isn't good enough." He asked, concern in his voice.

Finally, Rosemary said, "Wow. You did all this for me?"

"No, I did it for me, also. I'm just as hungry," replied Martin.

"This is so beautiful. I don't know what to say," she said.

"You don't have to say anything," Martin answered. "Just pick up your fork and eat."

Rosemary did just that. Twenty minutes later she sat back, patted her stomach and sighed. After finishing a delicious meal, Martin fixed them both a cup of coffee. They dawdled over coffee while Martin finished explaining about what her being 'connected' means. He told her than by being connected, she would have immediate communication with all of the team members anywhere in the world. All she had to do was say the word, "Computer." He also explained about her security clearance. As soon as he was finished, Rosemary said she understood everything he told her.

"I can't wait to be 'connected," she answered. "I guess that means I won't be going back to that hospital, anytime soon, will I?"

"I don't think so," Martin answered. "You'll work with Melinda until she says she doesn't need you around. I don't see that happening anytime soon. I've been told twins are a tough deal. Knowing Melinda, she will want to go on an assignment every now and then."

Rosemary yawned. "I guess I am more tired than I realized."

"Let's get some rest," Martin said. "What time do you want breakfast?"

"0800 sounds good to me," she said. Martin picked up the phone, ordered breakfast for two, said good night to Rosemary, went into his bedroom and closed the door.

Day 10   Monday at sea onboard the Valley Forge. Even though the teams did not think anything would be happening, they were still vigilant. Each team kept walking around the decks and through the passageways. Everyone knew that some of the crew on board were criminals. They had definitely identified four of the crew and one officer, and suspicions about one other person. All the teams were concerned that there might be more criminals onboard. No one could be trusted.

Melinda had New York double check the manifests against the bills of lading for all the material that were been delivered to the Valley Forge. They knew that the sealed cans were been used for shipping the drugs. That is how they got past the drug-sniffing dogs, but what about the boxes? How did they get the boxes aboard, and who brought them aboard? How did the boxes get by customs and the drug-sniffing dogs? New York said that it would take time to review the information and would get back to them the following day. They would start the search at Day 9 and work backwards.

In addition, they are doing a deep background search on all of the officers, starting with the Captain.

Each of the teams took some downtime. They were able to take a swim, use the gym or just lie out in the sun. By 1500, everyone was back in their cabins getting ready for dinner. After all, it was a formal night and they wanted to do it up right.

At 1800 hours, they all met in the dining room. The men were dressed in tuxedos, and the women were wearing gowns. It was a quiet dinner. The discussion centered again about Melinda, the babies and Martin. Martin had requested that no one call them. Martin and Melinda would call them when they were ready.

Day 10   At 0930 hours at the Greenville Hospital, Martin and Rosemary walked into Melinda's room. The nurse had just brought the babies back from the nursery. Rosemary went over to the babies and checked them. Melinda smiled when she did that.

"So how did it feel sleeping with my husband at a fancy hotel?" Melinda asked, with a chuckle in her voice.

Rosemary turned bright red and stammered, "I didn't sleep with him."

"Well, let's see. You went to a hotel with him?" asked Melinda, smiling.

"Yes. I did," answered Rosemary.

"You slept in the same suite?"

"Yes. I did."

"You showered in the same suite?" continued Melinda.

"Yes. I did."

"You slept in a bedroom?"

"Yes. I did."

"I rest my case. You went with my husband, period." Then Melinda started laughing.

Martin chuckled, shook his head, and patted Rosemary on the back. "Are you sure you still want to join us?" he asked as he started laughing.

Rosemary smiled and started laughing with them. "You had me

there. I really thought you were angry at me for going with your husband to a hotel."

"It would take more than that to make me angry. I know my husband, and he would never do anything to embarrass me."

"I know he wouldn't do that," answered Rosemary. "He made sure the door was locked, so no one would walk in."

Melinda opened her mouth, shut it and said. "You got me," Melinda said. Turning to Martin asked, "Where did you find this gem?"

"I'm going to get in trouble. I stole her from a hospital in Miami. At the time, she had no idea what she was getting into, but she came anyway. She tells me she is not only an Emergency Trauma Nurse but a jumper as well."

"Well, you can't take the babies jumping until they are at least a year old," Melinda said, laughing.

Rosemary smiled, walked over to Melinda, gave her a kiss on the cheek and squeezed her hand. "Thanks for having me. When did the doctor say they wanted you up and walking?"

"After lunch they want me up for a short time, especially if I am going to travel in four days. Until I can take care of myself, I can't take care of the babies." Rosemary and Melinda talked about a feeding and exercise schedule, while Martin sat next to the babies and admired them. They were sleeping. Edward was making faces in his sleep, while Annabelle opened and closed her hands. He reached over and put a finger in each one's hand and their little hands closed like a trap.

Chapter 4

Day 11 Tuesday 0530 hours onboard the Valley Forge. As they were fast approaching Georgetown, Grand Cayman, three teams were walking on deck. They still kept away from Deck 4. Ron and Lucinda were watching the monitor when they saw shadows moving through their field of vision. They switched the camera to night vision and saw two men moving boxes against the railing.

"New York, are you getting this?"

"That's affirmative. We will have a drone overhead in less than ten minutes. We have scheduled a drone every morning. This one is Special Three, connected."

"That's great. Special Three, do you have us in view?"

"Roger, Valley Forge, I see you. I just saw a box thrown over the side. Here goes another one. I see six boxes, total. I don't see any boats."

Ten minutes later Special Three said, "Okay Valley Forge, here comes a boat. It is red with a yellow stripe down its side. It's a cigarette speedboat. This is not like last week. This is one very fast looking boat. It looks like they cannot get all the boxes into the boat. They were only able to load four boxes. Would you believe it? It looks like they are shooting at the remaining two boxes. I guess they want to sink them. I cannot tell if they are hitting the boxes or not. One box appears to be lower in the water. Yes, one of the boxes sank out of sight. There goes the second box. I wonder what they sacrificed, that they couldn't afford a second speed boat. The boat is moving. It is going very fast in a northerly direction. I will keep it in sight."

"Charlie, did you get a team on the dock?" asked Ron. "I just found out that we are not going to dock. We are going to take a tender to shore. It will take us an additional couple of hours to get to shore."

"Yes Ron," said Charlie Pile. "I was able to fly three teams onto the island. We got here at dawn. I assumed they would do the same thing they did on the other islands, so we have set up the same way. I have one team on the dock, one team to the west, one team to the east, and I will roam. I would have had a fourth team, but they were left on St. Kitts. I finally found out why they never made contact. Their bodies were found floating in the water. They were both shot in the back of the head. I don't know if it was random or whether this was gang related. I have four men on the island doing an investigation. I'll keep you informed. This is the first time in a long time that I lost a man. Both of them had families."

"I'm sorry to hear that," said Ron. "Will you have enough men for now?"

"Yes," replied Charlie. "I've called for two more teams to meet us at the next island."

"I just got a call from Special Three," said Ron. "The boat that picked up four of the boxes is not coming to Georgetown. They are heading north. The only dock up that way is the dock at the Turtle Farm. Is there a way to get a team up there?"

"I don't know," said Charlie. "I have two men on motorcycles heading that way now. Have Special Three try to keep the boat in sight. Damn it, I hate it when the bad guys outsmart me."

"Don't feel bad," exclaimed Ron. "If we can't catch this batch, we still have four more shots; Jamaica, Haiti, St. Lucia and Curacao. At least we know how they're getting the material off the ship. We still don't know how they got the boxes onto the ship. New York is still checking the invoices and the manifests. We don't even know when they put the boxes on the ship. It could have been a month ago or it could have been the last time they were in the shipyard."

"Charlie Pile, this is Special Three. The cigarette boat has landed and they are offloading three boxes. They have put them on the dock at the Turtle Farm. The boat has moved offshore. They are about a quarter mile northwest of the dock. They seem to be waiting for something or someone. They have kept one box on their boat. I can see your two motorcyclists and they have a ways to go. They are passing Seven Mile Beach."

"The boat is still sitting a quarter mile off the dock," said Special Three. "Nobody has approached the three boxes that were left on the dock. Your men are only a quarter of a mile away. They are turning eastbound towards the Turtle Farm."

"Ron, did you copy all of that?"

"Yes I did," Ron replied. "What is happening with the remaining box that was kept on the boat?"

"The boat is still sitting out there," said Special Three. "I'll keep you informed."

Charlie remarked, "They have never done it this way before. I wonder if they are smuggling something else besides drugs. We have to get a look inside that box."

The Computer chimed in. "Harry Blank online"

"I was just going to call you," said Ron. "We have a situation developing. Six boxes were dropped off the Valley Forge, twenty miles off shore. A speedboat picked up four of the boxes and sunk the remaining two with gunfire. The boat did not come into Georgetown as expected. It went to the Turtle Farm dock instead. The men from the boat off loaded three boxes on the dock, and they moved offshore with the one remaining box. There is something else besides drugs in those boxes. We want to take a look inside of them."

"Okay. After the suspects have picked up the boxes, follow them to their destination and then arrange to shut the Grand Cayman operation down. Try not to let the natives know what you are doing. Use whatever assets you have at your disposal. When we get to Jamaica, I think we will do the same. For that island, we will have to wait until we can get the Charlie and Delta teams back. We found that they have three big warehouses. They have one warehouse in Falmouth, one warehouse in Montego Bay, and a small warehouse in Kingston. We have followed them up the ladder as far as we can go in Jamaica. Once the goods are delivered to the different warehouses we will raid them at the same time, capture all the suspects and take them to the airport. I want to leave Labadee until the ship goes back there in two days. Good luck with Grand Cayman."

"Charlie, have your team head back to the Turtle Farm dock," said Ron. "The boat might be coming ashore, or at least the box will. You might need a small van to pick up the other three boxes. Have one start out."

"Okay Ron."

"Special Three," asked Ron. "What ordinance do you have on board the drone?"

"I have a full load," replied Special Three. "I have four rockets and a full load for the machine gun. What would you have me do?"

"We want that last box," Ron said. "Do you think you can convince the boat to come ashore?"

"Standby, Valley Forge. They are making it easy. They aren't even moving. I'll run a line of bullets across their bow. Okay, they didn't see that one coming. I am coming around again. They are trying to start their engine. Oops. I ran another line across their stern. I think I hit their engine. It looks like they are on fire. The two men have jumped overboard and are swimming towards the dock. Okay, your people have them. I can see them on the ground. I am going to sink the boat to put out the fire. That was a perfect shot. I didn't even hit the box. You are lucky on this one. The tide is coming in, and the box is floating ashore towards you."

Five minutes later, Special Three said, "Your people have picked up the box that was in the water. It looks like a red van is coming from the west. I don't think it's yours. I suggest you scatter and stay out of sight. There is a large number forty-nine on the top of the van. They are heading right for the dock. Two men got out and are loading the three boxes into the van. They are looking around as if they know they are short one box. They got back in the van. They made a U turn and are heading east."

"I've told my men to follow." Charlie Pile said. "If my men get a chance they will put a tracker on the van. Once they do that, they are to break away and head back to town."

"Charlie, your guys are good," said Special Three. "I now have an active tracker. Tell them to break away." "This is Special Three. I have two hours on station. The van has pulled into a warehouse. I am sending you the coordinates. I'm circling the warehouse at twenty-six thousand feet."

"Charlie," said Special Three. "I see two garage doors opening. Two black cars are coming out. I'm designating them as bogey alpha and bogey bravo. I'm high enough that I can keep track of both of them. Bogey alpha has parked in front of a store on the main street in Georgetown. I am sending you the coordinates of the store. Bogey bravo is entering the parking lot of a large church. There are four cars parked there. I'm sending you those coordinates, as well. It's all yours. I'm bringing the drone home. Special Four is now on station, connected."

"Thanks for your help, Special Three," Ron said. "We will look for you when we get to Jamaica. Special Four, do you have a picture?"

"Yes I do," replied Special Four. "I see your men and the suspects' vans."

Charlie Pile spoke to his teams. Pointing to the first eight men he said, "You are team Echo. You will take bogey alpha. Use the dart guns." Pointing to the next group of men he said, "You are team Foxtrot and have bogey bravo. Same instructions as I gave Echo. The rest of you will come with me. We will be Team Hotel. We are going to the warehouse." He handed out the coordinates to each of the teams and informed Special Four of his plans. Each team got in their vans and headed to their assignments. Team Echo went east to the store. Team Foxtrot went down Main Street to the church and Team Hotel headed north towards the Turtle Farm.

Team Echo pulled around behind the store. Four men stayed in the back looking for a back door into the store. The other four went around the side of the building, and without pausing, broke the door down. There were three people standing around a table packing little cellophane bags into a shoebox and six young girls sitting at the next table filling little plastic bags with white powder. The table was loaded with little plastic bags filled with white powder and two electric scales. Everyone's heads turned towards the noise, and one man put his hand inside his jacket. All that could be heard was "p-f-f-f-t." Two men and one woman fell to the floor, unconscious. The six young girls were shot and fell asleep at the table.

The team leader took out his cell phone and notified Charlie that they had taken the objective. They have nine prisoners. He explained that the six young girls were chained in place. They were only wearing their underwear. He thought it would be better to just cut the chains and let them wake up after everyone is gone. Charlie acknowledged the information and told the leader of the team to use his judgement. Move the rest of the prisoners and the drugs into the van and head to the airport. Charlie forwarded the information to Ron. Ron contacted the airplane and told them that they would be getting some prisoners for Dr. Wellfleet.

Team Foxtrot parked in front of the St. James Church. Four of the men moved to the right of the church and hurried around the back of the building. The remaining four men moved to the left of the church. Both groups surrounded the four cars and the van. One of the suspects had been away from the group, and took out his gun and started firing at Team Foxtrot. Two of Charlie's men were killed before the suspect could be hit with a dart. The rest of the suspects were hit with darts and were on the ground. They searched the van and found twenty shoeboxes filled with clear plastic envelopes. Each envelope contained a fine white powder. They searched the men and the cars. Each car had a locked metal suitcase. When broken open, they found them full of Euros.

Foxtrot leader called it in. He told Ron that he lost two men in a firefight. Ron relayed the information to the airplane. They put the two men in body bags and placed them into the van. They could not get everyone and everything in one van, so they took the subjects' vans as well and headed to the airport.

Charlie Pile took his team to the warehouse. They broke in and found it empty. They searched the premises and found that even the garbage cans were empty. He reported to Ron. Ron acknowledged the report and told him to head for the airport. Falmouth, Jamaica will be his next stop.

Ron notified all of his teams. "All of my teams back to the ship. The rest of the day is yours, but keep your eyes open. We would like a volunteer to operate the monitor so we can take a break. Don't everyone yell at once. All he heard was laughter."

Day 12   Wednesday at 0400, it was Marsha's turn to watch the monitor. It was still dark, but they had left the camera in the infrared mode. Thirty minutes after she started to watch the monitor, she saw two people moving boxes to the railing, cover them up and leave. She notified New York and sent a message to everyone's tablet.

When the Valley Forge was twenty-five miles off the coast of Falmouth, Jamaica, eight boxes dropped over the side. The water was very rough, and the winds were at gale force. Ron knew they would put up a drone and it would be above the storm. He was thankful that the drones were equipped with infrared cameras. He contacted Charlie Pile and told him about the eight boxes.

"This is not the smartest bunch of smugglers," said Charlie. "I wonder where they are going to find someone stupid enough to go out in this weather to retrieve those boxes. I have four teams here with me. We hired two extremely large fishing boats to assist us. Even our skippers are concerned about the winds and the high seas. Unless they are going to take the boxes to the other side of the island, we will have them wrapped and tied up within a couple of hours. I understand the police raided the warehouse at Stingray City on the Caymans. They arrested twelve people and confiscated fourteen boxes. This delivery system must have been place a long time for them to have so much inventory on hand. Why it was all in one place makes me wonder. Twelve boxes each contained 4 kilos each of pure cocaine and the other two boxes contained currency. Each of those two boxes contained a half million dollars in hundred dollar bills. No wonder they had trouble lifting those boxes out of the water. The money will build some beautiful schools, if it makes it into the treasury. I don't know how we missed the fourth drop zone. I guess they weren't expecting a delivery today. I would have loved to be there just to see their faces. I guess three out of four isn't too shabby,"

After a rough night at sea, everyone wanted off the ship. Twenty minutes after the Valley Forge docked at Falmouth, Jamaica, and the ship was cleared by customs, the passengers started streaming off the ship. Thirty minutes later, it started to rain. The passengers rushed into the stores. All the stores were packed. The rains suddenly stopped and the sun came out. Everyone came out of the stores and started walking and visiting the outside booths. Thirty minutes later the rains came again.

"Valley Forge, Valley Forge. This is Special Four. We see a small boat approaching the boxes. The boat is bouncing all over the place. It is taking a beating."

Charlie Pile called Ron to tell him that the waves have not calmed down, and a small boat had stopped next to the boxes. Someone in the boat was trying to pick the boxes out of the water. The island had posted 'small craft warnings'. This person didn't look, didn't care, or the amount of money he was being paid overrode his common sense. Either this person was weak or the boxes were extremely heavy. This was a comedy of errors. He had finally gotten two boxes loaded on the boat. He got the third box on the lip of the boat, and the boat tipped over, dropping the driver and the three boxes back in the water. I had signaled one of my fishing boats to assist the man in the water. As they were approaching the man in the water, he took out a gun and shot one of my men, and put a second bullet through the wheelhouse window and wounded the wheelman. Would you believe he shot the man that was helping him out of the water? I don't know what the men's conditions are, but they tell me they think one of the men is dead. The shooter fell back into the water, and we retrieved all eight boxes. Six of the boxes were extremely heavy. The other two were much lighter. They had to use a crane to bring everything onboard The shooter finally gave up and threw his gun into the boat. They picked him out of the water with a fishing net and left him dangling over the water until they had tied up at the dock. They tied up to the dock and put our men in an ambulance. When they got them to the hospital, one of Charlie's men was pronounced dead. The shooter had been hit with a dart, became unconscious, and taken to the airport, along with the boxes they had retrieved from the boat. We won't need the Charlie and Delta teams. We'll take all the boxes to the airport. There is over four million dollars in this batch. That's too much money to turn over to the officials. With all the corruption on this Island I'm going to put the boxes on the plane. We cannot trust the officials on this island. Especially since two of the prisoners were high ranking police officials. One other prisoner worked for the mayor. I never liked the idea to involve outsiders because I would not want them to know about us. I'll load everything we can in our van. I probably will have to use one of their vans as well. We should be at the airport in an hour. How do you want me to deal with the boxes that we retrieved? Wait for one of our planes or send it Federal Express?"

"Hold off sending the boxes anywhere." Ron said. "As soon as our plane is available, we'll send it down to you. Do you have a place to keep the prisoners?"

"Yes. There is a small jail at the airport." Charlie Pile said. "It used to hold items for export that had a high dollar value. Since that kind of shipping isn't done anymore, it's vacant, so we can use it. I'll leave a couple of my people here to take care of the prisoners. Since we don't know when the plane will be here, we will make arrangements to feed them as well. If it were up to me, I would lock them up and throw away the key, but it is hard to punish a man because he's stupid. He will be well taken care of and be ready to transport as soon as the plane arrives. I'll leave the raiding party here in Jamaica and have another team ready for Haiti. At the rate I am leaving men on the different islands, I'll run out of troops if this keeps up for another week."

"I understand," Ron said. "I'll have Delta team flown down to St. Lucia instead. They will wait there for your instructions. Computer off."

Day 13 Thursday. At 0500 the Valley Forge tied up to the dock in Labadee, Haiti. Two couples were walking the deck, stopping every now and then to do stretching exercises. They stopped walking and stood by the railing on the starboard side of the ship. From that vantage point, they could see the action on the pier. They could see the kitchen staff moving supplies off the ship. They watched them load the small electric carts with coolers, pans and cooking utensils. The team was able to watch them move food to the cooking stations where they were preparing to cook lunch. By 0800, the sun had risen into a clear blue sky. The temperature was rising, and the sun was reflecting off the water. By 1000, people were already lining up for a barbecue lunch. The temperature had risen to eighty-five degrees and there was no sea breeze.

"We see one guy carrying a box that has a black diagonal stripe down its side," reported Marsha. "He is just passing the entrance to the park and heading down the walkway."

"We see him," Ron said.

"There goes a second man carrying a box with that same black diagonally stripe," Susan reported.

"Sheena is already in the park with Benjamin," Ron said. "They are sitting near where we all played ball the last time we were here. Sheena has remounted a digital camera under the bench. There is also a drone in the air at twenty-five thousand feet, call sign Special Two. Now we have to wait and see who else comes off the ship. Once we are satisfied that we have them all, Harry wants us to take them to the brig and then when we can have Dr. Wellfleet question them. He also wants us to close down this Haitian operation as well. We flew Charlie Team down last night so you should have enough assets to work with. Part of the team is near the house that you found last week. On your command, they will raid the house and retrieve whatever material is in the house. We have eight men and women in the park ready to raid the last drop zone."

"This is Special Two. We finally have some activity. It seems like a duplicate of last time. We see a sand buggy approaching the drop zone. He is slowing down but not stopping. He is turning around and leaving the park. I guess he figures he's too early, since there is only two boxes. Suggest everybody stay in place."

"This is Suzy Q. There is an electric truck from the park by the aft gangway. They are loading it with six boxes that have the black diagonal stripe. They are also loading eight-one gallon cans of Pinto beans from Colombia. This is the first time they have moved these gallon cans. Now I have to wonder how long these cans have been on the ship. Were they loaded when they brought the brown boxes on? My second in command is directing the loading. He has two members of the ship's crew assisting him. Now we know who else is involved in this operation. I don't want to stop them at this end, since we still have two more stops. Let them think that they are getting away with their game."

Ron said, "Charlie, Harry wants you can close the entire Haitian operation down after we leave here."

"The truck is leaving the pier loaded with six boxes and eight one gallon cans," Susy Q. said.

"I can see the truck coming." Sheena said. "They have stopped by the tree and are offloading the boxes and gallon cans. They are covering them up with a light blue sheet. They have finished and are looking around to see if anyone is paying attention to them. I have it all on the video. New York, are you getting all this?"

"That's a Roger, Sheena," New York replied.

"Heads up people," Special Two reported, "The sand buggy is heading back to the drop zone."

"I have them in sight," said Sheena. "They are loading all the boxes and gallon cans that were left by the tree."

"This is Charlie Pile. We have them in sight. The tracker is still working from last week. Special Two, are you getting the tracker?"

"Roger Charlie. We have them loud and clear on our screen. You can break off at this time."

"Roger that. I am breaking off and returning to the park to pick up Sheena and Benjamin. The rest of the team will meet at the northeast corner of the park. A bus will take them to the airport. A 737 will fly them to Curacao to await instructions from either me or Ron. I'll be flying to Castries in St. Lucia as soon as I can."

"There will be a meeting in the suite for all of my teams at 1600 hours," Ron said. "I want to make sure everyone made it back to the ship or that they are very strong swimmers." Everyone acknowledged the order and laughter could be heard in the background."

"Computer, get Ron online," said Charlie.

"I'm here," said Ron. "What's happening?"

"We just finished the raid in Haiti," said Charlie. "We confiscated twelve boxes and rounded up thirty-one people. This group is similar to the last group. We have one person that works for the mayor, one that is a captain in the police, one is a major in the police force and the rest are locals. One of the prisoners died after receiving a dart. It might be a reaction to the dart or it could be something that was in his system that reacted to the drug. Let Dr. Wellfleet know. One of my men ended up with a broken leg. He tripped over a bottle that was on the ground. We opened one of the heavy boxes. It contained hundred dollar bills in one-pound shrink-wrapped packages. I counted sixty packages. That figures that each box contains more than two million dollars. We are costing these cartel's a lot of money. We resealed the box and sent it to the airport with all the rest of the material."

Ron acknowledged the report and passed the information to the rest of his team.

At the end of the day, everyone lounged in the suite with refreshments in their hands. "It feels good to know we helped close up a large smuggling operation here in Haiti and the one in Jamaica," said Jose. "It is a shame we still have to deal with the five people whom we know are on the ship. I hope I don't react when I meet them on deck. Yeah, I know. They are not supposed to be on deck, but they do go on Deck 4."

"That's the thing," said Ron. "You have to stay away from Deck 4. We have it covered with the camera. We are watching it from here, and New York is watching it as well. Are there any questions or comments?" There weren't any. "Okay, that's it for today. Go relax. We are at sea all day tomorrow. I don't expect any action, but you never know. We will rotate the monitor watch every two hours. That will give you more time in the sun. Make sure to use sun tan lotion. I don't want to see you in sickbay with extreme sun burn. I'll put the schedule on your tablets after dinner. I still want you to patrol the whole ship. You can go to the production show at the Flamingo Theatre tonight. Stay near the doors in case I need you. I'm done." Everyone got up and left the suite. Ron and Lucinda sat back.

"At least we can rest for a day." Lucinda said. "I wonder how Melinda and Martin are doing."

"Don't call them. When they're ready, Martin told me that they would call us. We will have to be patient and wait."

That night Lucinda and Ron wandered around the ship. It was a formal night, and they got the chance to see all the passengers dressed in their finery. Well, not everyone was dressed up, but most were. The men wore tuxedos with vests or cummerbunds. Some men wore suits. However, the women's attire was outstanding. There were some beautiful gowns and pantsuits. Many a head was turned. John and Marsha sat at their usual table on the promenade and admired the parade while drinking their evening coffee.

"I don't know if I should be jealous or not," said Marsha. "Some of these outfits are spectacular. Look at that woman in the strapless red satin dress. Look at the other people watching her."

"Yes, I know," said John. "I've been watching her for a few minutes, myself."

Marsha turned to John, "Some 'husband' you are," she said. "Eyeing other women, and then admitting it to your 'wife.'"

John laughed, reached over and patted her hand. "Does that mean we're getting a divorce?"

"Don't be so smart. No divorce until this operation is over," Marsha said, laughing. "Besides, you can't get a divorce until your lawyer comes back from vacation." John let out a loud laugh and Marsha smiled.

Day 14 The day started with cold weather, gale force winds and heavy rain. The outside temperature dropped to forty degrees. Most of the passengers stayed indoors and walked around inside the ship. The captain made a safety announcement. He reminded the passengers about the ship's movement and to make sure they use the hand rails. At every elevator there were a small pile of little white bags.

The teams had the chance to relax. John and Marsha went back to the table in the coffee shop that they had occupied the day before. They sat admiring the people who were walking on the promenade. Even with the extremely cold weather, two of the teams were wandering around outside. The day was cold but peaceful. Even dinner was a quiet affair. They lingered over coffee until show time.

Day 15 Saturday at 0600 the Valley Forge docked in Ft. Lauderdale. It was an overcast day. Looking down from Deck 12, the buses and taxicabs were lining up to pick up passengers. The ground was wet, and it was still too early for a traffic jam. Taxis and vans were unloading passengers for the next cruise. Passengers that were staying on for the next cruise met in one of the designated rooms and escorted off the ship, through customs and passport control. It took twenty minutes and they were back on the ship. One team went forward and one team went aft on Deck 12. They stood there and watched the activities ashore. A third team went to the port side and watched for any action on the water. There were many small boats going back and forth in the channel even at that early hour. There were two Security boats from the Coast Guard keeping those small boats away from the side of the Valley Forge. The fourth team stayed on Deck 1 and watched the loading of fresh food, canned food, wine and water. They checked the manifest as each pallet of food was loaded.

At 1300 hours a very large van pulled up to the entrance to the dock. A member of the Sherriff's Department directed the van to pull into the V.I.P. parking lot. The van stopped inside the lot, the side door opened and Martin got out. He turned around and reached into the van for Melinda's hand. He assisted her out of the van. When Melinda was safely out of the van, Martin released her hand. Rosemary held Edward out to Martin. He took the baby and handed him to Melinda. Rosemary then reached out again, holding Annabelle. Martin quickly grabbed her and held her close to his chest. The tiny baby was lost in his big hands. Rosemary stepped out of the van and looked at the ship. Her jaw dropped.

Martin and Melinda watched her and laughed. "I gather you have never been on a cruise ship before," Martin said.

"I've been on a cruise ship before," Rosemary said. "I've just never been on a cruise ship this size before."

Two porters came to the van, and Martin started giving instructions. He told the porters that they were to take the contents of the van directly to their suite. The porters explained that they could not do that. Only the baggage handlers could move the luggage. Martin nodded. He turned away from the porters and said, "Computer, online.

"Computer online, Martin," said the Computer.

"Get me Suzy Q," said Martin.

"I'm online, Martin," answered Suzy Q. "How are you? How are Melinda, and the babies? Where are you?"

"If you stop talking and let me get a word in edgewise, I'll tell you," he said, laughing. "You're almost as bad as Melinda. We are dockside with our luggage, a ton of baby food and diapers, and a nurse. Is there some way you can expedite getting us on board the ship? We have two porters here who insist it can't be done."

"Where are you exactly?" asked Suzy Q.

"We are outside in the V.I.P. parking lot," replied Martin.

"Keep the porters there. I am on the way with a couple of cabin attendants. Keep the faith," said Suzy Q.

Martin did just that. He started to explain what the holdup was, when Suzy Q came around the end of the building riding on a forklift, which was carrying a luggage cage. The forklift placed the cage next to the van, and Suzy Q instructed the two porters and the two cabin attendants to load everything from the van into the cage. It took them twenty-five minutes to empty the large van. Suzy Q stayed with the trio, and the forklift turned and headed back to the ship with the two porters trailing behind.

"Now that is what I call service." Martin said to Suzy Q.

Suzy Q reached for the baby in Melinda's arms. She cuddled it and made the strange noise that only women make when holding a newborn. She looked at the other baby, tilted her head and said, "Which one is which? They both look the same, especially the way they are wrapped."

Martin laughed. "They are definitely not the same," he said. Annabelle is the quiet one. She waits to be fed, and waits to be changed. She smiles all the time. Edward, however, is a very impatient baby. He wants what he wants when we wants it. He always seems to be hungry. I don't recall ever seeing him smile since he was born. We are concerned, because he doesn't sleep well. We brought enough food and diapers to last ten days. I hope it will be enough. Melinda will be spending a lot of time resting. I wanted to go home, but she insisted that since we had a suite and a nurse, we should return to the ship, so here we are. I'm glad we will be flying home in our own plane."

Martin introduced Rosemary to Suzy Q. He explained that Rosemary had all the proper security clearances. She would be 'connected' this evening or tomorrow morning. Suzy Q raised her eyebrows and nodded her head. She turned to Rosemary and said, "Welcome to the team. If you need any help, let me know. Dr. Wellfleet is not aboard just yet. I'll let him know that you guys are back in your suite."

"It's great to be back." Melinda said. "Ron brought us up to date with your episodes. Harry Blank has also kept us up to date. All we have left is ten days. I can't wait to take the babies home when this operation is finished."

At 1630 hours, they all attended the abandon ship lifeboat drill. Melinda, Ron, Rosemary and of course, the babies stayed in the suite. When the drill was over, the rest of the teams went back to their cabins. While the drill was going on, Ron 'connected' Rosemary. He explained how the system worked and how the privacy mode worked. If she had any questions, she could ask the Computer. Everyone dressed and headed for dinner in the main dining room as the Valley Forge pulled away from the dock. They discussed the day's events as they waited for their food. They talked about how nice it was to have Melinda and Martin back. They talked about Melinda's twins. They talked about how proud Martin is with his new babies. They talked about how big Martin is and how small the babies are and talked about how tiny the nurse is and how young she looks.

Ron looked at his watch and said, "I guess the raids in Haiti have taken place. I wish they had called us to let us know what happened." Everyone nodded his or her head.

Just then, they heard the Computer come online, "Conference online to all team members," said the Computer.

"The raid on Haiti went off as planned," said Charlie Pile. "We were able to retrieve all the material that was in the house, and captured eight people. The raid on the warehouse gave us ten suspects in one room. In the second room we caught twenty young girls working at a packing table. They each had a metal cuff on one ankle and were chained to metal loops that attached to the floor. They were filling and weighing plastic bags. There was an assortment of equipment and packing material on other tables around the room. We found a machine for mixing chemicals in the back room. It looked like they were diluting the drugs. Just like the other port, we are not going to detain the young girls. They appear to be prisoners not volunteer workers. We put everyone to sleep. We went in with our faces covered so we couldn't be identified. We are moving all the material and prisoners to the airport to await transportation. I am sorry for the delay in reporting. We wanted to make sure we rounded up the entire group. We cut the chains that were holding the girls. When they wake up they will be able to walk away."

"We were just commenting about the raid," said Ron. "Thanks for bringing us up to date."

Everyone smiled at each other and enjoyed the evening meal. For some reason the meal tasted extremely good. Another smuggling unit shut down. After dinner everyone took a walk around the ship and met at the entrance to the theater. They found seats near the door in case there presence were needed elsewhere. Everything stayed quiet and they were able to enjoy the evening's entertainment. Afterwards they said their goodnights and went to their cabin. After all they had to get up at 0500 the next day to roam the decks.

Day 16   Sunday at 1000 hours, everyone met for breakfast at the buffet. They fixed their plates and sat down at a large round table. Jose looked around the table and said, "I overslept this morning. I didn't get my morning wakeup call." Everyone else nodded their head and admitted they also had missed their wakeup call.

Ron spoke up. "I cancelled your wakeup calls. We are going to be at sea today and tomorrow. Until we get close to shore tomorrow, I don't see that boxes will be thrown off the ship. We inspected almost everything that came on the ship and noticed a number of errors. New York informed me that they found 11 invoices that did not match the material brought onboard. They are going to continue looking at the past invoices to see what else they can find. There are still over seventy-one gallon cans to be offloaded, and there are still at least twenty-six boxes left, that we know of. There are too many lockers on this ship to check them all. It was suggested that the boxes could have been brought on inside another box. We have to see if anything matches."

As they were finishing breakfast, the sun came out and the temperature started to rise. "What a great day to do nothing." Marsha said. I think I'll put on a bathing suit and go swimming." Looking at Lucinda, Sheena, and Susan, she said, "Want to join me?" Lucinda and Susan got up and Lucinda said, "We'll meet in twenty minutes by the pool on Deck 11 port side."

Jose spoke up. "Hey! What about us guys? May we come too?"

The women laughed. "Sure, why not," Lucinda said. "Meet us at the pool on Deck 11 port side in twenty minutes." Everyone got up except Benjamin and Sheena. Benjamin turned to Sheena, "Don't you want to go swimming?"

"Not on your life. If I want to get wet, I'll take a shower."

Benjamin laughed. "I'll keep you company. That is, if you don't mind."

Sheena smiled and nodded her head.

"Would you like another cup of coffee?" he asked.

"I would like that," said Sheena. "Let's take our coffee on deck and sit in the lounge chairs."

Ten minutes later, Jose, John and Ron were on the pool deck setting up the chairs when Jose looked up, whistled, and said, "Oh my, oh my. Look what is walking our way."

John and Ron looked up, turned to see where Jose was looking and stopped what they were doing. Coming towards them were three gorgeous women. In the middle was a redhead wearing a very small yellow string bikini. On her right was a brunette beauty wearing a wine color bikini, and on her left was a blonde beauty wearing a sky blue bikini. The men stood there open mouthed. Each of the woman went to their 'husbands' and gave them a poke in the chest. They woke from their trance and directed their 'wives' to their chairs.

"I've never seen you without your clothes before," said Jose, as he sat next to Susan.

Susan laughed. "This is the only time you will," she said, blushing. They all started laughing.

With the tension broken, the couples had a great time. They ordered non-alcoholic drinks and took turns going for snacks. It was a great afternoon. By 1500 hours they were exhausted. The party broke up, and they headed back to their cabins.

On the way back to their cabins, the women started talking about the babies. "Let's stop in and see them," Marsha said. They walked down two flights of stairs and went to Martin and Melinda's suite. They stopped in to see Annabelle and Edward. They spent some time holding each one of the babies and making all kinds of silly noises. After a while, Rosemary chased them out so that Melinda could get some rest before dinner.

Instead of going to the main dining room, Ron had made reservations for the entire group to eat in the ship's specialty restaurant's private dining room. Everyone met there at six thirty. Melinda and Martin surprised the group by showing up unannounced.

"Who's watching the babies?" asked Lucinda.

"Rosemary and Stephen volunteered," said Martin. "They wanted us to have a night out."

The entire evening's discussion was about how the babies were faring and how Melinda was feeling. The men just sat there. They were not part of the discussion. Every now and then one of the women would glance at them and smile. The men did not know how to take that smile. With the exception of Ron, they were all confirmed bachelors, or so they told everyone.

They had a leisurely dinner. They kept each other amused telling stories. They told Martin and Melinda all that they had done in the week they were apart. They told Martin and Melinda how some of the material was smuggled on board the ship and how some of the material was smuggled off the ship. This went on for some time until Marsha noticed that Melinda was yawning.

"I think it is time to let our Den Mother get to bed," said Marsha. "You know how these 'old people' are. They need their sleep."

Melinda rolled up her napkin and threw it at her. "

'Old people', some nerve," Melinda said, with a smile on her face, as she and Martin got up to leave. Everyone at the table laughed as Martin and Melinda left the room.

They got back to their suite, and as they opened the door, they could hear one of the babies crying. "That's Edward crying," said Melinda as she rushed into the nursery and went to the cribs. Annabelle was sound asleep, and Edward's crib was empty. Melinda went into the other room and found Edward in Rosemary's arms. She was walking back and forth trying to soothe him. Melinda reached over, took Edward from Rosemary's arms and started walking, while whispering to the baby. He would not stop crying.

"Edward hasn't stopped crying all evening," said Rosemary. "I called down to the Medical Clinic and asked for Dr. Wellfleet. He should be on his way by now. Annabelle has slept through it all." A few minutes later, Dr. Wellfleet knocked, and Rosemary let him in. He walked in, went to Melinda and took Edward in his arms. Edward fussed, squirmed and kept crying.

After examining Edward he said, "There is nothing wrong with him. He will tire himself out with his crying and fall asleep. He will drive you nuts with the crying, but that's normal. Both the crying and driving you nuts." He gave the baby back to Melinda. "The only thing to worry about is if he starts to run a fever. I brought up a box of fever strips. You pull off the back and place it on his forehead. A minute later, you will have his temperature. If it goes to 100, call me." He said his goodbyes and left the suite.

Chapter 5

Day 17   Monday at sea they all met for a leisurely breakfast in the Rendezvous Café at 0900 hours, and over coffee discussed what they wanted to do with their free time.

"How about we use the hot tub?" Lucinda asked, looking around the table.

"How about we hit the gym for an hour and then the hot tub?" Jose remarked, with a wide smile on his face.

"I think that is an excellent idea." Susan said. "If we stay on the ship and lie around, and eat the way we have been, we will get so soft that Melinda's babies will be able to wrestle us to the mat." That got a laugh from everyone.

They finished their coffee and headed to the gym. Lucinda said, "Keep in mind I don't want to see any competition among you guys. If we were in our own gym, it would be all right. If you did it here, it would raise some eyebrows. We still don't want to raise any suspicions."

They took turns on the bicycle, the rowing machine and the treadmill. They used the arm-pull, the leg-pull and the free weights. After an hour of hard exercising, they headed towards the hot tub. After oohing and aahing in the hot water, they sat back, closed their eyes and relaxed.

By 1500 they had boiled themselves pink. They all got out of the hot tub and returned to their cabins. Jose and Susan went to the suite to relieve Sheena and Benjamin, the team that was watching the monitor.

The teams met in the dining room at 1800 looking rested. Their skin was still pink from being boiled in the hot tub, and you could feel the heat radiating off each of them. After a leisurely dinner and a show, they strolled through the promenade, admiring the people they passed. By 2000 hours none of them could keep their eyes open, they were exhausted. It was hard work, relaxing. Melinda and Martin gave the teams the night off and decided to watch the monitor themselves.

Day 18   At 0500 Tuesday, Melinda woke up to the sound of Edward screaming. She jumped out of bed, banged her leg into a chair, knocking it over. The noise woke Martin. He sat up and asked, "What's wrong?"

"Edward is screaming," she replied. "I'm going inside to see what's wrong." She walked into the main room and saw Rosemary with Edward on her shoulder, walking back and forth.   "What's wrong?" she asked Rosemary.

"Edward woke up an hour ago and started to cry. I checked his diaper and he was dry. I offered him a bottle, but he didn't want it. I don't know what else to do except walk with him and rub his back. He went from crying to screaming a few moments ago."

"Does he have a fever?" Melinda asked.

"No. I checked that, also," replied Rosemary. "I think he has colic and there isn't much we can do about it except to keep him comfortable."

Melinda looked at the clock and saw it was 0530 in the morning. "I'm going to call the Dr. Wellfleet. Maybe he can help us."

"Computer," Melinda said.

"Computer online," said the Computer.

"Get Dr. Wellfleet, please," said Melinda.

"Dr. Wellfleet online," said the Computer.

"What's wrong Melinda?" Dr. Wellfleet asked.

"It's Edward. He woke up over an hour ago, and Rosemary has not been able to get him back to sleep. He went from crying to screaming. All he does is scream and hiccup."

"Is he coughing?" asked the doctor.

"Let me check with Rosemary," Melinda said.

"Rosemary, has Edward been coughing?"

"No," answered Rosemary. "I even checked to see if he had a fever. He doesn't have one. I don't know what else to do."

"Okay," Wellfleet said. "I'll be up in ten minutes. Can you hold out until then?"

"Yes," replied Melinda. "I'll order some coffee for you." She picked up the phone and punched the button for 'room service'. Room service answered the phone on the first ring. Melinda ordered tea, coffee and some Danish. She hung up the phone and turned to Rosemary. "Let me have him awhile. I'll hold him until the doctor comes. Why don't you take a break?"

95

"It's okay. I'll go check on Annabelle." She reached over, rubbed Edward's back for a moment, left the room and entered the nursery. She leaned over and touched Annabelle's forehead. It was slightly warm, and she became concerned. She walked into the main room and told Melinda.

"Don't worry about it. The doctor will be here soon."

"At 0545 a call came in. "Valley Forge, Valley Forge, this is Special Two. Do you read?"

"Special Two, this is Ron. What's up?"

"We see boxes spreading out behind you. Looks like twelve in all. Do you have a visual?"

"Negative, Special Two. We are not at the monitor, at this time. Standby."

"Computer, get Martin," requested Ron.

"Martin has privacy. Standby," said the Computer.

"Martin online," said the Computer.

"What wrong, Ron?" asked Martin.

"We just got a call from Special Two. They spotted twelve boxes floating behind us. Are you and Melinda watching the monitor?"

"No, we aren't." Martin said. "We gave the crew the night off. We were doing fine until the babies started doing their thing. By the time we got them settled, we fell asleep. I'm turning on the monitors now. I'm rewinding. Okay, I see it. They put the boxes out on deck at 0500 and threw them over at 0525. I couldn't make out whom the people were who did the deed. I think we should rotate the assignment for someone to sit on the monitor at all times."

"Okay. I'll meet the rest of the team at breakfast and I'll set up a schedule. I'll get someone to you around 0700."

"We can hold out until then." Martin said. "We have extra coffee and Danish. Computer off," Martin told the Computer.

At 0600, the doorbell chimed in the suite. Rosemary walked to the door and looked through the peephole. She saw it was their regular cabin attendant. She unlocked the door and held it open for her. She wheeled a food cart into the room to the dining room table. She laid out four settings and put the tray of food on the table. She removed the food covers and placed them on the cart. She then said, 'Enjoy your breakfast', opened the door and wheeled the cart into the hallway.

The door no sooner closed than the bell chimed again. Rosemary walked quickly to the door, checked the peephole and opened the door. Dr. Wellfleet walked in carrying his familiar black bag. He put his bag down on the chair by the door and walked over to Melinda. He took Edward in his arms and put his lips to his forehead. "He seems to be a little warm," he said. "Let me check him." He carried Edward to the nursery and placed him on the changing table. "Would you bring my bag, please?" he asked of no one in particular. Melinda walked back into the living room, reached for the black bag, brought it into the nursery and put it on the table.

"Melinda," said Wellfleet. "Come over here and hold Edward so he won't roll off the table." Melinda walked over to the changing table and placed her hand on Edward's chest. Edward was still squirming, hiccupping, and crying. She started rubbing his belly and talking in a low voice.

The doctor took a temperature strip and placed in on Edward's forehead. A minute later, he had his answer. "He's running a slight fever," the doctor said. "One hundred degrees is not serious, but we will have to watch him very carefully." As the doctor was talking, Edward stopped crying and fell asleep.

"What about Annabelle?" Rosemary asked.

The doctor walked to Annabelle, and while she was sleeping, placed the temperature strip on her forehead. Then they waited. She also had a slight fever. Annabelle's temperature was 99.8. He took the tape off Annabelle's forehead and signaled everyone to go into the dining room. They sat down at the table as Martin walked in rubbing his eyes. Melinda looked at the clock and saw it was 0630. "What are you doing up so early?" asked Melinda. "I thought you went back to sleep."

"I don't think so," said Martin. "Not with the baby screaming, the doorbell chiming and a bunch of people talking. Not a chance. Besides, I smelled fresh coffee, and knowing my wife, there would be Danish."

Melinda smiled and said, "I got so concerned about Edward that I woke up Dr. Wellfleet. Both of the babies have a slight fever. Annabelle slept through it all. Edward is driving me and Rosemary crazy. He would not go to sleep or take a bottle. All he did was scream and hiccup. I didn't know what else to do."

Martin poured a cup of coffee for himself and a cup of tea for Melinda. Turning to the doctor, he asked, "What can we do about Edward?"

"Not much." the doctor replied. "We'll have to watch the fever. I will leave some temperature strips, and I want you to check both babies every two hours. Don't worry about Edward's screaming. It will drive you crazy, but he will eventually wear himself out and fall asleep. Call if there is a problem or the temperature goes up above 101. I'll stop by around 0930." So saying, he turned, opened the door and walked out carrying his old-fashioned well-worn doctor's black bag. The door swung shut and clicked as the lock engaged.

Martin said, "Since I had more sleep than you or Rosemary, why don't I take Edward and you two get some sleep. I'll wake you up at 0900, okay?" Both women nodded and left the room. Rosemary went to her room, and Melinda went to the master bedroom. Martin held the baby in the crook of his arm and walked the length of the cabin and back again. He moved Edward to his shoulder and kept rubbing his back. Edward cried, screamed and squirmed. An hour later, Edward fell asleep in Martin's arms. Martin walked into the nursery and gently placed Edward in his crib. Lowering the light, Martin pulled a lounge chair next to the crib. He sat down and leaned back. He placed his hand through the slot in the crib and rested it next to Edward's hand. Edward wrapped his fingers around Martin's pinky. Martin sighed, smiled, closed his eyes and fell sound asleep.

Day 19   At 0730 Ron called Charlie Pile. "Have you been monitoring Special Two?"

"Yes I have," replied Charlie. "I have been monitoring all the communications from the Specials. I have my teams spread out around Castries and Vieux Fort in St. Lucia. They have not seen any boats running out of either harbor. I mentioned it to Special Two, and she said she will keep an eye out for any boats as she makes the circle over both towns. She has the drone at 25,000 feet. So far, there has been no action from either harbor. Special Two said the floating material has spread out over a mile, and if the boxes are not picked up soon, they will be all over the ocean."

At 0740, Ron went into the Suite using his special passkey. He didn't want to ring the chime in case everyone was sleeping. He came in and it was very quiet. He walked to the monitor and saw that Martin had left it on. He walked to the dining room table, fixed a cup of coffee, picked out Danish and sat down in front of the monitor. He leaned back, sipped his coffee and watched the monitor for any movement. Occasionally he would monitor all the passageways. He would follow a crew member using the ships cameras. Deck 4 seems to have many broken cameras. He would notify Suzy Q and let her make the report.

At 0830, Ron put out a conference call to all the members of the team, except for Melinda, Martin and Rosemary. "Special Two called and told us that twelve boxes were thrown over the side, and no one has come to pick them up. Special Two said she is high enough to see both sides of the island. Customs has cleared Valley Forge. Passengers are starting to go ashore. I would like all of you to go ashore and wander around, except for John and Marsha. I would like John and Marsha to report to the suite around 0900."

At 0900, Martin woke up to the sound of women giggling. He opened his eyes, turned his head towards the sound and saw his wife and Rosemary standing in the doorway. "Are you enjoying yourself?" he said. "I worked hard this morning. I finally got Edward to fall asleep. I should be given credit for that."

"We will gladly give you the credit for getting Edward to sleep. Come into the dining room for a working man's breakfast while Rosemary checks on the temperatures of the babies."

Martin got off the lounge chair and moaned. "This chair was not meant for long term sitting."

"You weren't sitting my dear, you were sleeping," Melinda said, laughing. "Come, have some breakfast." She took his hand, leaned in and kissed him. "My Hero," she said, smiling. They walked together into the dining room. They passed Ron, who was drinking his third cup of coffee. They motioned for him to join them. He shook his head no. They both sat down at the dining room table and Melinda opened the heating tray. She took a couple of pancakes, two eggs, three slices of bacon, and a slice of pineapple. She put the plate in front of Martin. She fixed a similar plate for herself and started eating. Martin watched Melinda eat and said to her, "I love you." Melinda stopped eating, put her fork down and looked at Martin. She got up and walked around to his side of the table. She put her arms around his neck, sat on his lap, and gave him a slow, deep kiss. She broke the kiss and went back to her side of the table, saying nothing. She picked up her fork and continued eating her breakfast.

Martin smiled and said, "Another kiss like that and Edward and Annabelle might have a brother or sister." Melinda looked at him and smiled. "Are you threatening me?"

Before Martin could reply, Rosemary came into the dining room and said, "All's quiet, they're both sleeping."

"Sit down and eat some breakfast." Martin said. "I don't know when the three of us will get another chance."

Rosemary went to the heating tray, took a plate and started filling it with four pancakes, scrambled eggs, three strips of bacon and a slice of pineapple. Both Melinda and Martin looked at her in amazement.

"Are you going to eat all that?" asked Melinda.

"Yes," answered Rosemary. "I always eat a breakfast like this."

Both Melinda and Martin started laughing.

"What's so funny," asked Rosemary.

"You're eating a bigger breakfast than Martin eats. Look how big he is and look how tiny you are."

Rosemary burst out laughing. "You're right," she said. It does look funny."

It was very quiet at the table. All you were able to hear were cups touching a saucer or a fork touching a plate. Martin leaned back, smiled and said, "The beautiful sound of silence." Rosemary and Melinda laughed.

Just then, Edward let out a yowl, and even Annabelle started making noise. "You had to say something, didn't you?" Melinda remarked, sliding her hand around his neck and giving him a quick kiss. She followed

Rosemary into the nursery. When she got there, Rosemary already had Edward on the changing table checking his diaper.

"He's dry." Rosemary said, "Bring me Annabelle."

Melinda brought Annabelle to the table, took Edward away and placed him back in his crib. She stood there rubbing his belly and whispering to him. He kept crying. She picked him up, placed him over her shoulder and started walking around the room while rubbing his back. Nothing seemed to stop his crying.

As soon as Annabelle was changed, she went right back to sleep. Rosemary looked at her and smiled. She stood there running her finger lightly across Annabelle's cheek. She kissed her forehead and noticed she felt warm, warmer than she felt earlier that morning. She put Annabelle back in her crib, picked up a temperature strip, and placed in on her head. She handed another strip to Melinda, who placed it on Edward's forehead.

At 0930, the door chime sounded and Martin opened the door for Dr. Wellfleet. "We had quiet for about thirty minutes," Martin said. "Then Edward started up and he woke up his sister. Melinda and Rosemary are in the nursery."

Dr. Wellfleet went into the nursery and checked each of the babies. He checked the log that Rosemary had made and saw the temperatures were climbing. Annabelle and Edward both had temperatures of 101. "I don't like this. If the temperature goes up another degree, call me. Don't let Edward's fussing get to you. He'll cry for a while, just enough to drive you crazy, tire himself out and go back to sleep. I would suggest you move his crib into your bedroom so Annabelle will get undisturbed sleep." He asked Rosemary if Annabelle was taking her bottle. Rosemary nodded her head and the doctor left.

At 0940 hours, John and Marsha softly knocked on the door. Ron got up and checked the peephole. He opened the door and let them in. He offered them coffee which they declined. He walked them over to the monitor and sat them down. "It is a very strange day," he said. "Special Two is up there keeping watch. There is no action as far as boats going out and picking up the boxes. I want you to keep an eye out for anything unusual on the Valley Forge. I was using the joy stick to follow some of the crewmen around the ship, especially Suzy Q's assistant, Frank Barber. You know that there has to be more than the four men and one officer doing the smuggling. I'll try to get you relief around noon, or you can try to con one of the other teams to come in earlier, if you can.

At 1140, somewhere in the town of Castries, St. Lucia,

"Computer"

"Computer online, Susan."

"Get Ron please," she said.

"Ron online," said the Computer.

"What's wrong Susan?" Ron answered.

"I went ashore in Castries about 30 minutes ago," Susan said. "I am somewhere near an outdoor mall. I'm sick. I can't make it back to the Valley Forge. I need help."

"Help is on the way," said Ron. "Stay put."

"Jose," said Ron. "According to the built-in tracking device, she is less than five minutes away. Head out and the computer will direct you.

"Susan," said Ron. "Jose is already on his way to help you. Is there anyone near you that appears to be a threat?"

"Computer online," requested Ron.

"Computer online, Ron," said the Computer.

"I lost Susan," said Ron.

"Susan is still online," said the Computer. "Her pulse rate is very low. It appears she is unconscious at this time. I have Jose's tracker approaching Susan's tracker."

Five minutes later Ron said, "Computer, get me Jose."

"Jose online," answered the Computer.

"Jose, what is the situation?" Ron asked. "Have you found Susan?"

Jose answered, "Yes, I found her. She is sitting with her back against a wooden structure, out of sight of public view. If she was not connected and didn't have a tracker, no one would have found her for hours or even days. I wonder what made her so sick, so quickly. I saw her just before she left the ship this morning. She was fine then." Ron picked Susan up and carried her to the car. He went back, retrieved her shoulder bag and placed it in the car with her. He got behind the driver's wheel and headed back to the ship.

"Computer, get Ron online," said Jose.

"I'm online," said Ron. "What do you need?"

"Have a gurney ready," he said to Ron. "I'll be there in less than three minutes, if I can get through this heavy traffic at the Security gate."

Jose pulled up to the aft gangway at noon and screeched to a stop. A medical team came down the gangway with a gurney. They went to the car and lifted Susan from the back seat, grabbed her pocketbook, placed her on the gurney, and strapped her down. They pushed the gurney into the ship and onto the elevator. They took the elevator down two flights and raced with her to the Medical Center. One of the shore crew drove the car away and parked it at the head of the pier.

Jose headed for the Medical Clinic to find out what had made Susan so sick, so quickly. She was not the type of person to get sick. She was too careful with everything she did. He entered the clinic and spoke to the nurse. The nurse started asking questions.

"Is Susan allergic to anything?"

"What medicines is she taking?"

"Did he know her health plan?"

"Do you have her insurance card?"

He held up his hands in surrender. "I'll get you that information." He walked into the hall.

"Computer, get Ron," said Jose.

"I'm on, Jose," said Ron. "What's the problem?"

"The nurse at the Medical Clinic wants Susan's health information. I don't have that. Help me out here."

"Computer, override Privacy Rule for Susan Bart," Ron said. "Give Jose any information he requires."

"Privacy Rule override for Susan Bart in effect," replied the Computer.

"Thanks Ron." Jose walked back to the Medical Clinic. He approached the Nurse and said, "I have the information you requested," he said, and proceeded to give it to her. "Anything else you need?" he asked the nurse. She smiled and said she had everything she needed. She took the file and went through a narrow door behind her desk. The door clicked shut behind her.

Jose just stood there. *He gave a lot of information but got none in return. Some investigator he was.* This problem with Susan really bothered him. He had worked with her for some time and he had strong feelings for her. He went to the waiting room opposite the main desk and sat down. He would wait there until he had some information.

Dr. Wellfleet walked into the waiting room twenty minutes later, saw Jose and walked over to him. "Why are you here?" The doctor asked. "Are you injured?"

Jose explained what had happened to Susan and said he was waiting for some information as to what made Susan sick.

Dr. Wellfleet nodded and said, "I'll try to find out." He went through the same door as the nurse did. Ten minutes went by and then another ten minutes. Jose was growing concerned. Doctor Wellfleet finally came out and came over to him. "Susan is very sick," he said. "They took blood and pumped her stomach. They thought she had eaten something bad. It seems like she ingested some kind of poison. She is not responding to any medical procedures they are doing here on the ship. They have called for an ambulance to take her to the local hospital. Will you go back to the cabin and pack her things? Have the luggage at the gangway in fifteen minutes. I spoke to Ron. He said that if you want to go with her, you could. Pack up your things as well. Have the luggage out by the gangway to meet the ambulance. When the hospital finds out what the problem is, call Ron. You have known Susan for a long time so we feel it will be good for you to keep her company. Let me know what happens."

Jose got up, turned and left the Clinic. He headed for his room.

"Computer, get Marsha online," Jose requested.

"Marsha online," said the Computer.

"What's up Jose?" she asked.

"Could you meet me at my cabin?" replied Jose. He went on to explain that Susan can't be treated here on the ship and is being transferred to the hospital. He is going to the hospital with her and needs help packing Susan's things. Marsha said she would meet him in the cabin in five minutes. She was there in three, along with John Mason. Everyone worked smoothly together, and in five minutes had packed all of Jose and Susan's belongings and had the luggage ready to go. John grabbed two bags, Marsha grabbed one, Jose took the remaining one and both carry-on bags. He took one look around the cabin to make sure he had not left anything behind. He went out and let the door swing shut. They hurried down the gangway with the luggage just as the ambulance pulled up. Susan was lying on the gurney by the Security desk.

The driver and his assistant came onboard the Valley Forge. They quickly wheeled the gurney down the gangway and slid it into the ambulance. They loaded the luggage while Jose shook everyone's hand saying his, 'goodbyes'. Jose got in the ambulance. The door of the ambulance closed, its engine roared, and it started moving off the pier with its siren screaming. For a moment, everyone stood there looking after the ambulance.

"What the heck was that all about?" asked John, turning to Marsha.

"Jose asked for help to pack Susan's bags, and I came," said Marsha. "Of course, I grabbed you, since you were standing nearby." All I know is that Susan called in an emergency and then became unconscious while she was ashore. With the help of the Computer, Jose was able to find her quickly because she had the built in tracker that we all have. Jose found her and brought her back to the ship. The Medical Clinic wasn't able to help her. The doctors felt Susan needed more treatment than the Valley Forge could give her. Now you know as much as I do."

"So they don't know what made her sick in the thirty minutes she was off the ship? John asked. "That's very strange."

While John was pondering Susan's problem, another person was also deep in thought. This person was staring at a picture that she had taped to a mirror in front of her. She now had a side-by-side view of Susan and herself. She had less than two hours to make herself look as much like Susan as possible, so that the gangway Security would not recognize the difference.

Amy Gelz looked at the picture and did a comparison. They both had straight shiny hair. Amy's was black and Susan's was light brown. The only way to solve that would be a bleach job. ~~When the bleach job was finished she would dye her hair Susan's color.~~ She had better start on that first. Amy opened her bag, took out the proper chemicals and took them into her bathroom. She applied the chemicals to her hair and waited the required forty minutes. She rinsed her hair, washed it and combed it out. She then took the second chemical and applied it. She waited the required thirty minutes and then rinsed and washed her hair. She combed it out and quickly dried it. She walked to the mirror and compared the color. Perfect. She took out a contact lens case, opened it and chose the eye color that was as close as the real color in the picture.

Thoughts kept going through her head, *'Why did I take this contract? The money was good, of course. I don't like this job. I don't like messing with children, especially newborns. I should have let it go. I didn't need the money that badly. So what if I owe them a favor. I wonder what they will get out of this operation. What would they do if I don't succeed? When Susan wakes up, she'ill be able to tell them she was sprayed with something, but by that time the job will be finished.'*

At 1300 hours, Ron contacted New York.

"What do you need, Ron?" asked New York.

"Did you find out what made Susan sick so quickly?" he asked.

"Not yet," answered New York. "The doctors are analyzing the contents of her stomach. As soon as I get the results, I'll call you."

"Okay," said Ron. "It is not like our people to get sick on an operation, and then if it hadn't been for the tracker, we might not have found her before we sailed. Is there a way to increase security on the Valley Forge without it looking unusual?

"We are working on all of that," replied New York. "The problem is that we will have to let the Captain in on our operation. Harry Blank will be in touch with you and explain how it's going to work."

The Computer chimed. "Harry Blank is online."

"Harry," Ron asked. "What's going on? Do we know what made Susan sick? Are we going to a higher security level? Talk to me."

"Relax Ron. We are working on it as we speak. The Captain is now aware of the operation. He was a little peeved that he was not in on the operation in the beginning, but I was able to pacify him. The only thing is that he is not 'connected' and I don't want him to know that our people are. That is going to cause some problems, but your people are sharp enough to deal with it. I may as well tell you something, and you must keep it to yourself. I have a bodyguard coming to the Valley Forge for additional security for Melinda. No one is to know about him. He is being flown down on a private jet, and he will be coming onboard while you are still in St. Lucia. We rushed him down before we could 'connect' him. He has all the proper clearances. It will be up to you to connect him."

"What do you mean you hired a body guard for Melinda?" asked Ron. "What has happened since we spoke earlier today? Who is this bodyguard? Why does Melinda need one?"

"Slow down Ron," said Harry. "As soon as everything is put together here in my office, I will be able to explain it to you in better detail. Here is what I have right now. We got word through one of our assets in Columbia that an assassin was hired to go after Melinda. We do know the assassin is from one of the Mexican cartels. That cartel was working with the outfit called the Exchange in New York. We destroyed the Exchange's depot last year. That was the place where Melinda, Martin and Ron were wounded. The cartel is very angry that we shut down their operation before it really got up and running. They lost billions of dollars, and they want payback. Why they are picking on Melinda is something we don't understand. I am sending down one of my own bodyguards. His name is Stephen Blaine. He usually reports only to me but he is yours now. Keep in mind, Melinda does not know about the bodyguard. The Computer was given instructions not to include her in our conference calls. If I get any more information, I will get it to you. Computer off."

At 1400 hours at St. Jude Hospital in Vieux Fort, St. Lucia, two and a half hours after Susan got sick, Jose is pacing in the waiting room. It has been over an hour since he arrived at the hospital and he still can't get any information. Finally, a doctor entered the waiting room, walked over to him and said, "I'm Mathew Grant, Chief of Medicine here at St. Jude's. Our lab techs were able to identify the poison used on your friend. It was ricin. We were able to identify it quickly because our techs just came back from a course given by your C.I.A. in Miami. This poison has not been around since the 50's. We are trying to locate an antidote. None of the hospitals in the area have any."

Jose turned his head away from the doctor.

"Computer, get me Ron." Jose requested.

"Ron is online," said the Computer.

"What's happening, Jose?" asked Ron. "How is Susan?"

"They found that Susan was poisoned by an old poison from the 50's, called ricin. The poison was made from the oil of the Castor plant. The doctors do not have the antidote at the hospital but are trying to locate one. None of the hospitals in the area have the antidote. No one knows where to go to get it. The doctors tell me that Susan is already suffering from severe diarrhea and nausea. She is starting to have breathing difficulties. They put her on a ventilator. They are afraid these problems will affect her heart. Her kidneys are starting to shut down. My concern is that they have never tackled a case like this before. They are constantly checking her for nerve damage. Can you find an antidote and get it to them, or are we going to have to fly Susan to another hospital?"

"I'll get back to you as soon as I find out," answered Ron.

At 1500 hours at St. Jude Hospital in Vieux-Fort, St. Lucia, three and a half hours after Susan got sick.

"Computer, get Harry Blank," requested Ron.

"Harry Blank is online," said the Computer.

"Did you find an antidote?" asked Ron, with concern in his voice.

"Yes we did," answered Harry Blank. "It is being flown to you as we speak. We were able to get an F-18 to fly it down to you. However, we are not sure the antidote can be administered in time."

"What do you mean by 'in time'?" Ron asked.

"There is a thirty-six hour window for administrating this particular antidote," replied Harry Blank. "The time might be different, depending on the amount of poison she received and the method used to give her the poison."

"I'll notify Jose and let him tell the doctors," Ron said.

"That won't we necessary," Harry replied. "We already contacted everyone involved. The instructions were given to the doctor's on how to keep her comfortable until the antidote gets there. There are terrible side effects with ricin. The poison could have been put on her skin, or she could have walked into a spray. Ricin shuts down the organs and the nervous system. The doctors are going to put her in a drug-induced coma. That should slow down the poison. Since they are putting her in a coma, they will have to keep her on a ventilator. I understand Jose is going to stay with her. Have him get a hotel room so he can get some rest. We cannot have him getting sick. Have him keep New York informed. There is no one else in the area that is connected. When they give her the antidote, they will bring her out of the drug-induced coma. We don't know what damage the poison will have done to her. If she is able to talk, see if Jose can find out what happened. We played back the recording of her emergency call, and there was no information there."

"Computer, online," said Harry Blank.

"Computer online, Harry," said the Computer.

"Get Jose online," Harry Blank requested.

"Jose is online Harry" said the Computer.

"Jose," Harry asked, "Did you receive all the information I gave Ron?"

"Yes," Jose replied. "I heard it all. I will keep everyone informed. I'm trying to have them give me a room at the hospital so I can be close by."

"Harry," questioned Ron. "What are you trying to tell me about Susan? Are you saying that she might not make it?"

"I was hoping you wouldn't ask," said Harry. "This poison is one of the worst killers ever invented. We know the Bulgarian Secret Police used it on a dissident named George Markov. They shot him with a tiny plastic pellet contaminated with ricin. It took him two days to die. They did not find the pellet until they did an autopsy. We think the KGB gave the Secret Police the pellet. No one could prove it. It was used a second time, we believe, to assassinate one of our senior military officers who was stationed in South Korea. We were never able to confirm that either. That is why we have the ricin antidote at all our military bases all over the world.

What I am trying to say it that we don't know how much of this poison got into Susan. It only takes 22 micrograms to kill an average person. Our medical people are in contact with the doctors at St. Jude's in St. Lucia. They have been asked to examine every part of her body to see if there are any penetration marks. They already have done an MRI and a CT scan and sent us a copy. With both of us looking, it shouldn't take us too long to find a pellet, if there is one inside Susan."

"Where is the antidote now?" asked Jose.

"They are an hour from landing in San Juan for refueling," Harry Blank said. We did not have an air tanker available. If all goes well, they will be airborne by 1830 hours."

"How long will it take them to make the trip?" Jose asked, with worry in his voice.

"They will have to make a refueling stop to top off their tanks, and they should be there in less than five hours. I'll keep you informed."

At 1700 hours, Amy Gelz approached the gangway and showed her stolen cabin key card. Security scanned her card and it was accepted. She walked quickly to the elevator. She just stood there waiting for an outcry from Security. There wasn't any. The elevator opened and she entered. She pushed the button for the bottom deck. She made it onboard! *'To move around the ship unnoticed, I will need a uniform,'* she thought. *The only way I could obtain one would be to steal it. The only place to steal one would be from the laundry. Then she would worry about the next step.'*

Fifteen minutes later, Stephen Blaine got out of the taxi with a small carry-on bag. He walked up the gangway and handed the officer his 'key card.' His key card was scanned, and he was welcomed onboard. He walked to the nearest wall phone and called a number he had been given.

The phone was answered on the first ring. Ron said, "Hello."

"Stephen Blaine here."

"Where are you?" Ron asked

"Deck 2, aft gangway," Stephen replied.

Ron gave him his room number and hung up. Stephen hung up and walked to the elevator. Five minutes later, he was knocking on Ron's door. Ron opened the door and Stephen entered. They shook hands

Ron explained about being 'connected'. Stephen said he

110

understood and was willing to be connected. Ron walked to the safe, opened it and took out what looked like a very large hypodermic needle. He put on pair of magnifying glasses and picked up a pair of tweezers. With the tweezers, he picked up a very small object and placed it into the hypodermic needle.

"Take off your shirt," said Ron. Holding up the hypodermic he continued, "This won't hurt. It looks worse than it is."

Blaine took off his jacket and shirt. Ron injected the small object into Stephen's shoulder. Stephen Blaine was now 'connected'.

"I don't feel any different," Stephen remarked.

Ron laughed. "You are not supposed to feel any different. If you did, then there is something wrong."

"Computer," Ron said.

"Computer is online," said the Computer

"Connect Blaine, Stephen."

"Blaine, Stephen connected," replied the Computer

"Stephen, can you hear me?" Ron asked.

Stephen jumped up and looked around. "Was that you I heard in my head?" he asked, startled.

Ron smiled and continued giving Blaine instructions about the 'connection'. Once Stephen had gotten over the initial shock, he understood how it worked. Ron told him that he would be staying in Jose and Susan's room, since they were both staying ashore. He explained what had happened to Susan and why Jose is staying ashore. While Stephen was getting all this information, he put his shirt and jacket back on.

Blaine got up and started pacing for no reason. Finally, he stopped, turned to Ron and asked, "Have there been any Security checks at the gangway? Call down and see if Susan came back to the ship."

"She couldn't be back on the ship," said Ron. "She's in the hospital."

"Yes," Stephen said. "You know that, and I know that. The people at the gangway might not know that. What time do we get underway?"

Ron looked at the clock on the wall. "We should be getting underway right now. Why?"

"Call down and check if Susan is onboard, quickly" Stephen said. "Hurry."

Ron thought Blaine was nuts but he picked up the phone and called the special number for the Captain. When the captain came on the phone, Ron asked him to find out if Susan was onboard. He hung up the phone and sat down. One minute later the phone rang. Ron picked it up and answered it. The Captain told him that all passengers had checked in and the ship is moving away from the dock. Ron thanked him and hung up. He turned to Blaine and said, "You're right. Someone is on the ship impersonating Susan. She would have to look like her. Once she is on the ship, she could look like anyone. How are we going to go about finding one person out of 5000?"

"I would suggest that we have a meeting as soon as possible."

"Computer," requested Ron.

"Computer is online."

"Conference call for all team members."

"All members except Melinda are online."

"We just learned that someone came on the ship impersonating Susan," said Ron. "It doesn't mean that she would still look like her now, once she passed Security. We know she is after Melinda and possibly the babies. Now we have two operations. The first is the smugglers and second protecting Melinda. Both are important. At least one person is to be with Melinda at all times. Rosemary, are you armed?"

"No," replied Rosemary. "We never thought it would be necessary."

"I am sending Stephen Blaine with a weapon for you," said Ron."

"Who is Stephen Blaine?" she asked, with concern in her voice.

"He is a new member of our team. He's connected. He will be there in five minutes, "replied Ron.

Ron went to the closet, pulled out a small box and opened it. He took out two dart guns. "Are you armed?" he asked Stephen.

"I just have my knives," he replied.

"These are the dart guns," said Ron, holding out one of the guns. "It holds six darts. These darts with the blue tips will keep someone asleep for 30 minutes. The red tips are good for two hours. Usually, when the person wakes up, he has no memory of the incident. In the past year, we have had no fatalities, but that does not mean we won't. It is better than shooting them with bullets. The darts don't make any noise except 'p-f-f-f-t'. It is best to go for the leg, in case they are wearing armor. Do you have any questions?"

Blaine had none. He put both dart guns in his pocket and left the room. He didn't even bother with the elevator. He went up the stairs, two at a time. When he reached Deck 10, he saw Melinda's suite directly in front of him. He knocked on the door and stood back, allowing whoever was in the cabin to see him clearly through the peephole.

"Computer," asked Rosemary. "Confirm location of Stephen Blaine."

"He is three feet from you," the Computer answered.

There was a click and the rattle of chain, and the door opened. Standing in front of Stephen was this pixie of a woman with red curly hair and sparkling green eyes. His heart jumped, and his eyes expanded. He stood there frozen in place, looking at her.

Standing in front of Rosemary was this five foot ten inch sandy haired man with steel grey eyes. Her heart skipped a beat and she felt a flush throughout her body. "Are you going to stand out there all day, or are you coming in?" Rosemary asked, standing aside and smiling. She was amused watching him stand there. He was standing like a school boy, not knowing what to do. She looked him up and down and liked what she saw.

Blaine finally woke from his stupor and walked into the suite. He entered and turned to watch Rosemary close and lock the door. He admired the way she looked.

"Okay. Would you mind explaining to me what's going on? I've been in the privacy mode for the last four hours. I was working with the babies and didn't want to get disturbed."

"First of all," Stephen said, taking his hand out of his pocket with the dart gun, "this is for you. You only have to aim the gun and fire. Ron said you should aim for the legs, because the person might be wearing body armor. Secondly, I am Stephen Blaine," he said, holding out his hand to shake.

Without thinking, Rosemary reached out and took his hand. When their hands touched, it felt like she had put her hand in an electric socket. She could not let go. She looked into his eyes and saw that it had the same effect on him. They looked at each other for some minutes until the trance was broken when Edward let out a howl.

Rosemary jumped back and started blushing. She had never blushed before. She turned and rushed from the room. He followed her into the nursery. He watched her rush to one crib and pick up the crying baby. She moved quickly to a changing table and checked the baby's diaper. She did a quick diaper change, and returned the baby to the crib. She then went to a second crib, picked up another baby, and did the same. He admired her for the way she had handled the situation. There was no fuss, no bother, very professional. He continued to watch her. She soon realized that he had been watching her, and for the second time in her life, she blushed.

Blaine noticed the blush, but said nothing. He waited for her to finish working with the babies. Then they both walked out of the nursery and into the living room."

"Would you like some coffee?" she asked Blaine.

"Yes, that would be great," he replied. Stephen could not keep his eyes off her.

Rosemary served the coffee and sat down opposite him. "Okay," she said. "Tell me what's going on."

Stephen replied, "I received a call at 0430 this morning. Harry Blank told me to be at General Aviation at Kennedy Airport, and that there would be a private jet waiting for me. When I left my house, it was minus twenty degrees. I drove to JFK, parked in the short-term parking lot and went to the General Aviation gate. I boarded a private jet, and before I knew it, I was here and the temperature was seventy-two degrees. When I arrived on the ship, I was told that one of your team members was ashore and had given an emergency call. They found her by using the tracker that each of us has inserted under our skin. She was unconscious, and they took her to the hospital. Upon checking the passenger list, we found that everyone is onboard. That means…"

"That someone came onboard impersonating her," Rosemary finished the sentence.

"That's very good. Now for the second part. Ron told me that this person is after Melinda and/or her babies. Since my specialty is guarding bodies, live ones that is, and I was available, here I am. Ron has assigned one person to be with you at all times, and I guess that will be me. Now for the very bad part of this. Harry Blank does not want Melinda to know the reason I am here, unless it becomes absolutely necessary. Do you have any questions?"

Rosemary took a sip of her coffee, and put the cup down. She sat back and thought a moment. "This is not going to work," she said. "Melinda must be told! She will know something is up."

"Computer," said Rosemary

"Computer is online Rosemary," said the Computer.

"Get Harry Blank," she said.

"What's the matter, Rosemary?" Harry asked.

"I was just told about Melinda and the babies. You cannot keep Melinda out of the loop. She will know something is up five minute after she sees Blaine. Did you forget with whom you are dealing? If she is the target, then she has to be told that she is the target. Who says they are after Melinda? If I wanted to get even, I would not want to hurt Melinda. I would go after her babies. That would hurt Melinda more. I think we either have to move Melinda and the babies off the Valley Forge or bring on another team, and quickly."

"Melinda is online," said the Computer.

"Okay guys, what is going on? Melinda asked. "You don't think I can tell when radio traffic changes? Come clean."

"I warned you, Harry," said Rosemary. "Melinda has to be kept in the loop."

"All right, Melinda," said Harry. "The summary is that we received word from one of our assets in Columbia that there is a very big contract out on you. It is somewhere in the neighborhood of two million dollars."

"That's a nice neighborhood," interrupted Melinda.

"Yes it is," said Harry. "Let me continue. The contract wasn't picked up, it was assigned to someone. We don't know who it was assigned to. We didn't want to tell you until we had more information. While we were gathering this information, I sent Stephen Blaine down to assist Ron with your security. As the ship pulled out from St. Lucia, Stephen learned that someone came aboard the Valley Forge using Susan's identification. That brought Security to a higher level. The way we have it set up now, is there will be two people with you at all times. That will be Rosemary and one other. In this case, now that Stephen is aboard, it will be him. Everyone is to be armed at all times. No one is to go into the suite unless connected. In this way, we can continue looking for the smugglers and protect you and the babies. Rosemary seems to think that you are not the target, but that your babies are. We are assuming that this person is a woman. Otherwise, she could not have gotten past the gangway."

"I agree with Rosemary," Melinda said. "They would be after my babies. That would hurt me very deeply. She would have to be about Susan's height and build. How would she be able to move around the ship and not be noticed?"

"She would need a disguise," Sheena replied. "Just like we had in the upstate New York operation. Steal a uniform. No one looks twice at a person wearing a uniform on a ship. Where is the best place to steal a uniform?"

"The laundry," a number of voices sang out.

115

"Someone has to get on the monitor and check out the ship's laundry."

"This is New York. We are on it. We are running the recordings of the ship from 1600 hours to present time. Standby." Three minutes later New York continued. "We have it. A woman that appears to be Susan is approaching the gangway at 1730 hours. She handed her card to the guard and it scanned correctly. We noticed the guard did not even look closely at her. We didn't even think about that Security breach. We are following her through the ship. She took the elevator down. We could not see the floor. Standby." Moments later, "We found her. She is walking into the laundry on Deck 3. No one is paying any attention to her. She is taking an officer's uniform off the rack. She took a uniform with three gold stripes separated by two white spacers. No department markings are showing. So far, she does not seem to be paying attention to the surveillance cameras. We lost her again."

"Do you think she is heading for Susan's cabin?" asked Marsha.

"She has the key card. Why not?" replied Benjamin.

"There are no surveillance cameras in the staterooms, but they do have them in all the passageways," said New York. "We will keep tracking until we find her again. We forwarded a picture of what she looks like when she stole the uniform. Keep in mind she might change her appearance again. A wig would do it. You have to get more people on your monitors so we can have more eyes looking for her. Valley Forge is a big ship, and we are running two operations at the same time. While the suspect is finding a place to change clothes, we would suggest that you get your people in position. Melinda, I am sorry to say, but you have to stay in the nursery with the babies. Martin can wander around the ship in his special wheelchair. Rosemary and Stephen will remain in the nursery with you at all times. If possible, barricade yourselves in the nursery. Then you will need one other person to watch the monitor. Remember you are all connected. The only way she can get past your guard is if she grabs one of the team members and tries to use him or her as a bargaining chip. Stay sharp. New York will keep monitoring the ship's cameras. Computer off."

At 1900 hours, Harry Blank asked the Computer to contact Ron.

"Ron online," said the Computer.

"What's wrong Harry?" asked Ron.

"I have bad news," he said. "The military jet that was carrying the antidote had to land on the Island of Caicos. When they landed in San Juan, they had some minor fuel problem. It took them an hour to find the

116

problem and another hour to fix it. Obviously, they didn't fix it. They were not able to meet with the refueling plane. As soon as I find out more, I will let you know. I gave them permission to rent a plane, but Caicos is not a controlled airport. There is no one there after dark.

Chapter 6

At 1900 hours, sitting in the living room in the suite were Melinda, Martin, Rosemary, Stephen, Benjamin and Sheena. Sheena and Benjamin were watching the monitor. "I can't figure where she could be hiding," Sheena said.

"I know exactly where she is hiding," Stephen said. They all looked at him. "She is hiding in a bathroom. Another place they don't allow surveillance cameras."

"Computer," said Benjamin. "Get New York online."

"New York online," chimed the Computer.

"We thought of an additional angle," Benjamin said to New York. "She might have gone into a bathroom to change clothes. Either men's or women's bathroom."

"Okay," New York replied. "We will review the video again."

Melinda said, "I've been thinking about our security. Where are some of our weaknesses? We know the security at the boarding gate is bad. Where else is it lacking?"

No one said anything.

"You realize," Melinda continued. "Not to change the subject. We do not have enough food stocked in this suite to feed the six of us for the length of the cruise. We are going to have to order room service or have one of our people bring in food on a regular basis. That is going to be another major weakness in our security."

Martin said, "Let's get John to pick up enough food for all of us. We have drinks here in the suite. Have him followed by Marsha, and have Suzy Q follow Marsha. That should work one time, anyway." They made the call. John put together the meals and delivered them safely to the suite. All seven sat down at the dining room table and devoured dinner. After the cleanup was finished and the plates stacked on the cart, John wheeled it out and waited until the door closed and locked.

"New York online for Martin," the Computer said.

"What did you find out?" asked Martin.

"You were right," New York answered. "We reviewed the video. She went into the men's bathroom on Deck 3. We show her coming out at 1915 hours wearing an officer's white uniform. She went to Deck 14. It appears she is searching the ship for Melinda's cabin. I don't know who sent her, but they didn't give her a lot of information."

"Now the question is, 'What do we do?' Melinda asked. "Should we track her down and put a stop to it right now or let her wander around?"

The Computer interrupted Melinda.

"Harry Blank online for Melinda," said the Computer.

"Do you have any more information?" Harry Blank asked.

"We know what she looks like," Melinda said. "We see her wandering around the ship. What would you have us do? In the middle of the ocean, we don't have many choices. The ship does have a brig. Dr. Wellfleet has his truth serum, and we all have our dart guns. My preference would be to let her into the suite and shoot her with a dart. I would then have Dr. Wellfleet question her and get all the information he can from her. Then I would lock her in the brig. However, before we let her into the suite, I want to secure my babies in the nursery with Rosemary and Stephen. I want and put a couple of 'doll babies' in the cribs. We'll wrap up the 'doll babies' with a travel blanket and put a knit cap on their heads. We'll put them into the cribs and move them into the sitting room. She will never be able to see if the 'doll baby' is real or not." Melinda stopped talking and went into a trance.

"She's doing it again," said Martin as he came online. "When she comes out of the trance, she'll have a complete working plan for us."

Just as Martin predicted, Melinda soon came out of the trance and said, "Here's the plan. Secure the babies in the nursery with Rosemary and Stephen. Keep the suite dark. Let the assassin get into the suite. Have Sheena and Benjamin stand behind the curtain. As soon as the assassin is next to the curtain, have them shoot her with a dart. Let Dr. Wellfleet question her. Leave her alone to wake up in the living room. She will be groggy. We'll let her take one of the 'doll babies'. Before we let her escape, inject her with a tracker, and let her go. Let's see what her demands are. After all, she is getting paid two million dollars for this job."

"Harry, do you agree?" Melinda asked.

"Sounds like a plan to me," he answered. "Make sure all your people know what she looks like, and make sure everyone travels in pairs. The Computer will be on alert for any major medical changes on all the team members. If any medical levels change, everyone will be notified."

Stephen and Rosemary brought some food into the nursery. They carried extra blankets, made a bed on the floor for the babies and moved the empty cribs into the sitting room. They were waiting for Suzy Q to bring the dolls for the crib. They set up two monitors in the nursery so that they could observe the action in the sitting room as well as around the ship. Five minutes later, there was a knock on the door. Rosemary looked through the peephole and saw it was Suzy Q. She opened the door, took the two packages from Suzy, then closed and locked the door.

Rosemary and Stephen put the boxes on the table and opened them. Each contained a life-sized doll, the same size as Annabelle and Edward. Rosemary took the first doll, put a hat on it, wrapped it in a traveling blanket and handed it to Stephen to put in one of the cribs. She did the same with the second doll, as well. They looked around the room to make sure they didn't leave any paper or wrappings behind. Satisfied, Rosemary and Stephen went into the nursery, closed and locked the door. They were able to slide a chest of drawers against the door. They pulled two chairs to the table, sat and watched the monitors.

"Conference call," requested Rosemary.

"Conference call confirmed," the Computer announced.

"We are all secure in the nursery," said Rosemary. "Let the show begin."

It took a few minutes for Stephen to locate the suspect on the monitor. He informed all the team members of her location. As the suspect moved around the ship everyone was watching her movements on all the monitors. Stephen had Marsha stay on Deck 14 at the forward elevator, and John was on Deck 14 by the aft elevator. He had Sheena and Benjamin go to the suite and hide behind the drapes that covered the balcony doors. Finally, he had Martin, in his famous wheelchair, move around the promenade deck. The suspect would be observed, no matter where she went on the ship.

"Computer, get New York online," said Stephen.

"New York online Stephen," the Computer said.

"Have you identified our suspect yet?" he inquired.

"Yes. It took us some time to find her. She's not on any of our databases. We contacted Interpol, and they were able to identify her. Her name is Amy Gelz. She's a paid assassin. She works for the cartel that lost billions of dollars when you closed the New York depot that belonged to the Exchange last year. The cartel helped Gelz many years ago, so she owed them. Gelz has only been given credit for one kill that we know of. She assassinated a Russian diplomat who had five bodyguards and traveled in an armored car. The diplomat was wearing full body armor, and her shot went between the bodyguards and the armor plates in the diplomat's body armor. They estimated that she took the shot from twelve hundred feet. Interpol said she was active in a couple of other hits, but the information is only rumor. They have no proof, and she doesn't advertise her kills."

"Okay," said Stephan. "We are secure on the Valley Forge. Now it is a matter of waiting until she finds Melinda's suite. There is a problem with all this planning. I'm assuming this Amy Gelz has a time limit. I would think she has to finish her job before we get to the next port in thirty-six hours. That does not give us much time to lead her into the trap. We need a fast way to get her to Melinda's suite. The fastest way that I can think of is to have Martin wheel near her, talking with a member of the Staff discussing the beautiful babies in the Owners Suite. She should be smart enough to figure out where the Owner's Suite is. What do you think? Anyone have a comment?"

"Martin, what do you think?" asked Melinda.

"I like the idea," Martin replied. "Computer, get Suzy Q online."

"Suzy Q online," said the Computer.

"I'm here Martin," said Suzy Q. "What do you need?"

Martin explained what he needed, and Suzy Q quickly agreed. "Just let me know what deck you will be on and I can be there in five minutes."

"Stephen," asked Martin. "Where is Amy Gelz at the present time?"

"She is in the aft elevator going down," replied Stephen. "John happens to be in the elevator with her."

"Computer, connect me to John."

"John is online, Martin" said the Computer.

"John," Martin said, "Start talking to the other people in the elevator. Ask them if the saw those beautiful babies this morning. I hope that they will ask you where, and you tell them on Deck 10. Then get off the elevator." John did exactly that and got off the elevator on Deck 6.

Amy Gelz got off the elevator on Deck 5. She went to the large digital computer map that showed the location of all the cabins. She called up the floor plan for Deck 10 and studied it. There were five suites and four cabins on that deck. She thought, *'Which one would Melinda be in? I guess a little observation would be in order. She was still wearing the uniform, so no one would question her checking out the rooms. It is a shame that she could not steal a master key. Maybe she could talk one of the cabin attendants into opening up the rooms for an 'inspection.'* She got back on the elevator and pushed the button for Deck 10.

"Standby everyone," Stephen said. "She just got on the elevator and is heading for Deck 10. She still doesn't know where Melinda's suite is.

She will probably look for a cabin attendant to help her get in the rooms. Is there anyone on Deck 10 who can act as cabin attendant?"

Sheena chirped up, "Are you being funny? Has anyone looked at the color of our cabin attendants? You people are snowy white, and it would look strange. I cannot leave my position. Have one of the regular cabin attendants wheel the cart onto the floor and leave a master room key on the top of the cart."

"That's a great idea," Melinda said. Is there a cart close by that we can use?"

"Suzy Q, are you online?"

"I'm already on my way to Deck 10," Suzy Q replied. "I have access to the attendant's storage locker." A minute later she said, "I'm in the service corridor. Where is the suspect?"

"She is looking at the cabins in the aft part of the deck," said Stephen.

"Great," said Suzy Q. "I'm in the forward part of the ship. I'm wheeling the cart out into the corridor now. I left a master key on top of the cart. I'm going back inside the service corridor. I'm going to phone the cabin attendant and tell her to report to my office now. She said she doesn't understand. I told her it has nothing to do with her work, but that it was important that I see her right away."

"I see another attendant in the service corridor," said Stephen. "Did she leave her key?"

"No. I left one of my master keys for Deck 10 on the cart," Suzy replied.

"I would think this Amy Gelz has enough smarts to look over the entire floor before she tries anything," said Martin. "There she goes. She searched the first cart. I can see she's disappointed. She is walking down the hall towards the forward part of the ship. She should see the other cart in a moment. She spots it. She is moving very quickly towards it. She is searching the cart. The room key is right on top and she hasn't seen it yet. She searches the cart a second time, and she misses the master key again. She might be a great assassin, but she would make a lousy thief. Okay, she finally sees the key. She is looking around. She doesn't seem to be suspicious that there are no attendants on the floor. She is walking aft. I guess she thinks Melinda is in one of the smaller cabins."

"Do we know if those aft cabins are occupied?" asked Melinda.

"I checked before I came up here," Suzy Q said. "The people in all four aft cabins have reservations for dinner together at one of our specialty

122

restaurants tonight. They left fifteen minutes before the suspect came up to Deck 10. I called down to the restaurant. They have all been seated. When they get to the dessert I'll be called. They won't be finished with dinner for at least two hours."

"Amy just finished going through the four aft cabins," said Melinda. "I wish we had cameras in there to watch her. She is walking towards the suites. Suzy, what is the story with those suites?"

"New York checked the video and told me that all the forward suites are now empty," Suzy replied. "The occupants have all gone to dinner. One couple is celebrating their fiftieth wedding anniversary. The occupants in the other three suites are friends and relatives. Unless someone comes back to the room for something, we are clear for at least an hour."

"We can see Amy when she goes from one suite to another," said Melinda. "There is one blank spot in the hallway. We found that blank spot when Martin had his 'accident' on the first day of the cruise. It's about twenty feet aft of us. We will pick her up fifteen feet from our door. We have the living room completely dark. Here she comes now. She is opening the door to our suite, but she can't see anything. I can see everything because we have the infrared camera on. She is reaching for the light switch. She switched the light on and she is trying to get her vision back. She is just standing there as we did when we first saw the suite. She is moving towards the master bedroom. She opened the door and turned on the light. She walked in and checked the bathroom. She looked around and then closed the door. She didn't turn the light off. She tried the nursery door, but it was locked. She probably thinks it belongs to the next cabin. She is now walking into the dining room. Sheena, Benjamin, standby. Okay, she is on the other side of the drapes. She is all yours."

Sheena moved out from one side of the drapes, and Benjamin moved out from the other side. Amy did not hear them behind her. Sheena signaled Benjamin to do the honors. Benjamin fired a dart into Amy's thigh. Sheena caught her as she fell. They carried her into the bedroom, removed her clothes and tied her ankles and wrists with zip ties.

"Okay everyone," said Melinda. "The suspect is down. The dart did its job. Dr. Wellfleet, your presence is requested in the Owners Suite with your little black bag."

"The doctor replied, "I'm on my way. Five minutes."

"Martin," Melinda asked. "Will you rig a video camera in the master bedroom so we can see everything? We are still not coming out of

123

the nursery until we know just how dangerous she is, and what her plans are."

Martin went to the cabinet, opened it and took out a small digital camera. He went into the bedroom and mounted the camera on the ceiling in the corner. He went back into the sitting room and entered the code for the camera. "The camera is mounted. How is it being received?" he asked.

"This is New York. We have great reception. Everything is being recorded."

"This is Rosemary. We have excellent reception in the nursery."

"Just as a precaution," Melinda continued, "I think everyone should wear a mask for a disguise when dealing with this Amy Gelz. The less she sees, the better it will be, especially if she happens to remember anything in the future. We haven't been using these darts all that long to know how much suspects remembers, or if they remember anything at all."

There was a knock on the door. Sheena looked through the peephole and saw Dr. Wellfleet. She unlocked the door and the doctor came in. Sheena directed him to the master bedroom. She followed him into the bedroom and pulled a chair out for him. He opened his little black bag and took out two hypodermic needles. The first one contained the antidote to the sleep dart. The second contained a truth serum, a modified sodium pentothal. He injected the antidote and the truth serum into Amy's upper arm. He said, "It will take a few minutes for her to wake up." He reached into his bag and took out a facemask. He handed Sheena a mask also. Now they waited. Five minutes later, Amy started to wake up. She just lay there. Everyone knew what she was doing. She was trying to figure out where she was. They all could see her using her muscles, testing the ties.

"Since we know you're awake," said Dr. Wellfleet, "you don't have to pretend to be asleep. You can open your eyes." Sheena and Benjamin lifted her into a sitting position and then stood at the head of the bed. The doctor continued, "What is your name?

There was a hesitation and then she said, "Amy Gelz."

"Why are you here?" asked the doctor.

"To kidnap a baby," replied Gelz.

"Whose baby?" the doctor asked.

"Melinda Xavier's baby," answered Amy.

"Who hired you?" asked the doctor.

"The cartel."

"Which one?"

"The Mexican cartel and the Exchange."

Melinda chimed in, "We destroyed The Exchange last year. At least I thought we did. Computer, get Harry Blank."

"Harry Blank online," said the Computer.

"I'm here Melinda," said Harry. "I was listening in on all of the conversations and watching the pictures of our Amy Gelz."

"What do you think about what she said about The Exchange?" asked Melinda.

"I'm in the dark," said Harry. "I'll follow up on it, and get back to you."

"I thought The Exchange was destroyed in New York," Wellfleet said to Amy Gelz.

"I don't know anything about the Exchange being destroyed," Amy replied.

"What were you supposed to do with the baby?" asked Wellfleet.

"I was to call a special phone number."

"How were you to call this special number?" Wellfleet asked.

"I have a special satellite telephone."

"Where is this satellite phone?"

"I hid it in the bathroom."

"Which bathroom did you hide the phone?" Wellfleet asked.

"I hid it in the men's bathroom, on Deck 3."

"What number were you supposed to call?" asked the doctor.

"543 -555-1212"

"How much were you to be paid to do the kidnapping?"

"I am to get two million dollars. I got half when I started and half when I turn over the baby."

"Does it bother you, kidnapping a baby?"

"Yes. I really didn't want to do this job."

"Why did you take the job?"

"I owe them."

"For what reason?" questioned Dr. Wellfleet.

Amy replied, "A number of years ago my sister was kidnapped and forced into the sex trade. I tried for many years to find her. Then one day I received a note from this outfit, The Exchange. They told me where I could find my sister. I flew half way around the world to Hong Kong, found her and brought her back home. The people who kidnapped her made her a drug addict as well. The Exchange found a hospital that would treat her, and they paid all the medical bills."

"What happened to your sister?" asked Dr. Wellfleet.

"She died."

"Of what?" he questioned.

"She got a bullet to the brain."

"How did that come about?"

"She was mugged two weeks after she got out of the hospital."

There was silence in the room. The doctor walked away from the bed out of Amy's hearing. He then asked, "Does anyone have any additional questions?" No one answered. "New York, are you tracing that telephone number?"

"Yes we are," they replied. "The number is bouncing from cell tower to cell tower. We have traced it to Antwerp, Paris, Shanghai and Istanbul. It is still bouncing. I don't think we will get a trace, but we put a trap and trace on the number when she uses the phone."

"Computer, conference call, please confirm," requested Melinda.

"Computer confirms. All members connected," answered the Computer.

"Talk about a sad case," remarked Melinda. "I really feel sorry for her, even if she wanted to hurt me by kidnapping one of my babies. This does not solve the problem. Yes, we stopped the kidnapping, but they will send someone else after the babies, or after me. Does anyone have any ideas?"

There was silence on the line. Then Dr. Wellfleet spoke up. "Why not let the kidnapping take place? We have enough personnel to follow her. We can request a drone to cover the area. In fact, we will have a drone at first light at our next port."

"I'm not going to put my babies in danger," Melinda said, with an angry tone in her voice.

"No, I'm not talking about using the real babies," the doctor said. "We originally set it up with the 'doll babies'. They look like the real thing. They are soft, they make noise, they wet, their eyes open and close. Let us use them. You have to make the decision quickly." Looking at his watch, the doctor said, "The sodium pentothal is wearing off. She is going to get sleepy and then fall into a deep sleep for about ten minutes. Let's set up a little different scenario. After she falls asleep, I am going to bang her in the head. Not too hard, just enough to break the skin and let her bleed all over her nice white uniform jacket that she will be wearing. I'll leave her crumpled on the floor and see what happens. She will think she tripped, banged her head and became unconscious. Let us see what she will do when she wakes up. We left all of her things in the bathroom on Deck 3. I had

Ron mount a camera in there. I know it is not politically correct, and I will have it taken out after this part of the operation is finished. How does that sound?"

Melinda laughed. "You are a very devious person, Dr. Wellfleet. I like it. Is everyone set for this part of the operation?" No replies were forthcoming. "Okay. Let's set it up. The nursery will still stay secure with Stephen and Rosemary. Let Benjamin and Sheena stay behind the curtain until Amy leaves with the 'doll baby'. Ron, can you inject Amy with a tracker?"

"Sure," said Ron. "It will take me five minutes to get the tracking equipment out of my cabin and return. Doc, can you keep her asleep for 10 minutes while I do that?"

"Yes, I can do that," the Doctor replied. "But hurry. I want to do that only once. I still don't know how the sedative and the new sodium pentothal react with each other. It hasn't been widely tested."

Ron returned to his cabin, opened his safe, retrieved his equipment and hurried back to the Owner's Suite. He used his master key and reentered the Suite. He went to the bedroom and sat next to Amy Gelz. "Help me roll her over," Ron said. "I want to put the tracker in her behind. She won't be able to see any marks left by the hypodermic needle."

Sheena rolled Amy over and pulled her underpants down. Ron loaded the tracker into the hypodermic needle and shot it into Amy's butt. He removed the hypodermic and put a drop of skin glue on the puncture wound. Sheena pulled Amy's underpants in place and cut the zip ties off her ankles and wrists. She and Benjamin dressed Amy and brought her into the sitting room. They only put on one shoe.

Sheena and Benjamin held Amy by the arms, and Dr. Wellfleet smacked her in the forehead with a paperweight that was sitting on the desk. The skin broke and blood started streaming down Amy's face. They placed Amy on the floor, and everyone left the room except for Sheena and Benjamin, who went back behind the drapes. The last person out of the room shut the lights off. The door closed and the lock clicked in place.

"Now the waiting game begins again," said Melinda. Martin carried a portable monitor to the cabin next door. He knew that he had over an hour before the passengers returned to the cabin. They observed Amy as she regained consciousness. She got on all fours and stayed in that position for a few moments. She kept shaking her head. Then she tried to stand up and ended falling back to the floor and banging her head on the edge of the table. Amy made it to all fours again. She hesitated and then stood up. She

127

wobbled and almost fell down again. She grabbed the back of the chair to steady herself. She walked slowly with her hands out, until she bumped into the wall. She felt along the wall for the light switch. Finally, finding it she flipped it on. She started blinking until she got used to the bright light.

Amy felt her forehead and her hand came away covered in blood. She looked down and saw that her white jacket and skirt had blood all over the front. She looked at her feet and saw she was only wearing one shoe. She looked around the room and saw her other shoe under the dining room table. She walked over and bent down to pick up the shoe, and fell over and hit her head on the edge of the dining room table again. She sat down on the floor and put her shoe on. She sat for a few minutes on the floor, got up, stood and slowly walked around the room. She held on to whatever furniture was handy. She saw the two cribs and stopped. She stumbled to the first crib, leaned in, and picked up the 'doll baby.' She saw that the 'doll baby' was wrapped in a blanket and had a knit cap on its head. All you could see were the eyelashes, as the 'doll baby's' eyes were closed. As Amy moved the 'doll baby' the eyes opened and it made a noise.

Amy looked around the room. She could not find anything in which to carry the baby. She hugged the baby to her chest, opened the door and walked quickly to the elevator. There was no one waiting in the elevator lobby. She took the elevator down to the third deck and went into the men's bathroom. The team watched as she changed out of her bloody clothing, washed her hands and face, and dressed in her old clothes She wrapped the 'doll baby' in a blue beach towel and went back to the elevator. She checked that she had the special cell phone but did not check on the 'doll baby'. She took the elevator to Deck 14, went out on the deck and found a empty lounge chair in the corner. She covered herself and the 'doll baby' with a large beach towel, closed her eyes and fell asleep.

"She is acting very strange," Dr. Wellfleet commented.

"What do you mean? Melinda asked.

"She is acting as if she is on drugs, or she has a concussion. She never checked the 'doll baby' that she is carrying. Does she even realize that we are going to be at sea for two days? I wonder if she is reacting to the combination of drugs that I gave her, the sleeping drug and the modified truth serum. Don't forget, we have only been using the sleep darts for a little over a year. I don't recall testing it in combination with the modified truth drug. I would like to get some blood to test. This has never happened in the three years that we tested the drug."

128

"You might get the chance, if I can get my hands on her," Martin said.

"Computer, get New York," the doctor requested."

"Yes, Dr. Wellfleet," New York answered.

"Can you contact some of the doctors on my staff and ask them to review the video of Amy Gelz? I'm very concerned. Her actions are of someone with a concussion or someone who has a reaction to the sleep drug that I administered two hours ago."

An hour later, "Computer, get Dr. Wellfleet."

"Go ahead, New York. This is Dr. Wellfleet."

"Your staff reported that they did a quick test on the drugs using lab mice. They feel that you are correct, and that she is having a reaction to the drug. We cannot confirm that until we get a sample of her blood to test. No one here remembers a reaction of this kind on any prior tests. We are contacting the other researchers to see if they remember anything like this. In all the years of testing, they have never seen this reaction before. According to the records, they did discuss this back in the beginning of the testing, that someone might be allergic to the chemicals. We are checking the research records as we speak" They went on to tell Dr. Wellfleet how to test Amy's blood. That way he would have a definitive answer.

Dr. Wellfleet said to Martin, "Please go to the suite and see what blood samples you can get for me. I don't need much, but I have to run the blood tests." He went to his black bag, took out a sample kit and handed it to Martin.

"I'll go to the suite right away and get your samples," said Martin. "It shouldn't be difficult, seeing how much she bled in our living room."

"Doctor," said Melinda. "Her behavior might not be from the dart. It could be from the additional sedative you gave her so that she would remain asleep for those extra ten minutes. Can you test for that?"

Dr. Wellfleet thought a minute, and then said, "That's a great idea, Melinda. Computer, online."

"Computer is online, Dr. Wellfleet," said the Computer.

"Get me New York," said Dr. Wellfleet.

"New York is online," said the Computer.

"Yes Dr. Wellfleet," answered New York.

"Melinda came up with a good thought. It might be a combination of the drug in the dart and the sedative. Pass the information to my staff, and have them check it out."

129

"Doctor Wellfleet," asked Rosemary. "What would happen if you injected her with the long term sedative?"

"I'm not sure," he replied. "I'll have to have my staff look into that. Why are you asking?"

"We have two days before we get to Curacao. Amy cannot stay on deck for two days. She has to eat, bath, take care of her daily bathroom needs and take care of the 'doll baby'. If she stumbles around the ship in this condition she will bring attention to herself."

"Rosemary has a good point," Melinda said. "I think it is worth the gamble. Amy is no good to us in her present condition."

"It can't be any worse than it is now," said Wellfleet. "Martin, get a gurney and meet me on the portside on Deck 14. I'll get my bag." Both men met outside on Deck 14. They walked over to where Amy was sleeping with the 'doll baby' in her arms. Dr. Wellfleet looked around to make sure no one was watching. He took the prepared hypodermic needle out of his bag, stuck Amy in her thigh and pushed the plunger. Amy sat up and then collapsed. Martin lifted her out of the lounge chair and placed her on the gurney. Martin strapped her to the gurney. Dr. Wellfleet took the 'doll baby' and placed it next to Amy. He took a blanket and covered them both.

They checked that no one on deck observing their actions, they wheeled the gurney through a door behind the bar and into a short hall. They wheeled the gurney to the staff elevator, took it down to Deck 10 and wheeled it into the suite. Rosemary came out of the nursery to help Sheena undress Amy, bring her into the shower, scrub her down and dry her off. They put one of the ship's bathrobes on her. They placed her back on the gurney. Sheena secured one hand and one foot with the zip ties to the frame of the gurney. They attached a blood pressure monitor and a heart monitor to Amy's body.

"She is clean and hooked up to the monitors," said Rosemary. "All of her numbers are within nominal range."

Wellfleet came into the room and checked Amy's heart with his stethoscope. "Everything seems to be working the way it should," he said. "I'll hook up a sedative drip. I'll have to get an oxygen tank, mask and a catheter from the clinic, "he said.

Ron replied, "I'll go down to the clinic with Benjamin and get them. You had better call the Clinic and let them know we are coming down for the equipment. Dr. Wellfleet called the clinic and told them what he needed.

Benjamin carried the oxygen tank and Ron carried the rest of the medical equipment. They brought it into the suite and assembled all the parts. Rosemary inserted the catheter into Amy and then inserted a port into a vein into Amy's arm and secured it in place. She attached the saline solution to the port. She unpacked the sedative drip and attached it to the saline line. "Now we can control her more effectively," said Dr. Wellfleet. "We can take turns watching her. We will have to wake her up every six hours to feed her.

"Doc," said Martin. "I see another possible problem."

"What's that, Martin?" asked the doctor.

"Amy is a trained assassin. We do not know what she is capable of doing. I wouldn't trust my family's safety if she is not sedated. I would suggest that they bathe her while she is still unconscious. I know it is harder that way, but I feel it will be a lot safer for all of us."

"That makes sense, "said Wellfleet. "We can do it that way."

Another thought occurred to me," said Melinda. Amy had to know that there are two days between ports after we left St. Lucia. There has to be a way for her to leave the ship before we get to the next port."

"I didn't think of that," Martin said. "Let me check with the Captain." He got up and left the cabin.

Ron scratched his head. "I never thought of that, either. I always thought when a ship is underway it is sealed tight. Of course she could jump off the ship and be picked up by a boat."

"With the baby?" said Rosemary. "I don't think that's likely."

At 0200 on Day 19 at sea, the Computer chirped, "New York online for Ron"

"What is it, New York?" Ron asked.

"We decided to set up a twenty-four hour observation watch over the Valley Forge. With two operations going at the same time, we figured it would make it easier for you. If they try dropping any more boxes off the Valley Forge, we will let you know. As each drone comes online, they will call you."

At 0500, Special Three called and said that they sighted two very fast boats heading on a collision course with Valley Forge. Their speed is forty knots. They estimate collision in one hour.

"Valley Forge, Valley Forge. This is Special Three at 0530 hours. Two boats are approaching from the east. I designate the northernmost boat, bandit alpha. Southernmost boat is designated bandit bravo. Alpha is now in the lead. Estimate contact in thirty minutes. Be informed that a flight of

131

two from the U.S.S. Enterprise will be on station in ten minutes. Their call sign is Cobra Flight. The bandits have entered the safety exclusion zone of the Valley Forge and have been warned to turn away. They have ignored the warning. They are still on a collision course with Valley Forge."

"Valley Forge, Valley Forge. This is Cobra Leader. We are a flight of two. We have you in sight. We have the bandits in sight. We have come at them at water level, and they still have not turned away. We are weapons free."

"This is Cobra 2. The lead boat has fired on me as I made my approach. I have returned fire. Bandit alpha has been sunk. Bandit bravo has turned away from Valley Forge. Cobra 1 and 2 will remain on station for thirty more minutes."

"Valley Forge, Valley Forge. This is Special Three. We kept an eye on bandit bravo. He is heading into a cove on Marie Galante Island. There is one large house and two small structures on the island next to the cove. Behind the house is a medium sized runway with two aircraft parked at one end. We are sending pictures to New York for identification."

"New York," said Melinda.

"Go ahead, Melinda."

"You stopped the two boats. Now we have to be on alert to see what else they will try. All they know is that Amy is on board the Valley Forge. Don't forget, she is sedated, and unless we wake her up, there is no way they will know that she has succeeded in the kidnapping. We never did find out if she was supposed to call or text."

"Dr. Wellfleet, any comment?" asked New York.

"It would take thirty to forty minutes to wake her up, and another fifteen minutes or so for the medication to clear her system. Keep in mind that we still do not know what her reaction will be when she wakes up. She will have one heck of a headache. Until we can get her to a hospital, we won't know if she has a concussion or if she is having a reaction to the sedative that's in the dart."

"I think we should take the gamble and let her use the cell phone," Melinda said. Turning to Ron, she asked, "Ron, can you make it seem as if there is atmospheric interference?"

Ron thought a moment. "Yes, I can do that. Let me get her phone." He got up and left the room. Moments later, he returned with Amy's cell phone and his tool kit. He sat at the dining room table and opened the back of her cell phone. He made some adjustments, soldered something and closed the case. He got up, closed his kit and walked over to Melinda.

Handing her Amy's cell he said, "I made adjustments to her cell phone. It will make the cell phone sound scratchy, and it will break up during transmission."

"Okay," Melinda said. "Now what do we send?"

Martin said, "Let's figure out the full message and then decide what parts to eliminate for transmission."

Rosemary thought a minute and said, "The message should read, 'Have succeeded with project. Have package. Need pickup.'" She paused and then continued, "Then delete the entire message except, 'succeeded, package and pick'. I can imagine what it would sound like at the other end. I think that would work better than if we tried to send a text."

Ron listened to what Rosemary had said and then replied, "I like that idea. That would give them pause. Would they try to verify the transmission? I guess they would. Let us get Amy to make a digital recording of some of the possible answers. Let's figure out some of the questions they would ask her."

"I don't think we have to do that," said Lucinda. "Unless they are planning a pickup by helicopter, they will have to find out what is happening on this ship. Then they would have to make plans. I don't know what kind of an organization she works for, but remember, they sent her on board this ship without any information and as far as we can tell no backup. Amy was just unlucky that we were able to figure out that someone had come onboard impersonating one of our people, before we got underway."

Ron continued the thought, "Without our special communication system, we never would have found out that Susan had been replaced with Amy so quickly. That is our secret weapon. As Melinda said before, we could stop Amy right now. That wouldn't help us stop whatever cartel is after Melinda. We have to let this play out. Let's wake Amy up, let her use her cell phone and wait for a reply. We have enough assets to take care of almost any contingencies. Let's not overthink this operation. Speaking of which, we still have to work on the smuggling operation."

At 0600 Melinda said, "Doctor Wellfleet, wake up Amy Gelz. When she is awake and can follow instructions, work with Ron and have Amy make the phone call. In the meantime I am going to order us some food. It is one thing to do without sleep but I cannot do without food. Have you noticed that Ron has not said a word about food? I wonder if he has a secret stash." Everyone's eyes turned to Ron.

"I don't have anything," Ron said. "I'm too tired to think about food. Until Dr. Wellfleet is ready, I'm going to lie down." He went out on the balcony, sat in the recliner, and instantly fell asleep.

"Valley Forge, Valley Forge. This is Special Three. You are leaking boxes."

Martin acknowledged the message. Melinda said, "Could it be that those boats that were chased away from us were out here to pick up the boxes?"

"Special Three, this is Valley Forge. Keep a sharp eye on the boxes." Martin said. "We might have caused a disruption in one of their operations. We expect pickup will happen after we leave the area."

"This is Special Three. I understood all."

At 0700 Harry Blank spoke to Jose while he was in the waiting room at St. Jude's. Harry explained that the pilot was not able to fix the fuel lines on the jet, but was able to rent a Cessna aircraft and it is now in the air. The pilot doesn't know how long it will take him to reach Castries. I would guess less than three hours to reach the airport in Castries, St. Lucia, but it is only a guess. As soon as the pilot calls me with his ETA, I'll call you back. We are still within the safety period for the drug. How is Susan doing, Jose?"

"She is still in a drug induced coma," Jose replied. "She is being constantly monitored, but the doctors are very concerned. They are afraid that if they keep her sedated much longer, it might cause damage to her lungs. Her kidneys are not working the way they should. The faster they can wake her up, the better off she'll be. The fact that she was brought to the hospital so quickly is the only reason she has a chance."

"Valley Forge, Valley Forge. This is Special Three. You were right. Two fast boats are twenty-five miles behind you. They are heading toward the boxes in the water. The fast boats came out from Galante Island."

"Where the heck is Galante Island?" Ron asked Martin.

Martin answered, "It's a small island about 140 miles north of St. Lucia. It's a very tiny island. When I flew down to St, Lucia last year, it showed up on my computer. Would you believe it's smaller than Rhode Island?"

Ron said, "Come on, nothing is smaller than Rhode Island." They both laughed.

"Melinda," said Dr. Wellfleet. "Amy is coming around nicely. We fed her some food and something to drink. We explained to her what we want. She agreed without hesitation. She feels bad about this whole operation. I still don't know if we can trust her. Time will tell. We woke Ron up, and he is bringing Amy her adjusted phone. He told me he has attached a pause button, so that if she says the wrong thing, he has three seconds to stop the transmission. We didn't tell Amy about that attachment. We want to see her actions and reactions to her phone call."

At 0730, off the Coast of Marie Galante Island was heard, "Valley Forge, Valley Forge. This is Special Four. Twelve Boxes had been retrieved from the water and the boats returned to Galante Island. I am returning to base. I am low on fuel. You now have Special Five and Six in the air."

There was a knock on the cabin door at 0800. Martin and Ron got up quickly and walked to the door. Ron went to the left and Martin to the right. They pulled out their dart guns. Rosemary walked to the door and checked the peephole. She nodded to Martin and opened the door. John wheeled the food cart into the room as Rosemary closed and locked the door behind him. Ron and Martin put away their guns and followed John into the dining room.

"Come and get it!" John said, as he wheeled the cart into the dining room. "Get it while it's hot." Everyone but Rosemary got up and moved into the dining room. Martin did the honors and served the food.

Rosemary went back into the nursery and to the babies. Both babies slept through the commotion. She checked their temperatures and found the temperatures had dropped two tenths of a degree. At that rate, in two days, their temperatures would be normal.

Melinda walked into the nursery and relieved Rosemary. "Get something to eat and take a nap," she told Rosemary. "We will need you bright eyed and bushy tailed when the action starts." Rosemary nodded her head and walked slowly out of the nursery. She walked into the dining room and sat down at the table. She looked exhausted. Martin got up, fixed her a plate of food and put it in front of her. She stared at the plate. Martin looked at her and smiled. He got up, walked around the table and stopped alongside her. He lifted her in his arms, carried her into the nursery and placed her on the couch. Melinda came over, took out a blanket from the cabinet and covered Rosemary. They both stood and watched her sleep. "She is exhausted," Melinda whispered to Martin. "Besides not having much sleep these last two days, she was really worried about the babies." They both stood there and then Melinda turned to Martin and said, "I am glad you found her. She is going to be an asset to our organization."

"I didn't find her." Martin said. "She found me. I'm glad she did. She's not only been a big help to you with the babies, but she has come up with some great ideas. As an aside, did you see how fast she drew the dart gun when there was a knock on the door?"

"Valley Forge, Valley Forge. This is Special Five. I am over Marie Galante Island at 30,000 feet. We are watching them move the boxes from the boats into both aircraft." Ten minutes later she continued. "Both aircrafts are in the air. One aircraft is a small jet. It looks like an older Gulfstream 250. It is heading west. The first aircraft is designated as bogey alpha. The second aircraft is a small single engine plane. It is heading south. The second aircraft is designated as bogey bravo. I will follow bogey alpha and Special Six will follow bogey bravo. We will keep you informed."

Valley Forge, Valley Forge. This is Special Five. Bogey alpha is traveling southwest at 350 miles per hour."

Valley Forge, this is Special Six. Bogey bravo is traveling south at 120 miles per hour."

Fifteen minutes later Special Five transmitted, "Valley Forge, Valley Forge. Bogey alpha is preparing to land in Aruba. There is a small air strip west of Audicuri Beach. We have been instructed to disable the aircraft after it lands." Five minutes later Special Five continued. "The aircraft has landed and we have made a single machine gun pass. We have disabled the aircraft and are standing by for the authorities." Twenty minutes elapsed, and Special Five continued, "There are two military trucks heading across the runway towards the disabled aircraft. I have received instructions to break off and return to station."

"Computer, get Jose online," said Harry Blank.

"I'm online, Harry." Jose answered. "What is the story with the antidote?"

"The aircraft has just landed at Hewanorra International Airport outside of Vieux Fort in St. Lucia. They are waiting for medical clearance. As soon as that happens, it will only take them twenty minutes to get to St. Jude's Hospital. You can notify all the medical personnel at the hospital that the antidote has arrived."

"It really is cutting it close," Jose said. "I was getting worried."

"So were we," Harry answered. "I hope the antidote is in time, and that it works. Don't forget, we still don't know how strong the ricin was and how much she got. While you're at the hospital, keep us informed."

1030 hours at St. Jude's Hospital.

"Computer," said Jose.

"Computer online," said the Computer.

"Computer, get Harry Blank," said Jose.

"I'm here, Jose. What do you need?" asked Harry. "Did they administer the antidote yet?"

"The antidote just got here," replied Jose. "There was a delay at the airport. The pilot said that no one wanted to take responsibility for allowing the antidote into the country. It seems that the antidote was supposed to have an export clearance from the United States. The pilot was smart. He paid a bribe and received a medical release for the antidote. They are administering the antidote as we speak. They have decided to bring her out of the medically induced coma at the same time. I was told that it will be at least two hours before the doctors can determine her condition."

"That's making it tough," Harry said. "Keep me informed. I won't annoy you with questions"

Thirty minutes later the Computer chirped, "Melinda online for Jose."

"I'm here Melinda," replied Jose.

"Want to fill me in? Melinda asked. "Everyone here is very anxious."

José replied, "The antidote finally arrived."

"What took it so long?" Melinda said. "I was told the plane arrived over an hour ago."

"There was a misunderstanding at the airport," said Jose. "The pilot was able to straighten it out. The doctor is giving Susan the antidote. It will be about ninety minutes more before we know anything. They are also bringing her out of the coma. I will let everyone know as soon as soon as I know. What is happening at your end?"

"We captured the woman who gave Susan the ricin," said Melinda. "She doesn't know the strength of the poison. She used a spray that they gave her. She was to impersonate Susan to get on board the Valley Forge. Her job was to kidnap one of the babies and turn it over to someone from the Mexican cartel. We are setting up contact with the cartel now. We will let you know what happens. You just take care of Susan and leave everything else to us."

"Which cartel did she say she worked for?" Jose asked.

"The Mexican cartel and the Exchange," answered Melinda.

"I thought we closed the Exchange down last year," said Jose.

137

"We thought so also," said Melinda. "Harry Blank is checking it out. He will keep everyone informed when he knows what is happening on that front. Go take care of your partner. We'll talk to you later."

"Valley Forge, Valley Forge. This is Special Six. We still have bogey bravo in sight. We have watched him circle a small dirt runway outside a small town of Dunfermline in Grenada three times. He comes down low, buzzes a farmhouse that has a red roof, and then flies back over the ocean. We have instructions to shoot him down and make it look like an accident. We are weapons free and are making a run now, while he is still over the water." Three minutes later Special Six continued, "I don't know what else he was carrying on that aircraft, but when we fired on him, he exploded into one big fireball, as if he was carrying dynamite. We are returning to station."

Meanwhile, at St. Jude's Hospital, in St. Lucia, Jose was sitting next to Susan's bed. He was holding her hand and listening to all the sounds that the machines were making. They were noisy but were keeping Susan alive. He was dozing when he felt Susan's hand move. He stood up and leaned over her. He took a washcloth, squeezed it almost dry and wiped her face and forehead. She tried to lick the cloth. Jose grabbed the cup of ice and put a chip between her lips, and she moaned with pleasure. He pushed the call button, and within moments, a nurse entered the room. Jose told her what had happened. The nurse walked over to the intercom, picked up the phone and dialed a number. She spoke for a moment and placed the receiver back into the cradle. "I've notified the Chief of Medicine. One of her team will be here in a minute." The nurse started checking Susan's vital signs and making notes on her chart when the doctor walked in.

The doctor spoke to the nurse and then turned to Susan, who was lying in the bed with her eyes open. She checked her vital signs, just as the nurse had done moments before. The doctor said a few words to Susan, and Susan nodded her head. The doctor, with the nurse's help, removed the breathing tube. The doctor waited a full minute to see that Susan was breathing on her own. When she was satisfied, she handed the breathing tube to the nurse to dispose of. She checked Susan's lungs. "Her lungs are clear," she said to no one in particular. To Susan she said, "No talking for an hour or so because the breathing tube has irritated your throat. I would like you to sip hot tea with lots of honey in it." She turned without looking at Jose and left the room.

"Some bedside manner," said Jose.

Susan let out a hoarse laugh. "You got that right," she whispered.

The nurse smiled, but said nothing. She straightened Susan's bedclothes and left the room. She returned three minutes later with a cup of hot tea with honey. "Just what the doctor ordered," she said, handing Susan the cup.

Susan took the cup of tea and took a sip. "It tastes like liquid honey," she croaked.

"How are you feeling?" asked Jose.

Her reply startled him. "I feel fine," she whispered. "I feel like I just woke up from a good night's sleep. How long have I been here?" Susan asked.

"Would you believe less than 24 hours," Jose answered.

Susan asked, "What happened? I can't seem to remember anything. I know I went off the ship to buy a pair of flip-flops. That was the last thing I remember."

"I was told you went off the ship for an errand of some kind," Jose said. "Then about thirty minutes later you called in an emergency that you were sick, and then you passed out. The computer kept track of you. I was told where to go and was directed to your exact location. I had you back to the ship in less than ten minutes after your call and into the Medical Clinic. They examined you, hooked you to a saline drip, but they didn't have the foggiest idea what to treat you for. They did pump your stomach, believing you ate something that made you sick. A short time later, they realized that was not the problem. The doctor called for an ambulance, and you were brought here to St. Jude's Hospital. As soon as they examined you, they knew what the problem was. The funny part was that some of their doctors had just come back from a C.I.A. training facility, and one of the things they discussed was the poison that had affected you. They diagnosed that you had been poisoned with ricin. They didn't know how much you had or the strength of the poison. That was their main worry. As soon as they told me what poison was used, I contacted Harry Blank. He made arraignments to fly the antidote down here to us instead of flying you to another hospital. Halfway down here, the airplane developed problems and had to land on a small island. The pilot landed on the island as the airport closed and was not able to get another plane until the following morning. The pilot rented a small single engine plane and continued the flight. He flew into Hewanorra International Airport in Castries, St. Lucia. He had trouble getting medical clearance for the drug, but the pilot was able to bribe his way through customs. For some reason the drug was supposed to have an export sticker. Once the drug cleared customs, the pilot delivered it to the hospital. You were administered the antidote two hours ago. You were in a medically induced coma until then."

"I don't remember calling in that I was sick," said Susan. "How did you find me?"

"We all have a tracking device under our skin, along with the communication device. Without that, I might not have been able to find you. As it was, it only took me less than five minutes to find you with directions from the computer."

Susan smiled, reached up, pulled Jose down to her and kissed him. Sparks flew. Jose kissed her back. A few moments later, Jose stood up and said with a big smile on his face, "What just happened?"

Chapter 7

Susan looked at him and reached for his hand. She squeezed his hand, said nothing and just looked into his big brown eyes. Just then, the nurse came in and said to Susan, "The doctor said that if you feel up to it, you can take a shower. He said that your legs might feel weak, and that you should use a walker to get in and out of the shower. Do you feel up to taking a shower now, or would you rather wait?"

Susan did not look at Jose. She said to the nurse, "If you unhook all of these wires and tubes, I would love to take a shower now." The nurse started removing all of the connections and turning off the machines as she did so. Within five minutes, the room was quiet. No blood pressure noise, no heart monitor noise, nothing. In fact, the only noise was the sound of the tape being removed from Susan's body. The nurse finished removing all the tape and shut down the final machine. "The only thing I won't remove is the IV port," the nurse said. "That stays in until you are ready to walk out of here. I put an extra cover on the port so it will stay dry." The nurse smiled at the two of them, turned and left the room.

A moment later, the nurse wheeled in a metal walker for Susan to use in the shower. "If you run into trouble while you are in the shower, just pull the red cord. That will alert us at the nurse's station." The nurse lowered the bed, placed slippers on Susan's feet and stood up. "If you need me, call." She smiled at Jose and left the room.

Jose walked over to the bed and helped Susan sit up. He made her sit for a few minutes. She put her arms around his neck and rested her head on his chest. He started to reach for the walker when she stopped him. "I don't need the walker. I have you to help me."

"Are you sure?" Jose asked, having one hand on the walker and one hand holding Susan up.

"I'm sure," Susan said. I know this isn't the place where I thought about taking a shower, but it will have to do. I suggest you lock the door before we start."

Jose smiled, reached over and locked the door. He helped Susan sit up and then assisted her to stand. He walked her slowly into the shower room. He leaned her against the wall while he turned the shower on and adjusted the temperature. When he was satisfied that all was as it should be, he helped Susan take off her hospital gown and sat her down on a wooden stool. He undressed himself, helped Susan off the stool and they both went under the shower. They stood there with their arms around each other. A few moments later, Jose sat Susan on the wooden stool, took the shampoo from the rack and started shampooing Susan's hair. As Jose ran his hands through her hair, Susan purred and leaned back against him. He continued washing her, and she continued purring. He smiled as he rinsed her off, He stood her up, turned her around and kissed her.

She reached up, put her arms around his neck and returned the kiss. It was a long, deep kiss. Jose pulled her closer and kept moving his hands over her body. As he became aroused, he broke away and said, "I would love to continue this Susan but I don't think it's smart. I care for you very much. From the first week that we met I felt there was something between us. Every time I started to approach you something came up. We never operated on the same team before. When they assigned us to the same team for this operation I thought my heart would jump out of my chest. Then to my amazement they assigned you as my partner. I couldn't believe my luck. Then we had time together in the pool on the ship. I was in heaven. Just when I thought we had a chance to get together, you got sick. I asked to stay with you. There was no hesitation. Melinda gave instructions to pack both of our bags and for me to stay with you. It is almost as if someone is watching out for me. I want our lovemaking to be special. I don't feel this is the place. Besides, we're still in operational status. You remember the rule about 'togetherness'. It's okay to fraternize but not when you are on an operation. I wouldn't want to break that rule. How do you feel about it?"

"I have to admit I'm disappointed, but I understand," said Susan. After the sparks from that kiss, I wanted you. Even making love here in the hospital would have been okay. I don't understand the feelings I have for you. I didn't have them in the beginning when we first met. I didn't feel anything when we operated together on the Valley Forge. It wasn't until I kissed you while I was still attached to all those machines. I guess we aren't supposed to understand it, just accept it and go on with our lives. Just one thing though. I want this to work. How about you?"

"Does that mean we're a couple?" Jose asked, smiling.

"Yes," said Susan. She put her arms around his neck and kissed him again. A few minutes later, they broke apart and rinsed off. Jose dried her with a towel and sat her down on the stool. He dried himself and got dressed. He walked into the room, opened her suitcase and pulled out clothes for her to wear. He brought them into the bathroom and helped Susan get dressed. They walked into the room and Jose unlocked the door.

He no sooner unlocked the door when the nurse walked in pushing a wheelchair. She picked up the clipboard and said, "Here are all the release forms that you have to sign before you can leave. As soon as the papers are processed, you are free to leave the hospital. Make sure you use the wheelchair."

"Computer," said Jose.

"Computer online," said the Computer.

"Computer, get Ron," requested Jose.

"I'm here, Jose. What do you need?"

"I made arrangements for me and Susan to fly to Curacao tomorrow morning to meet the ship. What I need this afternoon is a reservation for a hotel and a taxi to take us there. We have our luggage with us at the hospital."

Ron answered, "I'll take care of it all. By the time you sign out of the hospital, there will be a car waiting for you at the main entrance. I look forward to seeing you people tomorrow afternoon."

Susan finished signing the release papers, sat in the chair and waited for the nurse to wheel her out of the hospital. Jose took the suitcases and the carry-ons and put them onto another wheelchair as he waited for the nurse. The nurse arrived and started pushing Susan's wheelchair towards the main entrance. Jose followed close behind. Twenty minutes later outside the hospital Susan said, "Computer, conference call."

"Conference call confirmed, Susan," chirped the Computer.

"I want to let everyone know that I am alive and well," Susan said. "The antidote worked better than the doctors hoped. They still don't know how much of the ricin I absorbed, but they feel it couldn't have been much, since I came out of it so quickly after the antidote was administered. According to all the tests there was no apparent damage to my organs, and they gave me a medical clearance to go back to work. Jose has arranged for us to fly out of here tomorrow morning and should meet the Valley Forge at Curacao on Thursday. I'll try to join you all for breakfast," she said, as she looked at Jose for confirmation. She saw him shaking his head. "Make that lunch," she continued. "Lunch is better. We will see you then. End conference call."

"Conference call ended," replied the Computer.

They came out of the hospital at the main entrance and sure enough, there was a car waiting for them. The driver and the nurse helped place Susan in the car, and the nurse buckled Susan's seat belt. Susan smiled and thanked the nurse. The driver took the luggage from Jose and placed it in the trunk. With the luggage loaded, the driver slammed the trunk closed and got behind the wheel. Jose got in the back seat and put his seat belt on. He put his arm around Susan and she leaned her head on his chest. The driver took off out of the parking lot as if he was a race car driver. He did not even apply his brakes when he made a right turn. One block later, he was on the main road heading north. Five minutes after that, he passed a sign that said **Castles in Paradise, turn right, next exit.** The car turned right and into *'Castles in Paradise Villa Resort'*. As soon as the car pulled up to the main entrance the doorman raced to the car and opened the back door. As Jose got out of the car, a bellman wheeled a cart to the back of the car and unloaded the luggage. The doorman assisted Susan out of the car. A bellman, whose nametag read 'Anthony' approached the couple and told them to follow him and that it was not necessary for them to sign the register.

They followed Anthony through the ornate lobby and out the back arch to a stone walkway. Next to the walkway was a pink golf cart. Anthony assisted Susan into the cart and Jose climbed in the other side. Anthony drove them alongside the golf course until he came to a small cottage. He helped Susan out of the golf cart and Jose followed. Anthony unlocked the door and waved the couple into the cottage. He followed them in. Moments later the second bellman came with the luggage. Anthony left the couple in the living room while he directed the other bellman into the master bedroom with the luggage. One of the bellmen put the luggage on racks, turned the cart around and went back to the living room. Anthony followed the first bellman and said to Jose, "Pick up the phone when you are ready for dinner." He followed the other bellman out of the room and closed the door.

Jose walked to Susan and put his arms around her. He bent down and kissed her lightly on the lips. Again, sparks flew. Susan stepped back. "It's happened again," she said, stepping away from him. "Every time you kiss me I feel sparks."

Jose looked at her. He cupped her face in his hands and kissed her again. "I can almost see the sparks every time I touch you," he said. "Let's look around this place, I know it can't be just a living room." Jose took Susan's hand as they walked through an archway into a short hallway. To the right was a very large master bedroom. Against the far wall was a California bed covered with a tan duvet. The walls were covered with tan patterned wallpaper. Silk drapes hung on one wall. They opened the drapes and saw a white sand beach. Opposite the bed was a large television screen mounted on the wall. They returned to the hallway and continued their walk. The second room was a tiled bathroom with a large glassed in

144

shower, two sinks, a toilet and a bidet'. Thick white pile rugs covered the floor.

"This is some place," Jose remarked. "I wonder what else there is." They returned to the hallway and entered the third door. This was another bedroom, smaller than the first. The room was decorated in light colors, and the floor was covered in a thick tan carpet. On one wall was a large screen television. Against the other wall a small desk and an upholstered chair. He reached for Susan's hand, and they walked back to the living room. Looking out the glass doors, they saw they had an enclosed private swimming pool.

"I thought they would have found us a Motel 6, not this," said Jose. "I can get used to this. Would you like to go for a swim?" he asked Susan. "We won't even need bathing suits."

Susan didn't hesitate. She did not answer Jose. She just undressed on the spot, walked to the pool and dived in. Jose followed moments later. They leisurely swam around the pool and finally stopped at the shallow end. Jose went to Susan and kissed her. She kissed him back, pulled away and smiled at him. He took her hand and led her out of the pool and into the outdoor shower. He turned the shower on and walked under the spray. Susan followed him, put her arms around him and held him tight.

"You make me so happy," said Susan, as she turned Jose around, put her hands on his cheeks and kissed him. Jose took the liquid soap and massaged Susan's back. She leaned into him as he moved his hands to the front of her body. Susan just stood there. She moaned with pleasure. When he was finished, Susan took the soap and did the same to him. When they were finished, Susan turned the water off and reached for the towel on the rack that stood alongside the shower stall. She massaged Jose with the towel until he was dry. Then Jose grabbed another towel from the rack and wrapped Susan in it. He rubbed her down until she was dry. When they were both dry, Susan took Jose's hand and walked with him into the bedroom.

Two hours later, Jose picked up the phone and notified the desk that they were ready for dinner. Thirty minutes later, there was a knock on the door, and Susan went to open it. Anthony was there with their dinner. He wheeled the food cart to the dining room table. He took two candles from the drawer, lit them and placed them in the middle of the table. He set two places with fine bone china and polished silverware.

Jose walked Susan to the table and pulled out a chair for her. They sat down and looked at each other. Anthony served the first course of lobster bisque, stepped back away from the table and left the dining room. Jose watched Susan as she started eating. She started eating slowly and then more rapidly.

"Slow down, Susan," said Jose gently. "I know you really haven't eaten solid food for more than twenty-four hours but I don't want you to get sick by eating so fast."

"I don't know what happened to me," she replied. "I'm embarrassed."

Anthony came back into the dining room and took the plates away. He tied bibs around their necks, placed nutcrackers and picks next to their plates, and served the second course, a four-pound Maine lobster for each of them. Susan's eyes opened wide. "I've never seen a lobster this size before."

"Jose laughed. "Neither have I," he said as he picked up the nutcracker. The waiter came over and offered to crack the shell for them. They both declined. Susan picked up a claw, placed the nutcracker on it and split it open. She looked over to Jose and saw he was having trouble. She reached over, took his nutcracker, split the claw open, splashing water over Jose's bib. He started laughing. Susan joined in.

Susan took a piece of lobster, dipped it into warm butter and fed it to Jose. His eyes lit up. He took a piece of lobster and dipped it into warm butter, and fed it to Susan. They both stopped eating. They looked at each other. Jose got up and pulled Susan's chair away from the table. He pulled her to her feet, put his arms around her and gave her a gentle kiss. "It's happening again," Susan said, smiling. She took his hand and pulled him towards the bedroom.

Anthony walked into the dining room and looked towards the bedroom as the door closed. He smiled to himself as he put the food back in the warmer. An hour later, they returned to the dining room table. Anthony returned to the dining room and took their food from the warming server. Not a word was said, except, "thank you," as Anthony left the room. They sat down and continued eating their dinner.

Anthony returned sometime later and served dessert. "If you need anything else," he said. "Just pick up the phone and ask for me. Goodnight." He turned and left the dining room. They lingered over the dessert and took their coffee out to the pool. They sat and watched the stars.

"Look," said Susan. "There's a shooting star." Jose smiled. He was content.

Day 20   Thursday   Martin started his turn at the monitors at 0400. At 0530, Martin noticed boxes being brought out on Deck 4 and secured against the railing.

At 0600 Martin heard, "Valley Forge, Valley Forge. This is Special Five and Special Six. We are with you at 30,000 feet. We see four boxes floating a quarter mile behind you. There is no boat traffic at this time. Out."

At 0630, Martin heard again, "Valley Forge, Valley Forge. This is Special Five. We have two small boats heading for the boxes." Ten minutes later, Special Five announced, "They are loading the boxes, two to each boat." A short time later Special Five called and said he could see the boats heading to Willemstad, Curacao.

Martin walked over to the monitor and saw the boxes were gone.

"Computer," requested Martin.

"Computer online," replied the Computer.

"Get Charlie Pile," said Martin.

"I'm online, Martin," answered Charlie Pile. "I'm still monitoring all the traffic from the Specials. We are setting up personnel the same way we did on the other island. We have two teams at the airport if they decide to send the boxes out by plane. There will be two teams at the dock if they plan to bring the boxes ashore there and I also have two teams standing by in two high powered boats in case they change their minds and don't follow the pattern."

"We are scheduled to dock at 0800 hours, or thereabouts," replied Martin. "I was expecting them to tender us ashore. They still might change their mind. I won't know for another hour. I will let you know as soon as I find out. Susan and Jose will be flying in this morning and will be joining us for lunch. If you can get away, let me know, and I'll meet you at the aft gangway if we dock or at the tender dock if we come in by tender."

"That sounds good," replied Charlie. "I'll see what I can do. When the boxes come ashore, I plan to have the boat skippers picked up. As soon as the boxes are delivered to their destination we will take all the personnel and the boxes to the airport. This time we are going to open the boxes when we get to the airport to see what's in them. According to the Specials, the skippers didn't seem to be having any problems taking the boxes out of the water. That would eliminate gold and guns. That would leave money and drugs. I would like to know what kind and how much. Did they open the other boxes we picked up from Haiti? I haven't been told. In any case, we should be finished here by the time you dock in Willemstad."

147

"I only know of one box being opened," said Martin. "It contained about two million dollars in hundred dollar bills. I haven't received any other reports."

At 0700, Martin walked to the kitchen and poured himself a cup of coffee. He took a sip and walked towards the nursery. He opened the door quietly and looked in. He was facing a gun that was being held rock steady in the hands of a red-headed doll. "Whoa, I'm a friend," he said, stopping so fast that he spilled his coffee over his hand. "Ow, that's hot," he said, as he put the cup down quickly. He reached for his handkerchief and wiped his hands. "I thought you guys would be sleeping, and I wanted to look in at my babies."

Rosemary put the gun down and said, "Sorry about that. As soon as the handle of the door moved, I was up." She reached for a towel and helped wipe up the spilled coffee.

"Melinda is napping," Rosemary said. "Edward was up part of the night. Melinda let me sleep for part of the night and she took care of Edward without my help. She must be exhausted by now. Come on in and look at your lovely sleeping children. I'm going to get a cup of coffee. Do you want a fresh one?"

"Yes," said Martin, "as long as the coffee is in a cup," he said smiling. He turned and went into the nursery. He saw Melinda sleeping on the day bed. He walked to her and kissed her gently on the lips. Melinda smiled and rolled over. She stayed asleep. Martin walked to the babies. Annabelle was sleeping and had a smile on her lips. Edward was sleeping but was squirming as he slept. Martin leaned in and gave each of them a kiss on the forehead. He noticed that they didn't feel as warm as yesterday. That was a good sign.

At 0730 hours, Valley Forge docked at Willemstad, Curacao. The sky was light blue with a slight breeze blowing onshore. The temperature was in the low 70's. Marsha and Mason were walking on Deck 14. They stopped to admire the scenery and noticed four multi-color vans parked near the entrance to the dock. They also saw a large group of people in full native costume walking around the same area.

"Computer online," said Marsha.

"Computer online, Marsha" said the Computer.

"Computer, get Melinda," said Marsha.

"I'm here, Marsha. What do you have?"

"We're on Deck 14," Marsha said. "We see four multi-colored vans parked near the entrance to the dock. There is a group of people dressed in native costumes wandering around the vans. We are wondering if these are the vans they plan to use to pick up the boxes."

"Charlie Pile called to tell us to expect the group in native costumes," said Melinda. "These are Charlie's people, and they are putting trackers on the vans. He is not sure if these vans are the ones the smugglers are going to use to move the boxes, but he isn't going to take a chance. Keep an eye out, and call Charlie if you see them moving the boxes. Do you see the small boats? Special Five told us they were heading to the same dock where we are."

"We see one of the boats. No, I can see both of the small boats now," Marsha said. "They are moving very slowly. They are tying up on the other side of our dock. They each have two boxes sitting on their decks. They have just moved the boxes onto the pier. One of the crew is walking towards the gate. He went outside the gate and is heading to one of the vans. He opened the rear of the green van with a large yellow flower on its side and took out a folding cart. He is wheeling it back through the gate. He is loading the four boxes onto the cart and wheeling it towards the gate without anyone stopping him. He has dropped a box at each van and is putting the cart back in the green van. The vans are pulling out. The man is heading back to the boat. The vans are now out of sight."

"Computer online," said Melinda.

"Computer online, Melinda," said the Computer.

"Get Charlie Pile online," said Melinda.

"I'm online," said Charlie.

"Charlie," said Melinda, "Did you hear the report."

"Yes," said Charlie. "All four vans have trackers on them. Special Five and Six are going to keep track of the vans. I just ordered one of my boats to standby in case he has to block the two small boats from leaving. The team I have on the dock is heading towards the boats to apprehend the skippers. After each box is delivered we will raid that location. I have enough people with me so that I can leave a team at each location for a week to see who comes for the merchandise. I checked with the Airport Security at Hato Airport, and they have a jail we can use until we get transportation. After each raid, we will open the boxes and let you know what we find. We are going to wait to see where the last delivery is made. We want to see what they plan to do with the merchandise. We expect them to repackage the merchandise like they did on the other islands."

Melinda said, "Okay Charlie. That sounds like a great idea." Turning to Marsha, she said, "You and Mason can take it easy. We don't expect any more action on the dock. Enjoy the rest of the day. Don't forget to relieve the team at the monitor. Charlie left a team at the dock to see if there would be any more action. If there is, he will call us."

At noon, everyone was in the suite waiting for Susan and Jose to arrive. Suzy Q said, "It is hard to believe that it has been a little over twenty-four hours since Susan was poisoned. She is a very lucky woman."

"It only goes to prove that it doesn't take much for one of us to be taken down," said Ron. "I've adjusted the computer to alert us when any one of us has blood pressure and heart rate changes beyond their recorded norms. We can't stop our members from being attacked, but we will be alerted more quickly.

"That's a good idea," Melinda said. "Keep in mind that you might have to tweak the numbers a little. We have a young active group," she said, smiling.

"Okay," Ron said, laughing. "I get the message. I'll make the adjustments to the program."

A call came from Special Six at 1300. "Valley Forge, one van has stopped by a small garage behind what appears to be a strip mall. It has been sitting there for twenty minutes with no activity."

Twenty-five minutes later Special Six came back on the air, "Valley Forge, a blue car just drove up. The driver of the van has gotten out, opened the rear of the van, took out a package and handed it to the driver of the blue car. We will designate this car as bogey 1. We will track it. Bogey 1 has pulled away from the van and made a U-turn and driven off."

Twenty minutes later Special Six continued, "Valley Forge, we have another bogey. I will designate this one as bogey 2. The car is green in color. It has pulled in behind the van. The driver of the green car has gotten out, walked to the driver's window of the van, received a small package and returned to his car. He has driven away. There are two vehicles approaching the van. One is a black SUV designated bogey 3. He was handed a package and he drove away. The yellow pickup truck designated bogey 4 has stopped and received a package from the driver of the van. The driver of the van has closed the rear door and gotten behind the wheel. He is pulling away from the garage. Special Five will track bogey 1 and bogey 2. Special Six will track bogey 3 bogey 4 and the van."

At 1330 the phone in the cabin rang. Rosemary picked it up, spoke a few words and placed the phone in its cradle. "Susan and Jose have just come on board," she said. "It shouldn't take them long to get to the suite. Should I order lunch, or are we going to use the specialty dining room?"

Melinda thought for a minute and said, "Order the food and have it delivered here. Once the food is here, we will not have to worry about security."

At 1340 another call came from Special Six. "The van has headed north. It stopped at a small marina next to the Hato airport. A man approached the driver's side of the van. The driver handed him a package and drove away. The man walked down the dock with the package and went aboard a blue and white motor boat. That blue and white boat is designated bogey 6. It is pulling away from the dock and heading east."

Twenty minutes later Special Six reported, "Bogey 6 (The blue and white boat) has docked at Kralendijk, Bonaire. Charlie Pile, do you have anyone there?"

"No," Charlie replied. "I didn't expect them to split the delivery. It will take about thirty minutes to get someone there. Keep tracking bogey 6."

"Charlie can you close down the three destinations that we know about?" asked Melinda.

"I need one more hour and we will be able to close down all four of the destinations at one time," Charlie replied. "This way they will not be able to warn anyone."

"Good idea," said Ron. "We have been lucky. Not one of the groups has gotten suspicious. They have not tried to communicate with each other."

Looking at the map on her tablet, Melinda said, "This is the last port. We have three days at sea before we arrive at Ft. Lauderdale. As soon as Charlie tells us that he has finished in Curacao and Bonaire, we can round up the four suspects on this ship and lock them in the brig with their friend from Holland. Then we'll let Dr. Wellfleet take over. Did anyone try to contact Amy?" she asked Ron.

"No," he replied. "Her cell phone has been silent and that does worry me. I don't think they'll forget about Amy Gelz. They know she made it to the ship because she made a phone call to the cartel. What else can we do?"

Martin scratched his chin and remarked, "I would not stop being vigilant. Don't forget we'll be at sea for three days. We are going to be close to many of the islands on the way home and anything can happen."

"What do we do about Amy?" asked Suzy Q. "Do we trust her enough to allow her to run free? There aren't many places she can go on this ship."

Melinda shook her head. "No," she said. "I don't want her running free. In fact, I want her secured and monitored as we are doing now. I will not put my babies at risk."

"I agree," Martin said. "We were very lucky catching her so quickly. I suggest she be kept secured and sedated, except for feeding. Make sure we are extra vigilant with our patrols on deck. Give everyone a pair of binoculars." Martin glanced over and saw Melinda leaning back and closing her eyes. "Here she goes again," he whispered.

Everyone turned and watched Melinda. Five minutes later, Melinda opened her eyes and said, "It's easy to watch the sides of the ship, but what about the back of the ship? We are vulnerable there. A fast boat can come up on us at night and we would never see it. I think we should mount a camera with motion sensors. Ron, can you take care of that?"

"Yes," Ron replied. "I'll take a walk to the back of the ship to see where the best place would be to mount cameras to give us the best view." He got up and left the suite.

Melinda said, "The only thing left to do would be to make sure that we watch the monitors and make sure New York is doing the same. As soon as Ron hooks up the aft camera, I'll check with New York. I don't expect anything to happen during the day, but you never know. Now is the time to go for a swim and to spend time in the sun. Everyone report back here by 1800 hours. Check your tablet for the times you have to be on watch in the suite."

Ron returned to the suite, walked over to the converter, entered the camera codes and watched the picture unfold on the monitor. "I had to mount two cameras on Deck 10 to get full coverage of the back of the ship," he said to Melinda.

"Computer, get New York online," said Melinda.

"We're here, Melinda," New York replied.

"We've just added two more cameras with motion sensors on Deck 10 covering the back of the ship. We feel that we are very vulnerable in that area. Make sure your people are vigilant for the next three days, especially at night."

"Roger, Valley Forge. We have four people watching the monitors at our end. If you want, you can shut your monitors down."

"Negative, New York," said Melinda. "We don't want to take that chance. The more eyes the better."

Charlie Pile called Melinda at 1600 hours. "Melinda," said Charlie. "We were able to catch the suspect who took the blue and white boat designated bogey 6 to Bonaire. He stayed with the boat drinking beer with the skipper. We scooped them both up with all their merchandise and are returning to Hato airport. I hope they send a plane soon. I would like to get these prisoners and this merchandise off my hands."

Melinda replied, "I understand. We chartered a special 727 yesterday, and started collecting prisoners and merchandise from each of the ports. We have already picked up prisoners from St. Maarten, St. Kitts and San Juan. I had Charlie's people open the boxes from St. Maarten for inspection. The heavy boxes weighed forty pounds and contained cash. Inside the box were bundles of one hundred dollar bills, shrink-wrapped, in one-pound bundles. We figured five hundred bills to the pound. That would total fifty thousand dollars a bundle. There were forty bundles in the box. That would be approximately two million dollars for each box. The other boxes contained mostly OxyContin. Each of the boxes weighed twenty pounds. They each contained four five-pound bags. Each bag had six thousand 80-mg. pills. Based on the last street value we received, that would mean the street value of each bag would be a half million dollars. Multiply it by four and the total value of the box of drugs is two million dollars. Our operation is going to cost the cartel a lot of money. I figured we have collected more than thirty boxes and forty suspects."

"I'm glad we're the good guys," said Charlie. "How are you doing with your assassin, Amy Gelz?"

Melinda replied, "It's a mixed bag. After Doctor Wellfleet finished with her she seemed to have switched sides. My father taught me years ago that if a person switches sides once, they just might switch sides a second time. There is that trust factor. We did make sure she didn't see our faces and we are keeping her sedated except for feeding times. We even keep her sedated to bathe her. I think that shows how much trust we have in her. Don't forget she's a trained assassin. I'm sure she had been trained to tell lies under the influence of truth drugs. We just don't know how much is truth. Wellfleet has assured me that with his new truth drug that cannot happen. I am not going to put my babies in jeopardy to find out. We had a conference a short time ago. One of the ideas that came up is that we are not secure just because we are out at sea. We will be at sea for three more days and we are less than six hours by boat from some of the small islands that we pass. We have set up two additional cameras to watch the rear of the ship, and New York will have four people monitoring the cameras. We're keeping a lookout on both sides of the ship twenty-four hours a day.

I'm glad it is only for three days. That brings you up to date. Do you have any questions?" she asked.

"I think you have it well in hand," Charlie replied. "You know, I could send a couple of teams out by helicopter."

"That came up in the conference," Melinda said. "I thought it would cause too many people to ask too many questions. Remember, we are supposed to be a covert operation. It was tough enough bringing the Captain in on this operation. He has been very good to us. He was a little annoyed that he wasn't told about this operation in the beginning, but now he understands the reasons. He is even putting his own lookouts on the bridge and an extra radar watch for the next three days. I think we have it covered. Of course, we do not have any idea what the opposition is going to do. As I find out, I'll let everyone know."

Continuing with that thought Charlie said, "How about I send a boat out? You can have them open the side hatch, and we can come aboard. None of the passengers will see a thing."

"That sounds like a good idea," Melinda said. "Let me discuss it with Ron, and I'll get back to you."

At 1700, Melinda went to the dining room table and made herself a cup of tea. She sat down with Ron and the rest of the team. "I just spoke to Charlie Pile," Melinda said. "He said he can send out a boat with a couple of teams, and if we have the Captain open the side hatch, they will be able to come onboard without the passengers knowing. What do you think?"

"I like that idea," said Rosemary. "We could use the extra people. If we have to stand watch twenty-four hours a day for three days, we are going to be exhausted and we might start making mistakes."

Martin said, "I like that idea but how long will it take him to get his people on board? Remember, the opposition will probably be trying to do the same thing."

"I think we should keep Amy locked up," Ron said. After each feeding session, she should be handcuffed and put back to sleep until the next session. If for some reason her friends get onboard the ship, they will look for her first. Another advantage we have is that they will not know where she is unless they have a tracking device on her. Did we ever check?"

"Computer, get Doctor Wellfleet," requested Ron.

"I'm on, Ron," said Doctor Wellfleet. What do you need?"

"Did you ever check to see if Amy Gelz had a tracker on her?" Ron asked. "I mean besides the one I put in her."

Wellfleet thought a minute. "No I didn't. I'll be up in five minutes to check," he said.

"Another thing to worry about," Martin remarked. "Now we definitely have to keep her under lock and key. Where are we going to do that? We can't keep her in the suite. It's a little crowded when everyone is in here."

Jose said, "Why not ask Suzy Q if she has any ideas."

"Computer, get Suzy Q online," requested Martin.

"I'm on, Martin," Suzy Q answered.

"We need a place to keep Amy Gelz locked up while sedated," Martin said. "We have to keep her sedated except when she has to be fed. Even when we bathe her, we will keep her asleep. There is a trust issue here. I think you understand. In addition, we just found out that we never checked to see if she came on board with a tracker on her body. Doctor Wellfleet is on his way up to check."

It was quiet for a moment and then Suzy Q said, "When were you planning on taking my assistant, Frank Barber and his assistant, Casandra Niki to the brig? If you do that now, then we can use his office. It is large enough for a gurney and six people. That office has bathing facilities. It is very secure, and no one will know she is there."

"Let's do it right now," Melinda said. "Let's tie up as many lose ends as we can. Have your Security people pick up all the suspects we know, including the three-crew members and your assistant, Frank Barber. I hate to recommend this, but I guess it is guilt by association. Have them pick up Casandra Niki as well. New York is especially interested in Casandra Niki. They have not been able to confirm any background information on her. I would recommend that you give your Security people dart guns to use. It would be a quieter way to apprehend them. They can join the first one we put in the brig, that person from Holland. I keep forgetting his name. I remember now, Van Deer. Stephen Van Deer. I just hope we got them all. New York is still doing background checks on the crew. It is a slow process when you are dealing with foreign governments. When Doctor Wellfleet finishes his work in the suite, I'll send him down to deal with the prisoners that are in the brig. When everything is secure, call me and I will have Amy brought down to you. Before I forget, we had a conference in the suite, and we decided to let Charlie send out a boat with a couple of teams. When his boats are next to the Valley Forge, we will need one of the hatches open. Can you handle that, or should I ask the Captain?"

155

"I can handle that," Suzy Q said. "Just give me a call. It will take five minutes to open the hatch at the speed this ship is traveling. I don't think it would be a good idea to slow the ship down. That would alert the passengers."

"Good thinking, Suzy," Martin said. "We'll tell Charlie to start out. I'll have him carry a radar reflector and an IFF transmitter set to 234.76. This way the Captain will know he is a friendly. As soon as I find out how long it will take him, I'll call you."

"What's IFF?" Rosemary asked.

"It is an 'Identify Friend or Foe," Martin explained. "In this day and age with high speed of boats and planes, you need some way to identify who is a friend and who isn't and it has to be done quickly. That's the way it is done."

"Computer, get Charlie Pile online," requested Martin.

"I'm on, Martin," he said. "What did you guys decide?"

"We can use your help," Martin replied. "We don't have enough people to cover everything we need to cover. How long will it take you to put together a team and get them out to us?"

"I'm like you," Charlie said. "I'm always thinking ahead. We started out two hours ago from St. Lucia. We should be with you in about five hours. We are traveling with three high speed racing boats. Each boat has two teams onboard. I will be transmitting IFF 234.76 as you requested, the entire time. Only the lead boat has a radar reflector. We will be monitoring Channel A. I am the only one that is connected. With the noise we will be making, I don't know if I will be able to communicate with the other boats until we are closer to you."

"Roger that. I will pass all this information to the Captain. We will see you in five hours or less. For your information, Special Five and Special Six will also be watching for you."

At 1730, Dr. Wellfleet examined Amy with his scanner. He started at her head and worked his way down. As he got to her left big toe, the beeper went off. He immediately took her to the Medical Clinic and had her toe x-rayed. The x-ray showed the outline of a foreign object that looked like a tracker.

"Computer, get Melinda online," he requested.

"What do you have, doctor?" asked Melinda

"I found what looks like a tracker in her big toe," replied the doctor. Do you want me to remove it?"

"Is there a way to shield it from being scanned?" Melinda questioned.

"I don't know," replied the doctor. "I think Ron would be the one to ask."

"Computer, get Ron online."

"I'm online, Melinda," said Ron. "In answer to your question, I don't believe we can shield the tracker completely when the tracker is still in the body. You either have to remove it or leave it alone. If you remove the tracker it can be put in a lead box and that will completely shield it."

"That means," said Melinda, "that we have to have her placed under guard in a defensible place. Suzy Q, is that office defensible?"

"Yes it is," Suzy Q answered. "The room was originally built to contain a safe and used to store valuables before they built a better facility behind the reception desk. The main door to the room is three inches of solid steel and can only be opened with a special key card. If there is a power failure, the door can only be opened from the inside."

"Okay, doctor," said Melinda. "Bring her to the special room. I'll have Marsha and John meet you there."

Turning to Marsha and John Melinda said, "Suzy Q will take you to meet Dr. Wellfleet and Amy. Once the doctor has left you, lock yourselves in. If we need you to do anything else, we'll call you. Remember, the tracker is active, so if they board us, they won't have a problem finding Amy. No matter what happens, do not leave that room."

"Special Five, Special Six, This is Valley Forge. Be on the lookout for three fast boats in formation coming from the east. They started from St. Lucia more than two hours ago. They are transmitting IFF 234.76. They are less than five hours away." Special Six and Special Five acknowledged the information.

An hour later, they heard in a conference mode, "Valley Forge, Valley Forge. This is Special Five. We have a formation of three high-speed boats on our screen. They are on a collision course with Valley Forge. They are transmitting IFF 234.76. At the rate of speed they are traveling, they are less than four hours out. Be aware, there is another formation of two boats coming from the southeast, tracking in your general direction. They are also on a collision course with Valley Forge. At their rate of speed they will not reach Valley Forge for seven plus hours.

At 1800 hours their dinner was delivered to the suite. Everyone sat down for dinner except Rosemary and Stephen. They stayed inside the nursery with Edward and Annabelle. Rosemary and Melinda decided the babies should never be alone, especially with Amy Gelz onboard, even though Amy was sedated, secured, and under guard.

The first team of watchers went out on Deck 14 at 1900 hours and watched the ship get underway and move away from the dock. The weather was mild, and they were able to admire the beautiful sunset.

At 2100, six hours south of San Juan, Special Five called. "Valley Forge, there is a formation of three boats approaching Valley Forge. They are transmitting IFF 234.76. We show another formation of two boats on a collision course with Valley Forge. If they maintain their course and speed they should be with you in a little over five hours."

More than two hours later, Charlie's boats pulled alongside the Valley Forge. Charlie called Suzy Q and asked her to open the hatch. As soon as the hatch was opened a rope ladder was placed over the side. Charlie's first boat pulled alongside, matched the ships speed, and the teams came on board the Valley Forge. After the people from the first boat were safely on board, the first boat pulled to the right and dropped back, acting as a safety boat for the remaining boats. This allowed the second boat to approach the hatch. Boats two and three unloaded their people without a mishap. The boats turned eastward and headed back to St. Lucia. Suzy ordered the hatch closed and sealed. Suzy Q called Melinda to tell her that Charlie Pile's boats had pulled alongside and his men have come on board. Charlie Pile introduced himself and his men. She acknowledged the introductions and escorted the twenty-four people and Charlie to Melinda's suite.

Day 21   Friday. Just past midnight Suzy Q called to Melinda, "I am outside the cabin with Charlie Pile and his twenty four men. Before I bring them in, do you want to secure the babies?"

"Suzy," replied Melinda. "That's a great idea. I know our Security has cleared Charlie's people, but the cabin door will be open, and anything can happen. Give me a couple of minutes."

Melinda spoke to Rosemary and Stephen. They made sure the doors to the nursery were secure. Stephen turned on the monitors so they could be part of the talk taking place in the next room. Melinda opened the door of the suite and let Charlie and his six teams enter.

Charlie Pile introduced his people. Melinda and Martin acknowledged the introductions. Melinda pointed to the dining room table and said, "I ordered food and drinks for you. You must have had a long trip by boat to reach us."

"It wasn't the length of the trip," one of men said. "It was the noise. Even wearing special earphones in an insulated cabin, the noise was difficult to handle."

After everyone settled in, Charlie asked, "Where do you want us to set up? My people need a few minutes to clean and check their weapons."

Melinda pointed to a table in the sitting room. "I'm sorry I didn't think of having a workspace for you and your people. We were occupied with the other operation."

Charlie answered, "I wouldn't worry about it. We can use the floor if they have to. We'll be using the dart guns on this operation so we won't have to worry about noise. These weapons have built in sound suppressors and each weapon has been fitted with a laser sight and a digital camera. You will be able to see what my people see, and New York can make a digital record." He handed Ron the codes for the cameras. Charlie continued, "I looked over the plans of the Valley Forge. I want to put two people on the top of the mast. That will give them the best view of the top two decks. I want to split one team between the two aft cabins on Deck 8. That will allow them to look directly down to the water. Can you make arrangements to have those cabins emptied?"

"Suzy, can that be arranged?" asked Melinda. Suzy nodded and took out her cell phone. She spoke a few minutes, disconnected and put the phone back in her pocket.

"It is being taken care of," said Suzy Q. "One of my people will be going to both cabins and informing them that there is a short in the wiring leading to their cabin and needs to be fixed. They were given a coupon for a specialty restaurant to compensate them for their inconvenience." Suzy continued, "I noticed the rifles, so I ordered six food carts to be wheeled up and left in the passageway. There are waiter's jackets inside the compartment. That will allow your people to get around the ship with ease. How you get them up to the crow's nest is up to you."

Charlie laughed. "That's good thinking, but my people are way ahead of you. The ones going up to the crow's nest have their weapons in a tube that looks like a folded fishing rod. The other teams have their weapons in small golf bags."

"My remaining people will be spread out throughout the ship," Charlie said. "Half of my people will be in civilian clothes and will be stationed on each deck. They are equipped with handguns that have sound suppressors, as well as the dart guns. I will have two men with rifles stationed by the access panels above the dining room ceiling that opens from

159

Deck 6. I will have two men on each of the bridge wings. I am placing two in the laundry room and six in the engine room. Can you think of anything I missed?"

Suzy Q reminded Melinda that they have Amy in the secure room, and Marsha and John are inside guarding her.

Charlie said, "I will have a team on each floor. Since access to the secure room is in the atrium, it can be covered from two different floors. According to the plans, those who try to come on the ship while we are out to sea can only do so from Deck 8 in the back of the ship or Deck 4 on the sides. Once they are on the ship they can only get to Amy from the inside crew staircase, the inside crew elevator, or the passenger elevator in the atrium. They could use the passenger staircase, but that would put them in the open for two levels. I don't think they would want to be that visible, do you?"

Martin spoke up, "No, I don't think they would. What I do think is that their part of the operation was put together very quickly and I don't see them having the manpower to do the job properly. How many people can they fit in a small boat? I believe they will come in shooting, and the devil be damned. Are all of your people wearing Kevlar vests?"

"Yes," answered Charlie. "They are combat veterans and are fully equipped. We even have our own medic with us."

Rosemary asked, "What about additional security in the nursery?"

Melinda chuckled. "We will have all of our people here except Marsha and John. Ron will be heading up to the bridge and staying alongside the Captain. What I don't like is that Charlie is the only one connected in his group."

Charlie replied, "All my men have encrypted radios and are in contact with me at all times. Ron set up the jammer in the communication room. Most cell phones won't work this far out without going through the ships system. Even satellite phones won't work."

"We have four monitors," Stephen said. "Including Sheena and Benjamin, we will have one person watching each monitor."

"Does that satisfy you, Rosemary?" Melinda asked.

"I just worry about the babies," replied Rosemary. "I would like a radio so we can listen in on Charlie's part of the operation."

Melinda said, "I like that idea. Sheena and Benjamin will stay with you for the duration. I hope you people don't get to hate each other."

Charlie walked over to the sliding glass door and opened it. He went out on the balcony, glanced around, looked over the side and came back in. "I would like to station a man out there, as well. He would have a great view of this side of the ship."

"Okay," said Melinda. "Let's get everyone in position." She paused, looked at the wall clock and continued, "Special Five has told me that there are two boats an hour away from us. We have to assume that these are Amy's people."

Some of Charlie's people left the room and headed to their positions. One opened the balcony door, stepped out and closed the door after himself. Martin walked over and closed the drapes making the balcony very dark.

"Now let's set up in here," Melinda said. "Rosemary, go into the nursery with Stephen. Sheena, you go with Benjamin. Take some food with you. Here is a portable radio set to Charlie's frequency. Secure the nursery door as best you can. I don't think they are even aware that we know they are coming."

Turning to the rest of the team she continued, "We still have a little time before the suspects are close enough to board the ship. Better get something to eat."

"Conference call, confirm" said Melinda.

"Conference call online, confirmed," said the Computer.

"This is Valley Forge," said Melinda. "We expect an unknown force to board in a short time. We have personnel placed throughout the ship with orders to take prisoners, if possible. Everyone is equipped with dart guns. There is no way we can clear the passenger areas if there is a gunfight. There are thirty-five hundred passengers on the Valley Forge plus another two-thousand crew members. There will be collateral damage. We would like to keep the collateral damage to a minimum if possible. We have kept the Captain up to date. It is my understanding that he is slowly changing course to make it difficult for the boats to catch up to us. By changing course slowly, the passengers will not be aware of any problems. He has also been able to increase his speed by another three knots. We don't know how much fuel the boarders have. It would be interesting if they ran out of gas before they were able to board our ship."

Melinda continued, "We have our prisoner, Amy Gelz, in a secure location, and she is still sedated. Dr. Wellfleet found a tracker in her big toe. We have left it active. We expect the boarding force to head to her location. We have armed personnel inside the room and teams outside the room. Once the enemy force has boarded, we intend to have Special Five remove their escape route. I expect the action to commence within the hour."

"Special Five, Special Six," Melinda continued. "Once we have the enemy force on board the Valley Forge, I want you to destroy their boats when they pull away from us. Do you foresee any problems?"

"This is Special Five. We will wait until they are at least a mile away. Otherwise, the passengers will see or hear the explosions. I will inform you when we start our run on the enemy's boats."

"Roger," Melinda said. "Let us know when they pull away. We are going to try to take prisoners. That was why I didn't request they be destroyed on the way to Valley Forge."

"This is Special Five. Hope you can keep the collateral damage to a minimum. I have to assume they will not care what kind of damage they do. Watch out for hand grenades. I will be standing by."

"Charlie, are you still online?" asked Melinda.

"Yes," he replied. "I'm on an open line until this is over. What do you need?"

"Have any of your people reported in yet?" she asked.

"Yes," Charlie answered. "The boats are in view. They appear to be having problems keeping up. It looks as if the Valley Forge has changed course and now has a forty mile an hour wind across its bow. The little boats are having a difficult time, bouncing and cutting into the fourteen-foot swells and now have to deal with that wind across their bows. Our Captain is one smart sailor. He is causing the small boats all kinds of grief."

"I passed your remark on to the Captain, said Ron. "He has not said anything, but I see a small smile on his lips. If I did not know better, I would think he's enjoying this operation. I hope he doesn't have to deal with any dead passengers when this is over."

At 0300 Charlie asked the Computer, "Conference call, confirm."

"Conference call confirmed," replied the Computer.

"My men on Deck 8 have reported that there are two boats alongside the aft end of the ship," said Charlie. "There is one boat on each side of the ship. They have been firing grappling hooks at the Valley Forge. They are bouncing very much in the wake of the ship. The first two times they missed. The third time they both were successful. Their grappling hooks have connected on both sides of the ship on Deck 9. There are three men climbing up ropes on each side of the Valley Forge. The boats they came in have let go their lines and are falling behind. The men have climbed to just below Deck 4 and have stopped. Does anyone see them on the aft cameras?" Charlie asked.

"This is New York. We have them on the screen. They have stopped just below Deck 4. Special Five has reported that they can see one man on each side of Deck 4, just inside the balcony railing. They can't be seen by the men climbing up the side of the ship."

Twenty minutes later Melinda asked Charlie if his men were ready.

"Yes," he said. "They are ready. My men on Deck 8 will not be spotted until the suspects are unconscious on the deck. Deck 8 is the first deck the suspects can reach from the back of the ship. I just received a report from Special Six that only one man on each side of the ship is continuing to climb. The other four are using some sort of climbing gear and are moving horizontally along the side of the ship heading forward. It looks like they are trying to gain access on Deck 4. That is where the boxes were thrown off the ship. Can you send someone to Deck 4?" Charlie asked. "I will contact one of my teams on Deck 6 to proceed to Deck 4 to assist. They are the closest team that I have available."

Melinda looked around the room. "Jose, you're the only one available. Go to the starboard side and I will have Charlie's men cover you." Jose nodded, took his backpack and left the cabin heading to Deck 4.

"Charlie," Melinda said, "I sent Jose to Deck 4 on the starboard side. See if one of your men can cover him, and have your other man check out the port side. If your man on Deck 8 sees the enemy, he should shoot him. We did not expect the suspects to split up this way. Prisoners be damned. I do not want anyone to hesitate. If one of your men has a shot he should take advantage of it."

"Melinda," said Rosemary. "We can see the two men climbing up the rear of the ship. They are on Deck 7, and they have stopped again."

"Charlie," said Martin. "Why haven't your men on Deck 8 fired at the climbers?"

"Their radios are turned off," said Charlie. "They will wait until they have a clear shot. They will then take them as prisoners."

"They are climbing again," continued Rosemary. "The one on the starboard side has put his leg over the railing. He appears to have fallen on the deck, out of my sight. The one on the portside has stopped again. He seems to be calling out to his climbing friend. He's being pulled up onto the deck by his hair and is now out of my sight."

It took Jose five minutes to get to Deck 4. He opened the door and came out on the starboard side of Deck 4 amidships. He quickly looked over the side and saw two men almost at the opening on Deck 4. There were people strolling on the deck. He could not take a chance of being seen firing a weapon, even though no one could hear it. He quickly walked to the back of the ship. Jose grabbed the climber's arm, pulled him aboard and fired his dart gun at the same time. He knelt down, lifted the man over his shoulder and carried him to a lounge chair. He walked back to the railing, looked over the side and saw that the other climber was moving up to Deck 5. Jose leaned over, aimed and fired his dart gun. He watched as the man let go of his climbing gear and fall into the water. Jose glanced around to see if anyone was paying attention. No one was even looking in his direction. He moved quickly to the port side to see if he could catch the other climbers. As he turned the corner, he tripped over a dark shape on the deck. Jose leaned over and saw the body one of Charlie's people. His throat had been slit from ear to ear. Jose reached down, grabbed the dead man's arms and pulled him into a corner.

"Melinda," asked Jose. "Is there a sighting of the two that came up the port side? I found one of Charlie's people dead on the Deck 4. His throat had been slit."

"Rosemary," asked Melinda. "Can you find those two men?"

"Rosemary replied, "The cameras on the port side on Deck 4 are not working."

"New York," asked Melinda. "What about you? Can you find them?"

New York answered, "No. We have the same problem with the cameras on the port side of Deck 4. As soon as the suspects open any doors and come in from the outside, we'll spot them."

"Rosemary," said Melinda. "I'm going to need Sheena and Benjamin. I'll have Susan and Lucinda take their place."

"Okay, but what about your security?" asked Rosemary.

Melinda laughed. "I have Martin and one of Charlie's men."

Chapter 8

The nursery door opened and Benjamin and Sheena came out. Susan and Lucinda walked into the nursery and secured the door. Rosemary said, "I spotted someone on Deck 5 port side, heading forward. He is moving very quickly. He just went in the doorway midships."

"This is New York. We see him. He is dressed in a black jumpsuit, black boots and a black watch cap. He has on a black backpack. He is carrying a weapon in his left hand. He's put the weapon in a shoulder holster and took off his backpack. He took a small black box out of his backpack. It's a scanner. He is scanning the area around the promenade deck. It is as if he had a general idea where Amy is being kept. He is now scanning the area near the Guest Relations desk. He stopped scanning. He is aiming that black box directly at the secure room. I should have checked what frequency the tracker in Amy's toe was. Our jammer is not working on his scanner."

At 0400 on a conference call, Charlie reported, "One of my men on the promenade deck reported that he sees the suspect, and he is heading slowly in that direction."

Rosemary reported, "I see the suspect. I see two of Charlie's men approaching the suspect carefully, one from each side. The promenade is not very crowded. The suspect has spotted one of Charlie's men. The suspect has reached into his backpack. He has thrown his backpack at the door of the 'secure' room just as one of Charlie's men shot him with a dart. The backpack exploded when it hit the floor on Deck 4 next to the Guest Relations desk. The suspect is down from the dart. Six passengers, no, seven passengers and one clerk are down on Deck 4. Two of Charlie's men are down. Passengers are running to the other end of the promenade. There is fire and heavy smoke. Two of the sprinklers near the Guest Relations desk have started spraying some kind of chemical."

Charlie said, "I am heading over to that location. Everyone keep alert. We still have at least one other man running around loose."

Over the loudspeakers was heard, "Foxtrot, Foxtrot, Foxtrot, Deck 4 midships. This is not a drill. Mike, Mike, Mike, Midships, Deck 4, Medical Squad bravo." This announcement was repeated two more times, and then there was silence. Two of Charlie's men ran down the stairs and started assisting those who had been injured by the bomb. Within minutes, two fire teams showed up and sprayed those areas that were still burning. They had the fire out in less than five minutes. They turned the sprinkler system off as the ship's medical team showed up and started treating those passengers who were injured. Within fifteen minutes all of those injured were transported to the Medical Clinic for additional treatment. A maintenance crew started cleaning up the damage and drying out the rugs.

Charlie inspected the damage as the last of the injured were transported to the Medical Center. He said, "I'm at the explosion site. There was no damage to the 'secure' room except for some scorched paint. The bomb severely damaged the Guest Relations desk. The fire destroyed all of the decorations. The fire team did a good job of quickly putting out the fire. There were seven or eight people injured. They've been taken to the Medical Center. I don't know the extent of their injuries."

"Melinda," Charlie continued. "I've left one man on Deck 8 with the two prisoners. They have been secured, but I don't want them moved since there is still one man on the loose. I have requested Dr. Wellfleet to check the suspects for trackers. I am having my people start a search for the missing suspect on Deck 14. I have assigned two men to search, and there is a third man behind them, protecting their back. I am leaving the two men on the mast and one on the balcony in your suite. I have left two men walking in the promenade. Since the bridge is secure, and we have Ron with the Captain, I am going to take the four from the bridge wings and start a search on Deck 12."

At 0430, Melinda requested the computer to get Mason online.

"I'm online, Melinda," said Mason.

"How are you doing in the secure room?" Melinda asked. "Did the bomb do any damage to the room? How is our prisoner, Amy, doing?"

"This room is pretty soundproof," answered Mason. "We heard a little noise but not enough to excite us. Amy is still sedated. This is a lovely room but there is no monitor for us to watch to see what is happening around the ship. What is happening?"

"Right after we moved you to the secure room," said Melinda. "Six men boarded us from two high speed boats. We thought they would all climb up to Deck 8 and try to enter the ship on that deck. We had a surprise waiting for them. It didn't happen that way. We were surprised by the suspects' actions. Two suspects climbed to Deck 8, and Charlie's men captured them. The other four moved sideways towards the front of the ship and tried to enter the ship at the same place where the boxes had been thrown overboard. Jose caught one man on the starboard side, shot him with a dart and laid him out on a lounge chair. He was able to shoot the second man as he was climbing up to Deck 5. That one fell off the side of the ship into the water. When Jose went to the port side, he tripped over a body on the deck. It was one of Charlie's men. That man had his throat slit. It meant that there were two suspects roaming the ship. The cameras were not working on the port side of Deck 4, so we had to wait until they came inside. They both came in midships on Deck 5. Rosemary spotted one of the men at the same time New York did. Charlie's men moved towards the suspect. The suspect spotted one of Charlie's men and threw his backpack over the banister. It landed by the 'secure' door on Deck 4 and exploded. The second suspect disappeared."

"Was anyone injured?" asked Mason, with concern in his voice.

"Yes," answered Melinda. "Eight people were removed to the Medical Clinic. I don't know the extent of their injuries yet. There was extensive damage to the Guest Relations area."

"We are still secure," said Mason. "Amy is still sedated and all her numbers are within the nominal range. The only thing that bothers us is that we don't know what is happening outside this room. We did hear the announcement for fire fighters and medical but we didn't know why. Please keep us informed."

"Computer, conference call, confirm," Melinda said.

"Conference call, confirmed."

"Just to keep everyone up to date," said Melinda, "Two boats have come alongside and six suspects have boarded the Valley Forge. We have stopped five of them. We don't know where the sixth suspect is. We have started a search of the ship. I don't know how effective the search will be, since we are not sure what the suspect looks like. All we know is that he is wearing a black jumpsuit, black boots and a black watch cap. New York is reviewing all of the digital images to see if we have a clearer picture of the suspect. New York is putting together pictures of the suspects. They will send them to Interpol to see if they can identify any of the men. Since these suspects work in groups, we might get lucky on the identification. I want everyone to stay alert. The babies are secure in the nursery with Rosemary, Stephen, Susan and Lucinda. Sheena and Benjamin are assisting Charlie. I am in the suite with Martin and one of Charlie's people. I will keep you informed if there are any changes. Computer off."

Melinda made a cup of coffee and brought it to Charlie's man on the balcony. He thanked her, sat back and sipped his coffee. She returned to the dining room and fixed a cup of tea for herself. She sat at the dining room table and thought. *There is something wrong. They only sent six men. Why did they send so few men? If I had to do this operation, especially from the water, I would need a team as large as Charlie's, at least twenty-five men. Even the explosion on Deck 4 was wrong. It should have been more effective. It wasn't a large explosion. Yes, it injured some people, possibly killed a few. Why so obvious? They didn't come to rescue Amy, because they did not know she needed to be rescued. So what was the reason? All they knew was that Amy had a tracker. They did look for her. Why? For the baby? Did they assume from the limited call that she had the baby? Was the explosion a diversion? Are the suspects being directed by The Exchange?'*

Melinda said, "Computer, conference call, confirm."

"Conference call confirmed, Melinda," chirped the Computer.

"All of this seems to be a diversion, Melinda said. "The suspects who boarded didn't do a lot of damage. They did get our attention, if that was their plan. I think they are here for another reason, and I can't seem to put it together."

Martin walked to Melinda, took her hands, pulled her into a chair and handed her another cup of tea. "You have to stop and rest," he said. "You won't be any help to us if you are exhausted."

After Melinda finished her tea and put her cup down, Rosemary came out of the nursery, walked to Melinda and handed her Edward to hold. "This will relax you better than the tea," she said, handing Melinda a bottle for her to feed Edward. Melinda snuggled her nose into Edwards's neck, breathed in his baby smell, and relaxed. Edward started sucking the nipple of the bottle as if he had not eaten for a week. Melinda smiled, leaned her head back and sighed. Rosemary watched for a few moments, returned to the nursery and closed the door.

"Smart move," Stephen said, while he stood at the changing table. Rosemary stood there, watching him change Annabelle's diaper.

"You do that well," Rosemary said, smiling, wondering if he had children of his own. He wasn't wearing a wedding band she noticed, but that didn't mean anything. She noticed that every time she got near him she felt a tingle, her pulse went into high gear, and she got warm all over. Her smile broadened when she thought of that. She liked what she saw. Maybe this might turn into something.

Stephen laughed and said, "I had many cousins that I babysat over the years. I have changed more diapers than I could count. I have discovered at a young age that fathers would rather sit with a child in a dirty diaper then change it. I found it was an easy way to make money. I used to charge a dollar to change a diaper. I was also sneaky about it. I used to hold the baby bottle as well."

"You are a sneaky one," Rosemary remarked, laughing. "I gather you like kids."

"I love kids," Stephen answered. "When I get married, I want a batch. If for some reason my wife can't have kids, we'll adopt them."

Rosemary stood there admiring Stephen even more. She took Annabelle from him and placed her in the crib. She turned, put her arms around Stephen's neck and gave him a kiss.

Stephen stood there, stunned. "What was that for?" he asked, running his tongue over his lips liking the taste.

"Because I just felt like it," Rosemary said, walking away. Stephen followed her, turned her around, put his arms around her waist, leaned down and gave her a gentle kiss."

"What was that for?" Rosemary asked, trying to catch her breath, feeling the heat course through her body.

Stephen smiled. He placed his hand under Rosemary's chin and lifted her face so that he was looking directly into her eyes. He said, "Something happened when our hands touched the first day we met. I felt electricity flow through me. I have never had that experience before. I have not been able to keep you out of my mind since then. I don't know what it is, but I like that feeling."

Rosemary then turned to Stephen and opened her arms. Stephen smiled, walked to her, wrapped his arms around her and held her tight. "Is this what I think it is?" Stephen said.

"I hope so," answered Rosemary as she put her head on his chest.

Just then Melinda walked into the nursery carrying Edward. She didn't say a word, just watched the two young people in an embrace. She smiled, turned around, closed the door quietly and went into the sitting room. She walked to Martin and told him what she had observed in the nursery.

"Don't tell me we're going to lose Rosemary," Martin remarked, with a smile on his face.

"I don't think so," answered Melinda. "Or at least not right away. I think we might end up with another operative and Harry will lose a bodyguard."

"Melinda, Dr. Wellfleet is online," chirped the Computer.

"What is it?" asked Melinda.

169

"I scanned the prisoners for tracking devices," said Wellfleet. "Every one of them has a tracking device in their right shoulder. I have removed the tracking devices from all five and put the trackers in the lead lined box. The lead box works in shielding the trackers once they have been removed. I am going to wake up one suspect at a time and question him. I will let you know what happens."

"Ron," asked Melinda. "Are you keeping the Captain apprised as to what is happening?"

"I keep walking to the wall phone on the bridge," said Ron. "I make believe that I am getting information from the person I call. This Captain is no dummy. He knows something is going on, but he has not figured it out yet. It will not take him much longer to learn that we have another way of communicating with each other."

"I have another question, Ron," said Melinda. "Can you make a scanner powerful enough to find the missing man? Dr. Wellfleet said that each of the other five suspects had a tracker in their right shoulder."

"If we were out in the field, I could probably build a unit," replied Ron. "We are on an all metal ship. I don't know how effective a scanner would be. It might be good for the length of a room."

"That would be good for a start," said Melinda. "How long would it take for you to build one?"

"It wouldn't take long," replied Ron. "I have a scanner. I would just have to design a booster for it. I might even have the parts in my cabin."

"I am going to send Martin to the bridge," said Melinda. As soon as he is introduced to the Captain I want you to go back to your cabin and start building that scanner. Is there a way to modify the jammer so if we have to jam the scanners we can?"

"No," said Ron. "The jammer was made for the communication frequencies not for the scanners."

She turned to Martin. "Take a walkie-talkie with you. We will communicate with each other using that so as to fool the Captain a little longer."

"If the Captain is as sharp as Ron says," Martin said, "he won't be fooled for long." He put the walkie-talkie in his pocket, put the earpiece in his ear, and left the suite, heading for the bridge.

Melinda made a cup of tea and went out on the balcony. She sipped her tea as she watched the sun come up. She was standing next to the guard when his face exploded. She ducked and looked around.

"Melinda, where are you?" asked Rosemary.

"I'm on the balcony," she replied.

"Get back in to the cabin," yelled Rosemary. "Someone is climbing down the side of the ship just above your balcony. New York, are you getting this?"

"Yes Valley Forge," New York replied. "We saw him the same time you did. Where is Melinda?"

"I made it back in the cabin," Melinda said, breathing hard. "Charlie's man didn't make it. He was shot in the head." She looked down and saw that her clothing was covered in blood. "The sliding glass doors won't stop this man for long. I am going back into the nursery. Rosemary, hurry, unlock the door."

Melinda ran to the nursery door just as Rosemary opened it. As soon as Melinda entered the nursery, Rosemary slammed and locked the door. She and Stephen slid the dresser in front of the door.

"That's the best we can do," said Stephen. "Unless he plans to use explosives, we should be safe."

"Conference call," requested Melinda. "Confirm."

"Conference call confirmed," the Computer chirped.

"We know where the sixth man is," said Melinda. "He is trying to enter our suite from the balcony. I have joined Rosemary in the nursery and we have barricaded the door. I don't know what kind of damage he is planning to do. We need some help up here. Who is available?"

"I have four men one deck above you," said Charlie Pile. "They will be there shortly. I guess we are not a covert operation anymore, are we?"

Melinda laughed. "We still are covert. The Captain made an announcement that pacified the passengers. He said that there was a mechanical problem, which caused the disruption and fire at the Guest Relations desk. He didn't mention injured passengers."

Rosemary yelled, "The suspect just fired his weapon and is now climbing onto the balcony. I have lost sight of him."

"Charlie," Melinda said. "The suspect has walked into the living room. We can see him. It looks like he shot out the glass doors. I see lots of glass on the floor."

"Ron is here with the room key," said Charlie. "Get everyone down on the floor, just in case and cover your heads." Ron put the key in the slot, looked at Charlie, who nodded, turned the handle and pushed open the door.

171

Charlie's four men rushed into the sitting room followed by Charlie and Ron, and stopped. There was no one there.

"He is in the master bedroom," said Rosemary. "That camera is still live and I can see him checking the room. Get him when he comes out. He won't be expecting anyone. Here he comes."

As the suspect came out of the bedroom, he saw Charlie's men and opened fire with his machine gun. At the same time, he was shot with two darts. He collapsed to the floor. One of Charlie's men took the suspect's weapon. He turned him over and secured his hands and feet with zip ties.

"Melinda," said Charlie Pile. "We need medical assistance. Three of my men have been killed and one is wounded. I've also have been wounded. Our intruder had his weapon on automatic, and many bullets were fired before we got him. Did any bullets penetrate the nursery?"

"No, Charlie," replied Melinda. "Both the doors and the wall are steel. Bullets would have ricocheted off the walls. I notified Dr. Wellfleet. He is on is way with a medical team from the ship's Medical Clinic. I told him to bring three body bags."

"That was too easy," remarked Lucinda. "It was way too easy. There has to be something else going on."

"Special Five, have you destroyed the escape boats?" Melinda asked.

"Valley Forge, that is an affirmative," replied Special Five. "We sank them thirty minutes ago."

"Do you see any other boats approaching Valley Forge?" asked Stephen.

"This is Special Six. There is a lot of boat traffic. There is no one closer than twenty miles and no one heading in your direction."

"Computer online," said Melinda.

"Computer online, Melinda," said the Computer.

"Computer, get me Charlie Pile," said Melinda.

"I'm online, Melinda," said Charlie.

"How are you feeling? Melinda asked. "Did Dr. Wellfleet get there yet?"

"Dr. Wellfleet got here five minutes ago and took care of my wounds. I took two hits, one in the shoulder and one in the waist. Both were through and through. I'm going to hurt for a while, but I can still function."

"Where do we stand with personnel?" Melinda asked. "I know you lost one on Deck 4 when this first started. Then you lost two at the

172

explosion. One of your men was killed on my balcony. That is a total of four. Have you lost any others?" She asked.

"Yes," replied Charlie. "I lost six more. One fell down a flight of steps and broke his leg. The other one got his hand caught in a door and crushed his fingers. I lost three more that were killed in the shoot-out in your suite and one was wounded in the same shoot-out. All were taken to the Medical Clinic."

"Do we have enough men left to continue fighting?" asked Melinda.

"I thought we stopped them all," said Charlie.

"I don't think so," continued Melinda. "Lucinda remarked that she thought it was too easy. Either they already have people on board, or they are going to send another group to board the ship. They don't know that we captured five of their people, or do they?"

"Computer, get Dr. Wellfleet," said Melinda.

"I'm online," said Dr. Wellfleet.

"Did you ever check Suzy Q's assistant, Frank Barber, for a tracker?" she asked.

"No I didn't," he replied. "I didn't think of it. Do you want me to check him?"

Melinda thought a minute then said, "Yes, I think you should check him. Check all of them. If they do have trackers, remove them and put them in the secure lead box. You don't have to be neat doing it. Just slice and use a Band-Aid. Report when you're finished."

"I'm on my way," said the doctor. "I'll let you know what I find."

"Charlie, are you still online?"

"Yes, I'm still here Melinda."

"You didn't answer my question," she said. "With your losses, do you have enough personnel to continue this operation?"

"To be honest Melinda," he replied. "I don't think so. This ship is extremely large. I only had twenty-four to start with. I had to spread my men very thinly to cover all the main areas."

"Charlie, can you get more men?" asked Stephen.

"I don't know," replied Charlie. "I don't operate in this area. Let me see if I can contact my counterpart on the South American desk."

"Computer online," said Charlie.

"Computer online," answered the Computer.

"Get New York online," said Charlie.

"New York online," said the Computer.

173

"New York, I need someone from the South American desk," said Charlie Pile.

"Standby, Charlie," answered New York.

Ten minutes later Charlie heard, "Charlie, this is Fred Rodriguez on the South American desk. What can I do for you?"

"We are on a cruise ship, the Valley Forge," replied Charlie. "We just left Curacao and are heading northwest towards Ft. Lauderdale. A group of men came on board whom we believe are from one of the Mexican cartels. We stopped them, but a number of my men were killed or wounded. I was also wounded. We expect they will try again. We have two more days at sea. As it stands, we do not have enough people to stop another boarding. Can you get me some assistance?"

Rodriquez was quiet for a moment and then said, "Yes, I can. Do you have air coverage?"

"The U.S.S. Enterprise can send a couple of fighters if I need them," replied Charlie. "I also have two drones that are fully armed in the air above us."

Fred Rodriguez said, "I have several suggestions. I can send a group by helicopter and get them to you in about an hour. I can send out a group by boat. I could also send a group in as a night paraglide drop. You would have to wait almost sixteen hours for the last two choices. The choice is yours, but in my opinion, sending the men by boat would be the best."

"What kind of boats do you have available?" asked Stephen.

"Rodriguez replied, "We have high speed motor boats, high speed zodiacs, and a tug boat. You have the choice."

"Could you use the tug boat and paint the word 'pilot' on the side? Stephen asked.

"I can do that," Rodrigues answered."

"How fast can it be done? Stephen asked. "How fast can you get a group out here? Can they be in civilian clothes? They will have to wear something that we will be able to tell they are friendlies."

"I won't have to have them wear something special," said Rodriguez. "You will recognize them as soon as you see them. If it will make you feel any better, they will be wearing a lanyard with small hearts imprinted on them."

"That's great," Stephen remarked. "How fast can you get to us?"

"It's being plotted as we speak," said Rodriguez. "Standby. Okay. If we start out now it should take us about three hours. According to my navigator, if you can have the Captain slow the ship down to ten knots and make a slow circle, we can be alongside in as little as two hours."

"I spoke to the Captain," said Martin. If he slows the ship down the passengers might think there is a problem. Making a slow turn will work. He is starting the turn now. Suggest you transmit IFF. Let me know the frequency when you dial it in."

"Roger, Valley Forge," said Fred Rodriguez. Our IFF is 960.1125."

"Special Five, Special Six," called Ron. "We have friendlies coming from the Port of San Nicolas in Aruba. They will be transmitting IFF 960.1125."

"Fred," called Martin. "Are you coming with the group?"

"You bet," said Fred. "It has been too quiet around here. All we have here are drug smugglers, and we know who they are. They go out, we catch them, take them before a judge and they are out before we get back to base. You know how it is. Money talks, everyone walks."

"Been there, done that," Ron replied." Have you worked with Charlie Pile before?"

"I've worked with him twice," said Fred, both times successfully, but they were both harrowing adventures. Ask him to tell you about it sometime. Ask him to show you his scars."

"You know he was just wounded in this last attack, and he lost three men," continued Ron. "He claims he is still operational. The doctors patched him up and he is on his way back to us. He is able to walk but with difficulty. He is the only one in his group who is connected. How many in your group are connected?"

"Two of my men and I are connected," answered Fred. "The two men are my team commanders. I will be bringing three teams. Each team has eight people. The call sign for Team One is Four-eight. Team Two's call sign is Four-four. Team Three will answer to Four-three. Each team leader is in contact with their men via encrypted radio."

Sometime later, Rodriguez called Valley Forge and said, "Ron, we have you in sight. We see the ship turning to its final leg. We will come alongside your port side in twenty minutes."

"Roger, Four-eight (Team one)," said Ron. "Door is opening now."

"We see it," said Fred. "You won't have to drop a net. We are the same height as the hatch."

"How many people did you bring?" asked Ron in amazement.

"I brought twenty-five people, including myself," exclaimed Fred. "I would have brought more, but I couldn't find another boat big enough

175

that would fool your passengers. They are used to seeing a pilot boat and we didn't want them to be suspicious when we pulled up."

"Now I see why you told me your men wouldn't need any special identification," said Ron. "They are all less than five foot tall and dark as ebony. I love it. If we give them white jackets they would be able to move around the ship as staff."

"That's a good idea," said Fred. "Here come my seconds in command." Fred introduced the leaders of Team Two (Four-four) and Team Three (Four-three).

"Now I understand their call signs," said Ron. Turning to Four-three he asked, "Is that your actual height?"

"Yes it is," Four-three, answered. "We found it easier than using our names. No one can pronounce them anyway," he said with a laugh. "We have trouble pronouncing your names, so I guess we're even. Besides, it gets a laugh when we use our call signs."

Fred started to introduce his men. Ron stopped him. "When we get upstairs, you can do the introductions," said Ron. "This way you will only have to do it once." He stopped and watched, as equipment was unloaded from the tugboat into the Valley Forge. "What have you brought onboard?" he asked.

"We fight differently than you do," said Fred. "We have our own weapons."

"I hope they have sound suppressors on them," said Ron. "We don't want to upset the passengers again. That explosion on Deck 4 three hours ago was enough."

"Oh, I guarantee you won't hear a sound," Four-three said with a laugh in his voice, "and neither will the enemy."

When all the men boarded the tugboat pulled away and dropped behind the Valley Forge. The hatch door started closing.

"Martin," said Ron. "Everyone is aboard. You can tell the Captain he can resume his normal course and speed. Make sure you thank him. I'm bringing Fred Rodriguez and his men up to the suite. Everyone is in for a surprise."

Ten minutes later, Ron, Fred, and his group of twenty-four gathered outside the suite. "Melinda," said Ron. "We're outside the suite. Let us in."

"Just a moment Ron," said Melinda. "I want to secure the babies in the nursery first." She made sure that Rosemary, Stephen, Lucinda and Susan were aware of what is happening.

176

Rosemary sat at the monitor to watch what was going to happen in the next room. Melinda went to the door, opened it and stood back with her mouth open. Standing before her in the hallway were twenty-five people, all under five feet in height carrying a duffle bag on their shoulder. Their ebony skin shone from the light. Melinda invited them in and waited for Ron to introduce everyone. Ron introduced Fred and said, "I'll let Fred introduce his people."

Fred laughed at that introduction and with hand signals told his people where to put the duffle bags. "The reason Ron wants me to do the introductions is that he can't pronounce the names of my people. They decided that they would use the name that represents their height. It works for them, so it should work for us." He waved over both of his team leaders. "This is Four-three and Four-four," he said, with a smile on his face.

Melinda shook their hands. She was amazed at the smallness of their hands, but could feel their strength. She looked at everyone and noticed that they were all dressed the same. They wore black pants and cream colored shirts. "Now I know why Suzy Q sent up the white jackets and black bow ties," she said. "They will be able to wander around the ship, and no one would pay attention to them. I notice that some of your fighters are women."

Rodriguez smiled. "You are the only one that noticed that. How did you?"

"The males and females have different features. Their eyes are shaped differently and their mouths are shaped differently. I gather they are as fierce as the men or you wouldn't have brought them."

"That's right," said Fred. "All of my people are fierce fighters. Because of their size, most people do not see the sex. It works to our advantage."

"Charlie, are you still online?" asked Melinda.

"Yes. I'm still at the Medical Clinic," he said.

"I thought you were on your way up," Ron said.

"I was," Charlie replied. "I got on the elevator and one of the waiters was in a hurry to get somewhere. He pushed his cart in without looking. He knocked me against the wall, my arm caught on a peg and ripped my bandage off and tore open a couple of stiches. I had to be taken back to the Medical Clinic for a couple of additional stiches and a new bandage."

"How long before you are able to get back to the suite?" Melinda asked.

177

"The nurse is just finishing taping the bandage," replied Charlie. "This time they are fastening my arm to my side so I cannot damage it again. Okay, she's finished. I'm on my way up now."

Melinda turned to Fred. "Charlie Pile is on his way up. Would you like me to order lunch for your people?" she asked.

"I don't think so," said Fred. "We are pretty much self-sufficient. We carry everything that we need with us. We even carry our own water. That is why these duffle bags are so heavy." Fred pointed to the stack of twenty-five bags against the wall and said, "There is enough in those bags to keep us in the field for five days."

"What about weapons?" Melinda asked. "I have only sixteen dart guns left."

"We have our own weapons," continued Fred. "They are also in the duffle bags. We are waiting for our assignments from Charlie Pile. It will be good to be working with him again. He really knows his stuff."

Just then, Charlie walked in. He greeted Fred, Four-three, Four-four, and the rest of the crew. "Is everyone ready?" he asked.

Everyone nodded and made a strange clicking sound with their tongues. "Get your weapons ready while I explain the situation," Charlie said. He unrolled the floor plans of the ship with his one good hand. Everyone gathered around him as he explained what he wanted them to do. When he was finished, he rolled up the plans, placed them in the cabinet and turning to Fred said, "It is up to you and your people to protect Melinda and her babies. Try not to take out any of the passengers if you can help it, but don't let that stop you. We don't know what they are going to try next, so be alert." He sighed, sat down on the couch and winced with pain. Ron brought him a cup of coffee.

"I think you have to sit out this part of the operation," said Melinda. "I can set you up in the nursery. You can guard the door."

"No," said Charlie. "I'll stay out here and keep an eye on things. I'll sit by this monitor."

"Martin," asked Melinda. "While it is quiet, why don't you invite the Captain to our suite and introduce him to everyone. After all, his ship was damaged, and he doesn't even know why. I think it is time for him to be informed."

"The Captain agreed to come with me to the suite," said Martin. "We'll be there in five minutes."

"Everyone, listen up," Melinda said. "The Captain is coming for a visit. I want all of Fred's men to go into the master bedroom. I want you to wait until I call you." She pointed to her left. They all filed into the bedroom and partially closed the door.

Moments later, the doorbell rang. Melinda went to the door, checked the peephole, opened the door and stepped back. She invited the Captain and Martin into the suite and closed the door. "Captain," she said. My name is Melinda Xavier. You have met Martin my husband. Standing next to him is Ron Sullivan, who is in charge of this group. The man sitting on the couch, with his arm wrapped in a sling, is Charlie Pile. He is in charge of our Caribbean desk. Standing next to him is Fred Rodriguez, the head of our South American desk. I was informed by our New York office that you have a top-secret clearance. That is why I am able to tell you about us. We have the responsibility of finding and stopping a very large smuggling ring that is using your ship to smuggle money and drugs throughout the Caribbean. If that were all we had to do, you would not even know we have been aboard your ship. However, a second problem has arisen."

Melinda paused, looked at the Captain and continued. "A contract was taken out on me. One of the cartels that we damaged last year has put out a two million dollar contract out on me. They want to hurt me. The only way they can do that is to take one of my babies. They were almost successful. One of my people, Susan, was attacked in Castries. She had been sprayed with a poison called ricin. She collapsed while ashore, but was able to alert us. We were able to get her to a hospital in St. Lucia. Her attacker was able to impersonate Susan and get on board this ship. Your Security people were not aware that Susan was taken to the hospital. Susan's attacker did a good job of impersonating Susan, and even had an excellent forged key card. Your Security people did not look very closely at the impersonator, so she walked right on. We found out as soon as we sailed and were able to capture her, learn what her job was, and who hired her. We secured her in the room next to the Guest Relations desk."

Melinda continued, "The Valley Forge was intercepted and boarded early this morning by six men from one of the cartels. We caught four of them immediately. The fifth man was able to get into the atrium, and before we could stop him he threw an explosive that damaged the Guest Relations desk. The explosion hurt a couple of your people, a number of passengers and two of Charlie Pile's people. We started a search of the ship starting with Deck 14. The sixth man climbed down the side of the ship, shot the man guarding the balcony of our suite, and walked into the living room after shattering the glass doors. Everyone had moved into the nursery before the

179

glass doors were shattered. He finished searching the bedroom and walked into the living room. At the same time, Charlie, Ron, and his team came in. There was a gunfight in the suite. The intruder killed three of Charlie's men before he was stopped. The gunman wounded Charlie, as well as a fourth man. With the loss of more than half of his men, Charlie needed replacements. He called on Fred for help. I think that brings you up to date. Do you have any questions? "Melinda asked the Captain.

"Yes," he answered. "I have a few. How is Fred going to replace Charlie's men?"

Melinda smiled and said, "I thought I explained. "Hey guys, everyone out of the bedroom," she yelled. The bedroom door opened all the way. Twenty-four men, all under five feet tall, walked out of the bedroom and stood beside Melinda.

The Captain stood there amazed. "I thought pygmies were only in Australia," he said, looking at the group of tiny men with ebony skin.

"Captain," Fred said quietly. "We don't like the use of the word 'pygmy'. If you have to describe us as a group, we like 'little people' better. We are all originally from Australia. A few hundred years ago, our relatives were shipped here as slaves. Most escaped into the jungles of South America and thrived. As time went by, many of them came out of the jungle, and became part of Australian society. Our organization realized the benefit of recruiting some of the little people. They were very skillful in jungle fighting. Many of them even have college degrees."

"I'm glad you invited me to meet everyone," said the Captain. "I have only one other question. How do you communicate with each other? I know you don't use that silly walkie-talkie. How long do you think you could have gotten away with that farce?"

Ron looked at Melinda. She nodded her head and Ron answered the Captain. "We have communication equipment under our skin. All of our people have it including Charlie, Fred, Four-three and Four-four. The rest of the men have regular encrypted radio links. It does make it a little awkward, but it has worked for us this trip."

"I was instructed by Harry Blank to offer the communication package to you," Ron said. He went on to explain what it meant to be connected and how the privacy mode worked.

"Does that mean that we will always hear each other?" the Captain asked.

Ron smiled. "No," he said. "There is a privacy mode. You just have to tell the computer what you want."

The Captain thought for a minute and said, "I like the idea. It will allow me to know what is happening on my ship faster. I'm ready."

Ron went to the wall safe, opened it and took out the hypodermic needle. He put on the magnifier glasses and opened a small box. He took the tweezers, took out a tiny pellet and put it into the hypodermic." Take off your jacket and unbutton your shirt," he said to the Captain.

The Captain did as he was requested, and Ron injected the pellet. Then he asked the Computer to verify that the Captain was connected.

The Computer replied, "Confirmed. The Captain is connected."

"Computer, get me the Captain."

"Captain online," said the Computer.

"Captain," asked Ron. "Can you hear me?"

The Captain smiled and answered, "I hear you loud and clear. This is marvelous."

"You don't have to talk very loud," said Martin. "You will be able to talk without moving your lips."

"Captain," said Melinda. "I wanted to ask, have you had many complaints from the passengers about their cell phone reception?"

"Not as many as I thought we would get," said the captain. "Having me make that announcement in the beginning calmed them down before rumors could be spread. After all, we told them the truth. The cell phones would be out for two days."

The Computer chirped, "Harry Blank online for Melinda."

Melinda raised her hand to stop everyone talking.

"Hi Harry, "Melinda said. "I was just going to call you. The Captain is now connected. I have explained to him who we are and what we are doing on his ship. I also explained how his ship was damaged and how some of his passengers got hurt.

"I guess we should have done that in the beginning," said Harry. "The reason I called was to let you know that the 727 stopped in Haiti, the Caymans and Jamaica, and picked up all the prisoners and all the merchandise. The plane was full. Based on the few additional boxes we opened, the merchandise in that plane is worth more than the plane. When it flew from the Caymans, I made sure it had an armed fighter escort. I had the fighter escort stay with the 727 until it landed at Ft. Lauderdale. The plane is now in Ft. Lauderdale and unloading. Security was a killer. I had Special Ops handle security. Once the new crew arrives, and the airplane has been serviced, and fueled, they will fly to St. Lucia and pick up the suspects and the merchandise that were confiscated. I'll get back to you if anything changes."

"Just so you know," Melinda said. "When we arrive in Ft. Lauderdale, we will need a morgue truck at the pier. Charlie lost many of his people, and we have a number of wounded. I had to ask Charlie to get additional troops. He was able to get them from South America. When we get organized, I will give you a call. Talk to you later. Computer off."

Turning to Charlie, Melinda said, "I think you had better work with Fred and get everyone stationed around the ship. I also have to get maintenance up here to fix the shattered door."

The Captain walked to the balcony door and looked at the damage. "That's a mess," he said, shaking his head. "I'll call maintenance and have the door replaced. I wish I could tell them a rogue wave hit the side of the ship and did the damage," he said laughing. "This suite is on Deck 10, which is almost seventy feet above the water. There is no damage to the rest of the ship, and there is no water in the cabin. I don't think they would believe me." He said his goodbyes to everyone, left the suite, and returned to the bridge.

"I'm glad he's finally connected," said Martin. "That will give us another pair of eyes on the bridge and faster communications."

"Rosemary," asked Melinda. "Since the babies are sleeping, why don't you and Stephen close your eyes for a few hours and let Susan and Lucinda watch the monitors. I don't know how long it will be before the action starts again."

"Okay," replied Rosemary. "We can use a nap."

"Charlie," said Melinda. "You should have your men stand down. They must be exhausted. Let Fred's people keep the watch."

"New York," said Melinda. "I am depending on you to keep an active watch on the monitors. My people are exhausted." New York acknowledged the request.

"Computer, get Melinda," said Suzy Q.

"What is it, Suzy?" Melinda answered.

"We found two bodies in the back of the laundry room," she said. "They are Charlie's people."

"I don't understand," said Melinda. "How were they killed?"

"It looks like they were both stabbed in the back with a small sharp object," Suzy Q. answered. "We found them while we were taking inventory. We were moving boxes around and they were found."

"Computer, get Charlie Pile and Dr. Wellfleet online," said Melinda. When they came online, she told them about the murders on the laundry deck. "I want you to help Suzy Q move the bodies to the morgue"

"Conference call," requested Melinda.

"We have just found two more of Charlie's men killed," said Melinda. "They were stabbed in the back. Suzy Q found them when they were moving boxes for inventory in the laundry room. I don't understand how two men could be killed at the same time. It means we have more suspects on the ship than we thought."

"New York," continued Melinda. "I need you to review all the recordings from Deck 3. See if you can find me the killers."

"Fred," said Melinda. "I know it will be difficult, but have your men stay in groups of three. I think it would be safer."

"Melinda," said Fred laughing. "Trust me. My men are well trained in jungle fighting. No one can sneak up behind them. Don't forget where they come from, and where they have been training."

"Everyone, be careful," Melinda said. "I think the last action was a diversion. I still wonder how many crewmembers belong to the cartel. How did we miss seeing the killing on the monitors?"

Martin cleared his throat and said, "Do you realize how many cameras there are on this ship? Even with ten people watching, we're bound to miss something."

Melinda nodded her head. "Yes, I know," she said. "I figured we missed it because we were tired. I don't think any one person in our group has had more than three hours sleep without interruption. Rosemary reminded us of that awhile back. As always, she was right."

"Melinda," said Marsha. "Someone is trying to get into the safe room. Can you see who it is?"

"We will check immediately, Marsha," said Melinda.

"I'll be damned," said Martin, looking at the monitor. "Look who it is. It's Stephen van Deer, the man from Holland. I thought he was locked up in the brig with the other prisoners. How did he get out?"

"Suzy Q," said Martin. "Can you check the brig? That man from Holland, van Deer, has gotten out."

Martin told her to be alert and to take someone from Security with her when she goes to check the brig. He told her not to go there until Dr. Wellfleet finished examining the bodies.

Dr. Wellfleet finished examining the bodies, and he, Suzy Q, and a member of ship's security placed the corpses in the body bags and moved them to the morgue. When they finished moving the bodies they all headed for the brig. When they got to brig, they found five more dead bodies. It appeared that van Deer had killed them. The doctor examined each of the five bodies. He said to Suzy Q, "Two of these men have broken necks. I see no signs how the other three were killed. How can one man kill five people in close quarters?" he asked.

The Computer chirped, "New York is online for Martin."

Martin answered, "Yes, go ahead New York."

"We suggest an immediate blood test on all the prisoners. We suspect drugs were put in their food."

"The better question is," asked Martin, "how did van Deer get out of the brig?"

"Valley Forge, Valley Forge. This is Special Five. We are tracking a large vessel traveling at a high rate of speed in your direction. This boat is approximately sixty feet long. Its speed is in excess of sixty knots. If this boat maintains its course and speed, it will be alongside in less than five hours. We are tracking a second vessel heading in your direction with the same course but much slower."

"Roger Special Five," said Martin. "Keep us advised."

"Alert, alert," chirped the Computer. "Emergency call! There has been an explosion in the forward engine room. There is heavy smoke on Decks D, E and F. Fire teams and sprinkler systems have been activated. All communications are with portable units channel five. The Captain has been notified. Exhaust fans are now venting the smoke through the smoke stacks. Two people are dead and one wounded. Entire emergency has been confined to lower decks.

"Charlie," said Martin. "Contact your men in the engine room and find out what's happening."

"I've been in contact with Evan, one of my men," said Charlie. "He said that six men dressed in white coveralls came into the engine room with machine guns. Before Evan could draw his gun, he was pushed down the stairs onto the lower deck. He sustained a broken arm. He saw a satchel thrown against the outer hull. It exploded and destroyed two steam pipes and one water pipe and whatever wiring was alongside the steam pipes. Evan said that two of his team was blown apart by the bomb, and shrapnel hurt one other. He does not know how badly. After the satchel bomb exploded, there was heavy smoke. The sprinklers activated and the exhaust fans started. There wasn't any other damage. Evan said that the damage did not affect the engines. Medical and fire assistance is needed immediately. I told him that fire and medical were on the way and to call me if he needed anything else."

"Charlie," said Evan. "I see the fire team. "They are spraying some kind of foam. The smoke is almost gone. Here comes the medical team."

Turning to Melinda, Charlie said, "You were right, Melinda. The first attack was a diversion. It seems that they are going all out to come on board this ship. Why? Who are these men in white coveralls? That doesn't make sense. How are they communicating with each other?"

"I think," said Martin, "that there are more crew members that are part of the cartel on this ship than we realized. Who knows how long they have been on board the Valley Forge. That ship that is approaching us must have been paid a lot of money for them to try to board this cruise ship. Look how many men have been sacrificed for this operation. Have you noticed how different each group is?"

"Computer, get Melinda," said Fred.

"I'm here, Fred," said Melinda.

"I'm in the engine room with one of my teams. We were able to stop the six men that entered the engine room and threw the bomb. They never knew what hit them."

"Great," replied Mclinda. "Get them to the brig so they can be questioned."

"I don't think so," said Fred. "My men don't use sleep darts. We use something more lethal. I contacted Dr. Wellfleet. He is bringing a team from Security to wrap the bodies and put them in the morgue."

"At this rate," said Rosemary, "the morgue is not going to be big enough."

"Valley Forge, Valley Forge. This is Special Six. The large boat is still on a collision course. It is a large hydrofoil and it's three hours away from you. The second boat has changed course and is no longer a threat."

"Melinda," said Dr. Wellfleet. "We have moved the bodies out of the engine room to the morgue, and the wounded have been taken to the Medical Clinic."

"Computer, conference call," said Melinda.

"Conference call confirmed," replied the Computer.

"There is a sixty foot hydrofoil approaching us," said Melinda. "It has been on a collision course for the last three hours. It should be alongside in less than ninety minutes. I do not know how these people plan to get on board this ship. I don't even know why they want to get on this ship. We have been attacked by people dressed in white coveralls, just like the men in the engine room. There is no way to distinguish them from the real crew. Fred and his men have killed them. I don't know how many others on the ship work for the cartel. Be alert."

"Valley Forge, Valley Forge. This is Special Five. That large ship is thirty minutes away. It is fifteen minutes away from invading your safety zone. We have been given permission for weapons free at your call."

"Roger, Special Five," Melinda said. "We want them to continue. I think that is the only way to stop them. We were able to take a few prisoners and put them in the brig, but before we could question them, they were killed. We have two other prisoners that have yet to be questioned. They are still unconscious. We don't think they will be able to tell us much, however."

"Computer, get Harry Blank," said Melinda.

"I'm online," said Harry Blank. "What do you need?"

"We have a hydrofoil that is sixty minutes away heading in our direction," said Melinda. "The Specials have been tracking it for the last five hours. We expect them to try boarding the Valley Forge. We haven't figured out how they plan to board this ship. Special Five and Special Six are weapons free. I have asked them to hold off. I want to let the ship come alongside and try to board us. We have enough personnel to stop this *invasion*."

"What do you need from me?" asked Harry.

"I would like some naval support," replied Melinda. "I understand that the Enterprise is close by. Is it possible for you to have one of the missile boats come this way? If my thinking is correct, there will be people in the water before this operation is over."

"Okay, Melinda," said Harry. "I have asked the Battle Group Commander to move in your direction. They will parallel your course. What else do you need?"

"That should do it for now," she said. "Charlie lost most of his men. It is a good thing that he was able to get Fred and his people. I don't think the cartel even realizes that we have combat troops on board. I would still like to know what is so valuable on the Valley Forge, that they are using all their hidden assets to assault us."

"I have been asked the same thing," Harry said. "No one in my office has any idea."

"I have asked the Captain to keep the helipad clear in case we need it. The passengers are still not aware of what is happening on this ship. The fire and explosion in the forward engine room was confined to that area. The fire and medical teams used walkie-talkies for communications. My concern now is the ship that is heading our way. When it gets close enough for its men to board, what are they are going to do? When the ship comes close, it will alarm the passengers. I asked the Captain to make an announcement to keep the passengers from the starboard side. He was very funny. He told the passengers to keep off the open decks on the starboard side because refueling will be taking place. Martin just made a suggestion. Can you have a couple of marine platoons stand by? I might have to call on them if the action on the Valley Forge gets any worse."

"I've notified the Battle Group commander," said Harry. "He has increased their speed and is just over the horizon. The Enterprise will be only fifteen minutes flying time to your vessel. All you have to do is call."

"Fred," asked Melinda. "Are your men ready?"

"We are ready, Melinda. Are you going to allow the ship to come alongside?"

"Yes," she answered. "I don't know of any other way to deal with them. I don't know where all these fighters are coming from. We have not had time to question the two prisoners that we do have on Deck 8. We are still trying to find out how one of our prisoners escaped from the brig and killed everyone else that was in the brig with him. New York is reviewing all the digital recordings."

"Valley Forge, Valley Forge. This is Special Five. The big hydrofoil has stopped five miles off your starboard side and is putting small boats in the water. We see six boats heading in your direction. We see rocket launchers on their decks. We are still weapons free."

"Special Five, Special Six," said Melinda. "Destroy four of the boats. Let two of the boats get through."

"Roger, Valley Forge. We are attacking now."

Ten minutes later Special Five called, "Valley Forge, four boats destroyed. We show two destroyers heading toward the ship that launched these boats. The ship has turned and is trying to outrun the destroyers. One destroyer put a shell across his bow. He is not stopping. They have gotten up to full speed. One of the destroyers' fired a rocket. It hit that speeding boat in the stern. They are slowing down. They have stopped. The destroyer has put four boats in the water. They are heading towards the hydrofoil. Something is happening. The four boats have stopped. They are turning around and heading back to the destroyer. The hydrofoil is on fire. It has exploded. All of the boats are clear of the explosion. No, I'm wrong," continued Special Five. "I see two of the boats have capsized.

There are people in the water. The other two boats are picking the sailors out of the water. They are towing the overturned boats back to the destroyer."

"Thanks for the report," said Martin.

"Having only two boats coming to us instead of six should make it a little easier," said Fred. "My men are ready."

"The two boats are alongside our ship," said Rosemary. "I have them on the monitor. There are four men in each boat. They are firing grappling hooks at the ship and have failed to connect. They both are trying again. One boat succeeded. Now the second boat has succeeded in getting a grappling hook onto Deck 4, midships. Three men from each of the boats are starting to climb up the lines."

"Fred," asked Melinda. "Are you getting all of this?"

"Yes, I am," said Fred. "I have three teams heading to Deck 4. They are going to use the dart guns. They don't like it, but they will do as you asked. They are much better with their own darts. If it causes a problem, they will use their own weapons."

"I understand, Fred," replied Melinda. "All we need is one or two prisoners for questioning."

"The last man climbing up the line has stopped and attached something to the hatch on Deck 2," said Rosemary. "He is continuing to climb. The others are almost to Deck 4. There is an explosion at the hatch. There is a lot of smoke. I can't see the hatch. Now I see it. There doesn't seem to be any damage, just a large black mark on the hull. The six men have made it to Deck 4. The cameras on Deck 4 were never fixed. I have lost sight of the six men. The two boats have moved away from the Valley Forge. Special Five, they are all yours."

"This is Special Five, Valley Forge. We are still guns free. We are taking a run at both boats." Five minutes later, Special Five reported that both boats had been sunk and that there doesn't appear to be any survivors.

"Melinda," said Fred. "We have the six men. You have two that you can question. The other four didn't make it. Sorry about that," he said.

"Suzy Q, are you online?" asked Melinda.

"Yes, I'm online, Melinda," she answered.

"We need a place to keep the prisoners," said Melinda. "The brig doesn't seem all that secure, especially with van Deer still running around."

"We reviewed the digital recordings," said Suzy Q. "He had a key to the brig."

"I thought he was searched before he was put in the brig," said Melinda.

"He was. My Security people were very thorough," said Suzy Q.

"Then how did he get the key?" Melinda questioned.

"Looking at the recording, it seems that the key was passed to him by a woman who works in the laundry. We are trying to identify her. I showed her picture to New York, and they have put it into the facial recognition program. They will call me as soon as they get results."

"Has anyone found the Dutchman on the monitors yet? Melinda asked.

"I see him," said Rosemary. "He is strolling down the inside passage. He is walking as if he doesn't have a care in the world. Fred, can you get a team down there?"

"They are already down there in the inside passage," said Fred. "They are waiting for him. They are not equipped with the dart guns. They are using their own weapons. Sorry about that, Melinda."

"I understand, Fred," Melinda answered. "Let your people put him out of action. When they put him down, will there be any traces of blood?"

"Absolutely not," answered Fred. They use a dart that is so fine, that it goes between the cells of the skin, just like going to an acupuncturist. The poison on the dart is instantaneous. Every one of my men carries an antidote in case of an accident. The antidote has to be administered within five minutes for it to be effective. Otherwise, that person is dead. You might want to send a gurney to Deck 4 aft and have it left outside on deck. My men will come for it."

"This is getting very strange," said Melinda. "The suspects do not seem to be very efficient. For the labor that was being used, they haven't done a lot of damage. What are they trying to accomplish? What I don't understand is the way they are going about it. Nothing was happening on the Valley Forge until Martin and I came back on the ship with the babies in Ft. Lauderdale. Only our people knew we were coming back. The teams on the ship were still dealing with the smugglers. They were shutting down the smuggling that was going on as we came to each of the islands. We did not do the work on the islands. Charlie Pile and his men did that."

"I agree with you, so far," said Martin. "What is your point?" he asked, reaching for her hands.

"I'm trying to see if I missed anything," Melinda continued. "There has to be something."

Martin picked up the narrative. "For three days after we came back on board, nothing happened until the morning before we landed in Castries, St. Lucia. We watched boxes being put over the side and listened to the drones telling us how the boxes were being retrieved by boat. Charlie was aware of the boxes being brought ashore. His people followed the smuggled goods to their destinations, captured the suspects and shut the smuggling operation down for that island. He took the material and the prisoners to the airport. Charlie was able to secure the prisoners at the airport until a plane could be sent to retrieve them."

"That's when things started happening," said Melinda. "First, Susan is poisoned in St. Lucia and she is taken to a hospital. Jose stays with her. They discover the type of poison that was used on Susan. Harry Blank finds the antidote and sends it down to St. Jude's Hospital in Castries. He hears about the contract on me by one of the Mexican cartels. Because of that, he sends a bodyguard down for me without telling saying a word about it. I figured there was something going on, and I questioned Harry about it. He finally told me about the cartel hiring an assassin and him sending his bodyguard, Stephen. Stephen figured that the assassin impersonated Susan and alerted us. Rosemary thought that the assassin was coming after one of the babies. Remember, they wanted to hurt me, and that would have been the best way. The cartel put together this operation in three days. Once New York was able to identify the assassin, we laid a trap for her. We caught Amy Gelz, questioned her and kept her sedated. Dr. Wellfleet found a tracker in her big toe. We left the tracker there. We moved her to a secure room and kept her under guard where she is now."

"That was more than enough action on that day," said Martin. "The next two days at sea were very quiet. We captured the four other suspects that were part of the crew and put them in the brig with the person from Holland. Then we had action in the engine room. Charlie lost three of his people, and one of his men was wounded and so was he. Two boats came alongside, and two groups of men came on the ship. Charlie's men captured two of the suspects that had climbed up the back of the ship. Jose captured one more and killed one. Another one of Charlie's men was killed on deck. Two suspects entered the atrium, and one threw a satchel bomb at the secure room. The suspects didn't get in, but they damaged the Reception Desk and killed one of the clerks. When the bomb went off, it killed six passengers and wounded eight others. Two more of Charlie's men were killed by the bomb."

190

"This is the part I don't understand," said Melinda. "We were able to kill or capture all of the suspects that got on the ship. It was very easy. Lucinda thought that the cartel must have had many people working on the ship. I can't picture them assigning Amy alone to kidnap the babies. If they had so many people working on the ship, why didn't they come into the suite and accomplish their mission at any time."

"Maybe it isn't the babies they are really after," said Rosemary. "I think it is time to talk to the Captain. He might have an idea."

"Good thinking," said Lucinda.

"Computer online," said Melinda.

"Computer online," said the Computer.

"Get the Captain online," said Melinda.

"I'm online," answered the Captain.

"We are trying to figure out what is going on," said Melinda. "We have summarized everything that has happened since we came back on board the Valley Forge. It still does not make any sense. There has to be something else going on. It is not just about my babies and me. Before I call Harry Blank, I wanted to talk to you."

"Since I'm connected," said the Captain, "I suppose I should tell you. When we were in Curacao, we loaded a very special cargo. No one was supposed to know what the cargo was, except for the person who packed it, Harry Blank, the person who was the be the receiver and me. The cargo was listed on the manifest as '*machine parts*'."

"Is that what all this fighting is about?" asked Martin.

"Yes," said the Captain. "Harry Blank is aware of the cargo. That is why the U.S.S. Enterprise is just over the horizon. As good as the security was word must have leaked."

"What is so important about this particular cargo?" Rosemary asked.

"The cargo is a material called 'graphene'," replied the Captain. "The full name of the product is *Nitrogen-Doped Graphene powder*."

Martin asked," What's so important about graphene powder?

"Graphene has extraordinary properties," replied the Captain. "It is one hundred times stronger than steel, conducts heat and electricity with great efficiency, and is almost transparent when treated a certain way. There was a small company in Curacao manufacturing the material for the last six months. It costs almost four hundred dollars a gram to produce. We are carrying ten pallets. Each pallet weighs six hundred pounds. That means each pallet is worth over a billion dollars."

"Are you saying billion, with a b?" asked Martin.

"Yes," replied the captain.

Lucinda asked, "What is it used for?"

"It is used for all the things that 'rare earths' are used for," said the Captain. "Nano-technology needs it. Without it, we could not miniaturize cell phones, cameras, or any electronics. One of our fighter planes uses over 400 pounds in its electronics. We have only one mine in the United States that produces rare earth. China mines most of it and they have threatened to cut off our supply. Graphene was originally developed and used in medical equipment. In the development process, someone tried to coat a piece of copper with it. They were able to make the coating one cell thick. In the process, they found that it made the metal a hundred times stronger. Overnight, they found that the material became translucent as well. Harry and his group found out about this and were able to buy the entire production run of the company for the last six month. What we have on the ship is its first shipment."

"Why didn't they have a destroyer pull up and take the load?" asked Stephen.

"Harry didn't want people to question what the destroyer was doing in Curacao," the Captain said. "That is not a usual port of call for the U.S. Navy."

"I'm sorry," said Melinda. "This entire thing still doesn't make sense. Different groups have attacked us. We could not question the first group because the Dutchman killed them when they were in the brig together. When we did question the Dutchman, we found out that he worked for a cartel in Holland. At the time, we thought it odd. We assumed he from another cartel and placed on this ship. Dr. Wellfleet questioned the two from Deck 8 that Charlie's men caught and learned they were from a cartel from France. Even then we did not think it was strange for the same reason. We were able to question one man from the fight in the engine room before he died. He was from a South American cartel. Now here is the strange part. Each group is looking for a different cargo. One told us he was looking for diamonds. A second was looking for plutonium, and a third was looking for the Graphene. Not one of them knew what the shipping containers looked like. It was almost like a circus."

"I don't think it is over, either," said the Captain. "We have less than thirty-six hours before we get to Ft. Lauderdale. Until then we cannot let our guard down. When we get to Ft. Lauderdale NASA takes over and will supply security to their testing facility."

"Conference call," said Melinda.

"Conference call confirmed," replied the Computer.

"Everyone has been informed what has happened in the last three hours," said Melinda. "I don't know when or if we will be attacked again. I suspect that there are others on the ship that we have not caught. I want everyone to stay alert. Eat when you can. Keep on the move. Remember, a moving target is more difficult to hit."

Melinda continued, "The captain has informed me that the cargo that has to be protected is in the aft cargo hold and Deck 1. If we aren't attacked by sundown, we have asked the battle group to send some marines. It is only six hours until sundown."

Chapter 9

For six hours, nothing was happening. Special Five reported that the safety area around Valley Forge was clear and the Enterprise was fifteen miles away, paralleling Valley Forge.

On **Day 22** at 0100, Martin went to the ship's communication room. "Enterprise, this is Valley Forge. Over." called Martin.

"This is Enterprise. Go ahead Valley Forge."

"This is Valley Forge. Request the marines. Have them come up on the starboard side aft. Over,"

"Roger, Valley Forge," replied Enterprise. "They are on the way. We are sending six boats. Lieutenant Norma Pitman is in charge."

"Valley Forge, Valley Forge," called Special Six. "There are six small boats approaching your starboard side. Lead boat is broadcasting IFF 293.170."

"Roger, Special Six," said Martin. "Let me know when they are alongside Valley Forge."

Twenty-five minutes later was heard, "Valley Forge, Valley Forge, this is Special Six. Six boats are alongside your starboard side now."

"Roger Special Six," said Martin.

"Suzy Q, can you have the starboard side aft door opened?" asked Melinda.

"Door coming open now," said Suzy Q. "The troops are boarding."

"Have the troops stand down," Martin said. "Bring the lieutenant up to the suite."

"We'll be up in ten minutes," said Suzy Q.

Ten minutes later Suzy Q entered the suite with Lieutenant Pitman. Introductions were made to everyone in the suite. Melinda saw a short svelte woman with short black hair and a pleasant looking face. She was wearing a uniform of dark colored pants and shirt with a wooly pulley sweater. She wore her weapon in a chest holster.

Martin offered her a cup of coffee and invited her to sit at the dining room table. "Lieutenant, did they tell you what you will be doing on this ship?" he asked.

Pitman answered, "Yes, sir. I was told to follow your orders, but under no circumstances was I to allow anyone to remove the material in the aft hold."

"How many people do you have with you?" asked Ron.

"I have thirty-six people, including myself," she answered.

194

"Here is the problem, as I see it, "said Melinda. "Your weapons make noise. That is going to upset the passengers. As of now, the passengers know only of a small explosion in the atrium, and the Captain was able to explain it away. The passengers were told that the cell phone transmitter was broken, that was the reason given for no reception. They accepted that."

"Before we left the Enterprise we had all our hand weapons fitted with suppressors," said the lieutenant as she removed her weapon to show the suppressor.

"That's better than I thought," said Melinda. "We are not only expecting problems from outside this ship, but we have found that we are having problems from within the ship. We are dealing with four different cartels that we know of. The secret is out that we are carrying something very valuable. The cartels don't know what it is or what it looks like. They have sacrificed many of their men to get it. We have been able to stop them so far. We are not looking to take prisoners. We would like you to be aware that we have over thirty-five hundred passengers and fifteen hundred crewmembers on this vessel. I don't know how you will be able to tell the friend from the foe."

"We will do our best," said the lieutenant.

"Fred," said Melinda. "Show the lieutenant where she and her men can bunk down for the next two nights and then take the lieutenant's people and station them around the ship. I don't know how we will be able to disguise their uniforms."

Suzy Q said, "I'll get them white jackets that will cover their uniform shirts, and with their black pants it will look like they are cabin stewards."

"That is a good idea," said Melinda. "As soon as you can get the jackets to the marines, they can be deployed wherever Fred needs them. Charlie will be here in the suite if anyone needs additional information. He will be manning the monitors as well as the encrypted radios."

Charlie said, "I'm concerned with the amount of dead bodies that we have. The morgue has room for only thirty bodies, and we already have twenty-eight in there. Has anyone thought of where we will put the extra bodies?"

"Since this trip is almost over," said Rosemary, "they will have room in the ship's cold storage room. We will have to get the bodies off the ship before the inspectors come on board."

"I have a better idea," said Charlie. "Why don't we call the small boats back and offload some of the bodies to the Enterprise. They have a much larger morgue, and it would free up space in our morgue."

"Computer, get the Captain online," asked Melinda.

"Captain online, Melinda," said the Computer.

"Captain, please call the Enterprise and have them send the small boats back. We are going to transfer all the dead bodies to the Enterprise. We don't want dead bodies on a cruise ship with the inspectors coming on board when we dock in Ft. Lauderdale. Since the morgue is almost full, I thought it would be a good idea to move the bodies off the Valley Forge and onto the Enterprise."

The Captain acknowledged the request and got on a secure channel to the Enterprise. He explained the reason he wanted the small boats back. The boats had gotten half way back to the Enterprise when they turned around and started back to the Valley Forge.

"Valley Forge, Valley Forge. This is Special Six. The six small boats have turned around and are heading back to you."

"Roger, Special Six," said Martin. "Sorry we didn't notify you of the change. Is the area around Valley Forge clear of shipping?"

"There is a medium sized ship slowly gaining on you," said Special Five. "The ship is twenty-five miles off your port side. You have six small boats coming alongside your port side."

"Captain online," said Melinda.

"What is it, Melinda?" asked the Captain.

"We have a ship gaining on us. It is twenty-five miles off our port side," said Melinda. "Would you notify the Enterprise? Explain to them that we have two drones at thirty thousand feet, and their calls signs are Special Five and Special Six."

"Suzy Q," said Melinda. "The small boats are alongside the port side. Open the aft hatch and have them load the bodies and take them back to the Enterprise."

"Portside aft hatch coming open," said Suzy Q.

"Harry Blank online for Melinda," said the Computer.

"Yes Harry," said Melinda.

"I have been listening to the communication between Valley Forge and Enterprise," said Harry. "I didn't realize that you had so many dead. It is a good idea to transfer the bodies to the Enterprise. How are the marines working out?"

"Fred is positioning them around the ship now," said Melinda. "Between Fred's men and the marines, we have over fifty fighters. That had better be enough. We are not concerned about people coming on board this ship from another ship. With our digital cameras all over the ship, we can watch for any trespassers. Our main concerns are those who are already on the ship that work for the cartels."

"Melinda," said Rosemary. "Lieutenant Pitman is trying to reach you on channel six."

Melinda picked up the walkie-talkie and changed the channel. "Yes, lieutenant?"

"I went to check on the placement of my people and found two of my men dead."

"Where are you?" Melinda asked.

"I'm on the starboard side Deck 9 aft," she replied. "Both bodies had stab wounds in the back."

"Dr. Wellfleet online," said Melinda.

"Yes, Melinda," answered Dr. Wellfleet.

"Contact Lieutenant Pitman on channel six," she said. "She has found two of her men dead on Deck 9 aft."

"Computer, conference call, confirm," said Melinda.

"Conference call confirmed," replied the Computer.

"I just received a call on channel six from Lieutenant Pitman. She found two of her men dead. They both had been stabbed in the back. She found them on Deck 9 aft. Be on the alert. Fred, relay this information to your people on channel five."

"Melinda," said Fred. "Two of my people just reported that they were attacked on the Deck 7 inside corridor."

"Was anyone injured? "Melinda asked.

"None of my people were hurt," Fred replied. "I have three bodies waiting for Dr. Wellfleet. We will move them to the outside deck and cover them with a blanket. No one is paying any attention to our actions. They probably think it is part of the entertainment."

"Computer, get Dr. Wellfleet online," said Melinda.

"Yes," said Dr. Wellfleet. "I heard Fred. I'm almost there. I have four Security people and two gurneys with me." Dr. Wellfleet approached the covered bodies. Making sure no one was paying attention to his actions, he uncovered the bodies, examined them and helped put them in body bags.

"Fred online," Said Dr. Wellfleet.

"I'm online doc," said Fred.

"I don't know what poison you use in your darts," said Dr. Wellfleet, "but these men are stiff as a board." He filled the body bags, and with the help of Fred's men, was able to lift them on the gurney.

"Do you want me to give one of them the antidote, so you can question him later? Fred asked."

"I think that would be a good idea," replied the doctor. "These men seem to be from a different group than the ones we caught earlier."

Fred called to one of his men to give one of the suspects the antidote for the poison. "Make sure he is secured to the gurney. I don't want any accidents when he wakes up. One of you stay with him."

"Dr. Wellfleet," said Fred. "Where do you want my men to take the prisoner? I was told that the brig isn't secure."

"It's secure now," said Dr. Wellfleet. "Additional locks were added that no one can access except our people. Ron has added another camera with motion sensors outside the brig. We can view both approaches as well as the brig itself. Ron also installed microphones in the brig incase the prisoners decide to talk to each other."

"By the time we get these two bodies into the morgue," said Fred, "the third suspect will be waking up. I would suggest you question him as soon as possible. I don't want any accidents to happen to him while he is in the brig. Suzy Q called and told me that they still have not been able to identify the woman from the laundry room who gave van Deer the key. We have to assume she also had access to their food. They still have not been able to match her picture with the ID cards in the Security office. I hope that doesn't mean we have more impersonators on the ship."

"Melinda," said Fred. "Pitman's men of Deck 3 are under attack. I have sent two teams to assist."

"Computer, conference call," said Melinda.

"Conference call confirmed," said the Computer.

"Pitman's people are under attack on Deck 3. Fred has sent assistance. We have secured the nursery and the suite. Pitman has already lost two of her people. Keep alert."

"Melinda," called Dr. Wellfleet. "I questioned the last suspect who was given the antidote. He is a sergeant in charge of twenty men and five women. They had various jobs on the Valley Forge. They were placed here six weeks ago. His instructions from his captain were to learn how drugs were being smuggled to the Caribbean using the Valley Forge. Then a week ago, he received a change in his orders. His captain wanted him to investigate a special shipment that was going to be loaded on the Valley

Forge in Curacao. As soon as he was able to locate the shipment and where it is was being stored, he was to contact his captain. That is all he was told. He notified his captain that he watched a truck unload four pallets of material. Two dozen men with machine guns were also watching the loading process. He had been unable to find out which cargo hold they are using for those pallets. He has not observed any increase in security since the material had been loaded on the ship. He was told by his captain that there are people on the ship from other cartels who want that cargo, and he was to use whatever means he had at his disposal to stop them."

Day 23 At 0300 hours.

"Computer, get Harry Blank online," said Martin.

"Harry Blank online, Martin," said the Computer.

"Harry," said Martin. "We now have four different cartels on the ship fighting over an unknown cargo. All they heard were whispers that the Valley Forge was carrying a cargo that was extremely valuable. I guess there were too many people who knew about the shipment. If more than one person knows about it, it's not a secret. It appears that each cartel wants the cargo. They are killing each other, and our people ended up in the middle of the fight. A cartel attacking a cruise ship is piracy on the high seas. Charlie lost more than half of his people that be brought on board. Lieutenant Pitman has started losing some of hers within six hours of coming aboard. Fred is the only one that has not lost any people. They seem to be in the right place at the right time and know who the bad guys are. I don't know how they can tell the difference. One of our concerns now is the passengers. The fighting has extended into the passenger areas."

"What do you need?" Harry asked.

"I don't really know at this point," said Martin. "I'm just keeping you up to date. We have enough personnel. The Captain has been a big help. He has allowed us to install the jammer in the communications room and has explained to the passengers why they are not getting service. He has literally turned the ship over to us. It bothers him that many of his crew are members of the cartels and that some of the passengers have lost their lives because of the fighting."

"Fred," this is Pitman. "I just received a report from one of my people. She found two bodies on Deck 15, starboard side, forward. The bodies were laid out on lounge chairs covered with blankets. There was one male and one female. Each had been stabbed in the heart. What do you want me to do?"

"I'll contact Dr. Wellfleet," said Fred.

"Computer, get Dr. Wellfleet," said Fred.

"What do you need, Fred?" asked Dr. Wellfleet.

"One of Pitman's people has two dead bodies on Deck 15, starboard side, forward. She is standing by until you get there to retrieve the bodies."

"Okay," said Wellfleet. "I'll get Security and head up to Deck 15. We should be there in ten minutes."

"Pitman," said Fred. "Dr. Wellfleet is on his way. He will be there in ten minutes. Notify your people."

"Charlie," asked Fred. "Are you missing any people? We have two dead bodies on Deck 15."

"No," replied Charlie. "I paired the rest of my men with Pitman's people."

"Melinda," said Fred. "Passengers are being killed and we don't know why."

"I'll contact Harry and see if he knows why," said Melinda.

"Computer online," said Melinda.

"Computer online, Melinda," said the Computer.

"Get Harry Blank," said Melinda.

"I'm online, Melinda," said Harry.

"Do you have any idea why passengers are being killed?" Melinda asked.

"We just had a meeting," replied Harry. "It was brought to our attention that some of the passengers are part of different cartels. I would think they have good intelligence and know who belongs to what group. All you can do at this point is to quickly transport the bodies to the morgue. It is a good thing you removed the other bodies to make room."

Rosemary turned to Melinda and said, "So now we are garbage men. We are tasked with removing the trash."

"I know it seems harsh," said Melinda. "It has to be done, and we seem to be the only group equipped to do it. I can't see leaving the bodies around the ship for the passengers to find. That would really get the passengers' knickers in a knot."

"Valley Forge, Valley Forge. This is Special Five. That ship is now twenty miles off your portside."

"Computer, conference call, confirm," said Melinda.

"Conference call confirmed," replied the Computer.

"We have another ship approaching us on the portside. It is less than twenty miles away and coming on slowly. We do not know her intentions at this time. According the Special Six, there are eight small boats on its deck, and no heavy weapons are visible. Keep in mind that we still have many people on the ship who are not our friends. At the rate we are losing people, we will not have anyone left by the time we get to Ft. Lauderdale, We only have to keep going for twenty-four more hours. Stay alert."

"Valley Forge, Valley Forge. This is Special Six. That ship is fifteen miles away coming up on your port side."

"Computer, get Melinda and Dr. Wellfleet," said Fred.

"Melinda and Dr. Wellfleet online, Fred," said the Computer.

"One of my men has informed me that they now have seven bodies that need to be retrieved. It's too late to administer the antidote. We are moving the bodies to an inside elevator and sending them down to Deck 1. That should make Dr. Wellfleet's job easier."

"I wish there was a way to lock the passengers in their cabins until the fighting is over," said Martin.

"Or until we pull into Ft. Lauderdale," added Lucinda.

"With so many groups fighting," said Rosemary. "I think we should all go into the nursery. The sitting room is not secure. The door to the hallway is only a two-inch aluminum hollow door. In won't stop a fire ax or a bullet. The nursery door is solid steel and should stop everything except a fifty caliber bullet. Luckily no one carries that kind of weapon on an assault."

"I agree with Rosemary," said Ron. It is only a matter of twenty hours before we dock. If the fighting gets worse, we call the Enterprise and tell her the situation. They can have more marines come here by helicopter. It would only take them less than twenty minutes."

Melinda said, "I agree with you but I think using helicopters will alarm the passengers. Some of the passengers are aware that we have some problems. There are over thirty-five hundred souls on this ship, plus the crew. As long as the killings do not take place in the middle of the atrium, no one is going to be any the wiser. All of the killings have been quiet. Even the people coming on board are using suppressors on their weapons."

"Melinda," said Lucinda. "There is a report of a gun fight on Deck 3 between two different groups. I now see Fred's people coming up behind both groups."

Ten minutes later, Lucinda continued. "The gunfight is over. There are bodies all over the corridor. I'm waiting for Fred to give me a final body count."

"Lucinda," said Fred. "My people report that they have stopped a gunfight on Deck 3. There are fifteen bodies portside between the middle and forward elevators. There is no way we can cover up the bodies. We are going to move them to the inside corridor. We need help."

"Help is on the way," said Melinda. "Just drag the bodies out of the passenger area. Gather up all the weapons and have them brought to cabin number 2309. Benjamin will meet you there. Sheena will bring you the body bags. Dr. Wellfleet is working down by the morgue. He will check the bodies before they are put in the morgue."

"Rosemary," said Melinda. "I'm glad you had that idea to move the bodies to the Enterprise. Fred will fill the morgue before the day is over. Where did you say we will have to put the bodies when the morgue is full?"

"The Captain told me that he has had the cold storage room partitioned," Rosemary said. "That is where they store the fresh vegetables. More than half the room is available in which to put the bodies. However, before we get to Ft. Lauderdale, we have to remove them. He is not allowed to have bodies and food in the same room, even if it is partitioned."

"Valley Forge, Valley Forge, this is Special Six. That ship is ten miles off your port beam, slowly closing. We have permission to fire on that ship, at your call. Over."

"Roger, Special Six," said Melinda. "We still do not know their intentions. The Captain has warned them that they are within the Valley Forge's safety zone. They have ignored the warning. If they come within five miles of us, I would request a gun run down their starboard side."

"Roger Valley Forge. We are standing by, said Special six."

"Charlie," said Pitman. "We are forward outside Deck 7. There is another gunfight on the starboard side between people in white coveralls and black jumpsuits. We are staying back and just watching. It is like watching a movie. One group knows how to use weapons. The other side doesn't. The fight won't last long. When it is over, we will take out the winners. Are you seeing this on the monitor?"

"This is New York. We are watching it all. I wish we had audio. How many people are on board that we know that are part of the cartels?"

"We thought you could tell us," said Charlie. "They seem to be coming out of the woodwork. Now we have to deal with the ship that is approaching off our port side. We can see it. The ship is about two hundred feet long, has a white top, and a black hull. It has a helipad, but I don't see a helicopter. I can see four boats strapped to its deck. It seems to be intent to come alongside the Valley Forge. Special Six has made a gun run down its starboard side, but this isn't stopping them."

"Fred," said Charlie. "Stand by. The white ship is on our port side. They have thrown grappling hooks. They are sending people onto the Valley Forge on Deck 4. It looks like two platoons, at least. They are all dressed in khakis. That should make it easy to identify them."

"We see them," said Fred. "We have a surprise for them as soon as they all get on board. Let me know if any additional troops come off the ship. I will try to keep a few of them alive for questioning. Are we allowed to dump the dead ones over the side?"

"Sorry Fred," said Martin. "I can't allow you to throw bodies in the ocean. It might sicken the fish. We have plenty of room to store the bodies. Give Dr. Wellfleet a couple of prisoners to question."

"We are going to need help on Deck 4. The bodies are getting in our way. That ship sent thirty-six people onto the Valley Forge. I now have thirty-four dead and two that will be ready for questioning in five minutes."

"Fred," said Lucinda. "It looks like they are getting ready to send some more soldiers. I am unable to count them. There are too many. I see them mounting fifty caliber machine guns on their starboard side. Special Six, can you make a run down their starboard side and kill the fifty calibers?"

"This is Special Six. Special Five is making the run now at high speed."

"Good shooting, Special Five," said Lucinda. "The three fifty caliber guns were destroyed. The men are looking around wondering where the shots came from. How fast were you going?"

"This is Special Five. I only went three hundred miles an hour. I could have done it faster. If you didn't have men on the deck on the Valley Forge, I could have made a gun run down the deck and ended this attack."

"Thanks, Special Five," said Mclinda. "We can't let you have all the fun."

"Harry," said Melinda. "We are still trying to find out who they are. We have taken prisoners from this group, and when Dr. Wellfleet has a chance, he will question them. He is so busy with all the dead bodies, that he has not had much time for the questioning. We asked the Captain to allow us to use the ship's doctor and he has agreed. All we know is that these suspects heard that we had an extremely valuable cargo on board, and they want it. One cartel already had men and women on the ship to learn about the smuggling operation. Their orders were changed and they were told to find out what the valuable cargo looked like but were never able to find out where the cargo was stored. That part of the secret was well kept."

"Charlie," said Fred. "We need some help on Deck 4. We are holding our own, but a couple of the suspects have gotten past us and into the ship."

"We couldn't see what is happening on Deck 4," said Lucinda. "We can see what is happening inside the ship. We are directing Pitman to go after those that get past you. She is sending a squad that will come out midships on the port side. Make sure your men stay low."

"They can't get any lower unless they have a shovel," remarked Fred, laughing. "We have been able to deal with those on deck. I am concerned with those that got away. I see that a few of them are trying to sneak around to the front of the ship. Direct Pitman's squad to split up and come around the ends of the deck. Catch them before they get to an entry door."

"Good suggestion," said Lucinda. "Charlie will pass it on to Pitman."

"Fred," said Martin. "That was a good idea. Pitman's people were able to stop them from both ends. She lost three of her people in the process. Watch for her people coming around the aft end of the deck."

"Roger, Martin," said Fred. "I see them. You have to see the surprised look on the suspects' faces. They did not expect any problems. I can see my men are getting mad. They are not used to a scrimmage lasting so long. I don't even have to do anything. My people are that good. With Pitman's people surprising them by coming around the end of the deck, we were able to kill the rest of them. We took two of them and administered the antidote. When they wake up, Dr. Wellfleet will be able question them."

"Melinda," said Fred. "We see many passengers watching what's happening on the deck. Is there any way to get them away from the windows? If we have an explosion on deck, or a stray bullet, there will be a lot of flying glass."

"Harry," said Melinda. "We asked the Captain for an idea. He came on the speaker system and explained to the passengers that a movie is being made and filming on Deck 4 has been completed for the day, except for the cleanup. It worked. Everyone went about their business, and our Security people were able to move the bodies down to the morgue. The morgue is now full. Any additional bodies will have to go in the vegetable cold storage room."

"Fred," called Pitman on channel 5. "There are snipers on Deck A. I have two people down. They are alive, but seriously wounded. Medical assistance is needed on the inside corridor aft. We have no cover. If you can spare some of your people, send them down the aft staircase. We are one level below Deck 1."

"Pitman," said Fred. "I'm sending down a squad on the aft stairway and a squad down the middle stairway. Keep your heads down."

"I see your men," said Pitman. "It looks like they are floating in the air. How do they do that? Two of your men floated by, distracted the sniper, and the sniper fell down. Watch out! There is another sniper shooting from Deck B. One of your men is down," Fred. "The sniper is down. We need medical assistance on Deck A, aft. We also need body bags and Security to help move them to the morgue. I have never seen anything like this before. This is more like jungle fighting. We never trained for this. I have never lost so many men before either. Our job was to make sure the special cargo is secure and we have never seen the cargo."

"Jose," asked Melinda. "Do you and Susan feel up to helping Pitman?"

"Jose turned and asked Susan, "Do you feel rested enough to join the fight?

Susan smiled and said, "Yes, I'm fine. I rested in the hospital."

"Do you feel like a little shoot-em-up, bang, bang?" said Jose.

"It has to be better than sitting here," answered Susan as she checked her weapon. "I'm ready. Open the door." The door was opened and Susan and Jose left the nursery, checked the sitting room and left the suite.

"Charlie," asked Melinda. "Where are you sending them?"

"I want them to work with Pitman," he said. "Maybe show her a thing or two about warfare on a ship. It might save her life. She has lost twenty-five percent of her team in less than three hours. That has to be tough on a first time commander."

Day 24 At 0200 "Computer, get Melinda online," said the Captain.

"I'm online, Captain," said Melinda.

"Melinda," said the Captain. "I just received a call from the battle group commander aboard the Enterprise. He told me that they have captured the ship and arrested their captain and crew for piracy. There were almost one hundred more soldiers down below in their hold. The battle group commander doesn't know why these soldiers didn't join in the attack on the Valley Forge."

"Okay," said Melinda. "I'll pass the information to the rest of the teams."

"Melinda," said Charlie. "I guess it was a good thing. At least they are alive."

Melinda turned to Martin. "I am getting worried about all this sniping and open warfare on all the decks. There has to be a way to stop it. We only have twelve more hours before we dock. No one has attacked the aft storage room where that special cargo is located. Special Six says that there are no ships within twenty-five miles of us except for the battle group which is twelve miles away. Dr. Wellfleet has reminded me that we need to remove the additional bodies before we dock in Ft. Lauderdale. According to the Captain, the weather has deteriorated, so we cannot use the small boats to move the bodies to the Enterprise, as we did earlier today. Do you have any ideas?"

Rosemary said, "Before the pilot boat gets here, call for a large tugboat. When it gets here, we can load the body bags on its deck, cover them with a large canvas and have the tug meet the morgue trucks at another dock."

Melinda walked to Rosemary and gave her a hug. "Now I know why we keep you around. You are so smart," she said. "Computer, get Harry Blank online,"

"I'm online, Melinda," said Harry.

"The battle commander said that he has discussed the weather with our Captain. The winds have picked up, and he cannot safely send the small boats back to us. Rosemary came up with a perfect solution. Have a large tug come out to us before the pilot boat does. We can then offload the bodies and cover them with canvas. The tug can meet the morgue trucks at another pier out of sight of the Valley Forge."

"You want me to get a tug?" asked Harry.

"Yes," said Martin. "You really are smart. Now I see why you are the boss."

"Don't be smart, Martin," Harry answered with a laugh in his voice. "I can still pull your pilot's license."

"Aw...,"cried Martin. "You wouldn't do that, would you?"

Everyone in the nursery laughed. The tension, which was so thick that you could cut it with a knife, was broken.

"Fred," asked Melinda. "How are your men holding up?"

"It is like a picnic for them," answered Fred. "It is like an extension of their exercise. They are taking a break and getting something to eat.

They can be ready at a moment's notice. We timed them. They can get to any point in the ship in less than three minutes and be ready to fight."

"Pitman," asked Melinda. "How are your people holding up?"

"It is a new experience for them," answered Pitman. "Even my sergeants have never seen warfare like this. They are already working up a new training procedure to cover this when we get back to base. They have already made changes on how we operate on this ship. It might save lives. They like the dart guns."

"Charlie," asked Melinda. "How are your troops holding up?

"Not well," he answered. "They are exhausted. They have been fighting for more than forty-eight hours, and the ones in the Medical Clinic want out. I told the medic that if they can walk, he should send them to me here in the suite. They can watch the monitors and stand guard."

Melinda said to Charlie, "Special Six said that there are no ships in a twenty-five mile radius and that the skies are clear of any bandits. At the speed that boats, ships and planes travel, that doesn't say much. In less than one hour, we could be under attack. Luckily, with our communications, we can act promptly. I would suggest that you have half your remaining people take a break, but stay ready. Have them get some food. Trust no one that you do not know. Expect the unexpected. I think the suspects will try at least one more time, because once we are close inshore, they know we can get all kinds of help. What they don't know is that we have extra troops on board."

"Pitman, this is Fred. We are under attack on Deck 2 aft by the elevators. They have us pinned down. This was a well-planned ambush. They are picking off my people one at a time. How fast can you get here?"

"We're on our way," answered Pitman. "Keep your heads down."

Five minutes went by and Fred said, "I see your people. They are doing a great job of sneaking up on the suspects. Those dart guns make less noise than our suppressed weapons. There is a sniper hiding in the drop ceiling directly in front and up fifteen degrees. Do you see him?"

"I see him," said Pitman. "I don't think he expected to be shot through the ceiling tiles. These dart guns are powerful. How will we know if they have been shot with the dart guns or with your weapons?"

"If they are shot by my men, their bodies will be stiff as a board," said Fred. "Enough of this chatter, let's finish up here so my men can get a little rest."

"Yeah," said Pitman. "Yeah, so they can get a little rest. I have never seen your people rest. They are always on the move."

"That's why most of them are alive," said Fred. "It is hard to hit a moving target."

"Watch behind you lieutenant," said a voice in her earpiece. Pitman whirled and fired. Her shot caught the suspect in the eye and he dropped like a stone.

"Whoever warned me, thanks," said Pitman. "How many people are we fighting, anyway? It seems it never ends. I will be glad when tomorrow comes. I can say I have been to war, even if they don't issue ribbons for this kind of fighting."

"Melinda," said Fred. "Pitman is down and her first sergeant is down. We are under attack again on Deck 2 aft central corridor. The pirates seem to be coming out of the woodwork. Some of them are coming out of the drop ceilings. Have a medical team standing by near Deck 3 aft. It is still a hot zone. No safe place to put our wounded and we have a lot of them. I can't reach Pitman's medical team. See if you can reach them and have them get to us. We need help."

"Susan and Jose," asked Melinda. "What is your location?"

"We are midships on Deck 2," Susan said. Jose and I are heading towards the fighting and will assist Fred."

Melinda picked up the walkie-talkie and said, "Who is in charge of Pitman's troops?"

"Corporal Roberts, Sir," came a reply. "We just joined up with two of your people. I have eight people with me. Two are wounded but able to fight. We have a medic with us and will try to get to the wounded as soon as we can."

"We are sending as many people as we can," said Melinda. She looked at Martin. He got up, picked up four dart guns and handed one to each of them. "Martin, Ron, Lucinda and I are going to join Susan and Jose on Deck 2. Keep everything secure and guard my babies." Stephen unlocked the nursery door and opened it. Martin, Melinda, Ron and Lucinda quickly left the suite as Stephen secured the nursery door behind them.

The group no sooner left the suite, than four men broke through the hallway door and entered the sitting room. They checked the master bedroom and the balcony. They tried the nursery door and found it locked. They fired a pistol at the lock, and the bullet ricocheted and hit one of the men in his arm, causing him to drop his weapon and fall onto the couch.

Rosemary and Stephen watched the intruders on the monitor. Stephen kept a running dialogue to keep everyone informed. They heard one man, whom they thought was the leader, say something in a language they did not understand. One of the three remaining men took a first aid kit from his belt and started dressing his wounded comrade's arm. When he was finished, he helped the wounded man to his feet, and they all started to leave the room. As they exited the sitting room, they collapsed in the hallway.

Rosemary watched as two of Fred's men started dragging the bodies into the sitting room and closed what was left of the door. She heard Fred say, "It would be so much easier if we could just dump the bodies over the side. This killing them in one place and having to take them somewhere else is really a bother." His men knelt and secured the prisoners' hands and ankles with zip ties.

"Dr. Wellfleet," said Fred. "I have four more for you. Do you want me to give any of them the antidote?"

"Yes," said the doctor. "Save the one that was carrying the pistol. He would be the leader."

"Okay," said Fred. "I injected that one with the antidote. He will wake up in about five minutes with an awful headache. I hope you get here before then to take them all away."

"I can't come," said the doctor. "Your people are dropping so many bodies around the ship that I don't have time to move about the ship to pick them up. I will send Security to you with body bags and gurneys to move the bodies to the morgue. You keep this up and there won't be anyone left to run the ship."

"That's okay," laughed Fred. "We can do that, also."

Rosemary asked Fred, "What made you come back to the suite?"

"I suspected that someone would try to take a hostage," said Fred. "If they had good intelligence, they would know that Melinda or the babies would be the best ones to grab."

"Melinda," said the Computer. "The pulses of Marsha Abrams and John Mason have dropped below normal."

"What about Amy Gelz?" asked Melinda.

"She is still on the net," said the Computer. "Her pulse is high."

"I'm trying to find the correct camera," said Stephen. "We have lost power for some of the cameras on Deck 5. I'm trying to find a bypass circuit. I have the camera outside the secure room. That door was blown off its frame. I don't see anyone in the room."

"Computer, conference call, confirm," said Melinda.

"Conference call confirmed," replied the Computer.

"The secure room has been compromised," said Melinda. "Stephen reports that he doesn't see Mason, Marsha, or the prisoner, Amy Gelz. Do we have anyone near that room? Stephen," she continued, "Better turn the tracker on and see where Amy Gelz is."

Stephen turned on the tracker and watched as the computer sent out a pulse. "The computer is slow to track because of all the steel on the ship. Oh, there she is! She is passing the middle elevator on Deck 3. She is passing the laundry room. She is heading towards the forward elevator."

"Fred," said Melinda. "Can you get a crew down to the forward elevator on Deck 3? Stephen says Amy is headed that way. I don't think she is moving under her own power because she was sedated when she was in the secure room and it has only been a few minutes since they blew the door off. Stephen says he cannot follow her on the monitors. Many of the cameras are broken in the stairwells between Decks 2 and 3."

"We are going down to Deck 2 and heading for the aft elevator," said Fred. "We plan to come up the inside corridor stairwell and catch all of them unawares. I know they will be looking behind themselves. They would want to see if they are being pursued. I don't think they will be looking ahead to see where they are going."

"Melinda, this is Pitman. I sent two of my people to look in the secure room. It should take them a few minutes to get there."

"Roger, Pitman," said Melinda. "How are you feeling?"

"The suspects got us good," replied Pitman. "They were waiting for us. I don't know how they set up these ambushes so quickly. I was wounded and then my sergeant was hit. We were both dragged out of the line of fire. A couple of my men didn't make it."

"How badly were you hit?" asked Melinda.

"Once in the shoulder and once in the hip," replied Pitman. Both shots were through and through, but the hip hurts like a bastard. I'm not able to walk, but I can still use a weapon. They hit my right shoulder, but I am left handed. I might not be able to walk, but I can still stand guard duty."

"The special tugboat that we ordered is one hour away," said Rosemary. "I told Security to start moving the bodies to the aft hatch, port side, on Deck 2. I don't even know how many bodies there are, especially after these last few shootouts. The Captain notified me that the pilot boat just left Ft. Lauderdale. That means we will have only thirty minutes to load the bodies and have the tug pull away. I don't think we can move all those bodies in that short period of time."

Martin said, "Don't worry about it Rosemary. We'll have the pilot come aboard on the starboard side, give him breakfast, and then take him to the bridge. That will give us at least forty-five minutes. Make sure our tug comes up on the port side."

"That should work," said Rosemary. "I guess that happens when you think like a sailor."

"I'm not a sailor," said Martin, with a scowl. "I'm Air Force."

Rosemary laughed.

"Computer, conference call, confirm," said Melinda.

"Conference call confirmed," answered the Computer.

"Martin, Ron, Lucinda and I are headed to Deck 3," said Melinda. "We'll keep you informed."

"We didn't get very far," said Ron. "We are under attack, again. It looks like three women in steward's uniforms. There weapons have suppressors. Their first shot broke a fixture in the ceiling. Luckily, they are not very good shots. Martin went through the crew's corridor to try to come up behind them. I misjudged them. They have us pinned down. I can see Martin sneaking up behind them. One of them heard him. She has turned and fired. She hit him. Martin is down. The four women have stopped firing. They are down. I don't see anyone in the hallway. We are going to investigate."

"Melinda," said Fred. "I hope Martin isn't hurt too bad. We couldn't stay around, Pitman's people needed help."

Melinda jumped up and ran to Martin. "Where are you shot?" she asked worriedly.

"I'm hit in the leg," he said. A medic ran up, tore Martin's pant leg, cleaned the wound and applied a pressure bandage. "It doesn't look bad," said the medic. "The bullet went right through his thigh and it didn't hit anything important. Another couple of inches and you would be singing soprano." He laughed at his own joke. He picked up his walkie-talkie and called for a wheelchair or a stretcher. He asked Security to bring body bags and gurneys to move the four bodies to the morgue.

A Security team showed up with the gurneys and a wheelchair. Martin got into the chair and Melinda wheeled him to the elevator.

"I guess when they finish with you in the clinic," Melinda said, as she pushed the wheelchair into the Medical Clinic. "You will need your special wheelchair. I'll go get it and bring it here while they fix you up." Melinda raced to the elevator, took it to Deck 10 and entered the suite. She took the special wheelchair and returned to the Medical Clinic. Martin was sitting in a chair in the waiting room.

"The doctor said that the wound is minor," said Martin. "It will hurt like hell and will leave a scar in the front and back of my thigh. The bullet missed everything important. It just went through the thigh muscle." Melinda helped him get out of the chair and into his special wheelchair. She turned the chair around, nodded to the nurse and left the Medical Clinic. She took the elevator to Deck 10 and entered the suite.

Charlie Pile was sitting on the couch with his arm taped to his side. Sitting next to him was Norma Pitman with her arm and leg in a cast. They had four guns sitting on the table in front of them. "It didn't take you long to get yourself shot, did it Martin?" said Charlie. "Now you can join us on the couch."

"No thanks," said Martin. "I want to stay inside the nursery. I want to be with our babies. That was the first thought I had when I was shot. *What about my babies*? That scared me. I'll have to be more careful."

"That's what I always say," said Charlie. "I have to be more careful."

"Let's get in the nursery," said Melinda. "I want to be secure. Being in the sitting room is not secure, even with you guys sitting out here on guard."

"Were staying out here," said Charlie. "It gets too crowded with all of us in the Nursery."

Rosemary unlocked the door, and Melinda wheeled the chair into the nursery. After they came into the nursery, Rosemary locked the door and came over and gave Martin a hug. "Are you all right? Do you need anything?" she asked.

"No," said Martin. "I'm fine. It was just a scratch. I just have to be off the leg for a week and keep the wound clean."

Melinda walked to Martin and gave him a light kiss on the lips. "My hero," she said, with a big smile on her face. She walked to the cribs to check on her babies. Annabelle was wide-awake watching the hanging mobile. Edward was moving from side to side and whimpering. She picked him up, checked his diaper, and walked to the changing table. "He's wet again," she said, smiling. "As fast as he takes liquids in, he lets liquids out. She started humming a tune while she changed him. "Now you are nice and dry, my little man," she said as she kissed him on the cheek and returned him to his crib.

212

"I am so glad Edward has gotten over the colic," said Rosemary. "With all that is going on, it would have really been crazy to fight and deal with the babies being sick. I'm also glad we decided to make this room the nursery. It makes me feel better that we are surrounded by thick steel. Even the locks and hinges are heavy metal. They held up nicely against an attack."

"I don't know about the rest of you, but I am tired," said Stephen. "I feel like I haven't slept since I came on the ship four days ago. I am going to take a nap on the couch. Yell if you need me."

Melinda looked at Stephen and said, "You do look like you haven't slept in the four days. At least Ron got a nap. We'll have to depend on him to stay awake."

"New York," said Martin. The surveillance cameras on Deck 4, starboard side, are still out. Many of the surveillance cameras on Deck 3 have been broken. We still have the cameras for both approaches to the brig and the approach to the laundry room. We need you to be extra vigilant for the remaining Deck 3 cameras. Our special tug is due alongside in thirty minutes. That will give us time for a cup of coffee."

"Roger, Valley Forge," said New York. "We have a special watch on those areas. Be advised, there is a small group of men coming up the crew stairs forward. They have passed Deck 8. They are wearing tan uniforms and are heavily armed."

"Okay, New York," said Martin. "I guess we are not going to get our coffee break."

"Fred," called Melinda. "New York just told us that we have a group of men in tan uniforms coming up the forward crew stairwell. The suspects are near Deck 8. They are still climbing."

Melinda picked up the walkie-talkie and said, "Corporal Roberts. Can you spare a few people? We show suspects passing Deck 9 heading in our direction. Fred has some of his people moving towards us from Deck 12. Where are you?"

"We're on Deck 6, moving forward," said Roberts.

"Can you come up on the midship passenger stairway to Deck 12? Then move forward, come down the forward stairway and meet at our suite? said Melinda. "New York called it. They are heading for our suite. We are still secure. Charlie and Pitman have moved into the nursery."

"Melinda, this is Roberts," I have four people able to move quickly. They are on Deck 6 moving forward. They will come up the passenger stairway and move to the forward stairway."

213

"Melinda, " said Fred. "We are on Deck 11. Let them come."

"We don't see you on the screen," said Rosemary. "Where on Deck 11 are you?"

"You forget," said Fred. We know where the cameras are. We like to be invisible. We don't know what kind of electronics the enemy has. It could be they can tap into the ship's surveillance cameras and see where everyone is. That might be the reason for all the ambushes. I'm glad they don't have cameras in the bathrooms or in the staterooms. We hear them coming up the stairwell. They are not as quiet as they think they are. A couple of them are smokers. We can smell them before we hear them. I'm going to allow them to breach the suite door. It is broken anyway. If we hit them on the stairs, it will be a tough job to move the bodies. If we attack them in the suite, it will be easier."

"Okay," said Rosemary. "They have now opened the hallway door. They tore it off the hinges. They aren't very quiet about it. There are eight of them. The leader has long blond hair tied in a ponytail. He must be six foot four or five. He is clean-shaven. His uniform looks spotless. The other seven are unshaven and dirty looking. They don't look like soldiers. They look like gang bangers off the street. If possible, let's keep the tall blond and one of the others alive. I don't care about the rest of them."

"Let me know when some of them go into the master bedroom," said Fred. "I want to cut them down before they can fire a shot. I should stay in the sitting room. This is the third time I have come here to clean out vermin."

"They are starting to go into the master bedroom," said Rosemary. "They seem to be admiring the size and décor of the room. Six of them are in the master bedroom."

"Here we come," said Fred. His team moved silently into the sitting room. Using the dart guns, they shot the two men that were still in the sitting room. They waited until the six other men came out the door and dropped them with the blowguns. All eight men were lying on the sitting room floor.

"Dr. Wellfleet, this is Fred. "I have eight more bodies for you. I have six for the morgue and two for you to question when they wake up." Fred had his men secure the two live prisoners' ankles and wrists. Fred started searching them. He searched the dead ones first. He pulled out wallets, money, cigarettes, lighters and condoms from them and put everything in a pile. He then searched the other two live ones. The first one had the same material in his pockets. The tall blond one was searched, and

Fred found a walkie-talkie, a cell phone and a wallet. He opened the wallet and saw an identification card. He reached over and removed the prisoner's hat. It was not a he, it was a she. According to her identification card in her wallet she is a colonel in the *Fuerza Pública de la República de Panamá,* The Panamanian Public Forces.

"Melinda," said Fred. "You won't believe who we have out here. Can you see me on the monitor?"

"Yes, Fred," said Melinda. "I can see your back. What do you have out there that I won't believe?"

Fred moved away from the body. "Can you see what is lying here?"

"All I can see is that it is a woman," said Melinda.

"Let me introduce her to you," said Fred. "May I present Colonel Isabella Ramirez of the Panamanian Public Forces Military Intelligence, otherwise known as the Panamanian Secret Police."

"Now my curiosity has gotten the better of me," said Melinda. "What in the world does the secret police of Panama want with us? Now that's a stupid question," continued Melinda. "They want what's in the aft storage room. I wonder if they know what it is that we are carrying, or just that it is a very valuable cargo. For them to send a colonel, shows how important this whole operation is to them. When she wakes up, get her to Dr. Wellfleet. We need her questioned as soon as possible to find out what else they have planned for us."

"I won't have to wait long," said Fred. "I injected her with the antidote five minutes ago. She should be waking up any second. When she is fully awake, I will walk her down to Dr. Wellfleet on Deck 3. Security should be up here soon to remove the rest of the bodies." Fred started putting all the material on the table, when he noticed the colonel testing her bonds. "You won't be able to break them," he said as he walked to her. "Do you speak English?" he asked.

She just glared at him and kept trying to break the ties. Fred stood near her but had to jump back when she tried to kick him. "I guess we are going to have to do this the hard way," he said, as he took out the dart gun. He aimed it at her, and she went quiet. "Are you going to work with me, or do I shoot you where you lie?"

She lay there a moment until Fred could see she had given up. He still did not trust her. After all, she was a colonel in the secret police. She couldn't be a stupid woman to have gotten that high in that organization.

"Are you going to cooperate?" Fred asked, again.

She didn't say anything, just nodded her head.

"Do you speak English," Fred asked again.

"Yes," the colonel said with a sneer on her face. "I speak English."

"What is your name?" Fred asked. *I wonder if she will lie or tell the truth,* he thought.

"My name is Isabella Ramirez."

"What is your title?

"I am a colonel in the Panamanian Public Forces," she answered.

"Is that a military or a police organization?" Fred asked. *He did not think she would answer that question, but she surprised him.*

"I am part of the military police," she announced proudly.

"Is that like the secret police?" Fred continued.

"We don't have a secret police," she answered.

"What are you doing on this cruise ship?" he asked.

"I was given orders to find and remove cargo from this ship."

"What cargo?" Fred insisted.

"We know that you have an extremely valuable cargo in the aft hold," said Isabella Ramirez.

"Do you know what the cargo is that is stored in the aft hold? What it looks like? What its size or weight?

"No, I only know where the valuable cargo is stored," continued Isabella.

"Do you have any idea how large the aft cargo hold is?" asked Fred.

"No, I'm in the Army, not in the Navy."

Fred turned away, and using the subcutaneous communication unit, said to Melinda, "What do you think? Most of her answers were truthful, except for her position in the Army. I'm going to put her to asleep with the dart gun. I think she is too dangerous to be walking around loose. Do you have any questions you want answered now?" he asked.

"No, Fred," said Melinda. "Shoot her with a dart. Do it from behind. The less information she has about our weapons, the better. I am so glad that Dr. Wellfleet made the dart guns look like handguns."

Fred walked behind Isabella Ramirez and shot her in the neck with the dart gun. She became unconscious immediately. Fred called Dr. Wellfleet and told him what he had done. Just then, there was knock on the door, and six Security people came in wheeling three gurneys. Fred pointed to the blond woman on the floor and told the men that she had to go first to Dr. Wellfleet. He then pointed to one of the men on the floor who was moving around. He instructed Security to make sure that the prisoner gets to Dr. Wellfleet as well. The rest of the bodies could be doubled up on the gurneys. The men unrolled the six body bags, moved the bodies and zipped up the bags. They loaded three bodies on each gurney. They put the man and the sleeping colonel together on the third gurney.

"Be careful with those two," said Fred, pointing to the blond woman and the squirming man. The man started moving so violently that he almost tipped the gurney over. Fred walked to him, put the dart gun to his head and said in perfect Spanish, "Do you want to die here and now?" The man stopped squirming.

"Fred," said Melinda. "Shoot him with a dart. He will be a problem, otherwise."

Fred walked over to the man in the gurney and said, "Good night," and shot him in the neck. Security smiled and started wheeling the gurneys out of the sitting room.

"Fred," said Rosemary. "What happened to Amy Gelz?"

"My men are still tracking her," he said. "It shouldn't be long now."

Melinda asked, "Has anyone found Mason or Marsha? They were guarding Amy."

"Melinda," Charlie said. "Two of my men are following a blood trail out of the secure room. They tell me the blood is fresh. As soon as I get their report I will call you."

"Valley Forge, Valley Forge. This is Enterprise. We are leaving you at this time. If you need further assistance, please feel free to call on us. We will be operating fifty miles south of Ft. Lauderdale for the next twelve hours. It has been an interesting two days."

"Roger, Enterprise," said the Captain. "Thanks for your assistance. Where do you plan to drop the bodies?"

"We expect to be at sea for another seventy two hours," said the Enterprise. "We will pull into one of the naval bases and off load all the bodies. We know where to ship your people. We were informed of the different destinations when the bodies were delivered to us. We are sorry for your loss, Valley Forge. Enterprise out."

"Melinda," called Suzy Q. "The special tug boat is here, and the bodies are being moved very rapidly to their deck. They put up an awning so the passengers cannot see them move the bodies onto the tug. As soon as they are finished, they will drop the awning to cover all the bodies and head to the dock at Inlet Drive. The morgue trucks will meet them there. That area is fairly deserted at this time of day."

"I'm glad that's taken care of," said Martin. "Now we only have to worry about Marsha, Mason and Amy. I wonder where they are."

Charlie touched Melinda's arm and said, "I just got a report. They found Marsha Abrams. She's dead. It appears she crawled behind the damaged desk, through the door, into the inside passage and bled out. At some time her body slid down the stairs. They are still looking for Mason. My men are following his blood trail and said that he has lost a lot of blood. The Computer said that Mason's tracker does not show a heartbeat. His tracker shows him on Deck 6 aft."

"Melinda," said Fred. "Four-four has reported that his team is under attack again. He doesn't know where the small arms fire is coming from and three of his men have been wounded. The medics report the wounds don't look serious. They are fighting on Deck C, aft of the forward engine room."

"What are your men doing in the engine room?" Melinda asked.

"They were checking to see if they could find any suspects hiding down there," Fred said. Four-four said that it was like kicking a bee's nest. Bullets were coming from everywhere. His men were being forced to crawl under the boilers and generators in the forward engine room. It is a good thing they are little people. If they were full size they wouldn't be able to get under the machinery."

"Fred just told me that he is sending another team to assist Four-four," said Charlie. "Pitman doesn't have enough people left to even attempt to help. Her men have moved her near the forward stairs. She cannot move her legs, but she can still fire a weapon. She will do a rear guard with her people."

"I don't know what these suspects think they can gain with this last attack," commented Martin.

"We are within throwing distance of the dock," said Charlie. "We have stopped in the channel while the Independence of the Seas is docking. Then it will be our turn. I see more than ten military trucks on the dock unloading a lot of troops."

"I spoke to Harry earlier," said Melinda. "I had explained to him what was happening on the ship. He said that he ordered the military to intervene with a battalion. The Valley Forge will be in lockdown. Passengers will be allowed to leave the ship only after their passports and custom declarations have been doubled-checked. New York has not finished the background checks on the ship's crew. With so many of the crew involved in shootouts, none of the crew will be allowed off the ship.

That might be the reason they are fighting. Maybe they think they can fight their way off."

Melinda continued, "The Captain has just made an announcement that the ship is infested with a bug from the islands. He wants all passengers to stay in their cabins until the spraying of the hallways has been completed. It should not take more than an hour to finish the spraying. After each deck has been sprayed, the passengers on that deck will be escorted off the ship."

Chapter 10

"As soon as we dock," Martin said, "soldiers will come on board and seal off the engine rooms. I told Fred to have his men prepare for a gas attack from our own. This is the fastest way to stop the fighting in the engine room. There are just too many places to hide. When the gas attack stops the fighting in the engine room, any bodies found will be moved to Deck 1. The dead bodies will be loaded into a luggage carrier and covered with canvas. Two more squads of soldiers will be coming on board to assist Fred and the doctor move the rest of the bodies. It will look like we are moving recycled material. As soon as two luggage carriers are put on a truck, it will leave. These are not refrigerated trucks, but with speed and dispatch, it shouldn't matter. We have four doctors coming on board to treat the wounded. The wounded suspects will be taken under guard to a prison hospital for additional treatment."

"Fred," asked Rosemary. "Is there anything special the doctors have to know about treating your wounded?"

"No," Fred replied.

"Would they know how to deal with this type of native population?" Rosemary asked.

"I would hope so," said Fred. "They would need smaller equipment to work on them. Remember, they are smaller than you, and a heck of a lot blacker than you are."

Melinda laughed. "You still have your sense of humor, Fred. I'm sorry for all your losses. I wish I could say it was for a good cause, but I don't know why your men were killed. I will leave it up to Harry Blank to find out why we lost over fifty men and women. This was supposed to be a quiet, relaxing cruise for Martin and myself. Of course I wasn't expecting to give birth in the middle of this operation. When we came back on the ship with the babies, we thought it would still be a relaxing cruise with nothing to do but watch for smugglers. If I had known we had a secret cargo on board, I don't think I would have brought my babies on the ship. I am still concerned about coming out of the nursery. We still don't know if we have caught everyone that has been sent to the Valley Forge to highjack the cargo. The suspects blew up the safe room where Marsha, Mason and Amy were. They found Marsha but not the other two. We know Amy couldn't be walking without assistance. The drugs could not have worn off. That means she is being carried somewhere. We don't know anything about

Mason except that he is leaving a trail of blood. That safe room really wasn't very safe."

Rosemary said, "I think we are too close to docking at Ft. Lauderdale for any more pirate adventures. The Captain told me the Coast Guard has sent two of their boats to guard the channel."

"Melinda," said Dr. Wellfleet. "I have treated Pitman, and we are planning to move her down to the Medical Clinic. She wants to be with her people until we are finished treating them. We have two more dead on this deck. With all the shooting, no one was able to get to them. They bled out before any medical personnel could get to them. I notified Security and they are bringing two body bags and a gurney to transport the bodies. We have four more doctors coming on board in about ten minutes. They are coming directly to the Clinic to take care of our wounded first."

"We are secure to the dock," said the Captain. "Soldiers are coming on. The soldiers notified me not to open any hatches until I receive directions to do so. From here, it looks like they are placing a soldier every hundred feet along the deck. I see six squads of soldiers dressed in protective gear coming aboard. That must be the 'spraying' teams. I hope they can do the job quickly. The stewards are telling me that the passengers are getting restless. Some of them have already come out of their cabins and are congregating in the atrium and along the promenade."

Stephen said, pointing to the monitor, "there is a gun battle taking place on Deck 15. It doesn't look like any of our people are involved. It's those people in white coveralls. They are fighting with a group of civilians."

"I bet these are the people Harry told us about," said Rosemary. "He said that the cartels probably had booked cabins for their people once they knew about the valuable cargo."

"I see some of the soldiers going up in the elevators," said Lucinda. "It didn't take them long to spread out and attack the pirates from both sides. The pirates have been caught in a pincer movement. They stopped fighting each other and started firing at our soldiers. The shooting has now stopped. All of the pirates are either dead or wounded. Our troops have gathered all the weapons. They are securing the wounded with zip ties. They are dragging the dead to one side, out of sight of the passengers."

"Dr. Wellfleet," said Melinda. "I think you should send a couple of doctors up to Deck 15. Have Security go up there with a few gurneys. I don't know how many dead or wounded there are on the deck. Have them put the bodies in the bags and take the bags directly to Deck 1 where they will be loaded onto luggage carriers and moved to the trucks on the pier. This should be done as quickly as possible. With the weather getting warmer, the bodies will start to ripen."

"Charlie," said Fred. "We see the gas grenades coming through the hatches. All of my men have masks. How long will it take for the gas to incapacitate the enemy?"

"I asked one of the soldiers," Charlie said. "He said they will open the vents in ten minutes. You can start the search in ten minutes, but keep the masks on. Did you ever find Mason?"

"Yes," said Fred. "After he was shot, he managed to crawl into an elevator and push the button for a lower deck. Two of my men found his body in a corner on Deck 1. He's dead."

"Melinda," said Charlie. "Fred just told me that they found Mason in a corner on Deck 1. He's dead."

"So the only person still missing is Amy Gelz, "said Melinda. "Does anyone know where she is? Computer, what does her track show?"

"Melinda," answered the Computer. "I show her pulse ninety six over fifty four. According to the medical program, she is tachycardiac. She might be bleeding out. I show her moving up the aft staircase starboard side between Decks 3 and 4."

"Fred," said Martin. "Do you have anyone near the aft staircase?"

"Yes, Martin," said Fred. "I have a team on Deck 8 and another team on Deck 1."

"The Computer shows that Amy Gelz is moving up the aft staircase starboard side between Deck 3 and 4. Deck 4 is the only deck that can be used to leave the ship. None of the lower hatches have been opened."

"I sent two teams to that location," said Fred. "It should take a few minutes for them to reach that deck."

"I see them coming up to Deck 4," said Pitman. "They don't see me or any of my people. They are carrying something in a body bag. My men are sneaking up on them. One of Fred's men just signaled us to stand down. His men are going to take a shot. I don't know what they are using to kill the pirates, but it works fast and is silent. We didn't even see them shooting, and we are right here. The four that were carrying the body bag are on the deck. They dropped the body bag. The four bodies and the bag slid down to Deck 3. Fred and his people carried the body bag to this deck. One of his people has opened the bag. The body looks like the prisoner you showed us when we came aboard, Amy Gelz. Fred's men are performing some medical magic. From what I can see, she is still alive. They are bandaging her wounds with the gel packs as fast as they can. That has slowed the blood flow from her wounds. There was a lot of blood when they opened the body bag. She is still unconscious. Additional holes were cut in the upper part of the body bag. Fred's people zipped the bag closed and are using it as a stretcher. Fred informed us that they are going to take Amy Gelz down to the Medical Clinic on the elevator. He wants a gurney waiting at the aft crew elevator when he gets there."

"I notified Dr. Wellfleet," said Melinda. "He will have a medic and a gurney at the aft elevator. He is sending Security to pick up the four dead bodies. We will be coming for you in about five minutes. Can you hold out?"

"My people have taken good care of me," said Pitman. "I am proud of the way they performed, especially after our first surprise encounter. Losing comrades in the first battle did not stop them. It did bother them, but they did not let it stop them from doing their job."

Twenty minutes later, Dr. Wellfleet called Melinda. "Amy Gelz will live. When the suspects blew open the door to the safe room, the shrapnel hit Amy and severed her spine just above her hip. Fred's medics was able to stop the blood flow in time, and that saved her life. I had the tracker removed. She is going to need at least three pints of blood. I am going to leave her in the Clinic for a while to make sure she is stable."

"What about the Panamanian colonel?" Melinda asked. "Did you get a chance to question her?"

"As soon as she came down here," said the doctor. "I gave her the antidote for the dart Fred fired at her. When she came awake, I gave her the truth drug. I questioned her extensively. I don't think Harry is going to like what I found."

"Do you want me to get Harry online?" asked Melinda.

"No," said Wellfleet. "Let me tell you what I found. You can pass it on if you think Harry is the right person to tell."

"You make it sound serious," said Melinda.

"It is very serious," replied Dr. Wellfleet.

"Do you want to tell me?" asked Melinda.

"It seems that Harry has a mole in his organization. The colonel, Isabella Ramirez, knew everything about the cargo except for the name of the material that is in the hold. She knew the plans for shipping it from Curacao. She was shown pictures of the cargo on the pallets. She knew where it was being stored on the ship. She even knew that the Enterprise was nearby. The only way she could know this was if she had the information from someone inside of Harry's group. She even knew the value of the cargo and was thinking of keeping some of it for herself. A couple of pounds of that chemical would make her a very rich colonel in the secret police. The only thing she didn't know about was that we installed a jammer in the communication room. Because of that she had no way to contact anyone."

"Is she secure in the Medical Clinic?" asked Martin.

"Yes she is," said the doctor. "I haven't removed the zip ties. I feel she is just too dangerous. For a woman to become a colonel in the secret police, she has to be smart and crafty. I asked the Captain to send additional Security people to guard all the prisoners that are here in the Medical Clinic. The only one that doesn't need a guard is Amy Gelz. She is still asleep from the anesthetic. I checked the colonel for a tracking device. She had two of them. I removed both of the trackers and put them in the lead box. I have to assume the dead pirates have devices under their skin as well. I told the receiving morgue to scan the bodies before they cremate them. That way we won't have to worry about visitors in the night trying to claim the bodies."

"Did you tell them to cremate only the bodies of the pirates? Melinda asked.

"Yes, I did," said the doctor. "I explained which ones were the enemy and which ones were ours."

"I don't think this is the end," said Rosemary. "I'm getting like Melinda. I get this feeling that we should not let our guard down until this material is at its final destination. I would not be surprised if the trucks come under attack after they leave the pier. It might be a good idea to give them an escort."

"If you feel that they should have an escort," said Melinda, "then an escort they shall have."

"Computer, get Harry Blank," said Melinda.

"I'm online, Melinda," said Harry.

"Rosemary has one of those feelings," said Melinda. "She thinks the trucks that we are using to transport the bodies should have an escort until the cremation is finished."

"If she feels that way, then I will make arrangements for an armed escort," said Harry. "I'll get back to you."

Ten minutes later Harry was back on the line. "Melinda, tell Rosemary that the trucks on the dock will have an armed escort. I even sent soldiers to meet the tugboat and escort those morgue trucks. Everything is secure. I hope she feels better about that."

Melinda passed the information to Rosemary, who said, "I am thinking of all of our dead. Charlie lost so many people, and so did Pitman. How is she doing, by the way? Has anyone checked on her?"

"I haven't spoken to her in a while," said Melinda.

"Charlie," asked Melinda, "are you in contact with Pitman?"

"Yes," Charlie answered. "She is still in the Medical Clinic along with corporal Roberts. He is not doing well. He will be one of the first ones off. They wanted to get her ready to go ashore, but she wants to stay until all of her wounded are ashore. She has learned a lot this trip, but it will be awhile before she is able to go on another mission. I understand that she will need a hip replacement."

Martin turned to Melinda and said, "The Captain told me that the Valley Forge is alongside the pier. He is having the aft hatch opened, so the bodies can be moved before the passengers get off. They don't have to see that."

"Melinda," said Charlie. "You are not going to believe this. One of my teams is being fired upon in the engine room aft."

"Order the soldiers to gas the aft engine room," said Melinda. "This fighting has to stop. We're tied to the pier. Some of the passengers are getting off, and we have another gunfight onboard. That is outrageous. What do pirates think they can accomplish? There is no way than can take the merchandise off the ship."

"Unless," said Rosemary, "they want to take over the ship. Better warn the captain."

"Captain," said Melinda. "We have another gunfight in the aft engine room. I ordered the soldiers to gas the engine room. Is there any chance that this ship can be taken over by the pirates?"

"Are you serious?" replied the Captain.

"Serious like a heart attack," Martin said. "How hard would it be for one of the cartels to take over the ship?"

"It would be difficult to do now," said the Captain. "I've already shut down the main engines. They won't be started again until 1700 hours. After that, it would be very easy to take over this ship. All they would have to do is take my executive officer or me hostage. Either one of us can take the ship out of the harbor. If they have anyone with basic ship handling skills, he or she would be able to operate the ship and besides there would be a pilot onboard."

"I would suggest you get some security up on the bridge," said Martin. "I don't know how long this gunfight is going last. We don't have a lot of people available to fight. I notified Harry. He has arranged for a battalion to meet the ship. Some should already be on the dock. "

"That's good," remarked the Captain. I now have six Security people on the bridge, and they are all armed. All the doors to the bridge are secured and will not be opened until the troops arrive."

"Sheena and Benjamin have gone to the aft engine room," said Lucinda. "They went to help Fred's people. I tried to stop them, but to no avail."

"Sheena," said Melinda. "What is happening in the engine room? Have the troops gotten there with the gas?"

"No they haven't, Melinda," Sheena said. "Fred's people are really taking a beating. I also see a few of Pitman's people. They are also taking part in this firefight. Benjamin has snuck down into Deck C and has gotten himself in a protected position. He is doing a lot of damage. The pirates did not expect gunfire from that direction. They are turning their guns on him. He has stopped firing. I think he's been wounded. Here come the soldiers with the gas grenades. I see Susan and Jose with them. I have to back away. I don't have a gas mask with me, so I'm coming back to the suite."

"I think we should double check that the nursery is secure," said Stephen. "I know that the dining room, the sitting room and the master bedroom are not secure. We will have to stay here in the nursery until we can get an armed escort off the ship. These people from the cartels are crazy. They keep throwing men into the fight and are not succeeding in whatever they think they are doing."

"When Amy made that remark about the Exchange, you said you would explain it," Rosemary asked.

Melinda smiled. "That's a long story," Melinda said. "Since we are secure in the nursery, let's fix something to drink and find a comfortable place to sit. They fixed something to drink and sat in the upholstered chairs.

Melinda continued. "About eleven months ago, one of my agents, Tom Markus, was doing an investigation for one of our clients. During that investigation, he was killed. We thought it was an accident until the local authorities notified us that it was not an accident, and Markus's death would be listed on the report as a homicide. We investigated the accident ourselves, and found that Markus was killed by mistake. Peter Mancuso was the intended victim. For some reason, they had swapped cars. In delving further, we discovered that a contract had been issued by a cartel named the Exchange."

"What was the Exchange?" asked Stephen.

"The Exchange started in Zürich more than thirty years ago. Ramos Shomo ran a small legitimate import export business. He was Hildo Shomo's father. When Hildo was old enough, his father sent him to the United States for schooling. That is where he met Norman Hillman. They became very good friends. Hildo opened an extension of his father's business in the United States, and Norman followed in his father's footsteps and went into the electronics business. During this time, Norman bid on and won many government contracts to supply all kinds of electronics for the military, both in this country and overseas. In the 70's, our government announced that it was not allowing certain electronics to be shipped out of the country. That ruling almost put Norman Hillman out of business. To keep making money, Norman convinced Hildo to join him in a partnership. They started illegally shipping electronics through Shomo's firm. This illegal activity went on for many years. Norman Hillman met Conrad Allen at an electronics convention in Las Vegas. They hit it off like brothers. Since Conrad had contacts all over the world, he suggested they do business together. He was moving small amounts of illegal substances through these contacts. He wanted to expand and wanted Shomo's firm to ship guns for him."

"These three men, Hildo Shomo, Norman Hillman and Conrad Allen were working together smoothly. Everything was going well until Arlene Watchett, who was on the Armed Forces Committee, entered the picture. Her signature was required for a government contract approval. She approached Hillman for a payoff, which he gladly paid. Thereafter, the partnership expanded. Because of Watchett, many additional contracts were won. Business got better and better. Mina Yarborough and Frank Visconti were the next to join. They needed money to expand, and Shomo and Norman had the money to loan. They started expanding into other ventures. Milton Pearl had additional connections for drugs. They bought drugs on the open market and shipped them around the world, using Shomo's facilities. The arms business became their biggest moneymaker. The arms business was so good, that they set up their own manufacturing facility. They were able to make the weapons without serial numbers. With the money they were making, they were able to bribe people. They even took over a number of pharmaceutical companies. As they got larger and larger, they had to open more depots around the country, and around the world."

"In the beginning each depot was set up as an independent operation. The problem was that they became too big, too quickly, and they could not find people they could trust to run each depot independently. Having no other option, they consolidated the operation and used a chain of command structure to run them. This consolidation worked well for over twenty years. They were able to help each other get into powerful positions."

"I still don't understand," Rosemary said. "They had enough money for five lifetimes. What is it they were trying to achieve?"

"It wasn't the money," said Melinda. "It was the power. After the first billion, The Exchange became nothing more than a power organization. They could do whatever they wanted. They had blackmailed and bribed so many people that they were able to take over small towns. They would then open a depot in the town and warehouse the weapons, and in some cases, the gold. It made it easier to ship without suspicion. They were even being asked by the drug cartel to ship small amounts of drugs to test their smuggling routes."

"As our teams closed some of the other depots throughout the United States, we found additional records. The Exchange was into slave labor, drugs, gunrunning, prostitution and counterfeit tax stamps. They even set up a number of these illegal activities as a venture and sold the operation to different cartels. The names of some of the investors are still not known. They are buried in the records. There was so much paper that it will take years to get through it all. The Exchange's profits were greater than most countries' gross national products. They had dealings, according to the records, in twenty-seven different countries."

"We found a secondary depot in upstate New York," continued Martin. "Sheena and her group closed it down and blew it up. It left a big hole in the ground. A main depot was in New York City. When we raided the New York City depot, we thought we had finally put the Exchange out of business. We had all their records, we thought. Melinda, Ron and I were wounded in that raid. We didn't find out until much later, that in shutting down the Exchange, we had shut down one of the Mexican cartels."

"That Mexican cartel was extremely upset. We cost them many billions of dollars. They had paid for a running operation and we shut it down. They had paid millions of dollars and were expecting to earn billions. We think that is the reason for the contract on Melinda. How they found out that Melinda is the head of The Company has yet to be determined.

"That still doesn't explain why we are having all these attacks on the Valley Forge," said Lucinda. "We have been attacked by at least four different cartels; France, Holland, Columbia and Mexico. They must think the material we are carrying in the aft hold is worth all these men's lives. They want the cargo. It must be extremely valuable for them to sacrifice so many people to get it. They could have hijacked this entire ship with all the men they lost."

"I don't know if you were here when we discussed this with the Captain," said Melinda. "The material we are carrying in the aft cargo hold is worth five hundred dollars a gram. That is about a quarter of a million dollars a pound. Each pallet weighs six hundred pounds. We are carrying ten pallets. That means we are carrying more than ten billion dollars' worth of product. Can you see why these cartels want it?"

"If I was one of these cartels," said Rosemary. "I would have brought people on as passengers, waited until we had a sea day, and take over the ship. How many people would it take? I would put a couple of armed men in the engine room and a couple of armed men up here. I could have another ship join us and transfer the material. I could do the entire operation in less than four hours without firing a shot."

"Maybe they should have hired you," Stephen remarked, patting her on the shoulder. She turned and punched him in the arm.

"Hey," Stephen said. "That hurt."

"It was meant to," Rosemary said, smiling.

"Okay," said Melinda. "We have to figure out what is going to happen next. Rosemary and I both agree that something is going to happen. Rosemary feels that there will be an attack on the ship before 1700 hours. I feel that the pirates are going to try to hijack the trucks. That being the case, let's prepare for both, the hijacking of the ship and an attack on the trucks heading to the NASA depot. This ship will be leaving the dock at 1730 hours. We have to be off just before they single up the lines. I figure that would be 1700 hours. We have to have guards at the gangways from now until the ship leaves."

"Harry," said Martin. "Can you contact the army battalion that is supposed to be here and have a couple of squads at the gangways from now until the ship leaves?

"What's happening that you need troops at the gangways?" asked Harry.

"Rosemary and I feel there is going to be more action, and we want to be prepared," said Melinda.

"Use a couple of squads from the army battalion that should be there now," said Harry. "I don't know the name of the person in charge of the army battalion. I don't even know if he is connected. All I do know is that he is a battalion commander. His security clearance is high enough should you want to 'connect' him."

"Melinda," reported Fred. "We have some big Army brass coming up the gangway. It looks like a lieutenant colonel and two captains are trying to come on board, and ship's Security will not let them pass. I am going to assist the colonel and the captains."

"Colonel," Fred said, glancing at her nametag, 'Barrister'. "My name is Fred Rodriguez. I've been asked to escort you and the captains aboard." Security stepped aside and let them pass. Fred escorted Colonel Barrister and her two captains to the elevator and up to Deck 10.

"Martin," said Fred. "I'm outside the suite with the colonel and two captains."

Martin opened the door and invited them in. Once they were inside and the door closed, introductions were made. "Colonel Barrister, this is Ron Sullivan. He's running this operation."

"Mr. Sullivan," the colonel said. "I've been told you need some help."

"Yes we do," said Ron. "But first, let me introduce the rest of the team." He introduced everyone except Melinda, Rosemary, Stephen and the babies. They stayed in the nursery, listened in and watched what was happening in the sitting room.

"Has Harry explained our situation?" asked Ron.

"He told me about the fire fights that have been going on for the last four days," said the colonel. "I've also received reports from my men in the engine rooms, forward and aft. I think you will have to explain what else is happening."

"Melinda," said Ron. "Would you like the job of explaining everything to the colonel?"

"Computer online," asked Melinda

"Computer online," replied the Computer.

"Is Colonel Barrister connected?" asked Melinda.

"Colonel Barrister is connected," replied the Computer.

"Computer, connect Colonel Barrister," said Melinda.

"Colonel," said Melinda. "My name is Melinda Xavier. I am in the room next door. Ron will show you."

Rosemary unlocked the nursery door and swung it open. The colonel walked into the nursery followed by the two captains. Once inside, Rosemary secured the door.

"Colonel Barrister, I would like you to meet Melinda Xavier," Rosemary said. "Melinda, this is Colonel Elizabeth Barrister."

Melinda stood there in awe. She looked Barrister up and down and said, "Liz, when did you get those oak leaves?"

Elizabeth Barrister walked over to Melinda and put her arms around her. "I haven't seen you in over ten years. Where have you been? What have you been doing? How is your father? Is he still running The Company?"

"Sit down," said Melinda. "We don't have time for a long drawn out story. I'll try to give you a short version. My father was killed more than ten years ago. I have been running the organization since he was killed."

"I'm sorry about your father," said Barrister. "I liked working with him. I didn't know he had been killed. I've been out of the country for over ten years and have lost contact with almost everyone I knew."

"I got married last year," continued Melinda. "Here's my husband now." Martin walked in with a tray of refreshments and set it down on the table.

Melinda held out her hand to Barrister and led her to the cribs. "And these are my babies."

Barrister reached down, picked Annabelle up and cuddled her. Annabelle made cute little mewing sounds. She kissed Annabelle on the forehead and put her back in the crib. She walked over to Edward's crib. Before she could pick him up, he started howling. Barrister leaned in, picked him up and cuddled Edward in her arms. She whispered in his ear, and he stopped howling.

"How did you do that?" asked Rosemary. "When he starts howling, he usually keeps going for an hour or so. What did you whisper in his ear?"

"Very simple," said Barrister. "I told him that if he continued to howl I was going to send him to the Navy."

Everyone started laughing.

"It's good to see you, Liz," said Melinda. "We need your help."

"Harry called me on my private cell phone," the colonel said. "Either he didn't know, or he forgot that I was connected. He explained most of the problems you were having and the reason he needed the troops in Ft. Lauderdale when the Valley Forge pulled in. Two days ago

I received a call to drop everything and to move my battalion from Colorado to Ft. Lauderdale by whatever expeditious way I could find. We rounded up seven C130's and here we are."

"Just so you know," said Melinda, "the fighting is still continuing around the ship. I have people all over the ship, and they are reporting small gunfights, sniper fire and some hand to hand. We send teams to help, they solve the problems and then they move on. The biggest fights are in the engine rooms. Your people are taking care of that with gas. Fred's people are gathering up any bodies they can find, securing them and moving them to the Medical Clinic. Dr. Wellfleet is questioning the suspects when they wake up. Now we have to go deck by deck to find them. We are not letting any of the crew off the ship."

"Why are they still fighting when they know they can't win?" asked Lucinda.

"The people from the cartels have nothing to lose, so they keep fighting," said Melinda. We have been fighting four different cartels that we know of. With that valuable cargo, everyone wants it. During a conference call, it was suggested that some of the passengers are members of the cartels, and that is another reason they do not seem to run out of people to fight. Charlie Pile has lost more than half of his men and…"

"Charlie Pile?" interrupted Colonel Barrister, surprised. "That old reprobate, is he still on the Caribbean Desk?"

"Yes, he's still on the Caribbean Desk" said Melinda. "You know Charlie Pile?"

"Yes I do," said Barrister. "When I was a lieutenant in Special Ops," continued Colonel Barrister, "he was my mentor. He taught me how to stay alive and keep my men alive. Women were not popular in the army back then. We were looked down upon, and everyone felt we slept our way into whatever position we held. We had to work extra hard to move up the ranks. Charlie and people like him helped pave the way for women in the military. Where is he?"

"Are you looking for me?" asked Charlie, as he limped into the nursery.

Elizabeth Barrister got up from the table, walked over to Charlie Pile, put her arms around him and gave him a hug and then a kiss. He moaned and she stepped back. "I'm sorry," she said. "I didn't see the cast. You got that on this trip?" pointing to the arm cast.

"Yes," said Charlie. "Didn't Melinda tell you what has been happening?" he asked.

"Melinda started telling me what's happening," said Barrister. "When she mentioned your name, I interrupted her. You are still causing me to lose my train of thought." She reached for his good hand and gave it a squeeze. "It's good to see you, Charlie." She leaned over and gave him a kiss on the cheek.

"That's considered sexual harassment," Charlie said with a smile, not letting go of her hand.

"Okay," said the colonel. "Let's finish the story. Charlie lost more than half his men and then what?"

"After Charlie lost his men, he was able to get in contact with Fred Rodriguez on the South American desk. Fred and his people were operating in Aruba on a training exercise, and they were able to get on board without the passengers knowing about it. They came on board just in time. We were under attack by the different cartels for two days. That was in addition to having Susan Bart incapacitated and having someone come on the ship impersonating her. Stephen Blaine, Melinda's bodyguard, figured it out. We were able to capture the impersonator and put her in a safe room under guard. What we did not anticipate was the 'invasion'. The last group of invaders came prepared. They carried Semtex, and they knew how to use it. They blew the safe room open. Two of my people were badly wounded, and the impersonator was severely injured by the shrapnel. The enemy wrapped the impersonator in a body bag and tried moving her off the ship. Fred stopped that from happening. So now, you are up to date. That is your debriefing. Do you have any questions?"

"Yes," said Barrister. "I have just one question. Why didn't you ask for help sooner?"

"We did," said Melinda. "We asked the Enterprise, and they sent Lieutenant Pitman and three squads of marines. As soon as they came on the Valley Forge, she lost four of her people. She was wounded as well as her sergeant. Corporal Roberts stepped in and took her place. Pitman is down in the Medical Clinic being treated. We have another guest you might be interested in."

"And who would that be?" asked the colonel.

"We have a colonel from the Panama Secret Police," said Melinda. "We have her secured and under guard in the Medical Clinic. Fred was responsible for her capture. Only she and one of her men survived."

"Do you have a name for this colonel?" asked Barrister.

"According to her papers," said Melinda, "her name is Isabella Ramirez."

"I have heard of her," said the colonel. "She has a bad reputation. She likes to torture her prisoners and leave them in the jungle tied to a tree. I would like to meet her."

"I would introduce you," said Melinda, "but there is a slight problem."

"What is that?" asked Barrister.

"There is a two million dollar contract out on me and my babies," said Melinda. "This room is the only safe place for us. I have a nurse," pointing to Rosemary, "and a body guard," pointing to Stephen. "Even though we have the assassin in the Medical Clinic, we don't know if there is another one. We can't leave here unless we have an armed escort, and even then, it doesn't mean we're home free. A good sniper can get me from almost anywhere around the port."

"Not on my watch," said Colonel Barrister. "I will make sure that when you are ready to leave the ship, you will be protected. In the meantime, let me bring on additional troops to relieve Pitman's people."

"You can do that," said Martin. "But Pitman won't leave. She is going to wait until all her wounded are moved off the ship. She is a mother hen. I think she is younger than most of those soldiers that are with her, but they would follow her anywhere. She was badly wounded, and she wouldn't let them take her off the ship. She wanted to stay and help. She had been shot twice but would not leave her troops. When she couldn't command because of her wounds, Corporal Roberts stepped right in. Pitman's people are well trained. For three days we were in a war, and they did a fantastic job."

"I want to meet this Pitman," said the colonel. "Is she a lieutenant?"

"Yes, she is," said Melinda.

"Get Harry Blank online," said Colonel Barrister.

"Elizabeth Barrister," said Harry. "How are you doing?"

"I just listened to a summary of what these people have gone through," said the colonel. "This is a war zone."

"No one would deny that," said Harry. "No one would believe that we would have a war zone in Florida."

"I need you to do me a favor," said Colonel Barrister.

"What do you need, Liz?" asked Harry.

"You know the story about Lieutenant Pitman, don't you?" asked the colonel.

"Yes," answered Harry. "Melinda has kept me informed. Charlie has, also. Why?"

"I know this ship is not officially a combat zone," said the colonel. "But I want to reward Pitman and her men for their actions. Find out what I can do for her. See if I can move her up in rank. You know what I mean. If the request comes through you, it will happen right away. If I do it, it might take a month or more. Is there anything I can do for Fred and his people?" They have put up a fantastic fight. I understand he lost a few of his people as well."

"They all work for Melinda," said Harry Blank.

"I don't understand," said Colonel Barrister.

"It is the same organization," said Harry. "It is the same organization you worked with before. The only difference is that Melinda now runs it."

"But they introduced Ron as their leader," said Colonel Barrister.

"Melinda," said Charlie. One of Fred's men just called me. Two of your people have just been shot."

"Who?" Melinda asked. She looked around the room. Everyone is accounted for."

"No," said Rosemary. "Susan and Jose are not here. They ducked out twenty minutes ago to help in the engine room."

"Martin," said Melinda. "Would you check on those two people. Find out who they are and call me."

Martin got up and left the room.

Harry continued, "That was before she knew it was you," Harry said. "She is semi-retired because of the babies."

"What is the rest of the story?" asked Barrister.

"I should let Melinda tell you," said Harry.

"Never mind," said the colonel. "You tell me."

"Okay," said Harry. "Here is a short version. Last year one of her investigators, Tom Markus, was killed by mistake. Melinda's people captured the killers, and Dr. Wellfleet questioned them. They found out that a group called the Exchange had hired them to kill Peter Mancuso. Melinda tracked the group all over the world. She found crooked politicians, crooked police, and crooked judges. The Exchange was smuggling guns, drugs, and young children for the sex trade. Melinda's group followed the trail of corruption. In the process, she lost her heart to Martin. Finally, Melinda's people found the secondary depot in the Berkshires and Sheena and her people raided it then blew it up. Left some hole in the ground, I understand. Then they found the main depot on the east coast and raided it. Martin and Melinda, as well as Ron, was wounded in that raid. When the operation was finished and everyone was recuperating Martin proposed to Melinda, and Ron proposed to Lucinda. A double wedding took place at the New York Center, and both couples decided to take time off. Jason was given temporary command of The Company, and Sheena was given operational command while she recuperated from her injuries. She had been badly hurt during one of their last operations in the states. She was injured badly, but was able to command from a wheelchair. Three weeks ago, I asked Lucinda to put together a crew for a trip on the Valley Forge. Their job was to find out how material was being smuggled to the islands. Just before the ship was to sail, I was notified that there was an empty suite available. I pulled some strings and got it for Melinda and Martin. I wanted Melinda to act as Den Mother. I didn't know at the time how far along Melinda was in her pregnancy. At the beginning of the second week on the ship, Melinda became unconscious, and she was medivacked to Ft. Lauderdale. Ft. Lauderdale couldn't help her, and she was flown to a Miami hospital. The operation that was called for couldn't be done there, and she was flown to a hospital in South Carolina, which could perform the procedure. The operation was a success. Six hours after the operation, while resting, she had severe cramps. She gave birth to twins, a boy and a girl. Knowing Melinda, she has shown you the babies already, hasn't she?"

"Yes, she has," said Barrister. "They are precious."

"So now I have brought you up to date," said Harry. "Is there anything else you need to know?"

"No," said the colonel. "I have everything I need. I thought I might move Melinda and her group out of here by helicopter, but with the fighting, I wouldn't take that chance. I'll get back to you when I've made a decision."

Colonel Barrister turned to both her lieutenants and said, "Take two platoons each and clean up this ship. Start at the top and work your way down. Put a platoon on each deck. Give no warnings. If you see anyone carrying a weapon, he is an enemy."

Turning to Charlie, the colonel asked, "How many men do you still have on deck?"

"I've teamed them up with the balance of Pitman's marines," said Charlie. "Pitman's people are all in uniform, so your people can't make a mistake."

"Fred," asked the colonel. "What about your people?"

"I don't think there will be a problem," he said. "They are all smaller than I am and just as black."

236

The colonel smiled. She turned to her lieutenants, "Let's get moving. I would like to finish the war before 1700 hours. If not, I will be forced to take a week-long cruise."

"You wouldn't want to take a week-long cruise?" asked Charlie.

"If I went on a week-long cruise without my husband," answered Barrister. "I would be looking at a long lonely winter as a single person."

Melinda laughed. "I didn't know you were married," she said. "When did that happen?"

"When I got my Captain's bars," said Barrister, "he proposed. "I only had forty-eight hours leave before I shipped out to Japan. I spent the weekend with him and slept all the way to Japan. I didn't think I would go any further up the chain of command, so we planned to get married the following year. The following year they shipped me to Alaska and I received my Major's leaves. When I finally got home from that tour of duty, he grabbed my hand, we jumped into a cab to city hall and we stood before a justice of the peace. That is how I got married. Four months later, I had to take a leave from the service."

"Why did you take a leave?" asked Rosemary.

"I found I was pregnant," said Barrister, smiling. "Five months after that, I gave birth to a beautiful daughter. The military, in their infinite wisdom, cancelled my leave thirty days later, and sent me to Greenland. I thank my lucky stars for my mother. She took my daughter in with her, and my daughter took over the household. With that transfer, I received my silver oak leaves. When I became a lieutenant colonel, I was assigned to command a desk, but I refused. I said I would make a fuss. Then Harry came to my rescue, and now I command a battalion. That's my whole story."

"I don't believe this," said Fred. "One of my men just reported shots being fired on Deck C aft engine room. I thought my men went through there an hour ago. I'll send another team to see what's happening. Charlie, do you have anyone near there?"

"I don't have anyone available," said Charlie. The ones I do have are working with Pitman's people, and they are on Deck 8. I have four people in the Medical Clinic assisting Dr. Wellfleet."

"I think Benjamin is still in the aft engine room," said Sheena. "He was there when your troops threw gas grenades. I know he didn't have a gas mask. I tried reaching him ten minutes ago. I still didn't get an answer. The gas must have knocked him out. When the gas cleared out, he must have awakened and started shooting again.

237

"Colonel," said Fred. "I guess it is time for me to borrow some of your men."

Colonel Barrister reached into her pocket, pulled out a walkie-talkie, and gave an order. Five minutes later a lieutenant knocked on the door. "I have three squads coming on board as we speak," he said. "Where do you want us to go?"

"Fred," said the colonel. "Take the lieutenant and get on with it. If you need additional help, let me know. See if they can find Benjamin Britain."

"Thanks, Colonel," said Fred. I'll keep you informed. Turning to the lieutenant he asked, "Do you have any gas grenades?"

"Sorry," said the lieutenant. "We weren't prepared for that kind of warfare. I'll pass the word to have the gas grenades' brought to us. Where will we be using the gas?"

Fred told the lieutenant, and they both left the suite heading for Deck C engine room aft."

Fred called Four-four and Four-three and asked them their situation. They both reported that they were under fire and were slowly reducing the enemy. Martin had come by and identified the two dead bodies. He was unable to move them. He left and said he was going back to the suite.

"Benjamin," said Sheena. "Can you hear me?"

"Yes," replied Benjamin, sounding groggy.

"What is happening where you are?" Sheena asked.

"When I first got down here," said Benjamin, "I was able to find a secure spot, and I started shooting at the bad guys in overalls. The next thing I knew, I was waking up and discovered that I had been shot in the leg. I was able to stop the bleeding with a tourniquet. I looked around and saw that some of the people in overalls were also waking up. I started shooting them. There seemed to be more of them shooting at me than when I started."

"There are some soldiers coming down to you," said Sheena. "Fred's people will be with them. Let them do their job. There are just too many of the enemy around the ship. We need an exterminator. I'll see you later. Take care of yourself."

"Now you know why I won't leave the nursery," Melinda said to Barrister. "The fighting keeps breaking out, even with all the soldiers on the ship. The Captain of the Valley Forge is letting those passengers who have cleared the background checks leave the ship. I have Pitman's marines escorting them to safety. Those passengers that did not pass the background checks are being escorted to Deck 12. Suzy Q arranged for food and drink to be available for them. The Security people are in civilian clothes. They are keeping an eye out for any troublemakers. The Security people are all armed. If you have a few extra men, I would like to have them go up there, as well. The passengers were patted down and escorted to Deck 12. While they are on Deck 12, their cabins are being checked, and their luggage is being searched."

Colonel Barrister took out her walkie-talkie, gave another order and put the walkie-talkie away. She walked out of the nursery and into the dining room. She poured herself another cup of hot coffee and returned to the nursery.

"We have drinks in here," said Rosemary.

"I have to walk as I'm thinking, said Colonel Barrister. "That's why I can't command a desk"

"Before you came on board, we were taking a break, especially since the babies are quiet. Thanks again for convincing Edward to be quiet. Will that trick work for me?"

"You never know," said Barrister, smiling at Rosemary. "You just never know."

"Fred just reported," said Charlie. "He lost two more men. Two of Barrister's men are down as well. Five of the enemy have been killed. These people just won't stop fighting. The gas grenades have just arrived. It will take a few minutes to give out gasmasks to the troops. Fred and his people haven't located Benjamin yet. He has requested two more squads. There are twenty or so enemy combatants in the aft engine room. They are doing some damage in the engine room. He said he can hear steam whistling out of the pipes, and he sees oil dripping down the wall."

"Melinda," said Dr. Wellfleet. "That Colonel Ramirez was able to break free and take a hostage. She has threatened to kill everyone in the Medical Clinic. I don't know how she broke the zip ties. She must have had help. She is dragging one of Fred's people to the door. You won't believe this. Amy somehow got a gun and shot the colonel and then passed out. Amy doesn't look well. She is very pale, and her lips are blue. She didn't kill Ramirez, just badly wounded her. I'll get back to you later," he said.

"Melinda," said Martin. "The Captain just told me that all the passengers are off the ship with the exception of the 42 he is holding on Deck 12. New York is having difficulty getting enough information to clear them. The two bodies were Susan and Jose. I haven't been able to move them because of the shooting."

"Can you lock them in the brig?" asked Colonel Barrister.

"I don't think our brig is large enough," said Lucinda. "It could hold twenty people, maybe."

"Is there a way to speed the checking process?" asked Rosemary. "Can we release those who are less questionable and put the rest in the brig?"

Melinda thought about that. "I don't think that is a good idea," she said. "If they are the enemy and are released, they could end up fighting us on the pier. I rather we err on our side caution and hold them on the ship." Turning to Barrister she asked, "Do you have extra men that we can use?"

"I have plenty of men," said the colonel. "How many do you want, and where do you want them?"

"I think two squads should be enough," said Melinda. "Have them go up to Deck 12 and relieve the Security people."

"Alpha Base, this is Barrister. "I need two squads on Deck 12 port side aft on the Valley Forge. Report when they are in place."

"Barrister, this is Alpha base. Two squads on their way to Deck 12 port side aft."

"Computer, conference call, confirm," said Martin.

"Conference call confirmed," said the Computer.

"One of our lookouts has reported three small boats have snuck past the Coast Guard ships that were stationed at the channel entrance. They are heading directly for us. One of the Coast Guard ships has started moving behind the small boats. Two of the small boats are firing on the Coast Guard ship. There is a gun battle in the channel. The second Coast Guard ship is also coming into the channel to assist the first Coast Guard ship. The Coast Guard is being very careful. There are many civilian small boats in the channel in addition to the cruise ships. Everyone has moved past the Valley Forge and into the southern channel. There is almost no room for the Coast Guard ships to maneuver around the small boats. One of the small boats has been hit and is on fire. It has exploded. I wonder what they were carrying. The second boat has been hit by gunfire from the lead Coast Guard ship and has stopped in the middle of the channel. The third boat has come behind the Valley Forge, thrown something in the water, and has sped away towards the south channel. There has been an explosion near the back of the Valley Forge."

"Colonel Barrister," asked Martin. "Can you get a situation report from your men in the aft engine room?"

"Echo Two, this is Barrister."

"This is Echo Two," replied the team leader.

"What is your situation in the aft engine room?" Barrister asked.

"There has been an explosion outside the hull, aft of us," Fisher replied. "I don't know what the damage is at this time. I sent a squad to check the rear of the engine room. The fighting is extremely heavy in our area. It seems there are more people down here than when we first arrived. As soon as I get the report, I will relay it to you."

"Sergeant Fisher reported that the fighting is heavy in the aft engine room," said Barrister. "He has sent a squad to inspect the rear of the aft engine room and report any damage from the explosion."

"Charlie," reported Four-Three. "There is a commotion on Deck 12. Can you see it on your monitor?

Martin turned on the monitor, sat down and moved the control stick until he could see Deck 12. He switched from camera to camera until he came to the one that showed the food court on Deck 12. It looked like the passengers were trying to take the soldiers' weapons.

"Colonel Barrister," said Martin, "your soldiers are being overwhelmed on Deck 12."

Everyone stood behind Martin and watched the fighting on Deck 12. For a moment, it seemed that the passengers were winning. Then something started happening. The passengers started falling down.

"Fred," said Martin smiling. "Are your men on Deck 12?"

"I guess so," he answered. "I didn't send them to Deck 12. Four-Three probably was up that way and jumped into the fighting. My people know who the good guys are."

"Well," said the colonel. "I'm glad we didn't send those passengers ashore. Those that survived will be handcuffed and put in the brig."

Chapter 11

Fred watched the screen. "Your soldiers have the fighting well in hand. It looks like only six suspects have survived."

The colonel turned to his lieutenant and asked, "Who is in charge on Deck 12?"

"Sergeant Candid is in charge, Colonel," replied the lieutenant. "He is Bravo Three."

"Bravo Three, this is Barrister, situation report."

"Barrister, this is Bravo Three," replied Sergeant Candid. "My squad and I got to Deck 12 aft just as the fighting started. I saw six passengers attack a single soldier. They tried to wrestle his weapon away from him. The soldier yelled for assistance, and then all the passengers started fighting the soldiers. One of the passengers was able to take a gun from a soldier and shoot him. I shot that passenger. As I walked over to check that he was dead, passengers around us started falling down. When I checked them, they were dead. Within minutes, the soldiers had everything under control. They are used to fighting with rifles, not the M11 pistols. I think they need a little more training and the holsters have to be modified for a faster draw. This entire operation is so strange. We're not used to dealing with civilians who are really combatants who are not in uniform."

"I agree with you, Sergeant," said Colonel Barrister. "It gets stranger and stranger. I'll send up body bags and instructions."

"Melinda," said Barrister. "My sergeant says we have eighteen bodies on Deck 12 aft."

"I'll have Security go up to Deck 12 with body bags and gurneys to help move the bodies," said Melinda. "Security knows to take the bodies to deck 1 port side aft. They will be put in luggage carriers and then taken out to the trucks."

"You have morgue trucks on the dock?" Barrister asked.

"No," answered Melinda. "We couldn't get that many morgue trucks. We are putting the bodies in the regular military trucks. We are trying to do it quickly because of the weather. As each truck is filled with the luggage carts it will be driven to the morgue. Harry said they have armed escorts for the trucks. Are they your people?"

"Yes," said Barrister. "I supplied the armed escorts, but I didn't know they were for the dead bodies. Why do you need armed escorts for dead bodies?"

"I think that the trucks will be attacked on the way to the morgue," said Rosemary. "I don't know the reason, yet."

"I sent soldiers to the pier where the tug is going to land," said Barrister. The bodies will be loaded into refrigerated trucks. As soon as the truck is full, they will be driven to the military morgue with armed escorts."

"I thought this pier was going to be cleared of all civilians," said Ron.

"That was my understanding," said Barrister. "Why?"

"I see a group of civilians on the west side of the pier," said Ron. "They don't seem to be following directions of the pier Security to leave the area. There is some pushing and shoving. I see weapons. Colonel, I think you had better warn your people. There is gunfire at the head of the pier on the west side. This is murder. Those Security people aren't armed."

"Alpha Base, this is Barrister, Red Alert," Barrister said. "There is gunfire at the head of the pier. The civilians are combatants. Assist Security. Security guards are not armed."

Martin clicked around the screen and moved the outboard camera to show the side of the ship. "Colonel," he said. "This might be another fake tactic. The combatants are trying to open the gangways. They want to send more people onto the ship."

"I see it," said Barrister. "I didn't get these oak leaves from a mail order catalogue," she said smiling. "Notice what my troops are doing. That's without me giving additional orders."

As everyone watched the monitors, they saw what the Colonel meant. Three squads rushed to the gangways and subdued those people trying to force their way onto the Valley Forge. Every fourth soldier standing in ranks fell out, formed on their sergeant and moved towards the head of the pier. As the soldiers approached the civilians at the head of the pier, the civilians turned and started firing on the solders. Once the soldiers were fired upon they returned fire. Within minutes, the fighting ended, and thirty-five civilians and three soldiers lay dead on the pier.

"I guess we have to send body bags to the head of the pier," said Lucinda. "The security people will need medical assistance. I'm glad that we released all of the passengers and no one saw what was happening on the pier."

"Your people won't have to do a thing," said Colonel Barrister. "My men know what to do, they are well trained. They know how to follow orders and they know how to think on their feet. In fact, Major Forcht figured out a way to safely move Melinda and her babies off the ship."

243

"That I would like to hear," said Martin.

"Why don't I wait until Major Forcht gets back," said Colonel Barrister. "I'll let him tell you."

"Where is he now?" Melinda asked.

"He's on Deck 12," answered Barrister. "Let me check." She took out her walkie-talkie and called him. He answered that he is available now. She directed him to come to the suite.

"I guess I have time for a cup of tea," said Melinda. "Care to join me?" she asked Colonel Barrister.

Twenty minutes later, there was a knock on the door and Major Forcht walked in. Melinda saw a man just as tall as she was with broad shoulders and a soldier's bearing. He had close cropped hair and was clean shaven. He walked to the Colonel and stood at attention.

"At ease," said Colonel Barrister. "Melinda, this is Major Forcht. Jon, I would like to introduce you to Melinda Xavier. She runs The Company. That's the outfit I told you about on the way down here from Colorado."

Forcht walked over and shook Melinda's hand. "I have to tell you Melinda, I've fought in many different types of combat situations but I've never fought a war like this," he said. "How long has it been going on?"

"It started less than a week ago," Melinda answered. "Before that, we had only smugglers to deal with. We had eight of our people on board this ship to do nothing but observe. When the fighting started we had to ask for help. Charlie came with twenty-four of his people. Three days ago the battling got worse and we started losing a lot of people. Charlie's group had the greatest losses. We asked the Enterprise for help, and they sent us a platoon of marines. They weren't on the Valley Forge four hours, when we came under attack, again. Charlie needed more personnel and was able to bring Fred and his 'little people' from Aruba to help us. They are unbelievable. The more people we bring on the ship, the more of the enemy shows up. We know that there are people from at least four different cartels aboard. We think they have come on as regular passengers as well as coming on as raiding parties. We know they are here for the cargo. However, in addition to the cargo, the Mexican cartel hired an assassin for two million dollars to hurt or kill me. The only way the cartel could hurt me was to have one of my babies kidnapped. Harry Blank told us about this plan, and we were able to thwart that effort and capture the assassin. When the cartels first attacked the Valley Forge, it was only a shooting war. After that, it got worse. The cartel attacked the safe room where we were keeping the assassin. They used an excessive amount of Semtex. The explosion was so fierce that it killed the guards, the men from the cartel themselves and badly injured the prisoner, Amy Gelz. A team of men from one of the cartels tried carrying Amy off the ship. Fred and his people stopped them and took Amy to the Medical Clinic. After they examined her they found that her spine had been severed above the waist by a piece of shrapnel. We also captured a Colonel from the secret police of Panama. She is not a very nice person. Now you're up to date. The problem is I want to get off the ship safely with my babies and my team. If I use the gangway, I'll be in plain view of a sniper. We have not thought of any other way for us to get off the ship safely, and I really don't want to stay on for another week. The colonel says you figured out a way to get us off safely. Tell us."

"It's easy," said Major Forcht. "We bring APC's onto the ship."

"Wait a minute," said Rosemary. "What's an APC?"

"Sorry," said Forcht. "I forgot I'm talking to civilians. An APC is an armored personnel carrier. I have a portable ramp on the pier that is strong enough to allow the APC to drive onto the Valley Forge through the aft hatch. I happened to 'borrow' four APC's from the National Guard here in Ft. Lauderdale as soon as the colonel mentioned the problem. I figured since we borrowed all of their trucks, four more items wouldn't be missed. Besides, I'll return them when we're finished."

"Elizabeth," said Melinda. "You have some sharp people working for you."

"If they weren't sharp," replied Barrister, "they wouldn't be working for me. He makes sure I'm connected to the rest of the world with all the electronics that are available."

"I'll be right back," Melinda said. She got up and left the room.

"Computer, online," said Melinda

"Computer online, Melinda," said the Computer.

"Is the Major connected?" she asked.

"Major Forcht is connected," replied the Computer.

Melinda returned to the nursery. "Just for your information, Major Forcht, everyone in this room is connected."

"Elizabeth," asked Melinda. "How many in your battalion are connected?"

"I, Major Forcht and my two lieutenants," answered Barrister. "No one else travels with me. The two lieutenants are also my bodyguards. They have saved my bacon more than once."

"Can we set up a schedule to get us off the ship?" asked Melinda. "I would like to be off the ship before they move the cargo. I want to observe the action from a distance." Turning to Major Forcht she asked, "When do you plan to bring the APC's aboard the Valley Forge?"

"I've already done that," Forcht replied. "I am having one of them especially prepared for you, Martin, Rosemary, Stephen and the babies. I've put extra blankets and pillows for the babies in that APC. I am having food and water brought to each of the APC's as well. One of the things my military training has taught me was to always plan for the worst. Lucinda, Ron, Charlie and Sheena will be in the second APC."

"Wait a minute," said Sheena. "What about our wounded?"

"I don't feel they are in any danger," said Forcht. "If they attract attention I'll bring on another APC."

"I understand Sheena's concern," said Melinda. "Her partner was wounded, and I believe he was moved to the Medical Clinic. Can you get a couple more APC's?"

"I already have two extra APC's in case they were needed," said Forcht. We can use them for the wounded. Let me make a call and I'll have them fitted out for the wounded." He took out his encrypted cell phone, punched a number on his speed dial and spoke for a few minutes.

"I've just been told that there are four more APC's on the road with a squad of soldiers in each. They are heading for the pier where the tugboat brought the bodies."

"Barrister," said Melinda, pointing to Forcht. "I understand why you keep him."

Barrister laughed. "I have to keep him," she said. "He knows where all the bodies are buried. Sorry about the pun. It was unintended."

"Since we have to wait awhile," said Ron. "I would like to order some lunch. For how many should I order?" he asked.

Everyone raised their hand. Melinda, Lucinda and Sheena started laughing. Barrister, Forcht, Rosemary and Stephen stood there, not understanding why those two were laughing so hard. After the laughter died down, Melinda explained that Ron is always asking for food. It did not matter where they traveled or the time of day. This is the first time in three weeks that Ron has asked for food. Ron smiled, picked up the phone and ordered lunch for everyone.

"Barrister, this is Echo Two," said the team leader in the aft engine room.

"This is Barrister. What do you have?"

"My squad just returned from the inspection of the aft engine room," said Echo Two. "There is water coming in through a shattered gasket on the starboard propeller shaft. Until the fighting stops, no one can get into the engine room to make repairs and start the pumps. This ship is not going anywhere. It will have to be towed to a dry dock for repairs."

Colonel Barrister turned to Melinda and said, "It was just reported that the ship is taking on water in the starboard aft engine room. That explosion damaged the gaskets on the propeller shaft."

"Harry, are you still online?" asked Melinda.

"I'm here," said Harry. "What's happening?"

"One of the three little boats that had passed into the channel threw an explosive of some kind, and it damaged a gasket on the propeller shaft of the Valley Forge. The ship is taking on water. Until the fighting stops, no one can get into the engine room to start the pumps. Everything was shut down when the fighting started."

"Computer online," said Melinda.

"Computer is online, Melinda," said the Computer.

"Get the Captain online," asked Melinda.

"I'm online Melinda," said the Captain. "What's happening? Are they still fighting in the engine room? I have emergency lights blinking on my control board. It shows water in the engine room."

"One of Colonel Barrister's squads was able to inspect the starboard aft engine room. He reported that the explosion damaged the gaskets on the propeller shaft and water is coming in. The pumps cannot be started until the fighting stops. I understand there are more suspects fighting than when we started two hours ago. I've asked Colonel Barrister to send three more squads to the aft engine room to try to overwhelm any suspects who are still alive. I asked Fred to assist them. Many of the surveillance cameras have been destroyed in the fighting."

"Melinda," said Dr. Wellfleet. "Amy's heart has stopped beating. She's in cardiac arrest. Three of the doctors are working on her. It doesn't look good. She lost a lot of blood when the suspects were trying to take her off the ship. They have pumped five pints of blood into her. They were able to restart her heart. One of the doctors told me that they found a small piece of shrapnel that had nicked the wall of her intestines. They were able to stop the bleeding in her intestines but they fear infection. They are pumping her full of antibiotics. Now it is just a waiting game. She won't be able to be moved for a while."

Edward woke up and started to cry. Rosemary picked him up and took him to the changing table. She changed his diaper and offered him a bottle, which he refused. He continued crying and fussing. Rosemary thought of what Barrister had done earlier and whispered those words into Edwards's ear. Edward stopped crying and fussing. Rosemary looked at Colonel Barrister, smiled and mouthed, 'thank you'. Colonel Barrister just smiled.

"Okay everybody," said Forcht, "I was planning to move everyone down to Deck 2 to board the APC's at noon but the fighting has started again on the promenade deck. The crew elevators are not working. That means we would have to use the passenger elevators, and that would expose everyone to gunfire. I recommend we wait an hour to see if Barrister's people can subdue the enemy and stop the fighting. The other choice would be to walk to the forward crew elevator. We would take it to Deck 2. I can move the APC's to the forward elevator but we can't leave by the forward hatch. I was told that the fork lifts have been damaged, so we can't move the ramp."

"Can you maneuver the APC's inside the ship?" asked Colonel Barrister.

"Yes, that's one of the things I like about this model APC," said Forcht. "It is like handling a large SUV."

"I think we should wait," said Melinda. "If it was just the adults, I would vote for the forward elevator. But we have the babies to carry, and that would make it a more dangerous."

"I agree with Melinda," said Rosemary. "I don't want to put the babies in harm's way. I vote we stay in the nursery until the very last minute."

"Based on what I was told," Barrister said, "this ship is not going anywhere, anytime soon, so we don't have to rush getting off the ship. I notified the Captain, and it is my understanding that he has contacted the main office to cancel next week's cruise. As soon as the main office gets back to him, he'll call me."

"Barrister, this is Bravo Three, Deck 12 is secured," reported Sergeant Candid. "All the bodies have been removed, and the six prisoners have been escorted to the brig."

"Roger Bravo Three," said Barrister. "Stay up there until relieved." Barrister turned to Melinda and relayed the information.

"Now, if they can stop the shooting in the engine rooms we would be home free," said Rosemary. "I don't feel that is going to happen any time soon. What I do not understand is where all of these people, that we are fighting, coming from? No one can get on the ship. Does that mean that the cartels have that many people on the ship as crew and passengers?"

"I've ordered eight more platoons to come on board," said Barrister. "It seems the only way we are going to stop the fighting is to overwhelm the fighters on every deck at the same time. I will have a platoon on each deck. All of the passengers that have been cleared have been escorted off the ship. With the exception of the bridge crew and the Captain, everyone else is a possible enemy."

"Barrister, this is Echo Two," said Fisher. "We could use additional help in the engine room. I have lost six people. We are being forced to move further aft. The water level has risen twelve inches on the lower deck. We still can't get to the pump room to get the pumps operating."

"Echo Two, this is Barrister. There is another platoon heading your way."

"Melinda," said the Captain. "The main office has called. They have cancelled the cruise for next week. They are sending a dive team to examine the propellers to see if the damage to the gasket can be repaired while we are at this dock. We are going to need protection for the divers, especially since three boats were able to sneak by the Coast Guard."

"Harry," said Melinda. "We are going to need protection for the dive team that the shipping company is sending to the Valley Forge. I am concerned, since three boats have already been able to sneak past the Coast Guard boats that were sitting in the channel."

"Melinda," said Harry. "I'll contact the National Guard unit to see who is available. Let me know when the divers arrive."

"Captain," Melinda said. "Let Harry Blank know when the divers are expected. He is contacting the National Guard in Ft. Lauderdale to see what is available to protect the divers."

"Colonel Barrister," said Major Forcht. "I'm going down to Deck 4. I am not able to see the entire picture on the monitor."

"Very well," said Barrister.

Forcht took the elevator to Deck 4. The inside deck was empty. He opened the outside midship door and went out on deck. He walked to the railing and studied the action on the pier. Everything seemed to be moving smoothly. Fresh food was being moved off the ship onto refrigerated trucks. His eyes followed one of the trailers as it moved to the head of the pier. He noticed a green and white van pull up to the fence and stop. He watched as the roof panel of the van slid open and a large pipe put on its roof. It took

Forcht a minute to recognize what that pipe was. He ducked down and moved away from the doors. He lay down on the deck and covered his head. The explosion, when it came, surprised him by its intensity. The doors behind him were blown in. Forcht found himself covered with broken glass and splinters from the doors. He sat up and touched the side of his face. He looked at his hands. They were covered in blood.

"Colonel Barrister," said Forcht. "I am on Deck 4 midships, starboard side. The ship was hit with a rocket. It exploded with an intensity that surprised me. It destroyed the doors and blew out a couple of the windows. No other damage seems apparent."

"Have you been hurt?" asked Barrister."

"Only some cuts from the flying glass, that's all," said Forcht. "I'm going to have to go to the Medical Clinic for to have the glass removed from my shoulder."

Forcht took the elevator down to Deck 1 and walked to the Medical Clinic. The nurse escorted him to the treatment room and helped him take off is shirt which was covered with blood. She put on sterile gloves and took out a tray that contained tweezers, swabs and an antiseptic.

"This is going to hurt," the nurse said, as she started picking the glass chards from Jon's shoulder. Jon just sat there while the nurse finished removing the glass chards, putting an antibiotic cream on the wounds, and covering it with a bandage. "Keep the wound dry and get back to me so I can check it for infection. I'm sure I have taken all the glass out," she said. She moved the magnified light. "Let me check the side of your face, the blood keeps dripping." She examined the area around his eye. "I'll have to get the doctor. There are a couple of splinters of glass that are very close to the eye.

The doctor came in, examined the area around the eye, picked up a fresh pair of tweezers and removed four slivers of glass. "You were very lucky, young man," he said. "Let the nurse clean and bandage your face and you are good to go." He smiled at Forcht, turned and left the room.

He nurse cleaned his face with an antiseptic and bandaged the side of his face. Keep it dry for as long as you can. Come back tomorrow and I'll change the bandage."

Forcht headed back on deck. "Computer, get me Martin."

"Martin is online," said the Computer.

"Can anyone see the end of the pier on the monitor?"

"No," answered Martin. "The one camera that I was able to

maneuver has been destroyed. We have no views of that part of the pier or the parking lot."

"Okay," said Forcht. "I'm going to try to get back on deck." Five minutes later Forcht continued, "I'm on Deck 4. The damage is extensive. I have a good view of the pier. The green van is still there, and the rocket launcher is still on the roof. Someone in that van just fired another rocket. It looks like they are trying to hit the bridge wing. Another rocket was fired and missed the bridge wing and has fallen in the water. There was no explosion. We need someone on Deck 15 with a rifle to stop these people. A black van has pulled up next to the green van. That van's roof is sliding opening. Another rocket launcher has being placed on its roof. Another rocket has been fired at one of the lower decks. I cannot see what it hit. These rockets are more powerful than any I've seen on the battlefield. I am going forward and up to Deck 8."

"I understand," said Barrister. "I'll try to get someone up to Deck 15 starboard side with a rifle." She turned to Melinda and said, "Any of your people qualified with a rifle?"

Melinda turned to Stephen and said, "Stephen, grab a rifle and go up on Deck 15 and help them out. Lucinda, you grab a rifle and back him up."

Lucinda and Stephen each picked up a rifle and a bandolier of ammunition. Rosemary unlocked the door, and Lucinda and Stephen left the nursery, walked out the door and entered the elevator. They took the elevator to Deck 15 and carefully went out on deck. Stephen took a quick look over the railing, and turned to Lucinda and said, "There are now two vans on the dock with their roofs open. On the count of three, we will stand up and fire. I'll fire on the green van and you fire on the black one. Ready?"

Lucinda nodded her head.

"One, two, three," Stephen said. They stood up, leaned over the railing, quickly sighted the enemy and started firing. What surprised both Stephen and Lucinda was that there was no return fire. They stopped firing and observed the action on the pier. The food trucks stopped moving after the first rocket had been fired. The drivers had gotten out of their trucks and had run to the side of the pier for safety. Now that the rifle fire had ceased, the drivers were getting back into their trucks, starting their engines and started moving off the pier. Soldiers from the battalion escorted the trucks to the gate. Two soldiers entered each van and dragged the bodies out. There were five bodies in each van. The bodies were searched and each one was carrying an identical identification card that showed that they lived in Ft.

Lauderdale, Florida, at the same address. Fingerprints of the dead were taken before they were placed into the body bags. The soldiers found a cart and used it to transport the dead to the truck that would take the bodies to the morgue.

"Melinda," said Lucinda. "We were able to stop them before they could fire any more rockets. The soldiers on the pier have taken five bodies from each van, put them in body bags and moved them to the trucks. They have removed ten rockets from the green van and five from the black van. The rockets have Chinese writing on the casing. That's a lot of firepower. I can't see the license plates from this angle. Can you have Ron come up here and put in a new camera? If not, we will need to have an observer to keep an eye on the pier."

"Good job, Lucinda," said Melinda. "Ron is on his way. I want you to stay there until he is finished installing the new camera."

"Melinda," said Stephen. "I'll stay up here, and Lucinda will be coming back to the suite. I don't think we need two people to stand guard."

"Good point," said Melinda. "Let me know if you need a relief."

"Colonel," said Forcht, "I'm on Deck 8 forward port side. I see four small boats coming north, up the channel. The Coast Guard have challenged them. Three of the boats are turning around and are heading south. The fourth boat has sped up, gone around the Coast Guard boat, and is coming this way. It looks like there are six men in the boat. The Coast Guard has fired at the boat. It has stopped dead in the water. There is smoke coming from their engine. One of the Coast Guard zodiacs is heading to the small boat. There is gunfire coming from the small boat. The men on the zodiac have returned fire. Now the firing has stopped. A Coast Guardsman is boarding the small boat. They must have found something. They are transferring small boxes to the zodiac. The zodiac is towing the small boat to the side of the channel and anchoring it there. The zodiac is going back to the Coast Guard boat and is transferring those boxes. They have now finished loading the boxes onto the Coast Guard boat and are moving back into the channel."

"Captain," asked Melinda. "Would you call the Coast Guard boat and find out what that small boat was carrying?"

"Melinda," answered the Captain. "The Coast Guard told me that the small boat was carrying two hundred pounds of Semtex. The captain of the Coast Guard boat asked what was going on. I told him I didn't know. I think you should tell Harry. Two hundred pounds of Semtex could do a lot of damage to a ship like the Valley Forge."

"Computer, get Harry online," said Melinda

"Harry Blank is online," said the Computer.

"Harry," said Melinda. "The Coast Guard stopped a boat that was carrying two hundred pounds of Semtex. The Captain feels we are still under attack and I agree. That amount of explosives would do a lot of damage to this ship. I think it is time to remove the graphene. Maybe then the Valley Forge wouldn't be the center of the attention."

"I agree Melinda," said Harry. "I'll contact NASA to find out where their trucks are. I'm surprised they aren't on the pier. They were told what time the ship was going to dock."

"Let Colonel Barrister know when you find out," said Melinda. "Her troops have been fighting since we docked over five hours ago. One of her men, Major Forcht, has figured how to get us off the ship safely. With the rocket attacks, we had to delay our departure by an hour. Now that it has quieted down, we are making our way to the APC's. There are two of them parked in the forward bay. All the cameras are still on except for Deck 4. The ship's maintenance crew never got around to fixing them. I think that was on purpose. I'll keep you informed."

"Colonel Barrister, this is Harry Blank. I just spoke to NASA dispatch. Their trucks are twenty minutes out. One of their trucks had a flat, and this was the reason for the delay. The trucks are being escorted by two state police vehicles."

"Thanks for letting me know," said Barrister. "I want to get Melinda and her group off the ship before the NASA trucks get here. I have a platoon on each deck looking for suspects. All the cabins and rooms on all decks except Deck 2, 1, A, B and C have been searched and sealed. We are waiting for the gas to dissipate on Decks B and C before we can send in teams to search those areas."

"Major Forcht," said Melinda. "We are ready to leave. Where should we meet you? The colonel Barrister called for two platoons of soldiers to escort us."

"Melinda," said Jon Forcht. "It will be a few minutes yet. I was injured in that last rocket attack and I had to go to the Medical Clinic. As I started back to Deck 8 and was injured again. They just finished bandaging me as we speak. I'm on my way to Deck 2 forward. Meet you there."

"The platoons have arrived," said Martin. He walked over to the platoon leader and discussed how they were going to go down to Deck 2. "The sergeant suggests that Rosemary carry Edward. Stephen will follow Rosemary. Melinda will carry Annabelle. Martin will follow Melinda. The

253

sergeant will have a squad in the front and a column of soldiers on each side of the passageway. The rest of you stay inside the columns. There is a platoon on each deck traveling aft to forward searching all the cabins and rooms. We are going to walk down the passenger stairway. It is a long way down, but safer than taking the elevator. If we are attacked drop to the floor. The soldiers know what to do. The sergeant is ready to move. Let's go."

The soldiers formed two columns, and everyone marched in between the columns. As they got to Deck 5, gunfire erupted. Rosemary and Melinda dropped to the floor and shielded the babies with their bodies. Stephen and Martin knelt and protected the two women. A squad of soldiers ran past them heading aft. After a few minutes, they heard more gunfire. Then they heard an explosion of a hand grenade. Then they heard a second explosion. Then silence. A few moments later, the squad came back and moved to the front of the column. The column proceeded down the stairs. They met Major Forcht at the APC's. Everyone was helped into his or her assigned vehicle.

"What about the wounded?" asked Sheena.

"I checked with the Medical Clinic," said Major Forcht. "They are moving the wounded as fast as they can. There is fighting still going on in the aft engine room, making it difficult to move the patients quickly and safely. We have accounted for every one of your people except Benjamin Britain. The soldiers have not been able to get into the aft engine room to search for him. They haven't been able to get into the pump room to turn on the pumps, either. I've been instructed to get you and yours off the ship before the NASA trucks get on the pier. We'll park you far enough away from the action to be safe and still see the Valley Forge. When the wounded get here, they will loaded on the remaining APC's and transported to the Broward Medical Center in Ft. Lauderdale. They will have their own armed escorts. The pier is clear. Let's get out of here."

"Computer, get Colonel Barrister online," said Major Forcht.

"Yes, Major," said Barrister. "What do you need?"

"Everyone is loaded into the APC's and we are ready to leave the ship," said Forcht. "We have not loaded the wounded. They were delayed because of the fighting near the Medical Clinic. There are two APC's for the wounded in the forward bay. There is still gunfire in the aft engine room. Benjamin Britain has still not been located. The Computer is unable to track him. Benjamin was able to tell us, before we lost communications, that he was wounded in his leg, and was able to apply a tourniquet. Then communications ceased. Everyone one else is accounted for. We are now on the pier heading for the gate. We are taking fire from outside the gate. Is there anyone able to help us?"

"Bravo Three," said Barrister. "Where are you?"

"This is Bravo Three," answered Sergeant Candid. "I'm up on Deck 10 with a squad of men."

"Can you give the APC's covering fire?" Barrister asked.

"We'll give them covering fire as soon as they clear the pier," said Candid. "I have Bravo Two and Bravo One with me. We will send them a surprise as soon as all the APC's are clear of the pier."

"We were told that the other two APC's are staying on the ship," said Forcht. "We are clear of the pier. Have fun."

"This is Bravo Three," said Candid into his walkie-talkie. "All troops on the pier, take cover." He waited two minutes, and then all three squads started throwing hand grenades and flash bangs (stun grenades). The noise was deafening. One hand grenade landed in the green van, and blew the van into the water. The black van caught fire, and the gas tank exploded. Two minutes went by and all that could be heard was the sound of the van burning.

"This is Bravo Three," said Candid. "All troops on the pier, all clear."

"That was some show," said Forcht. "Thanks." He had the APC's move to the center of the main road and wait. From where they were parked, they could see the Valley Forge and the approach road.

"Forcht," asked Barrister. "Can you see the NASA trucks yet?"

"They are just pulling up to the pier," said Forcht. "There are five trucks and two police cars. The police cars are blocking the entrance to the pier."

"Alpha company, this is Barrister. Proceed to Deck 2 aft, starboard side loading area."

Twenty minutes later, "Barrister, this is Alpha Company, we have assembled in the loading area Deck 2 aft."

"Alpha base, this is Barrister. Direct the first NASA truck to the ship."

"Barrister, this is Alpha base," We have not been able to fix the fork lifts."

"Alpha base, this is Barrister. The trucks will have to loaded by hand, one can at a time. No more than three pallets in each truck."

The storage room was unlocked, and the soldiers started passing the cans of graphene along the deck. One of the soldiers found a portable gangway on the dock. They moved it to the ship. The gangway helped speed up the unloading process. When the first truck was fully loaded, it was driven to the end of the pier, and a second truck pulled up. It took an hour to complete the loading. As the last trucked moved towards the end of the pier, the two APC's with the wounded followed. The five trucks and the two police cars lined up and moved away from the dock and toward the interstate.

"First two APC's," said Major Forcht. "We are going to follow the NASA trucks. When the APC's with the wounded are ready they will head to Broward Health Medical Center off route 1. The hospital is expecting you. They'll do triage."

Major Forcht started opening the cabinets mounted in the APC. He had opened about half of the cabinets when the driver asked what he was looking for. Forcht asked if they still carried the thirty caliber machine guns. The driver told him that there were two machine guns stored under the floorboards. The ammunition was stored in the cabinet in the back. He told the driver to contact the second APC and have them get their machine gun ready to mount. The driver did that, and then wanted to know what trouble the Major expected.

"I always expect trouble," Major Forcht said. "That's why I'm still alive." The driver nodded his head but kept his eyes on the road.

"Computer online," said Barrister.

"Computer online, Colonel Barrister," said the Computer.

"Get Major Forcht online," said Barrister.

"I'm online, Colonel," said Forcht.

"Forcht," said Barrister. "We finally stopped the fighting in the aft engine room. Let Sheena know that we found Benjamin Britain. He had been shot in the leg and the neck. The shot to his neck clipped his communication insert. He lost a lot of blood. We are keeping him in the Medical Clinic on the Valley Forge. He is too weak to move at this time.

"Forcht," said Dr. Wellfleet. "Call me on your encrypted cell phone."

Forcht took out his cell phone and called Dr. Wellfleet. "What do you need, doc?" he asked, concern in his voice.

"I need you to do me a favor," said Dr. Wellfleet. "I want you to call Harry Blank on your cell phone, and have him call me on my cell phone. Tell him not to tell anyone he is calling me."

"You had me scared, Doc," said Forcht. "I thought you were calling to tell me that some of my men had died. I'll call Harry Blank right now."

Forcht called Harry on his encrypted cell phone and passed the message from Dr. Wellfleet.

Harry thanked him and called Dr. Wellfleet. "What is so important that you wanted me to use my encrypted cell phone and not to tell anyone?" he asked.

"You are not going to like this," said Dr. Wellfleet. "You have a mole in your organization."

"How do you know this?" asked Harry Blank.

"When I questioned Isabella Ramirez," said Wellfleet, "that Panamanian Secret Police colonel. She knew everything about the graphene powder. She knew it was on the ship, she knew the name of the chemical and she knew its value. In short, she knew everything. The only way this could happen is if she got the information from someone in your organization. Until you find out who the mole is, you have to be careful. We don't even know if it is only one mole. I have asked Ron to set up a scanner that will record the frequencies of the trackers we found embedded in each of the dead. If he can do that, then we can send it to you, and you can check each person that works with you."

"I like that idea," said Harry. "Tell him to hurry."

"I can't do that," said Dr. Wellfleet. "He is in an APC on the pier. As soon as the graphene is off the ship, he might be able to return to the Valley Forge and build a scanner/recorder."

"What's happening with the fighting?" asked Harry.

"I just received a report from Colonel Barrister," said Wellfleet. "The fighting has ended in the aft engine room. The soldiers are removing the wounded and bringing them to the Medical Clinic. The dead are being finger printed, placed in body bags and removed to the trucks on the pier. A maintenance man got into the pump room and fixed half of the pumps. The water had risen two feet. The pumps will be working hard for a while. The Coast Guard has loaned us some of their portable pumps to help get rid of the water. That will speed up the process. The divers from the National Guard are still in the water. They reported that none of the propellers have been damaged. One gasket on the starboard shaft was shattered and they are pumping some sort of sealant to stop the water flow. The Valley Forge may have to be moved to a dry dock. The company is sending a tugboat to stand by, just in case. If the Valley Forge has to go into a dry dock, the engineer said it would take four days to remove the damaged gasket and replace it with a new one. That is still within the period of time allowed to be able to take on passengers for the following week's cruise. All the graphene has been removed from the ship. It was loaded into the five NASA trucks. They are on the road with two police cars as escorts as well as the two APC's."

"Does he know how much longer the fighting on the decks is going to last?" asked Harry.

"No," said Wellfleet. "Barrister no sooner has her troop's clear one area, when fighting breaks out in another area. She is slowly losing people, and she is angry about that. The only men that have been successful are Fred and his men. However, even Fred has lost a few men, even though it was by accident. Barrister said he has three hundred soldiers going deck by deck, cabin by cabin and room by room. They have found small groups of men and women hiding in some of the public rooms. The suspects never got the word that all passengers were off the ship. It has made it easier to spot the enemy. Every now and then, one of Barrister's men was being fired upon. The return fire was deadly. Fred's men are roaming around the ship as well. Based on the speed with which Barrister's people are moving, they should complete the search of the ship in a few hours. The pier is quiet. There are four squads roaming around the pier. All we have to worry about is the water side."

"The NASA trucks have reported that they are now on the interstate," said Harry. "They can see the APC's following them."

"I don't know what Major Forcht and his band of merry men can do if there is an attack," said Wellfleet. "Unless I can convince Barrister to have a couple of squads follow the APC's."

"Colonel Barrister," said Wellfleet. "Can you spare four squads? I would like to have them follow the NASA trucks in case they are attacked. Two APC's are all that is following the NASA trucks. I don't even know if the APC's are armed. I haven't spoken to Major Forcht since they started following the NASA trucks."

"Barrister," said Major Forcht. "We are twenty miles from the dock. Both of the police cars has been hit by rocket fire and are burning. The driver and his assistant could not have survived the explosion. The first NASA truck was hit with a rocket has exploded. It has stopped in the middle of the road. The remaining four NASA trucks have pulled around the burning vehicles and have stopped a quarter mile down the road. We have one thirty-caliber machine gun on each APC. We are going to assist. Standby."

Major Forcht opened the forward hatch and pushed his way through. The thirty-caliber machine gun was passed to him through the hatch. Forcht mounted the machine gun into its turret and attached the ammunition belt. He turned and noticed the second APC was doing the same thing. Forcht called down and told them to close the shutters. A hand reached up and handed him a helmet that had a microphone and earpiece. He now had contact with his driver. He told the driver to contact the other unit and have them drive down the left side of the road, and we would drive down the right side of the road. When the APC was two hundred feet from the burning trucks, he opened fire and raked his side of the road. The enemy returned fire and Forcht was hit. He let go of the machine gun and slipped down through the hatch. His helmet caught on the edge of the hatch and was pulled off his head causing his head to bang on the crossbeam. He was knocked unconscious before he hit the floor. Rosemary and Melinda pulled Forcht out of the way. Stephen grabbed the helmet, put it on his head and struggled up through the hatch. He reached the machine gun and continued firing. A short time later Stephen was also wounded. He too let go of the machine gun and slipped to the deck, unconscious. Rosemary and Melinda pulled him away from the hatch. Rosemary scampered through the hatch, seated herself on the edge of the hatch and started firing the machine gun. The APC reached the head of the line, turned around, and stopped. The second APC pulled alongside and stopped. Rosemary climbed down into the APC and Martin took her place behind the machine gun. Rosemary handed up the helmet to Martin. She took out the combat first aid kit and started treating Major Forcht. Forcht was wounded in the neck, and was bleeding from a scalp wound. Rosemary quickly cleaned and bandaged his scalp wound then started treating the neck wound. The bullet had gone all the way through. It did not look like the bullet had damaged anything vital. She applied a battle dressing, taped it in place and then moved over to treat Stephen's wounds. Stephen had sustained serious wounds to his neck and shoulder. A piece of shrapnel nicked his skull. Rosemary was almost in shock when she saw how badly Stephen had been wounded. His face was covered with blood. She carefully cleaned his face and discovered that Stephen's head wound was minor. It was just a bleeder. She applied pressure and was able to stop the bleeding. The neck wound was serious but not life threatening. The bullet had gone all the way through. It was a small entry wound but a large exit wound. She was able to stop the bleeding and put a battlefield dressing on it. The second bullet had gone into his shoulder, but had not come out. She was going to have to make a decision. *Wait until they can get Stephen to a hospital or do the surgery in the APC.*

Chapter 12

"Melinda," asked Rosemary. "I need to make a decision about Stephen. I'm not worried about the wound to his head. I am worried about the shoulder wound. The bullet is still in him. Do I wait until we can get him to a hospital or should I remove the bullet now? The longer the bullet is in his body, the more chance of additional damage to his shoulder."

"Contact Dr. Wellfleet," said Melinda. "Let him make that decision."

"Computer, get Dr. Wellfleet online," asked Rosemary.

"I'm online, Rosemary," said Dr. Wellfleet. "What do you need?"

"Stephen has been wounded," Rosemary said. "The bullet is still in his shoulder. Do I wait until we get to a hospital, or should I take the bullet out now?"

"Is he conscious?" asked Wellfleet.

"No," said Rosemary. "When he was shot, he slipped through the hatch, banged his head and passed out."

"I want you to remove the bullet," said Dr. Wellfleet. "The longer it is in his body, the greater the chance for an infection. Do you have a medical kit with you?" he asked.

"Yes," said Rosemary. "I have a full field medical kit."

"Okay," said Wellfleet, "Have you ever done this type surgery before?"

"Yes, doctor," said Rosemary. "I've have done this a few times."

"Then let's get started," said Wellfleet. "Hook up the intravenous port. Attach the saline drip. Piggyback a morphine drip. Clean the wound. How deep is the bullet?" he asked.

"It is about three inches in," said Rosemary, after probing the wound.

"Try and grasp the bullet with the forceps," said Wellfleet, "and pull straight out. You might have to enlarge the opening to get a better grip."

Following Dr. Wellfleet's instructions, Rosemary was able to remove the bullet without increasing the size of the wound. There was a small amount of bleeding. She cleaned the wound again and debrided the damaged tissue. She applied a bandage over the wound. She then took his pulse and found it strong and steady."

"How soon can you get him to a medical facility?" asked Wellfleet.

"I don't know," said Rosemary. "I don't think we can leave the four remaining NASA trucks. When the gunmen started firing, they destroyed both police cars. Both APC's are still being fired on. Martin is operating our machine gun. Is there any chance of getting some help out here?"

"I'll check with Barrister and get back to you," said Wellfleet.

Rosemary placed a blanket over Stephen, leaned over and gently kissed him on the lips, and went to check on Major Forcht. She saw that the Major had opened his eyes and was watching her. She blushed, again. *'I don't know what is happening to me,'* she thought. *'I never, ever blush'.* She walked over to Forcht and checked his pulse.

"This is some strange war," said Forcht. "I've done three tours of duty in Afghanistan and come away without a scratch. Here, I am wounded twice. What is going on?"

"It has to be the cargo that the NASA trucks took from the Valley Forge," said Melinda. "How did the enemy know which road we would use? How many men did they have out here in this awful place? It must be ninety-five degrees. How long have they been waiting here? None of this makes sense."

There was a loud bang on the side of the APC, and they could hear Martin firing the machine gun.

"What was that?" asked Rosemary, startled.

"Sounded like a rocket bouncing off the side," said Major Forcht. "It must have been a dud."

"Rosemary," said Wellfleet. "Barrister said there are two squads speeding to you. They left ten minutes after you did. Keep an eye out for them."

"Ron, are you online?" asked Rosemary.

"Yes," said Ron.

"Barrister said there are two squads coming our way," she said. "They are ten minutes behind us. I don't have any way to contact them. Do you?"

"No," I don't. I see a vehicle coming down the road," said Ron. "I hope it's the soldiers. I'm out of ammunition, so I can't fight any more. Our driver was hit by shrapnel but is still holding on. How are you doing?"

"Not too good," replied Rosemary. "Both Major Forcht and Stephen were wounded. Martin is operating the machine gun. I don't know how much ammunition we have left for the guns."

Rosemary opened the rear view port and watched the vehicle approach. It was an army truck. It stopped two hundred feet down the road, and soldiers started jumping off the truck. She could tell from the uniforms that they were part of Barrister's battalion. They spread out on both sides of the road and slid down the embankments. She closed the view port, not wanting to put anyone in danger with a bullet bouncing around inside. She could hear bullets bouncing off the side of the APC. *'I hope Ron is okay'* she thought, as she walked back to Stephen. She sat down next to him, placed her hand on his cheek, leaned over and kissed him. He stirred, opened his eyes and smiled.

"Hi," he whispered.

"Hi, yourself," Rosemary said, leaning over and kissing him again.

He smiled again, closed his eyes and fell asleep.

Rosemary checked his vitals and then called Dr. Wellfleet. "All his numbers appear to be normal," she said. "He woke up for a few moments then went back to sleep. The antibiotics are still piggy backed with the saline. I didn't give him any more morphine. I want to wait until he wakes up and asks for it."

"That's great," said Wellfleet. "Can you get him to a hospital?"

"The soldiers just arrived," said Rosemary. "It shouldn't be long now. I'll let you know."

Everyone waited. They still heard occasional gunfire. Twenty minutes later it was quiet. The driver turned and told Melinda that one of the soldiers wanted to speak to her. She lowered the back ramp, and blinking from the sun, stepped down onto the roadway. A soldier wearing sergeant's stripes came up to her and introduced himself.

"I am Sergeant Anderson," he said. "Colonel Barrister told me that he would like you and the other APC to accompany us as we escort these remaining trucks to the NASA depot. I sent one of my men to the other trucks. They will be turning around and returning here. We are going to try to remove whatever cargo we can from the first truck and put it on the others. If any of the cans are damaged, we've been instructed to destroy the material and the damaged truck. I'll have one of the trucks push the damaged truck to the side of the road. Then I'll have an explosive charge set to go off when we are about a thousand yards down the road. The two police officers in each of the police cars are dead."

"Martin," said Melinda. "How much ammunition do we have for the machine gun?"

"It looks like we have twelve cases," replied Martin. "We only used three."

Turning to the sergeant, Melinda said, "Sergeant Anderson. If you can have six of these ammo cans taken to the other APC, we will be able to go with you. I do have a slight problem, though. I have a seriously wounded man inside. Is there a medical facility on the way to the NASA depot?"

"Yes, ma'am," said Sergeant Anderson. "There is a hospital fifteen miles down the road. I'll lead the column to the hospital and wait. I won't be able to call ahead so they won't have someone waiting for us at the emergency door."

"That is going to be tough," said Melinda. "Have someone on the truck keep an eye on us. If we want you to stop before we get to the hospital, we will blink our lights."

"Great idea," said the sergeant. "We don't have any communications equipment with us. When Colonel Barrister says move, we move. It was more important to catch up with you than it was to talk to the colonel. Do you have communications with the colonel?"

"Yes we do," said Melinda. "Do you want us to give her a message?"

"Just tell her we caught up with you," said the sergeant, "and that we had a little to-do when we did."

"Okay," said Melinda. She turned and yelled into the APC, "Rosemary, contact Colonel Barrister and tell her the soldiers have caught up with us and that we had little fighting. All is secure, and we are heading to the nearest hospital for one of our people who was injured, and then onto the NASA depot. Have him call the hospital and let them know we are on our way. We are thirty minutes out." Rosemary didn't question the order, just acknowledged it.

Melinda turned to the sergeant and asked if there was anything else. The sergeant signaled for two of his men to take the ammunition cans over to the second APC. That completed, the sergeant saluted Melinda, walked to the truck, opened the passenger door and got in. Melinda got back on the APC, closed the hatch and returned to her seat. The APC followed the truck. Melinda looked out the view port and noticed that the sergeant had left six soldiers to guard the bodies. The four remaining NASA trucks pulled in behind Melinda's APC, and Ron's APC pulled in line at the end. The line slowly picked up speed. Twenty-five minutes later the line of vehicles pulled into the emergency lane at the hospital. A gurney was waiting at the door. When the orderly saw the type of vehicle the wounded man was in, he turned, went back through the doors and returned with a collapsible stretcher. Melinda had the hatch open as soon as the APC stopped. The orderlies came in, placed Stephen gently on the stretcher, and took him out of the APC. They placed the stretcher on the gurney, fastened a strap around Stephen and moved quickly into the emergency room. Rosemary followed the gurney. The emergency room nurse tried to stop Rosemary from coming into the emergency room. Rosemary identified herself and allowed to enter.

A doctor came over to the gurney and unstrapped Stephen. They slid him across onto a bed. As the gurney was wheeled away the doctor started examining Stephen. Rosemary started giving the doctor all the vitals she had taken just before the APC had stopped.

The doctor stopped, looked at Rosemary and asked, "Who are you?"

"I'm Rosemary Klein," she answered. "I'm an emergency trauma nurse who is traveling with this circus."

The doctor smiled. He liked her. She might be tiny but she was a spitfire. The doctor undid the bandages. He examined the wound. "This is beautiful work. You did this?" he asked.

"Yes," Rosemary answered. "That's what trauma nurses do."

"I agree," the doctor said, "but they usually have a lot of equipment and people to help."

"Not when bullets are flying," said Rosemary, with a smile. "I'll let you get on with it."

Rosemary walked out into the hall and said, "Computer, get Melinda online."

"I'm online, Rosemary," said Melinda.

"Melinda, I'm here at the hospital with Stephen. If it okay with you, I would like to stay with him."

"That's alright," said Melinda. "You can stay with him."

"According to the Sergeant," continued Rosemary, "They will be back here in about three hours."

"Is that going to be enough time?" said Melinda.

"No," said Rosemary, "but I guess it will have to do. I'll ask the doctor if Stephen will be strong enough to be moved at that time." Rosemary went back into the hospital, walked into the emergency room, stood at the foot of Stephen's bed and watched the doctor finish his work.

"You did a nice job," said the doctor. "I didn't have to do any additional work. I put on a fresh bandage and gave him another dose of antibiotics. I would like to keep him overnight, but I can see from your face that you prefer he be discharged."

"My people will be back in about three hours," said Rosemary. "Will he be able to travel by then?"

"He's young, he's healthy but he has lost a lot of blood," said the doctor. "It will be rough on him. He is going to be in a lot of pain because of his shoulder wound. I can give you some pain meds to give him. I hope you notice I haven't asked from where you are coming, or where you are supposed to be going. I was in the army not too long ago. I can tell when something is going on. I even recognized the chariot that brought you here."

Rosemary smiled. "Thanks Doc," she said. "Now I don't have to make up a bunch of lies to explain the bullet hole in my partner's shoulder."

"How do you want me to record this?" the doctor asked.

"I will have someone call you," said Rosemary. "At what number can you be reached?"

The doctor gave Rosemary his phone number, and Rosemary walked into the hall. When she was out of sight of the doctor she said, "Computer, get Colonel Barrister."

"I'm online, Rosemary," said the colonel.

"I am at the hospital with Stephen," said Rosemary. "The doctor who is treating him wants to know how you want the bullet wound to be recorded. Here is his number." She recited the phone number and disconnected. She walked back into the emergency room just as the doctor's phone started to ring.

The doctor stopped what he was doing and answered the phone. He listened, looked at Rosemary, said yes and few times and hung up. "That was fast," the doctor said. "This must be an important operation. I'm impressed. I'll make sure your young man is ready to travel in three hours. I'll have him moved into the room across the hall. You will be able to rest, as well." He signaled an orderly, gave him instructions, and the bed was moved across the hall into a small private room. When the door was closed, Rosemary took off her shoes and climbed into Stephen's bed, put his head on her shoulder and fell asleep. An hour later, the doctor walked in to check on his patient, saw the couple in bed, smiled to himself and quietly walked out of the room.

Stephen woke up, turned his head and was surprised to see Rosemary sleeping next to him in the hospital bed. He smiled, leaned over and kissed her. She smiled, opened her eyes and looked deeply into Stephen's eyes. She liked what she saw. She put her arm around his neck, carefully pulled him close and gave him a kiss that caused him to moan. She quickly pulled back and looked at him.

"Did I hurt you?" Rosemary asked, with concern on her face.

"No," Stephen said. "It was just the power of that kiss. "What is happening between us? Every time I get near you my heart jumps, and I have trouble keeping my hands to myself."

"I feel the same way," said Rosemary. "When you got shot, I froze. For a moment, I couldn't do my job. If it wasn't for Melinda bringing me out of the trance, you might have died from blood loss. Now I understand why you should not work on someone you love."

"Are you saying you love me?" Stephen said.

"You know I do," Rosemary said. "You knew it the first time we touched and the sparks flew. I wanted to jump into your arms right then and there."

"Now what do we do?" asked Stephen. "We are still in the middle of an operation, and I have been warned that the members of The Company can't fraternize with each other when they are working an operation. Will we be able to hide the way we feel from everyone?"

"I don't think that will be a problem," said Rosemary. "I think Melinda and Martin already know. They were there the first time we met. As for the rest of the team, I don't know. I don't think anyone will say anything as long as we are available to do our job."

"When are they going to release me?" asked Stephen. "Are they going to fly me home?"

Rosemary looked at her watch. "The team should be returning here in about thirty minutes," she said. "Those of us who are not wounded are going back to the ship. The remaining wounded will be taken to the hospital for twenty-four hours and then be prepped to travel. If all goes well, we will fly home. That is all the information I have. I'll go to the desk and sign you out now. How is the pain? The doctor gave me pain pills for you, if the pain gets too bad."

Rosemary went out to the nurse's desk, signed the papers, spoke to the doctor, got a wheelchair and returned to the room. She helped Stephen get up and out of bed without tearing out his intravenous line. Stephen got comfortable in the wheelchair, Rosemary moved the saline drip onto the frame, and wheeled him outside. They waited in the sun for the APC. Twenty minutes later, the two APC's and the five army trucks pulled up. Martin and Melinda helped Stephen into one of the APC's and assisted him in lying down on the cot. Stephan grunted with pain and then sighed as his head hit the pillow. Rosemary walked over to him and punched his good arm.

"Why did you do that?" Stephen asked. "I'm a wounded soldier."

"The doctor warned me you would play hero," Rosemary said. "Take the pain pills." She held out the pills and a bottle of water.

Stephen was going to object when he looked in her eyes. He saw that Rosemary would not stop hounding him until he took the pain pills. He sighed again and reached for the pills and the water bottle. After he took the pills, Rosemary smiled and sat next to him on the cot.

"Isn't that better than fighting me?" Rosemary said.

Melinda let out a laugh and said, "You children sound like you're married. All that seems to be missing is the ring and the ceremony."

Stephen looked at Rosemary. "That sounds like a good idea," said Stephen. "Don't you agree?"

"I'll have to think about it," replied Rosemary. "Okay, I thought enough. Yes, it is a good idea."

"Rosemary," said Stephen, "I can't get on my knee, but I'll say the words. Will you marry me?"

She looked at him and smiled. She was about to answer him when she noticed his eyes had closed and his breathing had slowed. She looked at Melinda, who smiled at her.

"Now what do I do?" she asked Melinda. "He fell asleep before I could answer him. I don't know if I should be upset, or just glad that he's alive."

"When he does wake up," said Melinda, "you could tease him about it. Besides, you could always say that you are disappointed that he doesn't remember your answer. You can also say that Martin and I were witnesses to what you said. Martin will go along with the joke. Won't you Martin?" she said turning to him.

"I don't know if I like the idea of teasing him," said Martin. "After all, he is wounded."

"Let's play it by ear," said Rosemary. "I'll let him sleep it off, and then let's see what he says."

The sergeant came over to check that everything was secure. "We are going to head back to the ship," he said. "If you have any problems, blink your lights. Let the colonel know we are forty minutes out."

When the rear ramp closed, and everyone was secure, the column moved onto the main road and headed towards where the Valley Forge was docked.

"Computer, get Colonel Barrister," said Melinda.

"I'm online," said Barrister. "How was the trip to the NASA depot?"

"We were attacked about twenty miles down the road," said Melinda. "Luckily we had the thirty caliber machine guns and lots of ammunition. Major Forcht was wounded twice. Stephen took his place on the machine gun, and he also was also wounded. His wounds were a little more serious. Rosemary did battlefield surgery with the help of Dr. Wellfleet. The soldiers you sent caught up to us and helped quell the fighting. We lost one of the trucks to a rocket attack. The two police cars were destroyed by rocket fire and their occupants were killed. We were able to save all the graphene from the first truck before it was completely destroyed by fire. The two APC's and the truck full of soldiers escorted the four remaining trucks to their final destination. We stopped on the way to drop off Stephen and Rosemary at the hospital. We picked them up on the way back. The other APC did not sustain any injuries. We should be back in about thirty minutes."

"Do you want to drive directly to the hospital to have Stephen and Forcht checked out?" asked Barrister.

Melinda turned to Rosemary and asked her what she thought of the idea of going to the hospital first, or going back to the ship first. Rosemary said she would prefer to go back to the ship. She then asked Melinda when they planned to fly home. Melinda told her she would like to fly out about 1700 hours. Melinda thought a moment and then she answered Barrister.

"Have you secured the Valley Forge?" Melinda asked.

"Yes," said Barrister. "We have gone over the entire ship and collected whatever suspects were still in hiding."

"We are coming back to the ship," said Melinda. We will stay in the nursery until 1700 hours, and then I would like the APC's to take us to the airport. I will be leaving Fred and his people with you. We will take all the wounded with us, since the aircraft is still configured for medical transport."

"I'll notify the Medical Clinic to prepare the wounded for transport," said Barrister.

"We are at the main gate," said Melinda. "We should be at the ship in ten minutes."

"Computer, get Dr. Wellfleet online," said Barrister.

"I'm online," said Dr. Wellfleet.

"I just spoke to Melinda," said Barrister. "She will be here in about ten minutes. She said she is going to take all the wounded with her when she flies out of Ft. Lauderdale. She'll leave the ship at 1700 hours. Are all the wounded able to travel?"

"Yes," said Dr. Wellfleet. "Everyone can be moved off the ship in wheelchairs except for Benjamin Britain and Amy Gelz. They have to be moved by stretcher."

"How many wounded are we talking about?" asked Barrister.

"We have thirty-one wounded plus Benjamin and Amy," said Wellfleet.

"I had better tell Melinda," said Barrister. "I don't know what kind of plane she has."

"Computer, get Melinda online," said Barrister.

"I'm here, Colonel," said Melinda.

"I just spoke to Dr. Wellfleet," said Barrister. "He told me that there are thirty-one wounded plus two stretcher cases. Is your plane big enough to hold all of the wounded?"

"I didn't think there would be that many wounded," said Melinda. "Martin is calling the airport to see if he can lease a larger plane for the wounded. If he has trouble getting a plane, I will order our 727 from New York. In any case, we will be ready to fly out of Ft. Lauderdale in three hours. I have room on the Gulfstream for Amy and Stephen on stretchers. Major Forcht will stay in a recliner. With Ron, Lucinda, Sheena, Martin, Rosemary and I, we have a full plane. How badly damaged was the Valley Forge?"

"The Captain told me," said Barrister," that as soon as I declare the ship safe, he is going to have the ship repaired, repaint the damaged areas, and put the ship back in order. He told me that he has five days to get the ship ready for the next cruise. I'm just waiting for the last two squads to report."

"What about the damage from the explosion in the water near the propellers?" Melinda asked.

"I asked the Captain about that," said Barrister. "He told me that he is waiting on the report from the divers. There was a delay in putting the divers in the water. It took two hours to get a seal team here to guard them. Everything seems to be going smoothly. The Captain wants to get the repair crews on board the ship. Let me get back to you."

Barrister, Fred and the Captain discussed the best way to expedite the final reports. Before the reports could be delivered, it was decided that as a precaution, it would be better to leave the two squads and Fred's people on the ship while it was being repaired. The Captain suggested that the soldiers be put in coveralls so that the repair people wouldn't ask questions.

"How can we disguise your people?" Barrister asked Fred.

Fred started laughing. "You can't disguise my people," he said. "They are less than five feet tall and black as ebony. They are going to stand out no matter what you do."

"I still think, if you give them white jackets and let them carry a tray, no one would think twice about them moving about the ship," said the Captain.

"We did that before and it worked," said Fred. "We'll try it again."

"I called the main office," said the Captain. "The work crews have been standing by waiting for us to tell them that it was safe for them to come on board the ship. They are waiting in the parking lot."

"I just thought of something," said Barrister. "How do we know that these repair people are who they say they are? I know I must sound paranoid, but after all we have been through this past week, I think I am going to start looking under the beds."

"I can't stop the repair crews," said the Captain. "I have to get the ship repaired and ready for the next cruise. My suggestion is that all the repair people be patted down, scanned, and then be allowed to board the ship. Have all of the materials that they bring on board x-rayed. You can tell them there was a bomb scare."

"That will work for me," said Barrister. "Let's get on with it. Bring the repair crews on. I just received a report from one of my squads. Four people were caught walking in the hallway and have been taken to the brig to be questioned later. I only have one more squad that has not reported in, yet. As soon as they report, I'll notify you."

The repair crews started lining up on the pier and were patted down as they came on deck. Each went through the scanner, and their tools and supplies were x-rayed. Even the boxes of nails were opened. Each repair crew moved to his assigned area and started working. There were four hundred workers moving around the ship.

"Computer, get the Captain online," said Barrister.

"I'm online, Colonel," said the Captain.

"I just received a report from my last squad," said Barrister. "The sergeant said his squad caught two women trying to plant explosives in the forward generator room. He estimated they were using five pounds of Semtex. Each of the women was carrying a detonator. He questioned each of them, but they would not talk. He wonders if they could have planted other explosives or were going to use two detonators on this one bomb."

"I'm glad you insisted to have your people make another sweep of the ship," said the Captain. "If the generator had been blown, this ship would be out of commission for some time."

"As far as I am concerned," said Barrister, "your ship is clear. I am going to take all my men home. I asked Fred if he would stay until you start taking on passengers for the next cruise. He agreed to keep his men on board, just in case. Since the last report leaves some doubt, Fred is going to have his men do another sweep of the ship, especially in the engine rooms. I think you should instruct your engine room people to watch for anything out of place."

"That's a good idea," said the Captain. "I'll make sure there are cabins available for Fred and him men. Thanks again for keeping us afloat. I'm sorry for all the losses you took, Colonel Barrister."

Colonel Barrister gathered his men together on the pier. Everyone was loaded in the trucks, and with a beep of the horn, the column of trucks proceeded out the gate heading towards the airport. The Captain and Fred watched the trucks move through what was left of the gate and onto the main road.

"I'm glad that's over," said the Captain. "I'm going to need a vacation after what we went through this past week. It was one thing to deal with smugglers, but to fight four different cartels was something I never expected in all my years sailing the seas. Five years ago, we had to fight off Somali pirates. All they had were rockets, and not very good ones, either. Fortunately for us, they were pirates that were given sophisticated equipment that they didn't know how to use. We didn't lose anyone and all they did was scratch the paint. These people from the cartels had trained people who knew how to use the equipment. My second in command did a tally of the enemy dead. He figures that between you, Charlie, Barrister and Pitman, there are approximately two hundred dead and one hundred fifty-three enemy wounded. We lost one hundred-six men and women. This wasn't a firefight, it was a war."

"I agree," said Fred. "New York called me a short time ago. They had received a report from Dr. Wellfleet. He was able to question one of the men that survived the shootout. The doctor used his special truth drug. The man he questioned said he was a sergeant. He said his captain was killed as soon as they boarded the Valley Forge. They were Russian Ex-Special forces. We were able to confirm the identity of this group by using pictures of their tattoos combined with their fingerprints. The soldiers had been carrying AK 74's, not the standard AK 47's. Dr. Wellfleet was not able to learn who sent them to the Valley Forge."

"Computer, get Colonel Barrister online," said Melinda.

"I'm online," said Barrister.

"Colonel," said Melinda, "we're not coming back to the ship. We're going directly to the airport. Our plane is there, fueled, and ready to take us home. A 727 will be landing in about one hour. It will be able to take all the wounded. It will have a doctor and two nurses on board to continue treatment for those who still need it. When the plane lands in New York, the wounded will be transferred to Kingsbridge Military Hospital in the Bronx. I've already spoken to the hospital, and doctors there will be prepared to do triage when the wounded arrive. I've made arrangements for a hospital bus to be at the airport when we land. Did I miss anything?" she asked.

"No," said Barrister. "You covered it all. I'm sorry we won't get a chance to sit down for a quiet dinner. Maybe you will get a chance to get out to Colorado and visit."

"I would like that," said Melinda. "It will be awhile. I have two babies that will keep me busy. It was nice working with you. When will you be leaving?"

"We are already heading for the airport," said Barrister. "In fact, we are driving through the gate. Where are you parked?"

"We're at General Aviation on the west side of the airport," said Melinda. "We are parked next to seven C130's."

"That's very funny," said Barrister. "That's our aircraft. Maybe we can have a cup of coffee before you head out."

"I think I can do that," said Melinda. "When you get your troops settled, come on the G650 that is parked next to the C130. Our tail number is November two zero two tango."

"The troops and supplies are being loaded," said Barrister. "I'm heading your way now. See you in a couple of minutes."

Barrister turned to her lieutenants and gave them their instructions. They saluted, turned and headed towards their aircraft. Barrister headed for November two zero two tango. She walked up the stairs and entered the cabin. She stood there in amazement. The first thing she saw was the two gurneys. One held Stephen Blaine, and the other held Amy Gelz. They both still had their IV's attached. The rest of Melinda's team was sitting in the cabin, relaxing. Melinda saw Barrister standing in the doorway and walked over to her. She took both her hands and drew her into a hug.

"I'm glad that is over," said Melinda, releasing Elizabeth Barrister. She stood back and looked Barrister up and down. "You look tired," she said. "Didn't you get any sleep?"

"Not this trip," said Barrister. "These were the roughest four days I have ever had. I had a briefing with all my officers and non-coms. They all agreed. They would rather have been out in the field than fighting on the Valley Forge."

Martin came in with a tray of coffee and tea and set it on the table. Everyone took a cup and sat down at the two tables. Barrister asked how Melinda came to be on the ship. Melinda told her the entire story, from being invited at the last minute to act as a den mother to her team, keeping track of the suspects on the Valley Forge, passing out, needing a special operation, giving birth to the twins, and then coming back to the Valley Forge with the babies. Who knew it would turn into a war zone? It would have been better if she didn't have the babies with her. That made for extra worry, but it all worked out in the end.

"Stephen had been seriously wounded," Melinda said. "The doctors say he will recover, but he is going to be in a load of pain for a long time, especially when he goes through rehab. I think Rosemary will help take his mind off the pain."

Melinda turned around and looked at Stephen. Rosemary was sitting next to him, holding one of his hands next to her cheek. Barrister turned, saw the couple and smiled.

"I see what you mean," said Barrister. "How long have they been working together?"

"They met five days ago for the first time," said Melinda. "Rosemary came to us just two weeks ago. She has been terrific. She was with Stephen when he was wounded and she performed battlefield surgery on his wounds. The doctor said she saved his life. I guess he owes her."

Still looking at the couple, Barrister said, "I don't think that will be a problem. Just look at them. When you meet the right person, everything clicks in place. I bet they will have a wedding very soon. Look at their faces."

"Computer, get Colonel Barrister online," said Lieutenant Peterson.

"Yes," Lieutenant Peterson," said Barrister.

"All the troops have been loaded," said Peterson.

"Thank you, Lieutenant," said Barrister. "I'm on my way. Have them warm up the engines.

"Melinda," said Barrister. "I have to run." She picked up her coffee cup, took the last mouthful, put the cup down, waved to the group and left the airplane.

"I'm glad this is finished," said Martin, placing his arms around her waist. Melinda leaned against him and sighed.

"I guess it is time to get this show on the road," Melinda said as she turned around, put her hand on Martin's neck and pulled him down for a quick kiss.

Martin walked into the cockpit and gave the pilots their instructions. He walked back and pushed the button to raise the stairs. When the stairs were retracted, he closed and locked the door. He checked that all the passengers had their seat belts properly fastened. He checked that the babies were secure in their special cribs mounted on each side of Melinda. He sat down next to Annabelle and put his hand in her crib. She grabbed his little finger and held it tightly. Martin smiled, leaned back and closed his eyes. He said to himself, *'I'm such a lucky guy'*.

"Computer, get Dr. Wellfleet," said Melinda.

"I'm online," said Dr. Wellfleet. "How is everyone?"

"I was going to ask you that same question," said Melinda. "Everyone here is fine. Rosemary is taking care of Stephen. Forcht is sleeping. The rest of the crew is munching on food, drinking whatever they drink, and generally relaxing. How are all your patients?"

"Before Barrister left the Valley Forge," said Dr. Wellfleet, "she came down and met with Lieutenant Pitman. They spent thirty minutes talking. Then I introduced her to that woman from the secret police. Barrister spent another thirty minutes talking with her. They got along very well. Then she visited the rest of the wounded who could not be moved. She teased some of them with the threat that they might have to stay on the ship for another week. Not one of the soldiers complained. She is a good commander. I am going to stay on the ship for this next week. I can help treat the wounded and relax at the same time."

Melinda laughed. "I guess we can spare you for a week," she said. "Just don't get sunburned. What is the final situation with Pitman?"

"I've made all the arrangements for her," said Dr. Wellfleet. "She is going to need a hip replacement. That bullet shattered her hip. We are keeping her asleep until everything else has healed. When she wakes up she is going to be in extreme pain. The doctor at the hospital recommended that we don't wake her up until after the hip operation."

"Computer, get the Captain," asked Melinda.

"I'm online, Melinda," said the Captain.

"We are getting ready to take off," said Melinda. "I wanted to know about the water in the aft engine room. Have the pumps been fixed?

"We were very lucky," said the Captain. "Not only were the pumps fixed, but the divers were able to fix the gaskets, and there was no damage to the propellers. In three days we will take on a new group of passengers, and no one will be the wiser."

"What about the passengers that missed this week's cruise?" Melinda asked.

"I understand they were offered a week's cruise for free plus their money back," said the Captain. "I think they got a good deal."

"Melinda, Barrister is online," said the Computer.

"What is it, Liz?" asked Melinda.

"One of our C130's just exploded," said Barrister. "We are breaking formation and making an emergency landing at the next available airfield. I was told that we lost sixty-three men and women. I don't understand what happened. We took only our own equipment with us. I'll talk to you after we are on the ground."

"Martin," said Melinda. "Liz just told me that one of her aircraft exploded. She lost sixty-three people."

"Melinda, are you still online?" asked Barrister.

"Yes," said Melinda. "I'm still online. What is happening?"

"Harry just told me that he had arranged a flight of two fighters as an escort," said Barrister. The pilot of one of the fighter planes said that he saw the rocket trail come up from the ground. He is circling to see if he can find the shooter. I have cancelled our emergency landing, reforming on the lead aircraft, and are continuing to our base in Colorado. I'll keep you informed. All my troops are in shock. One of our fighter escorts just informed me that he has spotted the shooter. The shooter is in a black pickup truck. The pilot is trying to get permission to fire on the truck. The pilot tells me that his base is in contact with the state police. He has only fuel enough for thirty minutes. He has contacted his commander to try to get another plane in the air."

"The pilot told me the state police have done a good job," said Harry. "They were able to follow his instructions. The pilot had to leave the area. I'll try to find out what is happening."

"Melinda, Harry Blank online," said the Computer.

"Yes, Harry," said Melinda. "Have you heard what is happening with the C130's?"

"I have been in contact with our friends at the Pentagon. An air exercise with drones is taking place just north of Topeka, Kansas. The drones have been diverted from their exercise to assist the fighter plane that had to leave the area. Call sign for the drone is Special Nine. The fighter directed Special Nine to the suspect's truck. The fighter plane had to leave because he was low on fuel. It would have been nice if we could have had an aerial refueling tanker, but everything is happening too fast.

"Melinda, this is Special Nine. I have the suspect's truck in sight. He is heading west on the expressway. He has now exited the expressway and is heading southwest on route 74. He is on a two-lane road, still heading southwest. There is a police car heading east. The police car has stopped and is blocking the road. There is another police car coming up behind the suspect. The police have blocked the suspect at the junction of 74 and 295. There is no place for him to go. There is a police helicopter heading to the area. The chopper has landed and six people have jumped out. The helicopter is leaving. The police have surrounded the suspect. The suspect is shooting at the officers. The police are returning fire and have wounded the suspect. I can maintain station for another hour."

Harry said, "I have asked one of Dr. Wellfleet's medical people from Tucson to meet with the state police and assist them in questioning the shooter. The sent a helicopter for the doctor. It will still take him two hours to arrive. That will give them an hour to do the questioning before the F.B.I. gets there. I'll keep you informed. When do you expect to be back in New York?"

"We just took off," said Melinda. "We should land in New Jersey in about three hours or less. Martin notified Dennis, and he will have two helicopters waiting for us. The wounded will go directly to Kingsbridge hospital, and the others will go to the New York office. I still have some wounded back on the ship, but they will be staying an extra week. I know it will be a hardship for them, but they are strong enough to deal with it."

Harry laughed. "Yes," he said, "that's a real hardship. Wait until they come home and have to start training. Then we'll sit back and see how strong they are."

The plane landed on time, and the wounded transferred to the helicopter that was to take them to the Kingsbridge hospital. The rest of the team boarded the remaining helicopter and headed east to the New York center. They took the elevator to the basement and boarded the electric carts that took them to their building. They took the elevator to the top floor and entered the conference room. Everyone except Melinda grabbed a cup of coffee and sat down.

"We're home," said Lucinda. "When you are finished with your drinks, you have forty-eight hours to take care of your own stuff and report back here."

Forty-eight hours later the team met in the conference room. Melinda looked around the room. Everyone was there except Rosemary, Stephen and Benjamin. Rosemary was at home with Melinda's babies and Stephen was in rehab with Benjamin.

"I glad to see everyone has recovered from there twenty four day cruise," said Melinda. "It has been a tough three and a half weeks for most of you. Now you see why we train for all possible contingencies. Both the ten-minute and two-hour dart guns worked the way Dr. Wellfleet said they would. Any comments before we go any further?"

Everyone looked at each other, waiting to see who would start the comments.

"What's the story with Stephen?" asked Lucinda.

"He was wounded twice on the way to deliver the material to NASA," said Melinda. The convoy stopped at a hospital on the way to NASA. A doctor at the hospital treated Stephen. Three hours later, the convoy returned and picked up Stephen and Rosemary and brought them back. The doctor informed me that Stephen will recover fully after a long rehab."

"That wasn't what I was questioning," said Lucinda, smiling at Melinda. "What about Stephen and Rosemary?"

"I don't think it is any of our business," said Melinda. "I think we should wait and let them tell you."

"We won't see them for a while," said Sheena. 'You tell us."

"Alright," said Melinda. "Stephen asked Rosemary to marry him."

"And what did she say?" asked Lucinda.

"That's the thing," said Melinda. "Before she could answer him, he fell asleep from the drugs."

There was silence for a moment, and then everyone started laughing.

"I wonder when and where the wedding going to be." said Ron, trying to keep from laughing.

"I'm pretty sure the wedding will take place here at the Center," said Melinda. "I don't know when. As soon as I know, you'll know. Don't forget, they met only a week ago."

"I know we don't set these operations as match making scenarios," said Lucinda, "but look what has happened last year. Ron and I were married, and Martin and Melinda were married. Now we have Stephen and Rosemary. Who will be next?"

Everyone looked at Sheena. "Don't look at me," she said. "I'm single and plan to stay that way. Yeah, I like Benjamin, but give me a break. I met him only three weeks ago. Ask me again in a year or two."

Just then, there was a knock on the door. Ron got up, walked to the door and opened it. There was Beth pushing a food cart. She pushed the cart into the conference room with Ron's assistance. As they both entered the conference room, everyone started laughing.

Following Ron into the conference room was Rosemary, pushing Stephen in a wheelchair followed by Suzy Q.

Everyone got to their feet and greeted the newcomers.

"Now we can eat," said Ron, as he rubbed his stomach.

The room burst out laughing.

"Okay," said Melinda. "Now that everyone is here, who is minding the store? I mean the babies."

Rosemary laughed. Looking at Melinda she said, "Do you think I would ever let the babies out of my sight?"

"Where are they," asked Melinda.

"They're in the office," Rosemary said. "They are both in my line of sight."

"Martin," did you get a report from Dr. Wellfleet's colleague from Tucson?" asked Melinda.

"Yes I did," he replied. "The suspect who fired the rocket was hired by one of the Mexican cartels."

"How did he know which airplane to shoot at?" asked Ron.

"He was given a tail number and the position in the formation," said Martin. "He told the doctor that he couldn't see the tail number because the planes were too high so he fired at a plane based on its location in the formation. Under further questioning, he told the doctor where he got the rocket. The questioning was finished just as the F.B.I. pulled up. All of our people were able to leave as the F.B.I. came in."

"What about the plane that was hit?" asked Rosemary.

"I received a second report," said Martin. "The plane that was shot down by the rocket is spread out over the northwest corner of Arkansas. The rescuers have been able to retrieve thirty bodies so far and many more body parts. They are bringing in cadaver dogs to assist. Every county in

Arkansas is sending rescuers with dogs to assist the military. Barrister said she would contact us when she has more information. She is trying to find out how the cartel knew what plane was in what part of the formation. Only a dozen people knew that information."

The room became quiet.

"There is news, good news and more good news," said Melinda. "The news is that memorial for Susan Bart, Jose Martinez, Marsha Abrams and John Mason will be held in the chapel tomorrow morning. Their families will be attending. They will notify us when and where the funerals will be held."

"The good news is that I am turning this meeting over to Stephen and Rosemary."

Rosemary looked at Stephen and she stood up. He smiled at Rosemary and nodded. "Stephen and I have an announcement to make," Rosemary said. The room got very quiet. "Stephen has asked me to marry him. The problem is he fell asleep and he doesn't remember my response."

Everyone started laughing and Stephen blushed. *'And I thought I was the only one who blushed,'* thought Rosemary.

"So what did you answer?" shouted the rest of the team.

"Of course I said yes." Rosemary said, "Didn't I, Melinda?"

"I'm not talking," said Melinda. "Now tell us the very good news."

"We're going to have the wedding here at the Center and you're all invited."

Everyone cheered.

"When is it going to be?" asked Martin.

"Stephen and I wanted the wedding today but we were thought that a week from tomorrow would be soon enough," said Rosemary, leaning over and kissing Stephen.

There was a knock on the door. Ron walked back into the office and opened the door. There was Benjamin in a wheelchair with his leg in a brace. Ron held the door wide and motioned Benjamin and Harry Blank in. He directed them to the conference room.

"Look who I found," said Ron, as Harry wheeled Benjamin into the conference room.

Sheena saw Benjamin, squealed and rushed over to him. She leaned down and gave him a kiss. Everyone else started humming the wedding march. Harry stood there admiring Melinda and her team.

"Just to let everyone know," Harry said. "It was a job well done. "I'm talking about the smuggling operation. I am sorry about the graphene.

I should have informed you about it but my hands were tired. Pitman sends her regards. She wanted to let you know that she is going to be retiring from the service. I asked her to join your organization and she has agreed. I made arrangements for her to complete her rehabilitation here at the New York center after she is released from the VA hospital."

"How long do you think she will be in the hospital," asked Rosemary.

"Dr. Wellfleet told me that it will be at least three weeks before she is released," said Harry. "He is going to call you in a while to discuss Amy Gelz. I'm sorry you walked into the middle of this war. The cruise was supposed to be a reward for all the work you did in Europe. It really was for you to have a nice vacation and at the same time watch over the four couples. I didn't mean to put you and your babies in danger."

"Sometimes you never know what is behind the next door," said Melinda. "It is going to take some time to get the Caribbean desk and the South American desk back up to full strength."

"I've already passed the word to the National Guard," said Harry. "That's where I was able to get men for the Caribbean desk last time. It will be up to Fred to replace his losses. I spoke to him earlier and he told me that it won't be a problem. They will be going back to Aruba and start training again."

"Melinda, Dr. Wellfleet online, conference call," said the Computer.

"I'm online, Dr. Wellfleet," said Melinda.

"I want to give you a summary of what's happening here on the Valley Forge," said Wellfleet.

"Okay," said Melinda. "Tell us about Amy Gelz first."

"I met with two of my colleagues and we discussed Amy Gelz's case. They have developed a new process that can repair the spine and connect the nerves. They have discussed the procedure with Amy and she is going to have the operation next week."

"What are her chances?" asked Rosemary.

"The doctors tell me that there is a 60% chance of a successful outcome. Amy said that she is willing to accept those odds. If she does nothing she will be bed ridden the rest of her life and she is very young. At least with the operation she has a chance of recovery."

"That is pretty good news," said Martin. "Now tell us about the Valley Forge."

"The repairs are almost finished," said Dr. Wellfleet. "The first thing they did was replace the Guest Relations desk. You would never know there was a gunfight and an explosion there. I walked around the rest of the ship. All the repairs are finished and the paint is almost dry. They replaced the rugs in all the areas that needed it. The new passengers will be coming on the ship tomorrow. As to our wounded that stayed behind. They are doing well. They are suffering with the food that is being served, but someone has to do it. I've made arrangements for massage therapy, physical therapy and whatever else they need. The captain has set aside a small dining room for us to use. The military police came and took the Panamanian person away. She will have her own medic all the way to our Tucson prison. We are going to move Amy off the ship and take her to the hospital where she will undergo surgery for her spine. I don't know how long she will be here to recuperate before she is strong enough to be moved to New York. Fred has stationed him people around the ship, just in case. That's all the news I have except the captain says, 'thank you for saving his ship'.

"The only news we have here is that there will be a wedding next week."

"Who is getting married?" asked Dr. Wellfleet.

"Rosemary and Stephen," said Melinda.

"He has only been on the ship a week," said Dr. Wellfleet. "Is there something in the water?"

Everyone laughed.

"This meeting is over," said Melinda. "Everyone has two weeks to rest up. We already have another assignment. Hope everyone likes Chinese food. Don't be late."

THE END

If you enjoyed The Smugglers at Sea
you will enjoy
Book 1- The Company
Book 3 - The Company in Asia

hfink6434@aol.com